THE SECR[

Hugh Walpole was born in New Zealand in 1884. After moving to England he swiftly established a reputation. His output was vast, and included the novels *Fortitude* and *The Dark Forest*, as well as *Mr Perrin and Mr Traill* and *The Secret City*, both published by Capuchin Classics. He died in London in 1941.

Bridget Kendall, the broadcaster, made her name internationally as a Russian specialist covering the break-up of the Soviet Union under Gorbachev and Yeltsin. She is the host of the talk show *The Forum* on BBC World Service radio.

The Secret City

The Secret City

———————————

Hugh Walpole

FOREWORD BY BRIDGET KENDALL

CAPUCHIN CLASSICS

CAPUCHIN CLASSICS
LONDON

The Secret City

© Hugh Walpole 1919

This edition published by Capuchin Classics 2012

2 4 6 8 0 9 7 5 3 1

Capuchin Classics
128 Kensington Church Street, London W8 4BH
Telephone: +44 (0)20 7221 7166
Fax: +44 (0)20 7792 9288
E-mail: info@capuchin-classics.co.uk
www.capuchin-classics.co.uk

Châtelaine of Capuchin Classics: Emma Howard

ISBN: 978-1-907429-28-6

Printed and bound by CPI Group (UK) Ltd. Croydon CR0 4YY

Contents

Foreword

It is December 1916, on the eve of the year that would turn Russia upside down and usher in a Revolution which would change the world. But Russia's old imperial capital is not yet ready to give up its secrets.

At least not to a fresh-faced young British diplomat called Henry Bohun nor to his more seasoned travelling companion Jerry Lawrence, both newly arrived from London to take up posts in the city.

Within days the two men, one naïve and the other wary, are swept into the embrace of a shambolic but mesmerising Russian family called Markovitch, drawn in by the warmth and energy of two sisters, Vera and Nina.

For these diffident, perplexed Englishmen the Markovitch flat is soon to be the centre of the universe.

Like characters in a story by Tolstoy they become entangled in the family's love dramas, unhappy marriages and frustrated ambitions, while the currents of impending revolution swirl around them.

Meanwhile beyond the bright, comfortable hospitality of the Markovitch flat on Anglisky Prospect, ghostly figures queue for bread, dark buildings loom out of mists and the cold waters of the great river Neva flow silently. The city is an eerie stage setting, a reminder that – in the metaphor of Alexander Pushkin's poem 'The Bronze Horseman' – the flood waters are rising and a cataclysm is inevitable.

****

Hugh Walpole was probably best known during his lifetime for his romantic history of family life set in the Lake District, *The Herries Chronicles*, which he wrote in the 1930s. He was a prolific and successful writer. I remember much-loved and well-thumbed editions of his novels on the bookshelves of both my father and my grandmother.

But this earlier novel, '*The Secret City*', is a different sort of tale and particularly deserves to be resurrected.

It is not only a powerful love story and a cracking yarn, masterfully written – it was awarded the inaugural James Tait Memorial Prize for fiction when published in 1919.

It is also an elegant tribute to the Russian literary tradition of the 'Petersburg myth' that so fascinated writers like Pushkin, Dostoevsky and Gogol.

The imperial capital was renamed Petrograd in 1914 to remove the Germanic associations of its original name Saint Petersburg. This was not the last name change for the city; in Soviet times it became Leningrad. But its aloof, unreal charm was unaltered: an artificial fog-wrapped construct built on a swamp at a tsar's whim, enigmatic and elemental, like a monster guarding a mysterious destiny. Hugh Walpole's contribution to the myth was to imbue that sense of mystery with a lurking fear of revolution.

If this makes '*The Secret City*' sound like a Gothic horror tale it is not meant to. What is refreshing about this book is that it also comes across as an honest account of an extraordinary moment in history. If you compare it to excerpts from Hugh Walpole's diaries and letters, reprinted by his first biographer, it is clear that much is drawn from his own experiences. (1)

He spent three years in Russia, arriving as a young author in search of adventure in 1914, intent on writing about the 'Slav peril' as he put it; and leaving in 1917 as the outgoing head of the Anglo-Russian Propaganda Bureau in Petrograd, packing his bags and hurrying out of town for the last time as the Winter Palace was literally being besieged by Lenin and his Bolsheviks.

The Russian family he lived with on arrival in order to learn the rudiments of the language matches many of the characteristics of the Markovitch family. Vignettes of volatile eccentricities that were to be worked into the novel– the histrionics, the slightly pathetic attempts at inventing – appeared in letters home:

'All Monday and Tuesday husband and wife don't speak. Wednesday morning he cries at breakfast and is forgiven, Thursday morning it begins again…. He's an inventor and in the last month has invented a new kind of grey sock, a new paint to be extracted from the bark of trees, a new ink and a sort of soap.'

Later diary entries from 1917 when he was in Petrograd, nominally in charge of the British propaganda effort and desperately trying to keep a grip on the fast moving politics, painted a vivid snapshot of a city sliding into chaos –and also provided useful material for the novel:

'One of the most exciting days of my life,' he wrote on March 12 1917. 'At lunch Ambassador reported Government in great state of panic. Afterwards walking back heard loud firing. Then saw whole revolutionary mob pass down our street. About two thousand soldiers, many civilians armed, motor lorries with red flags'.

Dodging the bullets, he jotted down his impressions daily, as much elated as terrified. Though two days later on March 14 he noted the mood was becoming uglier:

'Lunch was interrupted by a lively battle in the street under our windows. Finally had to run down the street for my life, an unpleasant experience. Afternoon, much firing around us. Twice invaded by revolutionaries who insisted on searching our place as a policeman is hidden somewhere.'

How do you make sense of revolution when you are in the midst of it?

Hugh Walpole's answer was to allow us to see it the way he and his friends did, as a surreal backdrop to ordinary life until the simmering unrest turned to violence and it could be ignored no longer.

Like his own experience of Russia, *The Secret City* ends before the Bolshevik coup has been played out. What fate awaits the Markovitch girls and those of their relatives and friends who stay on in Soviet Russia is left to our imagination.

Except, with the hindsight of history, we know what happened next. Civil war was round the corner, emigration for many aristocratic Russians, and for those who remained in Petrograd, the draconian strictures of War Communism and terrible epidemics of typhoid and famine.

In some ways this novel is also a lament: the cosy, lamplit, bourgeois world of pre-revolutionary Russia which Walpole describes so affectionately was about to vanish forever.

Bridget Kendall

NOTES

1. Letter and diary extracts all quoted from *Hugh Walpole: a biography* by Rupert Hart-Davis. Macmillan & Co, 1952.

Part I

Vera and Nina

Vera and Nina

I

. . . There are certain things that I feel, as I look through this bundle or manuscript, that I must say. The first is that of course no writer ever has fulfilled his intention and no writer ever will; secondly, that there was, when I began, another intention than that of dealing with my subject adequately, namely that of keeping myself outside the whole of it; I was to be, in the most abstract and immaterial sense of the word, a voice, and that simply because this business of seeing Russian psychology through English eyes has no excuse except that it *is* English. That is its only interest, its only atmosphere, its only motive, and if you are going to tell me that any aspect of Russia psychological, mystical, practical, or commercial seen through an English medium is either Russia as she really is or Russia as Russians see her, I say to you, without hesitation, that you don't know of what you are talking.

Of Russia and the Russians I know nothing, but of the effect upon myself and my ideas of life that Russia and the Russians have made during these last three years I know something. You are perfectly free to say that neither myself nor my ideas of life are of the slightest importance to any one. To that I would say that any one's ideas about life are of importance and that any one's ideas about Russian life are of interest . . . and beyond that, I have simply been compelled to write. I have not been able to help myself, and all the faults and any virtues in this story come from that. The facts are true, the inferences absolutely my own, so that you may reject them at any moment and substitute others. It is true that I have known Vera Michailovna, Nina, Alexei Petrovitch, Henry, Jerry, and the rest – some of them intimately – and many of the conversations here recorded I have myself heard. Nevertheless the inferences are my own, and I think there is no

Russian who, were he to read this book, would not say that those inferences were wrong. In an earlier record, to which this is in some ways a sequel,[1] my inferences were, almost without exception, wrong, and there is no Russian alive for whom this book can have any kind of value except as a happy example of the mistakes that the Englishman can make about the Russian.

But it is over those very mistakes that the two souls, Russian and English, so different, so similar, so friendly, so hostile, may meet. . . . And in any case the thing has been too strong for me. I have no other defence. For one's interest in life is stronger, God knows how much stronger, than one's discretion, and one's love of life than one's wisdom, and one's curiosity in life than one's ability to record it. At least, as I have said, I have endeavoured to keep my own history, my own desires, my own temperament out of this, as much as is humanly possible. . . .

And the facts are true.

II

They had been travelling for a week, and had quite definitely decided that they had nothing whatever in common. As they stood there, lost and desolate on the grimy platform of the Finland station, this same thought must have been paramount in their minds: 'Thank God we shan't have to talk to one another any longer. Whatever else may happen in this strange place, that at least we're spared.' They were probably quite unconscious of the contrast they presented, unconscious because, at this time, young Bohun never, I should imagine, visualised himself as anything more definite than absolutely 'right,' and Lawrence simply never thought about himself at all. But they were perfectly aware of their mutual dissatisfaction, although they were of course absolutely polite. I heard of it afterwards from both sides, and I will say quite frankly that my sympathy was all with Lawrence. Young Bohun can have been no fun as a travelling companion at that time. If you had looked at him there standing on the Finland station platform and staring haughtily about for porters, you must have thought him the most self-satisfied of mortals. 'That fellow wants kicking,' you would have said. Good-looking, thin, tall,

---

[1] *The Dark Forest.*

large black eyes, black eyelashes, clean and neat and 'right' at the end of his journey as he had been at the beginning of it, just foreign-looking enough with his black hair and pallor to make him interesting – he was certainly arresting. But it was the self-satisfaction that would have struck any one. And he had reason; he was at that very moment experiencing the most triumphant moment of his life.

He was only twenty-three, and was already as it seemed to the youthfully limited circle of his vision, famous. Before the war he had been, as he quite frankly admitted to myself and all his friends, nothing but ambitious. 'Of course I edited the *Granta* for a year,' he would say, 'and I don't think I did it badly. . . . But that wasn't very much.'

No, it really wasn't a great deal, and we couldn't tell him that it was. He had always intended, however, to be a great man; the *Granta* was simply a stepping-stone. He was already, during his second year at Cambridge, casting about as to the best way to penetrate, swiftly and securely, the fastnesses of London journalism. Then the war came, and he had an impulse of perfectly honest and selfless patriotism . . ., not quite selfless perhaps, because he certainly saw himself as a mighty hero, winning V.C.'s and saving forlorn hopes, finally received by his native village under an archway of flags and mottoes (the local postmaster, who had never treated him very properly, would make the speech of welcome). The reality did him some good, but not very much, because when he had been in France only a fortnight he was gassed and sent home with a weak heart. His heart remained weak, which made him interesting to women and allowed time for his poetry. He was given an easy post in the Foreign Office, and in the autumn of 1916 he published *Discipline: Sonnets and Poems.* This appeared at a very fortunate moment, when the more serious of British idealists were searching for signs of a general improvement, through the stress of war, of poor humanity. . . . 'Thank God, there are our young poets,' they said.

The little book had excellent notices in the papers, and one poem in especial, 'How God spoke to Jones at Breakfast-time,' was selected for especial praise because of its admirable realism and force. One paper said that the British breakfast-table lived in that poem 'in all its tiniest most insignificant details,' as no breakfast-table, save possibly that of Major Pendennis at the beginning of *Pendennis,* has lived before. One paper said, 'Mr. Bohun merits that much-abused word "genius."'

The young author carried these notices about with him and I have seen them all. But there was more than this. Bohun had been for the last four years cultivating Russian. He had been led into this through a real, genuine interest. He read the novelists and set himself to learn the Russian language. That, as any one who has tried it will know, is no easy business, but Henry Bohun was no fool, and the Russian refugee who taught him was no fool. After Henry's return from France he continued his lessons, and by the spring of 1916 he could read easily, write fairly, and speak atrociously. He then adopted Russia, an easy thing to do, because his supposed mastery of the language gave him a tremendous advantage over his friends. 'I assure you that's not so,' he would say. 'You can't judge Tchekov till you've read him in the original. Wait till you can read him in Russian.' 'No, I don't think the Russian characters are like that,' he would declare. 'It's a queer thing, but you'd almost think I had some Russian blood in me . . . I sympathise so.' He followed closely the books that emphasised the more sentimental side of the Russian character, being of course grossly sentimental himself at heart. He saw Russia glittering with fire and colour, and Russians, large, warm, and simple, willing to be patronised, eagerly confessing their sins, rushing forward to make him happy, entertaining him for ever and ever with a free and glorious hospitality.

'I really think I do understand Russia,' he would say modestly. He said it to me when he had been in Russia two days.

Then, in addition to the success of his poems and the general interest that he himself aroused, the final ambition of his young heart was realised. The Foreign Office decided to send him to Petrograd to help in the great work of British propaganda.

He sailed from Newcastle on December 2, 1916. . . .

III

At this point I am inevitably reminded of that other Englishman who, two years earlier than Bohun, had arrived in Russia with his own pack of dreams and expectations.

But John Trenchard, of whose life and death I have tried elsewhere to say something, was young Bohun's opposite, and I do not think that the strange unexpectedness of Russia can be exemplified more strongly than by the similarity of appeal that she could make to two so various characters. John was shy, self-doubting, humble, brave, and a gentleman, – Bohun was brave and a gentleman, but the rest had yet to be added to him. How he would have patronised Trenchard if he had known him! And yet at heart they were not perhaps so dissimilar. At the end of my story it will be apparent, I think, that they were not.

That journey from Newcastle to Bergen, from Bergen to Torneo, from Torneo to Petrograd is a tiresome business. There is much waiting at Custom-houses, disarrangement of trains and horses and meals, long wearisome hours of stuffy carriages and grimy window-panes. Bohun I suspect suffered, too, from that sudden sharp precipitance into a world that knew not *Discipline* and recked nothing of the *Granta*. Obviously none of the passengers on the boat from Newcastle had ever heard of *Discipline*. They clutched in their hands the works of Mr. Oppenheim, Mr. Compton Mackenzie, and Mr. O. Henry and looked at Bohun, I imagine, with indifferent superiority. He had been told at the Foreign Office that his especial travelling companion was to be Jerry Lawrence. If he had hoped for anything from this direction one glance at Jerry's brick-red face and stalwart figure must have undeceived him. Jerry, although he was now thirty-two years of age, looked still very much the undergraduate. My slight acquaintance with him had been in those earlier Cambridge days, through a queer mutual friend, Dune, who at that time seemed to promise so magnificently, who afterwards disappeared so mysteriously. You would never have supposed that Lawrence, Captain of the University Rugger during his last two years, Captain of the English team through all the Internationals of the season 1913–14, could have had anything in common, except football, with Dune, artist and poet if ever there was one. But on the few occasions when I saw them together it struck me that football was the very least part of their common ground. And that was the first occasion on which I suspected that Jerry Lawrence was not quite what he seemed. . . .

I can imagine Lawrence standing straddleways on the deck of the *Jupiter*, his short thick legs wide apart, his broad back indifferent to everything and everybody, his rather plump, ugly, good-natured face staring out to sea as though he saw nothing at all. He always gave the impression of being half asleep, he had a way of suddenly lurching on his legs as though in another moment his desire for slumber would be too strong for him, and would send him crashing to the ground. He would be smoking an ancient briar, and his thick red hands would be clasped behind his back. . . .

No encouraging figure for Bohun's aestheticism.

I can see as though I had been present Bohun's approach to him, his patronising introduction, his kindly suggestion that they should eat their meals together, Jerry's smiling, lazy acquiescence. I can imagine how Bohun decided to himself that 'he must make the best of this chap. After all, it was a long tiresome journey, and anything was better than having no one to talk to. . . .' But Jerry, unfortunately, was in a bad temper at the start. He did not want to go out to Russia at all. His father, old Stephen Lawrence, had been for many years the manager of some works in Petrograd, and the first fifteen years of Jerry's life had been spent in Russia. I did not, at the time when I made Jerry's acquaintance at Cambridge, know this; had I realised it I would have understood many things about him which puzzled me. He never alluded to Russia, never apparently thought of it, never read a Russian book, had, it seemed, no connection of any kind with any living soul in that country.

Old Lawrence retired, and took a fine large ugly palace in Clapham to end his days in. . . .

Suddenly, after Lawrence had been in France for two years, had won the Military Cross there, and, as he put it, 'was just settling inside his skin,' the authorities realised his Russian knowledge, and decided to transfer him to the British Military Mission in Petrograd. His anger when he was sent back to London and informed of this was extreme. He hadn't the least desire to return to Russia, he was very happy where he was, he had forgotten all his Russian; I can see him, saying very little, looking like a sulky child and kicking his heel up and down across the carpet.

'Just the man we want out there, Lawrence,' he told me somebody said to him; 'keep them in order.'

'Keep them in order!' That tickled his sense of humour. He was to laugh frequently, afterwards, when he thought of it. He always chewed a joke as a cow chews the cud.

So that he was in no pleasant temper when he met Bohun on the decks of the *Jupiter*. That journey must have had its humours for any observer who knew the two men. During the first half of it I imagine that Bohun talked and Lawrence slumbered. Bohun patronised, was kind and indulgent, and showed very plainly that he thought his companion the dullest and heaviest of mortals. Then he told Lawrence about Russia; he explained everything to him, the morals, psychology, fighting qualities, strengths, and weaknesses. The climax arrived when he announced: 'But it's the mysticism of the Russian peasant which will save the world. That adoration of God . . .'

'Rot!' interrupted Lawrence.

Bohun was indignant. 'Of course if you know better——' he said.

'I do,' said Lawrence, 'I lived there for fifteen years. Ask my old governor about the mysticism of the Russian peasant. He'll tell you.'

Bohun felt that he was justified in his annoyance. As he said to me afterwards: 'The fellow had simply been laughing at me. He might have told me about his having been there.' At that time, to Bohun, the most terrible thing in the world was to be laughed at.

After that Bohun asked Jerry questions. But Jerry refused to give himself away. 'I don't know,' he said, 'I've forgotten it all. I don't suppose I ever did know much about it.'

At Haparanda, most unfortunately, Bohun was insulted. The Swedish Customs Officer there, tired at the constant appearance of self-satisfied gentlemen with Red Passports, decided that Bohun was carrying medicine in his private bags. Bohun refused to open his portmanteau, simply because he 'was a Courier and wasn't going to be insulted by a dirty foreigner.' Nevertheless 'the dirty foreigner' had his way and Bohun looked rather a fool. Jerry had not sympathised sufficiently with Bohun in this affair. . . . 'He only grinned,' Bohun told me indignantly afterwards. 'No sense of patriotism at all. After all, Englishmen ought to stick together.'

Finally, Bohun tested Jerry's literary knowledge. Jerry seemed to have none. He liked Fielding, and a man called Farnol and Jack London.

He never read poetry. But, a strange thing, he was interested in Greek. He had bought the works of Euripides and Aeschylus in the Loeb Library, and he thought them 'thundering good.' He had never read a word of any Russian author. 'Never *Anna?* Never *War and Peace?* Never *Karamazov?* Never Tchekov?'

No, never.

Bohun gave him up.

IV

It should be obvious enough then that they hailed their approaching separation with relief. Bohun had been promised by one of the secretaries at the Embassy that rooms would be found for him. Jerry intended to 'hang out' at one of the hotels. The 'Astoria' was, he believed, the right place.

'I shall go to the "France" for to-night,' Bohun declared, having lived, it would seem, in Petrograd all his days. 'Look me up, old man, won't you?'

Jerry smiled his slow smile. 'I will,' he said. 'So long.'

We will now follow the adventures of Henry. He had in him, I know, a tiny, tiny creature with sharp ironical eyes and pointed springing feet who watched his poses, his sentimentalities and heroics with affectionate scorn. This same creature watched him now as he waited to collect his bags, and then stood on the gleaming steps of the station whilst the porters fetched an Isvostchick, and the rain fell in long thundering lines of steel upon the bare and desolate streets.

'You're very miserable and lonely,' the Creature said; 'you didn't expect this.'

No, Henry had not expected this, and he also had not expected that the Isvostchick would demand eight roubles for his fare to the 'France.' Henry knew that this was the barest extortion, and he had sworn to himself long ago that he would allow nobody to 'do' him. He looked at the rain and submitted. 'After all, it's war time,' he whispered to the Creature.

He huddled himself into the cab, his baggage piled all about him, and tried by pulling at the hood to protect himself from the elements. He has told me that he felt that the rain was laughing at him; the cab was so slow that he seemed to be sitting in the middle of pools and melting snow; he was dirty, tired, hungry, and really not far from tears. Poor Henry was very, very young. . . .

He scarcely looked at the Neva as he crossed the bridge; all the length of the Quay he saw only the hunched, heavy back of the old cabman and the spurting, jumping rain, the vast stone grave-like buildings and the high grey sky. He drove through the Red Square that swung in the rain. He was thinking about the eight roubles. . . . He pulled up with a jerk outside the 'France' hotel. Here he tried, I am sure, to recover his dignity, but he was met by a large, stout, Eastern-looking gentleman with peacock feathers in his round cap who smiled gently when he heard about the eight roubles, and ushered Henry into the dark hall with a kindly patronage that admitted of no reply.

The 'France' is a good hotel, and its host is one of the kindest of mortals, but it is in many ways Russian rather than Continental in its atmosphere. That ought to have pleased and excited so sympathetic a soul as Henry. I am afraid that this moment of his arrival was the first realisation in his life of that stern truth that that which seems romantic in retrospect is only too often unpleasantly realistic in its actual experience.

He stepped into the dark hall, damp like a well, with a whirring snarling clock on the wall and a heavy glass door pulled by a rope swinging and shifting, the walls and door and rack with the letters shifting too. In this rocking world there seemed to be no stable thing. He was dirty and tired and humiliated. He explained to his host, who smiled but seemed to be thinking of other things, that he wanted a bath and a room and a meal. He was promised these things, but there was no conviction abroad that the 'France' had gone up in the world since Henry Bohun had crossed its threshold. An old man with a grey beard and the fixed and glittering eye of the 'Ancient Mariner' told him to follow him. How well I know those strange, cold, winding passages of the 'France,' creeping in and out across boards that shiver and shake, with walls pressing in upon you so thin and rocky that the wind whistles and screams and the paper makes ghostly shadows and signs as though unseen fingers moved it. There is that smell, too, which a Russian hotel alone, of all the hostelries in the world, can produce, a smell of damp and cabbage soup, of sunflower seeds and cigarette-ends, of drainage and patchouli, of, in some odd way, the sea and fish and wet pavements. It is a smell that will, until I die, be presented to me by those dark half-hidden passages, warrens of intricate fumbling ways with boards suddenly rising like little mountains in the path; behind the wainscot one hears the scuttling of innumerable rats.

The Ancient Mariner showed Henry to his room and left him. Henry was depressed at what he saw. His room was a slip cut out of other rooms, and its one window was faced by a high black wall down whose surface gleaming water trickled. The bare boards showed large and gaping cracks; there was a washstand, a bed, a chest of drawers, and a faded padded arm-chair with a hole in it. In the corner near the window was an Ikon of tinsel and wood; a little round marble-topped table offered a dusty carafe of water. A heavy red-plush bell-rope tapped the wall.

He sat down in the faded arm-chair and instantly fell asleep. Was the room hypnotic? Why not? There are stranger things than that in Petrograd. . . . I myself am aware of what walls and streets and rivers, engaged on their own secret life in that most secret of towns, can do to the mere mortals who interfere with their stealthy concerns. Henry dreamt; he was never afterwards able to tell me of what he had dreamt, but it had been a long heavy cobwebby affair, in which the walls of the hotel seemed to open and to close, black little figures moving like ants up and down across the winding ways. He saw innumerable carafes and basins and beds, the wall-paper whistling, the rats scuttling, and lines of cigarette-ends, black and yellow, moving in trails like worms across the boards. All men like worms, like ants, like rats, and the gleaming water trickling interminably down the high black wall. Of course he was tired after his long journey, hungry too, and depressed. . . . He awoke to find the Ancient Mariner watching him. He screamed. The Mariner reassured him with a toothless smile, gripped him by the arm, and showed him the bathroom.

'*Pajaluista!*' said the Mariner.

Although Henry had learnt Russian, so unexpected was the pronunciation of this familiar word that it was as though the old man had said 'Open Sesame!' . . .

V

He felt happy and consoled after a bath, a shave, and breakfast. Always I should think he reacted very quickly to his own physical sensations, and he was, as yet, too young to know that you cannot lay ghosts by the simple brushing of your hair and sponging your face. After his breakfast he lay down on the bed and again fell asleep, but this time not to dream; he slept like a Briton, dreamless, healthy and clean. He awoke as sure of himself as ever. . . . The first incantation had not, you see, been enough. . . .

He plunged into the city. It was raining with that thick dark rain that seems to have mud in it before it has fallen. The town was veiled in thin mist, figures appearing and disappearing, tram-bells ringing, and those strange wild cries in the Russian tongue that seem at one's first hearing so romantic and startling, rising sharply and yet lazily into the air. He plunged along and found himself in the Nevski Prospect – he could not mistake its breadth and assurance, dull though it seemed in the mud and rain.

But he was above all things a romantic and sentimental youth, and he was determined to see this country as he had expected to see it; so he plodded on, his coat-collar up, British obstinacy in his eyes and a little excited flutter in his heart whenever a bright colour, an Eastern face, a street pedlar, a bunched-up, high-backed coachman, anything or any one unusual presented itself.

He saw on his right a great church; it stood back from the street, having in front of it a desolate little arrangement of bushes and public seats and winding paths. The church itself was approached by flights of steps that disappeared under the shadow of a high dome supported by vast stone pillars. Letters in gold flamed across the building above the pillars.

Henry passed the intervening ground and climbed the steps. Under the pillars before the heavy, swinging doors were two rows of beggars; they were dirtier, more touzled and tangled, fiercer and more ironically, falsely submissive than any beggars that he had ever seen. He described one fellow to me, a fierce brigand with a high black hat of feathers, a soiled Cossack coat and tall dirty red leather boots; his eyes were fires, Henry said. At any rate that is what Henry liked to think they were. There was a woman with no legs, and a man with neither nose nor ears. I am sure that they watched Henry with supplicating hostility. He entered the church and was instantly swallowed up by a vast multitude.

He described to me afterwards that it was as though he had been pushed (by the evil, eager fingers of the beggars no doubt) into deep water. He rose with a gasp, and was first conscious of a strange smell of dirt and tallow and something that he did not know, but was afterwards to recognise as the scent of sunflower seed. He was pushed upon, pressed and pulled, fingered and crushed. He did not mind – he was glad – this was what he wanted. He looked about him and found that he and all the people round him were swimming in a hazy golden mist flung into the air from the thousands of lighted candles that danced in the breeze blowing through the building. The whole vast shining floor was covered with peasants, pressed, packed together. Peasants, men and women – he did not see a single member of the middle-class. In front of him under the altar there was a blaze of light, and figures moved in the blaze uncertainly, indistinctly. Now and then a sudden quiver passed across the throng, as wind blows through the corn. Here and there men and women knelt, but for the most part they stood steadfast, motionless, staring in front of them. He looked at them and discovered that they had the faces of children – simple, trustful, unintelligent, unhumorous children, – and eyes, always kindlier than any he had ever seen in other human beings. They stood there gravely, with no signs of religious fervour, with no marks of impatience or weariness, and also with no evidence of any especial interest in what was occurring. It might have been a vast concourse of sleep-walkers.

He saw that three soldiers near to him were holding hands. . . .

From the lighted altars came the echoing whisper of a monotonous chant. The sound rose and fell, scarcely a voice, scarcely an appeal, something rising from the place itself and sinking back into it again without human agency.

After a time he saw a strange movement that at first he could not understand. Then watching, he found that unlit candles were being passed from line to line, one man leaning forward and tapping the man in front of him with the candle, the man in front passing it, in his turn, forward, and so on until at last it reached the altar, where it was lighted and fastened into its sconce. This tapping with the candles happened incessantly throughout the vast crowd. Henry himself was tapped, and felt suddenly as though he had been admitted a member of some secret society. He felt the tap again and again, and soon he seemed to be hypnotised by the low chant at the altar and the motionless silent crowd and the dim golden mist. He stood, not thinking, not living, away, away, questioning nothing, wanting nothing. . . .

He must of course finish with his romantic notion. People pushed around him, struggling to get out. He turned to go and was faced, he told me, with a remarkable figure. His description, romantic and sentimental though he tried to make it, resolved itself into nothing more than the sketch of an ordinary peasant, tall, broad, black-bearded, neatly clad in blue shirt, black trousers, and high boots. This fellow stood apparently away from the crowd, apart, and watched it all, as you so often may see the Russian peasant doing, with indifferent gaze. In his mild blue eyes Bohun fancied that he saw all kinds of things – power, wisdom, prophecy – a figure apart and symbolic. But how easy in Russia it is to see symbols, and how often those symbols fail to justify themselves! Well, I let Bohun have his fancies. 'I should know that man anywhere again,' he declared. 'It was as though he knew what was going to happen and was ready for it.' Then I suppose he saw my smile, for he broke off and said no more.

And here for a moment I leave him and his adventures.

VI

I must speak, for a moment, of myself. Throughout the autumn and winter of 1914 and the spring and summer of 1915 I was with the Russian Red Cross on the Polish and Galician fronts. During the summer and early autumn of 1915 I shared with the Ninth Army the retreat through Galicia. Never very strong physically, owing to a lameness of the left hip from which I have suffered from birth, the difficulties of the retreat and the loss of my two greatest friends gave opportunities to my arch-enemy Sciatica to do what he wished with me, and in October 1915 I was forced to leave the Front and return to Petrograd. I was an invalid throughout the whole of that winter, and only gradually during the spring of 1916 was able to pull myself back to an old shadow of my former vigour and energy. I saw that I would never be good for the Front again, but I minded that the less now in that the events of the summer of 1915 had left me without heart or desire, the merest spectator of life, passive and, I cynically believed, indifferent. I was nothing to any one, nor was any one anything to me. The desire of my heart had slipped like a laughing ghost away from my ken – men of my slow warmth and cautious suspicion do not easily admit a new guest....

Moreover, during this spring of 1916 Petrograd, against my knowledge, wove webs about my feet. I had never shared the common belief that Moscow was the only town in Russia. I had always known that Petrograd had its own grace and beauty, but it was not until, sore and sick at heart, lonely and bitter against fate, haunted always by the face and laughter of one whom I would never see again, I wandered about the canals and quays and deserted byways of the city, that I began to understand its spirit. I took, to the derision of my few friends, two tumbledown rooms on Pilot's Island, at the far end of Ekateringofsky Prospect. Here amongst tangled grass, old deserted boats, stranded, ruined cottages and abraded piers, I hung above the sea. Not indeed the sea of my Glebeshire memories; this was a sluggish, tideless sea, but in the winter one sheet of ice, stretching far beyond the barrier of the eye, catching into its frosted heart every colour of the sky and air, the lights of the town, the lamps of imprisoned barges, the moon, the sun, the stars, the purple sunsets, and the strange, mysterious lights that flash from the shadows of the hovering snow-clouds. My rooms were desolate perhaps, bare boards with holes, an old cracked mirror, a stove, a bookcase, a photograph, and a sketch of Rafiel Cove. My friends looked and shivered; I, staring from my window on to the entrance into the waterways of the city, felt that any magic might come out of that strange desolation and silence. A shadow like the sweeping of the wing of a great bird would hover above the ice; a bell from some boat would ring, then the church bells of the city would answer it; the shadow would pass and the moon would rise, deep gold, and lie hard and sharp against the thick, impending air; the shadow would pass and the stars come out, breaking with an almost audible crackle through the stuff of the sky . . . and only five minutes away the shop-lights were glittering, the Isvostchiks crying to clear the road, the tram-bells clanging, the boys shouting the news. Around and about me marvellous silence. . . .

In the early autumn of 1916 I met at a dinner-party Nicolai Leontievitch Markovitch. In the course of a conversation I informed him that I had been for a year with the Ninth Army in Galicia, and he then asked me whether I had met his wife's uncle, Alexei Petrovitch Semyonov, who was also with the Ninth Army. It happened that I had known Alexei Petrovitch very well, and the sound of his name brought back to me so vividly events and persons with whom we had both been connected that I had difficulty in controlling my sudden emotion. Markovitch invited me to his house. He lived, he told me, with his wife in a flat in the Anglisky Prospect; his sister-in-law and another of his wife's uncles, a brother of Alexei Petrovitch, also lived with them. I said that I would be very glad to come.

It is impossible to describe how deeply, in the days that followed, I struggled against the attraction that this invitation presented to me. I had succeeded during all these months in avoiding any contact with the incidents or characters of the preceding year. I had written no letters and had received none; I had resolutely avoided meeting any members of my old Otriad when they came to the town.

But now I succumbed. Perhaps something of my old vitality and curiosity was already creeping back into my bones, perhaps time was already dimming my memories – at any rate, on an evening early in October I paid my call. Alexei Petrovitch was not present; he was on the Galician front, in Tarnopol. I found Markovitch, his wife Vera Michailovna, his sister-in-law Nina Michailovna, his wife's uncle Ivan Petrovitch, and a young man Boris Nicolaievitch Grogoff. Markovitch himself was a thin, loose, untidy man with pale yellow hair, thinning on top, a ragged, pale beard, a nose with a tendency to redden at any sudden insult or unkind word, and an expression perpetually anxious.

Vera Michailovna, on the other hand, was a fine young woman, and it must have been the first thought of all who met them as to why she had married him. She gave an impression of great strength; her figure tall and her bosom full, her dark eyes large and clear. She had black hair, a vast quantity of it, piled upon her head. Her face was finely moulded, her lips strong, red, sharply marked. She looked like a woman who had already made up her mind upon all things in life and could face them all. Her expression was often stern and almost insolently scornful, but also she could be tender, and her heart would shine from her eyes. She moved slowly and gracefully, and quite without self-consciousness.

A strange contrast was her sister, Nina Michailovna, a girl still, it seemed, in childhood, pretty, with brown hair, laughing eyes, and a trembling mouth that seemed ever on the edge of laughter. Her body was soft and plump; she had lovely hands, of which she was obviously very proud. Vera dressed sternly, often in black, with a soft white collar, almost like a nurse or nun. Nina was always in gay colours; she wore clothes, as it seemed to me, in very bad taste, colours clashing, strange bows and ribbons and lace that had nothing to do with the dress to which they were attached. She was always eating sweets, laughed a great deal, had a shrill piercing voice, and was never still. Ivan Petrovitch, the uncle, was very different from my Semyonov. He was short, fat, and dressed with great neatness and taste. He had a short black moustache, a head nearly bald, and a round chubby face with small smiling eyes. He was a Chinovnik, and held his position in some Government office with great pride and solemnity. It was his chief aim, I found, to be considered cosmopolitan, and when he discovered the feeble quality of my French he insisted in speaking always to me in his strange confused English, a language quite of his own, with sudden startling phrases which he had 'snatched,' as he expressed it, from Shakespeare and the Bible. He was the kindest soul alive, and all he asked was that he should be left alone and that no one should quarrel with him. He confided to me that he hated quarrels, and that it was an eternal sorrow to him that the Russian people should enjoy so greatly that pastime. I discovered that he was terrified of his brother, Alexei, and at that I was not surprised. His weakness was that he was impenetrably stupid, and it was quite impossible to make him understand anything that was not immediately in line with his own experiences – unusual obtuseness in a Russian. He was vain about his clothes, especially about his shoes, which he always had made in London; he was sentimental and very easily hurt.

Very different again was the young man Boris Nicolaievitch Grogoff. No relation of the family, he seemed to spend most of his time in the Markovitch flat. A handsome young man, strongly built, with a head of untidy curly yellow hair, blue eyes, high cheek bones, long hands with which he was for ever gesticulating. Grogoff was an internationalist Socialist, and expressed his opinions at the top of his voice whenever he could find an occasion. He would sit for hours staring moodily at the floor, or glaring fiercely upon the company. Then suddenly he would burst out, walking about, flinging up his arms, shouting. I saw at once that Markovitch did not like him, and that he despised Markovitch. He did not seem to me a very wise young man, but I liked his energy, his kindness, sudden generosities, and honesty. I could not see his reason for being so much in this company.

During the autumn of 1916 I spent more and more time with the Markovitches. I cannot tell you what was exactly the reason. Vera Michailovna perhaps, although let no one imagine that I fell in love with her or ever thought of doing so. No, my time for that was over. But I felt from the first that she was a fine, understanding creature, that she sympathised with me without pitying me, that she would be a good and loyal friend, and that I, on my side, could give her comprehension and fidelity. They made me feel at home with them; there had been as yet no house in Petrograd whither I could go easily and without ceremony, which I could leave at any moment that I wished. Soon they did not notice whether I were there or not; they continued their ordinary lives, and Nina, to whom I was old, plain, and feeble, treated me with a friendly indifference that did not hurt as it might have done in England. Boris Grogoff patronised and laughed at me, but would give me anything in the way of help, property, or opinions, did I need it. I was in fact by Christmas time a member of the family. They nicknamed me 'Durdles,' after many jokes about my surname and reminiscences of 'Edwin Drood' (my Russian name was Ivan Andreievitch). We had merry times in spite of the troubles and distresses now crowding upon Russia.

And now I come to the first of the links in my story. It was with this family that Henry Bohun was to lodge.

VII

Some three years before, when Ivan Petrovitch had gone to live with the Markovitches, it had occurred to them that they had two empty rooms and that these would accommodate one or two paying guests. It seemed to them still more attractive that these guests should be English, and I expect that it was Ivan Petrovitch who emphasised this. The British Consulate was asked to assist them, and after a few inconspicuous clerks and young business men they entertained for a whole six months the Hon. Charles Trafford, one of the junior secretaries at the Embassy. At the end of those six months the Hon. Charles, burdened with debt, and weakened by little sleep and much liquor, was removed to a less exciting atmosphere. With all his faults, he left faithful friends in the Markovitch flat, and he, on his side, gave so enthusiastic an account of Mme. Markovitch's attempts to restrain and modify his impetuosities that the Embassy recommended her care and guidance to other young secretaries. The war came and Vera Michailovna declared that she could have lodgers no longer, and a terrible blow this was to Ivan Petrovitch. Then suddenly, towards the end of 1916, she changed her mind and announced to the Embassy that she was ready for any one whom they could send her. Henry Bohun was offered, accepted, and prepared for. Ivan Petrovitch was a happy man once more.

I never discovered that Markovitch was much consulted in these affairs. Vera Michailovna 'ran' the flat financially, industrially, and spiritually. Markovitch meanwhile was busy with his inventions. I have, as yet, said nothing about Nicolai Leontievitch's inventions. I hesitate, indeed, to speak of them, although they are so essential, and indeed important, a part of my story. I hesitate simply because I do not wish this narrative to be at all fantastic, but that it should stick quite honestly and obviously to the truth. It is certain, moreover, that what is naked truth to one man seems the falsest fancy to another, and after all I have, from beginning to end, only my own conscience to satisfy. The history of the human soul and its relation to divinity, which is, I think, the only history worth any man's pursuit, must push its way, again and again, through this same tangled territory which infests the region lying between truth and fantasy; one passes suddenly into a world that seems pure falsehood, so askew, so obscure, so twisted and coloured is it. One is through, one looks back and it lies behind one as the clearest truth. Such an experience makes one tender to other men's fancies and less impatient of the vague and half-defined travellers' tales that other men tell. Childe Roland is not the only traveller who has challenged the Dark Tower.

In the Middle Ages Nicolai Leontievitch Markovitch would have been called, I suppose, a Magician – a very half-hearted and unsatisfactory one he would always have been – and he would have been most certainly burnt at the stake before he had accomplished any magic worthy of the name. His inventions, so far as I saw anything of them, were innocent and simple enough. It was the man himself rather than his inventions that arrested the attention. About the time of Bohun's arrival upon the scene it was a new kind of ink that he had discovered, and for many weeks the Markovitch flat dripped ink from every pore. He had no laboratory, no scientific materials, nor, I think, any profound knowledge. The room where he worked was a small box-like place off the living-room, a cheerless enough abode with a little high barred window in it as in a prison-cell, cardboard-boxes piled high with feminine garments, a sewing-machine, old dusty books, and a broken-down perambulator occupying most of the space. I never could understand why the perambulator was there, as the Markovitches had no children. Nicolai Leontievitch sat at a table under the little window, and his favourite position was to sit with the chair perched on one leg, and so, rocking in this insecure position, he brooded over his bottles and glasses and trays. This room was so dark even in the middle of the day that he was often compelled to use a lamp. There he hovered, with his ragged beard, his ink-stained fingers, and his red-rimmed eyes, making strange noises to himself and evolving from his materials continual little explosions that caused him infinite satisfaction. He did not mind interruptions, nor did he ever complain of the noise in the other room, terrific though it often was. He would be absorbed, in a trance, lost in another world, and surely amiable and harmless enough. And yet not entirely amiable. His eyes would close to little spots of dull, lifeless colour – the only thing alive about him seemed to be his hands that moved and stirred as though they did not belong to his body at all, but had an independent existence of their own – and his heels protruding from under his chair were like horrid little animals waiting, malevolently, on guard.

His inventions were, of course, never successful, and he contributed, therefore, nothing to the maintenance of his household. Vera Michailovna had means of her own, and there were also the paying guests. But he suffered from no sense of distress at his impecuniosity. I discovered very quickly that Vera Michailovna kept the family purse, and one of the earliest sources of family trouble was, I fancy, his constant demands for money. Before the war he had, I believe, been drunk whenever it was possible. Because drink was difficult to obtain, and in a flood of patriotism roused by the enthusiasm of the early days of the war, he declared himself a teetotaller, and marvellously he kept his vows. This abstinence was now one of his greatest prides, and he liked to tell you about it. Nevertheless he needed money as badly as ever, and he borrowed whenever he could. One of the first things that Vera Michailovna told me was that I was on no account to open my purse to him. I was not always able to keep my promise.

On this particular evening of Bohun's arrival I came, by invitation, to supper. They had told me about their Englishman, and had asked me indeed to help the first awkward half-hour over the stile. It may seem strange that the British Embassy should have chosen so uncouth a host as Nicolai Leontievitch for their innocent secretaries, but it was only the more enterprising of the young men who preferred to live in a Russian family; most of them inhabited elegant flats of their own, ornamented with coloured stuffs and gaily decorated cups and bright trays from the Jews' Market, together with English comforts and luxuries dragged all the way from London. Moreover, Markovitch figured very slightly in the consciousness of his guests, and the rest of the flat was roomy and clean and light. It was, like most of the homes of the Russian Intelligentzia, over-burdened with family history. Amazing the things that Russians will gather together and keep, one must suppose, only because they are too lethargic to do away with them. On the walls of the Markovitch dining-room all kinds of pictures were hung – old family photographs yellow and dusty, old calendars, prints of ships at sea, and young men hanging over stiles, and old ladies having tea, photographs of the Kremlin and the Lavra at Kieff, copies of Ivan and his murdered son and Serov's portrait of Chaliapine as Boris Godounov. Bookcases there were with tattered editions of Pushkin and Lermontov. The middle of the living-room was occupied with an enormous table covered by a dark red cloth, and this table was the centre of the life of the family. A large clock wheezed and groaned against the wall, and various chairs of different shapes and sizes filled up most of the remaining space. Nevertheless, although everything in the room looked old except the white and gleaming stove, Vera Michailovna spread over the place the impress of her strong and active personality. It was not a sluggish room, nor was it untidy as so many Russian rooms are. Around the table everybody sat. It seemed that at all hours of the day and night some kind of meal was in progress there; and it was almost certain that from half-past two in the afternoon until half-past two on the following morning the samovar would be found there, presiding with sleepy dignity over the whole family and caring nothing for anybody. I can smell now that especial smell of tea and radishes and salted fish, and can hear the wheeze of the clock, the hum of the samovar, Nina's shrill laugh and Boris's deep voice. . . . I owe that room a great deal. It was there that I was taken out of myself and memories that fared no better for their perpetual resurrection. That room called me back to life.

On this evening there was to be, in honour of young Bohun, an especially fine dinner. A message had come from him that he would appear with his boxes at half-past seven. When I arrived Vera was busy in the kitchen, and Nina adding in her bedroom extra ribbons and laces to her costume; Boris Nicolaievitch was not present; Nicolai Leontievitch was working in his den.

I went through to him. He did not look up as I came in. The room was darker than usual; the green shade over the lamp was tilted wickedly as though it were cocking its eye at Markovitch's vain hopes, and there was the man himself, one cheek a ghastly green, his hair on end, and his chair precariously balanced.

I heard him say as though he repeated an incantation – 'Nu Vot . . . Nu Vot . . . Nu Vot.'

'Zdras te, Nicolai Leontievitch,' I said. Then I did not disturb him but sat down on a rickety chair and waited. Ink dripped from his table on to the floor. One bottle lay on its side, the ink oozing out; other bottles stood, some filled, some half-filled, some empty.

'Ah, ha!' he cried, and there was a little explosion; a cork spurted out and struck the ceiling; there was smoke and the crackling of glass. He turned round and faced me, a smudge of ink on one of his cheeks, and that customary nervous unhappy smile on his lips.

'Well, how goes it?' I asked.

'Well enough.' He touched his cheek, then sucked his fingers. 'I must wash. We have a guest to-night. And the news, what's the latest?'

He always asked me this question, having apparently the firm conviction that an Englishman must know more about the war than a man of any other nationality. But he didn't pause for an answer – 'News – but of course there is none. What can you expect from this Russia of ours? – and the rest – it's all too far away for any of us to know anything about it – only Germany's close at hand. Yes. Remember that. You forget it sometimes in England. She's very near indeed. . . . We've got a guest coming – from the English Embassy. His name's Boon and a funny name too. You don't know him, do you?'

No, I didn't know him. I laughed. Why should he think that I always knew everybody, I who kept to myself so?

'The English always stick together. That's more than can be said for us Russians. We're a rotten lot. Well, I must go and wash.'

Then, whether by a sudden chance of light and shade, or, if you like to have it, by a sudden revelation on the part of a beneficent Providence, he really did look malevolent, standing in the middle of the dirty little room, malevolent and pathetic too, like a cross, sick bird.

'Vera's got a good dinner ready. That's one thing, Ivan Andreievitch,' he said; 'and vodka – a little bottle. We got it from a friend. But I don't drink now, you know.'

He went off, and I, going into the other room, found Vera Michailovna giving last touches to the table. I sat and watched with pleasure her calm assured movements. She really was splendid, I thought, with the fine carriage of her head, her large mild eyes, her firm strong hands.

'All ready for the guest, Vera Michailovna?' I asked.

'Yes,' she answered, smiling at me, 'I hope so. He won't be very particular, will he, because we aren't princes?'

'I can't answer for him,' I replied, smiling back at her. 'But he can't be more particular than the Hon. Charles – and he was a great success.'

The Hon. Charles was a standing legend in the family, and we always laughed when we mentioned him.

'I don't know' – she stopped her work at the table and stood, her hand up to her brow as though she would shade her eyes from the light – 'I wish he wasn't coming – the new Englishman, I mean. Better perhaps as we were – Nicholas——' she stopped short. 'Oh, I don't know! They're difficult times, Ivan Andreievitch.'

The door opened and old Uncle Ivan came in. He was dressed very smartly with a clean white shirt and a black bow tie and black patent leather shoes, and his round face shone as the sun.

'Ah, Mr. Durward,' he said, trotting forward. 'Good health to you! What excellent weather we're sharing.'

'So we are, M. Semyonov,' I answered him. 'Although it did rain most of yesterday, you know. But weather of the soul perhaps you mean? In that case I'm very glad to hear that you are well.'

'Ah – of the soul?' He always spoke his words very carefully, clipping and completing them, and then standing back to look at them as though they were china ornaments arranged on a shining table. 'No – my soul today is not of the first rank, I'm afraid.'

It was obvious that he was in a state of the very greatest excitement; he could not keep still, but walked up and down beside the long table, fingering the knives and forks.

Then Nina burst in upon us in one of her frantic rages. Her tempers were famous both for their ferocity and the swiftness of their passing. In the course of them she was like some impassioned bird of brilliant plumage, tossing her feathers, fluttering behind the bars of her cage at some impertinent, teasing passer-by. She stood there now in the doorway, gesticulating with her hands.

'*Nu, tznaiesh schto?* Michael Alexandrovitch has put me off – says he is busy all night at the office. He busy all night! Don't I know the business he's after? And it's the third time – I won't see him again – no, I won't. He——'

'Good evening, Nina Michailovna,' I said, smiling. She turned to me.

'Durdles – Mr. Durdles – only listen. It was all arranged for to-night – the *Parisiana*, and then we were to come straight back——'

'But your guest——' I began.

However, the torrent continued. The door opened and Boris Grogoff came in. Instantly she turned upon him.

'There's your fine friend!' she cried; 'Michael Alexandrovitch isn't coming. Put me off at the last moment, and it's the third time. And I might have gone to Musikalnaya Drama. I was asked by——'

'Well, why not?' Grogoff interrupted calmly. 'If he had something better to do——'

Then she turned upon him, screaming, and in a moment they were at it, tooth and nail, heaping up old scores, producing fact after fact to prove, the one to the other, false friendship, lying manners, deceitful promises, perjured records. Vera tried to interrupt, Markovitch said something, I began a remonstrance – in a moment we were all at it, and the room was a whirl of noise. In the tempest it was only I who heard the door open. I turned and saw Henry Bohun standing there.

I smile now when I think of that moment of his arrival, so fitting to the characters of the place, so appropriate a symbol of what was to come. Bohun was beautifully dressed, spotlessly neat, in a bowler hat a little to one side, a light-blue silk scarf, a dark-blue overcoat. His face wore an expression of dignified self-appreciation. It was as though he stood there breathing blessings on the house that he had sanctified by his arrival. He looked, too, with it all, such a boy that my heart was touched. And there was something good and honest about his eyes.

He may have spoken, but certainly no one heard him in the confusion.

I just caught Nina's shrill voice: 'Listen, all of you! There you are! You hear what he says! That I told him it was to be Tuesday when, everybody knows – Verotchka! Ah – Verotchka! He says——' Then she paused; I caught her amazed glance at the door, her gasp, a scream of stifled laughter, and behold she was gone!

Then they all saw. There was instant silence, a terrible pause, and then Bohun's polite gentle voice: 'Is this where Mr. Markovitch lives? I beg your pardon——'

Great awkwardness followed. It is quite an illusion to suppose that Russians are easy, affable hosts. I know of no people in the world who are so unable to put you at your ease if there is something unfortunate in the air. They have few easy social graces, and they are inclined to abandon at once a situation if it is made difficult for them. If it needs an effort to make a guest happy they leave him alone and trust to a providence in whose powers, however, they entirely disbelieve. Bohun was led to his room, his bags being carried by old Sacha, the Markovitch's servant, and the Dvornik.

His bags, I remember, were very splendid, and I saw the eyes of Uncle Ivan grow large as he watched their progress. Then with a sigh he drew a chair up to the table and began eating zakuska, putting salt-fish and radishes and sausage on to his plate and eating them with a fork.

'Dyadya, Ivan!' Vera said reproachfully. 'Not yet – we haven't begun. Ivan Andreievitch, what do you think? Will he want hot water?'

She hurried after him.

The evening thus unfortunately begun was not happily continued. There was a blight upon us all. I did my best, but I was in considerable pain and very tired. Moreover, I was not favourably impressed with my first sight of young Bohun. He seemed to me foolish and conceited. Uncle Ivan was afraid of him. He made only one attack.

'It was a very fruitful journey that you had, sir, I hope?'

'I beg your pardon,' said Bohun.

'A very fruitful journey – nothing burdensome nor extravagant?'

'Oh, all right, thanks,' Bohun answered, trying unsuccessfully to show that he was not surprised at my friend's choice of words. But Uncle Ivan saw that he had not been successful and his lip trembled. Markovitch was silent and Boris Nicolaievitch sulked. Only once towards the end of the meal Bohun interested me.

'I wonder,' he asked me, 'whether you know a fellow called Lawrence? He travelled from England with me. A man who's played a lot of football.'

'Not Jerry Lawrence, the international!' I said. 'Surely he can't have come out here?' Of course it was the same. I was interested and strangely pleased. The thought of Lawrence's square back and cheery smile was extremely agreeable just then.

'Oh! I'm very glad,' I answered. 'I must get him to come and see me. I knew him pretty well at one time. Where's he to be found?'

Bohun, with an air of rather gentle surprise, as though he could not help thinking it strange that any one should take an interest in Lawrence's movements, told me where he was lodging.

'And I hope you also will find your way to me sometime,' I added. 'It's an out-of-place grimy spot, I'm afraid. You might bring Lawrence round one evening.'

Soon after that, feeling that I could do no more towards retrieving an evening definitely lost, I departed. At the last I caught Markovitch's eye. He seemed to be watching for something. A new invention perhaps. He was certainly an unhappy man.

VIII

I was to meet Jerry Lawrence sooner than I had expected. And it was in this way.

Two days after the evening that I have just described I was driven to go and see Vera Michailovna. I was driven, partly by my curiosity, partly by my depression, and partly by my loneliness. This same loneliness was, I believe, at this time beginning to affect us all. I should be considered perhaps to be speaking with exaggeration if I were to borrow the title of one of Mrs. Oliphant's old-fashioned and charming novels and to speak of Petrograd as already 'A Beleaguered City' – beleaguered, moreover, in very much the same sense as that other old city was. From the very beginning of the war Petrograd was isolated – isolated not by the facts of the war, its geographical position or any of the obvious causes, but simply by the contempt and hatred with which it was regarded. From very old days it was spoken of as a German town. 'If you want to know Russia don't go to Petrograd.' 'Simply a cosmopolitan town like any other.' 'A smaller Berlin' – and so on, and so on. This sense of outside contempt influenced its own attitude to the world. It was always at war with Moscow. It showed you when you first arrived its Nevski, its ordered squares, its official buildings, as though it would say: 'I suppose you will take the same view as the rest. If you don't wish to look any deeper, here you are. I'm not going to help you.'

As the war developed it lost whatever gaiety and humour it had had. After the fall of Warsaw the attitude of the Russian people in general became fatalistic. Much nonsense was talked in the foreign press about 'Russia coming back again and again.' 'Russia, the harder she was pressed the harder she resisted,' and the ghost of Napoleon retreating from Moscow was presented to every home in Europe; but the plain truth was that, after Warsaw, the temper of the people changed. Things were going wrong once more, as they had always gone wrong in Russian history, and as they always would go wrong. Then followed bewilderment. What to do? Whose fault was it all? Shall we blame our blood or our rulers? Our rulers, certainly, as we always, with justice, have blamed them – our blood, too, perhaps. From the fall of Warsaw, in spite of momentary flashes of splendour and courage, the Russians were a blindfolded, naked people, fighting a nation fully armed. Now, Europe was vast continents away, and only Germany, that old Germany whose soul was hateful, whose practical spirit was terribly admirable, was close at hand. The Russian people turned hither and thither, first to its Czar, then to its generals, then to its democratic spirit, then to its idealism – and there was no hope anywhere. They appealed for Liberty. In the autumn of 1916 a great prayer from the whole country went up that the bandage might be taken from its eyes, and soon, lest when the light did at last come the eyes should be so unused to it that they should see nothing. Nicholas had his opportunity – the greatest opportunity perhaps ever offered to man. He refused it. From that moment the easiest way was closed, and only a most perilous rocky path remained.

With every week of that winter of 1916 Petrograd stepped deeper and deeper into the darkness. Its strangeness grew and grew upon me as the days filed through. I wondered whether my illness and the troubles of the preceding year made me see everything at an impossible angle – or it was perhaps my isolated lodging, my crumbling rooms, with the grey expanse of sea and sky in front of them that was responsible. Whatever it was, Petrograd soon came to be to me a place with a most terrible secret life of its own.

There is an old poem of Pushkin's that Alexandre Benois has most marvellously illustrated, which has for its theme the rising of the river Neva in November 1824. On that occasion the splendid animal devoured the town, and in Pushkin's poem you feel the devastating power of the beast, and in Benois' pictures you can see it licking its lips as it swallowed down pillars and bridges and streets and squares with poor little fragments of humanity clutching and crying and fruitlessly appealing.

This poem only emphasised for me the suspicion that I had originally had, that the great river and the marshy swamp around it despised contemptuously the buildings that man had raised beside and upon it, and that even the buildings in their turn despised the human beings who thronged them. It could only be some sense of this kind that could make one so repeatedly conscious that one's feet were treading ancient ground.

The town, raised all of a piece by Peter the Great, could claim no ancient history at all; but through every stick and stone that had been laid there stirred the spirit and soul of the ground, so that out of one of the sluggish canals one might expect at any moment to see the horrid and scaly head of some palaeolithic monster with dead and greedy eyes slowly push its way up that it might gaze at the little black hurrying atoms as they crossed and recrossed the grey bridge. There are many places in Petrograd where life is utterly dead; where some building, half-completed, has fallen into red and green decay; where the water lies still under iridescent scum, and thick clotted reeds seem to stand at bay, concealing in their depths some terrible monster.

At such a spot I have often fancied that the eyes of countless inhabitants of that earlier world are watching me, and that not far away the waters of Neva are gathering, gathering, gathering their mighty momentum for some instant, when, with a great heave and swell, they will toss the whole fabric of brick and mortar from their shoulders, flood the streets and squares, and then sink tranquilly back into great sheets of unruffled waters marked only with reeds and the sharp cry of some travelling bird.

All this may be fantastic enough, I only know that it was sufficiently real to me during that winter of 1916 to be ever at the back of my mind; and I believe that some sense of that kind had in all sober reality something to do with that strange weight of uneasy anticipation that we all of us, yes, the most unimaginative amongst us, felt at this time.

Upon this afternoon, when I went to pay my call on Vera Michailovna, the real snow began to fall. We had had the false preliminary attempt a fortnight before; now in the quiet persistent determination, the solid soft resilience beneath one's feet, and the patient acquiescence of roofs and bridges and cobbles one knew that the real winter had come. Already, although it was only four o'clock in the afternoon, there was darkness, with the strange almost metallic glow as of the light from an inverted looking-glass that snow makes upon the air. I had not far to go, but the long stretch of the Ekateringofsky Canal was black and gloomy and desolate, repeating here and there the pale yellow reflection of some lamp, but for the most part dim and dead, with the hulks of barges lying like sleeping monsters on its surface. As I turned into Anglisky Prospect I found stretched like a black dado, far down the street, against the wall, a queue of waiting women. They would be there until the early morning, many of them, and it was possible that then the bread would not be sufficient. And this not from any real Jack, but simply from the mistakes of a bungling, peculating Government. No wonder that one's heart was heavy.

I found Vera Michailovna, to my relief, alone. When Sacha brought me into the room she was doing what I think I had never seen her do before, sitting unoccupied, her eyes staring in front of her, her hands folded on her lap.

'I don't believe that I've ever caught you idle before, Vera Michailovna,' I said.

'Oh, I'm glad you've come!' She caught my hand with an eagerness very different from her usual calm, quiet greeting. 'Sit down. It's an extraordinary thing. At that very moment I was wishing for you.'

'What is it I can do for you?' I asked. 'You know that I would do anything for you.'

'Yes, I know that you would. But – well. You can't help me because I don't know what's the matter with me.'

'That's very unlike you,' I said.

'Yes, I know it is – and perhaps that's why I am frightened. It's so vague; and you know I long ago determined that if I couldn't define a trouble and have it there in front of me, so that I could strangle it – why, I wouldn't bother about it. But those things are so easy to say.'

She got up and began to walk up and down the room. That again was utterly unlike her, and altogether I seemed to be seeing, this afternoon, some quite new Vera Michailovna, some one more intimate, more personal, more appealing. I realised suddenly that she had never before, at any period of our friendship, asked for my help – not even for my sympathy. She was so strong and reliant and independent, cared so little for the opinion of others, and shut down so closely upon herself her private life, that I could not have imagined her asking help from any one. And of the two of us, she was the man, the strong determined soul, the brave and self-reliant character. It seemed to me ludicrous that she should ask for my help. Nevertheless I was greatly touched.

'I would do anything for you,' I said.

She turned to me, a splendid figure, her head, with its crown of black hair, lifted, her hands on her hips, her eyes gravely regarding me.

'There are three things,' she said, 'perhaps all of them nothing. . . . And yet all of them disturbing. First my husband. He's beginning to drink again.'

'Drink?' I said; 'where can he get it from?'

'I don't know. I must discover. But it isn't the actual drinking. Every one in our country drinks if he can. Only what has made my husband break his resolve? He was so proud of it. You know how proud he was. And he lies about it. He says he is not drinking. He never used to lie about anything. That was not one of his faults.'

'Perhaps his inventions,' I suggested.

'Pouf! His inventions! You know better than that, Ivan Andreievitch. No, no. It is something. . . . He's not himself. Well, then, secondly, there's Nina. The other night did you notice anything?'

'Only that she lost her temper. But she's always doing that.'

'No, it's more than that. She's unhappy, and I don't like the life she's leading. Always out at cinematographs and theatres and restaurants, and with a lot of boys who mean no harm, I know – but they're idiotic, they're no good. . . . Now, when the war's like this and the suffering. . . . To be always at the cinematograph! But I've lost my authority over her, Ivan Andreievitch. She doesn't care any longer what I say to her. Once, and not so long ago, I meant so much to her. She's changed, she's harder, more careless, more selfish. You know, Ivan Andreievitch, that Nina's simply everything to me. I don't talk about myself, do I? but at least I can say that since – oh, many, many years, she's been the whole world and more than the whole world to me. Our mother and father were killed in a railway accident coming up from Odessa when Nina was very small, and since then Nina's been mine – all mine!'

She said that word with sudden passion, flinging it at me with a fierce gesture of her hands. 'Do you know what it is to want that something should belong to you, belong entirely to you, and to no one else? I've been too proud to say, but I've wanted that terribly all my life. I haven't had children, although I prayed for them, and perhaps now it is as well. But Nina! She's known she was mine, and, until now, she's loved to know it. But now she's escaping from me, and she knows that too, and is ashamed. I think I could bear anything but that sense that she herself has that she's being wrong – I hate her to be ashamed.'

'Perhaps,' I suggested, 'it's time that she went out into the world now and worked. There are a thousand things that a woman can do.'

'No – not Nina. I've spoilt her, perhaps; I don't know. I always liked to feel that she needed my help. I didn't want to make her too self-reliant. That was wrong of me, and I shall be punished for it.'

'Speak to her,' I said. 'She loves you so much that one word from you to her will be enough.'

'No,' Vera Michailovna said slowly. 'It won't be enough now. A year ago, yes. But now she's escaping as fast as she can.'

'Perhaps she's in love with some one,' I suggested.

'No. I should have seen at once if it had been that. I would rather it were that. I think she would come back to me then. No, I suppose that this had to happen. I was foolish to think that it would not. But it leaves one alone – it——'

She pulled herself up at that, regarding me with sudden shyness, as though she would forbid me to hint that she had shown the slightest emotion, or made in any way an appeal for pity.

I was silent, then I said:

'And the third thing, Vera Michailovna?'

'Uncle Alexei is coming back.'

That startled me. I felt my heart give one frantic leap.

'Alexei Petrovitch!' I cried. 'When? How soon?'

'I don't know. I've had a letter.' She felt in her dress, found the letter and read it through. 'Soon, perhaps. He's leaving the Front for good. He's disgusted with it all, he says. He's going to take up his Petrograd practice again.'

'Will he live with you?'

'No. God forbid!'

She felt then, perhaps, that her cry had revealed more than she intended, because she smiled and, trying to speak lightly, said:

'No. We're old enemies, my uncle and I. We don't get on. He thinks me sentimental; I think him – but never mind what I think him. He has a bad effect on my husband.'

'A bad effect?' I repeated.

'Yes. He irritates him. He laughs at his inventions, you know.'

I nodded my head. Yes, with my earlier experience of him I could understand that he would do that.

'He's a cynical, embittered man,' I said. 'He believes in nothing and in nobody. And yet he has his fine side——'

'No, he has no fine side,' she interrupted me fiercely. 'None. He is a bad man. I've known him all my life, and I'm not to be deceived.'

Then in a softer, quieter tone she continued:

'But tell me, Ivan Andreievitch. I've wanted before to ask you. You were with him on the Front last year. We have heard that he had a great love affair there, and that the Sister whom he loved was killed. Is that true?'

'Yes,' I said, 'that is true.'

'Was he very much in love with her?'

'I believe terribly.'

'And it hurt him deeply when she was killed?'

'Desperately deeply.'

'But what kind of woman was she? What type? It's so strange to me. Uncle Alexei . . . with his love affairs!'

I looked up, smiling. 'She was your very opposite, Vera Michailovna, in everything. Like a child – with no knowledge, no experience, no self-reliance – nothing. She was wonderful in her ignorance and bravery. We all thought her wonderful.'

'And she loved *him*?'

'Yes – she loved him.'

'How strange! Perhaps there is some good in him somewhere. But to us at any rate he always brings trouble. This affair may have changed him. They say he is very different. Worse perhaps——'

She broke out then into a cry:

'I want to get away, Ivan Andreievitch! To get away, to escape, to leave Russia and everything in it behind me! To escape!'

It was just then that Sacha knocked on the door. She came in to say that there was an Englishman in the hall inquiring for the other Englishman who had come yesterday, that he wanted to know when he would be back.

'Perhaps I can help,' I said. I went out into the hall and there I found Jerry Lawrence.

He stood there in the dusk of the little hall looking as resolute and unconcerned as an Englishman, in a strange and uncertain world, is expected to look. Not that he ever considered the attitudes fitting to adopt on certain occasions. He would tell you, if you inquired, that 'he couldn't stand those fellows who looked into every glass they passed.' His brow wore now a simple and innocent frown like that of a healthy baby presented for the first time with a strange and alarming rattle. It was only later that I was to arrive at some faint conception of Lawrence's marvellous acceptance of anything that might happen to turn up. Vice, cruelty, unsuspected beauty, terror, remorse, hatred, and ignorance – he accepted them all once they were there in front of him. He sometimes, as I shall on a later occasion show, allowed himself a free expression of his views in the company of those whom he could trust, but they were never the views of a suspicious or a disappointed man. It was not that he had great faith in human nature. He had, I think, very little. Nor was he without curiosity – far from it. But once a thing was really there he wasted no time over exclamations as to the horror or beauty or abomination of its actual presence. There was as he once explained to me, 'precious little time to waste.' Those who thought him a dull, silent fellow – and they were many – made of course an almost ludicrous mistake, but most people in life are, I take it, too deeply occupied with their own personal history to do more than estimate at its surface value the appearance of others . . . but after all such a dispensation makes, in all probability, for the Zgeneral happiness. . . .

On this present occasion Jerry Lawrence stood there exactly as I had seen him stand many times on the football field waiting for the referee's whistle, his thick, short body held together, his mouth shut and his eyes on guard. He did not at first recognise me.

'You've forgotten me,' I said.

'I beg your pardon,' he answered in his husky, good-natured voice, like the rumble of an amiable bull-dog.

'My name is Durward,' I said, holding out my hand. 'And years ago we had a mutual friend in Olva Dune.'

That pleased him. He gripped my hand very heartily and smiled a big ugly smile. 'Why, yes,' he said. 'Of course. How are you? Feeling fit? Damned long ago all that, isn't it? Hope you're really fit.'

'Oh, I'm all right,' I answered. 'I was never a Hercules, you know. I heard that you were here from Bohun. I was going to write to you. But it's excellent that we should meet like this.'

'I was after young Bohun,' he explained. 'But it's pleasant to find there's another fellow in the town one knows. I've been a bit at sea these two days. To tell you the truth I never wanted to come.' I heard a rumble in his throat that sounded like 'silly blighters.'

'Come in,' I said. 'You must meet Madame Markovitch with whom Bohun is staying – and then wait a bit. He won't be long, I expect.'

The idea of this seemed to fill Jerry with alarm. He turned back toward the door. 'Oh! I don't think . . . she won't want . . . better another time . . .' his mouth was filled with indistinct rumblings.

'Nonsense.' I caught his arm. 'She is delightful. You must make yourself at home here. They'll be only too glad.'

'Does she speak English?' he asked.

'No,' I answered. 'But that's all right.'

He backed again towards the door.

'My Russian's so slow,' he said. 'Never been here since I was a kid. I'd rather not, really——'

However, I dragged him in and introduced him. I had quite a fatherly desire, as I watched him, that 'he should make good.' But I'm afraid that that first interview was not a great success. Vera Michailovna was strange that afternoon, excited and disturbed as I had never known her, and I could see that it was only with the greatest difficulty that she could bring herself to think about Jerry at all.

And Jerry himself was so unresponsive that I could have beaten him. 'Why, you're duller than you used to be,' I thought to myself, and wondered how I could have suspected, in those days, subtle depths and mysterious comprehensions. Vera Michailovna asked him questions about France and London but, quite obviously, did not listen to his answers.

After ten minutes he pulled himself up slowly from his chair:

'Well, I must be going,' he said. 'Tell young Bohun I shall be waiting for him to-night – 7.30 – Astoria——' He turned to Vera Michailovna to say good-bye, and then, suddenly, as she rose and their eyes met, they seemed to strike some unexpected chord of sympathy. It took both of them, I think, by surprise; for quite a moment they stared at one another.

'Please come whenever you want to see your friend,' she said; 'we shall be delighted.'

'Thank you,' he answered simply, and went.

When he had gone she said to me:

'I like that man. One could trust him.'

'Yes, one could,' I answered her.

IX

I must return now to young Henry Bohun. I would like to arouse your sympathy for him, but sympathy's a dangerous medicine for the young, who are only too ready, so far as their self-confidence goes, to take a mile if you give them an inch. But with Bohun it was simply a case of re-delivering, piece by piece, the mile that he had had no possible right to imagine in his possession, and at the end of his relinquishment he was as naked and impoverished a soul as any life with youth and health on its side can manage to sustain. He was very miserable during these first weeks, and then it must be remembered that Petrograd was, at this time, no very happy place for anybody. Bohun was not a coward – he would have stood the worst things in France without flinching – but he was neither old enough nor young enough to face without a tremor the queer world of nerves and unfulfilled expectation in which he found himself. In the first place, Petrograd was so very different from anything that he had expected. Its size and space, its power of reducing the human figure to a sudden speck of insignificance, its strange lights and shadows, its waste spaces and cold, empty, moonlit squares, its jumble of modern and mediaeval civilisation, above all, its supreme indifference to all and sundry – these things cowed and humiliated him. He was sharp enough to realise that here he was nobody at all. Then he had not expected to be so absolutely cut off from all that he had known. The Western world simply did not seem to exist. The papers came so slowly that on their arrival they were not worth reading. He had not told his friends in England to send his letters through the Embassy bag, with the result that they would not, he was informed, reach him for months.

Of his work I do not intend here to speak, – it does not come into this story, – but he found that it was most complicated and difficult, and kicks rather than halfpence would be the certain reward. And Bohun hated kicks. . . .

Finally, he could not be said to be happy in the Markovitch flat. He had, poor boy, heard so much about Russian hospitality, and had formed, from the reading of the books of Mr. Stephen Graham and others, delightful pictures of the warmest hearts in the world holding out the warmest hands before the warmest samovars. In its spirit that was true enough, but it was not true in the way that Bohun expected it.

The Markovitches, during those first weeks, left him to look after himself because they quite honestly believed that that was the thing that he would prefer. Uncle Ivan tried to entertain him, but Bohun found him a bore, and with the ruthless intolerance of the very young, showed him so. The family did not put itself out to please him in any way. He had his room and his latchkey. There was always coffee in the morning, dinner at half-past six, and the samovar from half-past nine onwards. But the Markovitch family life was not turned from its normal course. Why should it be?

And then he was laughed at. Nina laughed at him. Everything about him seemed to Nina ridiculous – his cold bath in the morning, his trouser-press, the little silver-topped bottles on his table, the crease in his trousers, his shining neat hair, the pearl pin in his black tie, his precise and careful speech, the way that he said 'Nu tak . . . Spasebo . . . gavoreet . . . gariachy . . .' She was never tired of imitating him; and very soon he caught her strutting about the dining-room with a man's cap on her head, twisting a cane and bargaining with an Isvostchik – this last because, only the evening before, he had told them with great pride of his cleverness in that especial direction. The fun was good-natured enough, but it was, as Russian chaff generally is, quite regardless of sensitive feelings. Nina chaffed everybody and nobody minded, but Bohun did not know this, and minded very much indeed. He showed during dinner that evening that he was hurt, and sat over his cabbage soup very dignified and silent. This made every one uncomfortable, although Vera told me afterwards that she found it difficult not to laugh. The family did not make themselves especially pleasant, as Henry felt they ought to have done – they continued the even tenor of their way. He was met by one of those sudden cold horrible waves of isolated terror with which it pleases Russia sometimes to overwhelm one. The snow was falling; the town was settling into a suspicious ominous quiet. There was no light in the sky, and horrible winds blew round the corners of abandoned streets. Henry was desperately homesick. He would have cut and run, had there been any possible means of doing it. He did not remember the wild joy with which he had heard, only a few weeks before, that he was to come to Petrograd.

He had forgotten even the splendours of *Discipline*. He only knew that he was lonely and frightened and home-sick. He seemed to be without a friend in the world.

But he was proud. He confided in nobody. He went about with his head up, and every one thought him the most conceited young puppy who had ever trotted the Petrograd streets. And, although he never owned it even to himself, Jerry Lawrence seemed to him now the one friendly soul in all the world. You could be sure that Lawrence would be always the same; he would not laugh at you behind your back; if he disliked something he would say so. You knew where you were with him, and in the uncertain world in which poor Bohun found himself that simply was everything. Bohun would have denied it vehemently if you told him that he had once looked down on Lawrence, or despised him for his inartistic mind. Lawrence was 'a fine fellow'; he might seem a little slow at first, 'but you wait and you will see what kind of a chap he is.' Nevertheless Bohun was not able to be for ever in his company; work separated them, and then Lawrence lodged with Baron Wilderling on the Admiralty Quay, a long way from Anglisky Prospect. Therefore, at the end of three weeks, Henry Bohun discovered himself to be profoundly wretched. There seemed to be no hope anywhere. Even the artist in him was disappointed. He went to the Ballet and saw Tchaikowsky's 'Swan Lake'; but bearing Diagilev's splendours in front of him, and knowing nothing about the technique of ballet-dancing, he was bored and cross and contemptuous. He went to 'Eugen Onyegin' and enjoyed it, because there was still a great deal of the schoolgirl in him; but after that he was flung on to Glinka's 'Russlan and Ludmilla,' and this seemed to him quite interminable and to have nothing to do with the gentleman and lady mentioned in the title. He tried a play at the Alexander Theatre; it was, he saw, by Andréeff, whose art he had told many people in England he admired, but now he mixed him up in his mind with Kuprin, and the play was all about a circus – very confused and gloomy. As for literature, he purchased some new poems by Balmont, some essays by Merejkowsky, and André Biely's *St. Petersburg*, but the first of these he found pretentious, the second dull, and the third quite impossibly obscure. He did not confess to himself that it might perhaps be his ignorance of the Russian language that was at fault. He went to the Hermitage and the Alexander Galleries, and purchased coloured postcards of the works of Somov, Benois, Douboginsky, Lançeray, and Ostroymova – all the quite obvious people. He wrote home to his mother 'that from what he could see of

Russian Art it seemed to him to have a real future in front of it' – and he bought little painted wooden animals and figures at the Peasants' Workshops and stuck them up on the front of his stove.

'I like them because they are so essentially Russian,' he said to me, pointing out a red spotted cow and a green giraffe. 'No other country could have been responsible for them.'

Poor boy, I had not the heart to tell him that they had been made in Germany.

However, as I have said, in spite of his painted toys and his operas he was, at the end of three weeks, a miserable man. Anybody could see that he was miserable, and Vera Michailovna saw it. She took him in hand, and at once his life was changed. I was present at the beginning of the change.

It was the evening of Rasputin's murder. The town of course talked of nothing else – it had been talking, without cessation, since two o'clock that afternoon. The dirty, sinister figure of the monk, with his magnetic eyes, his greasy beard, his robe, his girdle, and all his other properties, brooded gigantic over all of us. He was brought into immediate personal relationship with the humblest, most insignificant creature in the city, and with him incredible shadows and shapes, from Dostoeffsky, from Gogol, from Lermontov, from Nekrasov – from whom you please – all the shadows of whom one is eternally subconsciously aware in Russia – faced us and reminded us that they were not shadows but realities.

The details of his murder were not accurately known – it was only sure that, at last, after so many false rumours of attempted assassination, he was truly gone, and this world would be bothered by his evil presence no longer.

Pictures formed in one's mind as one listened. The day was fiercely cold, and this seemed to add to the horror of it all – to the Hoffmannesque fantasy of the party, the lights, the supper, and the women, the murder with its mixture of religion and superstition and melodrama, the body flung out at last so easily and swiftly, on to the frozen river. How many souls must have asked themselves that day – 'Why, if this is so easy, do we not proceed further? A man dies more simply than you thought – only resolution ... only resolution.'

I know that that evening I found it impossible to remain in my lonely rooms; I went round to the Markovitch flat. I found Vera Michailovna and Bohun preparing to go out; they were alone in the flat. He looked at me apprehensively. I think that I appeared to him at that time a queer, moody, ill-disposed fellow, who was too old to understand the true character of young men's impetuous souls. It may be that he was right. . . .

'Will you come with us, Ivan Andreievitch?' Vera Michailovna asked me. 'We're going to the little cinema on Ekateringofsky – a piece of local colour for Mr. Bohun.'

'I'll come anywhere with you,' I said. 'And we'll talk about Rasputin.'

Bohun was only too ready. The affair seemed to his romantic soul too good to be true. Because we none of us knew, at that time, what had really happened, a fine field was offered for every rumour and conjecture.

Bohun had collected some wonderful stories. I saw that, apart from Rasputin, he was a new man – something had happened to him. It was not long before I discovered that what had happened was that Vera Michailovna had been kind to him. Vera's most beautiful quality was her motherliness. I do not intend that much-abused word in any sentimental fashion. She did not shed tears over a dirty baby in the street, nor did she drag decrepit old men into the flat to give them milk and fifty kopecks, – but let some one appeal to the strength and bravery in her, and she responded magnificently. I believe that to be true of very many Russian women, who are always their most natural selves when something appeals to the best in them. Vera Michailovna had a strength and a security in her protection of souls weaker than her own that had about it nothing forced or pretentious or self-conscious – it was simply the natural woman acting as she was made to act. She saw that Bohun was lonely and miserable and, now that the first awkwardness was passed and he was no longer a stranger, she was able, gently and unobtrusively, to show him that she was his friend. I think that she had not liked him at first; but if you want a Russian to like you, the thing to do is to show him that you need him. It is amazing to watch their readiness to receive dependent souls whom they are in no kind of way qualified to protect – but they do their best, and although the result is invariably bad for everybody's character, a great deal of affection is created.

As we walked to the cinema she asked him, very gently and rather shyly, about his home and his people and English life. She must have asked all her English guests the same questions, but Bohun, I fancy, gave her rather original answers. He let himself go, and became very young and rather absurd, but also sympathetic. We were, all three of us, gay and silly, as one very often suddenly is, in Russia, in the middle of even disastrous situations. It had been a day of most beautiful weather, the mud was frozen, the streets clean, the sky deep blue, the air harshly sweet. The night blazed with stars that seemed to swing through the haze of the frost like a curtain moved, very gently, by the wind. The Ekateringofsky Canal was blue with the stars lying like scraps of quicksilver all about it, and the trees and houses were deep black in outline above it. I could feel that the people in the street were happy. The murder of Rasputin was a sign, a symbol; his figure had been behind the scenes so long that it had become mythical, something beyond human power – and now, behold, it was not beyond human power at all, but was there like a dead stinking fish. I could see the thought in their minds as they hurried along: 'Ah, he is gone, the dirty fellow – *Slava Bogu* – the war will soon be over.'

I, myself, felt the influence. Perhaps now the war would go better, perhaps Stürmer and Protopopoff and the rest of them would be dismissed, and clean men . . . it was still time for the Czar. . . . And I heard Bohun, in his funny, slow, childish Russian: 'But you understand, Vera Michailovna, that my father knows nothing about writing, nothing at all – so that it wouldn't matter very much what he said. . . . Yes, he's military – been in the Army always. . . .'

Along the canal the little trees that in the spring would be green flames were touched now very faintly by silver frost. A huge barge lay black against the blue water; in the middle of it the rain had left a pool that was not frozen and under the light of a street lamp blazed gold – very strange the sudden gleam. . . . We passed the little wooden shelter where an old man in a high furry cap kept oranges and apples and nuts and sweets in paper. One candle illuminated his little store. He looked out from the darkness behind him like an old prehistoric man. His shed was peaked like a cocked hat, an old fat woman sat beside him knitting and drinking a glass of tea. . . .

'I'm sorry, Vera Michailovna, that you can't read English . . .' Bohun's careful voice was explaining. 'Only Wells and Locke and Jack London . . .'

I heard Vera Michailovna's voice. Then Bohun again:

'No, I write very slowly – yes, I correct an awful lot. . . .'

We stumbled amongst the darkness of the cobbles; where pools had been the ice crackled beneath our feet, then the snow scrunched. . . . I loved the sound, the sharp clear scent of the air, the pools of stars in the sky, the pools of ice at our feet, the blue like the thinnest glass stretched across the sky. I felt the poignancy of my age, of the country where I was, of Bohun's youth and confidence, of the war, of disease and death – but behind it all happiness at the strange sense that I had to-night, that came to me sometimes from I knew not where, that the undercurrent of the river of life was stronger than the eddies and whirlpools on its surface, that it knew whither it was speeding, and that the purpose behind its force was strong and true and good. . . .

'Oh,' I heard Bohun say, 'I'm not really very young, Vera Michailovna. After all, it's what you've done rather than your actual years. . . .'

'You're older than you'll ever be again, Bohun, if that's any consolation to you,' I said.

We had arrived. The cinema door blazed with light, and around it was gathered a group of soldiers and women and children, peering in at a soldiers' band, which, placed on benches in a corner of the room, played away for its very life. Outside, around the door were large bills announcing 'The Woman without a Soul, Drama in four parts,' and there were fine pictures of women falling over precipices, men shot in bedrooms, and parties in which all the guests shrank back in extreme horror from the heroine. We went inside and were overwhelmed by the band, so that we could not hear one another speak. The floor was covered with sunflower seeds, and there was a strong smell of soldiers' boots and bad cigarettes and urine. We bought tickets from an old Jewess behind the pigeon-hole, and then, pushing the curtain aside, stumbled into darkness. Here the smell was different, being quite simply that of human flesh not very carefully washed. Although, as we stumbled to some seats at the back, we could feel that we were alone, it had the impression that multitudes of people pressed in upon us, and when the lights did go up we found that the little hall was indeed packed to its extremest limit.

No one could have denied that it was a cheerful scene. Soldiers, sailors, peasants, women, and children crowded together upon the narrow benches. There was a great consumption of sunflower seeds, and the narrow passage down the middle of the room was littered with fragments. Two stout and elaborate policemen leaned against the wall surveying the public with a friendly if superior air. There was a tremendous amount of noise. Mingled with the strains of the band beyond the curtain were cries and calls and loud roars of laughter. The soldiers embraced the girls, and the children, their fingers in their mouths, wandered from bench to bench, and a mangy dog begged wherever he thought that he saw a kindly face. All the faces were kindly – kindly, ignorant, and astoundingly young. As I felt that youth I felt also separation; I and my like could emphasise as we pleased the goodness, docility, mysticism even of these people, but we were walking in a country of darkness. I caught a laugh, the glance of some women, the voice of a young soldier – I felt behind us, watching us, the thick heavy figure of Rasputin. I smelt the eastern scent of the sunflower seeds, I looked back and glanced at the impenetrable superiority of the two policemen, and I laughed at myself for the knowledge that I thought I had, for the security upon which I thought that I rested, for the familiarity with which I had fancied I could approach my neighbours.... I was not wise, I was not secure, I had no claim to familiarity....

The lights were down and we were shown pictures of Paris. Because the cinema was a little one and the prices small the films were faded and torn, so that the Opera and the Place de la Concorde and the Louvre and the Seine danced and wriggled and broke before our eyes. They looked strange enough to us and only accented our isolation and the odd semi-civilisation in which we were living. There were comments all around the room in exactly the spirit of children before a conjurer at a party.... The smell grew steadily stronger and stronger ... my head swam a little and I seemed to see Rasputin, swelling in his black robe, catching us all into its folds, sweeping us up into the starlit sky. We were under the flare of the light again. I caught Bohun's happy eyes; he was talking eagerly to Vera Michailovna, not removing his eyes from her face. She had conquered him; I fancied as I looked at her that her thoughts were elsewhere.

There followed a Vaudeville entertainment. A woman and a man in peasants' dress came and laughed raucously, without meaning, their eyes narrowly searching the depths of the house, then they stamped their feet and whirled around, struck one another, laughed again, and vanished.

The applause was half-hearted. Then there was a trainer of dogs, a black-eyed Tartar with four very miserable little fox-terriers, who shivered and trembled and jumped reluctantly through hoops. The audience liked this, and cried and shouted and threw paper pellets at the dogs. A stout perspiring Jew in a shabby evening suit came forward and begged for decorum. Then there appeared a stout little man in a top hat who wished to recite verses of, I gathered, a violent indecency. I was uncomfortable about Vera Michailovna, but I need not have been. The indecency was of no importance to her, and she was interested in the human tragedy of the performer. Tragedy it was. The man was hungry and dirty and not far from tears. He forgot his verses and glanced nervously into the wings as though he expected to be beaten publicly by the perspiring Jew.

He stammered; his mouth wobbled; he covered it with a dirty hand. He could not continue.

The audience was sympathetic. They listened in encouraging silence; then they clapped; then they shouted friendly words to him. You could feel throughout the room an intense desire that he should succeed. He responded a little to the encouragement, but could not remember his verses. He struggled, struggled, did a hurried little breakdown dance, bowed and vanished into the wings, to be beaten, I have no doubt, by the Jewish gentleman. We watched a little of the 'Drama of the Woman without a Soul,' but the sense of being in a large vat filled with boiling human flesh, into whose depths we were pressed ever more and more deeply, was at last too much for us, and we stumbled our way into the open air. The black shadow of the barge, the jagged outline of the huddled buildings against the sky, the black tower at the end of the canal, all these swam in the crystal air.

We took deep breaths of the freshness and purity; cheerful noises were on every side of us, the band and laughter; a church bell with its deep note and silver tinkle; the snow was vast and deep and hard all about us. We walked back very happily to Anglisky Prospect. Vera Michailovna said goodnight to me and went in. Before he followed her, Bohun turned round to me:

'Isn't she splendid?' he whispered. 'By God, Durward, I'd do anything for her. . . . Do you think she likes me?'

'Why not?' I asked.

'I want her to – frightfully. I'd do anything for her. Do you think she'd like to learn English?'

'I don't know,' I said. 'Ask her.'

He disappeared. As I walked home I felt about me the new interaction of human lives and souls – ambitions, hopes, youth. And the crisis, behind these, of the world's history made up, as it was, of the same interactions of human and divine. The fortunes and adventures of the soul on its journey towards its own country, its hopes and fears, struggles and despairs, its rejections and joy and rewards – its death and destruction – all this in terms of human life and the silly blundering conditions of this splendid glorious earth. . . . Here was Vera Michailovna and her husband, Nina and Boris Grogoff,

Bohun and Lawrence, myself and Semyonov – a jumbled lot – with all our pitiful self-important little histories, our crimes and virtues so insignificant and so quickly over, and behind them the fine stuff of the human and divine soul, pushing on through all raillery and incongruity to its goal. Why, I had caught up, once more, that interest in life that I had, I thought, so utterly lost! I stopped for a moment by the frozen canal and laughed to myself. The drama of life was, after all, too strong for my weak indifference. I felt that night as though I had stepped into a new house with lighted rooms and fires and friends waiting for me. Afterwards, I was so closely stirred by the sense of impending events that I could not sleep, but sat at my window watching the faint lights of the sky shift and waver over the frozen ice. . . .

X

We were approaching Christmas. The weather of these weeks was wonderfully beautiful, sharply cold, the sky pale bird's-egg blue, the ice and the snow glittering, shining with a thousand colours. There began now a strange relationship between Markovitch and myself.

There was something ineffectual and pessimistic about me that made Russians often feel in me a kindred soul. At the Front, Russians had confided in me again and again, but that was not astonishing, because they confided in every one. Nevertheless, they felt that I was less English than the rest, and rather blamed me in their minds, I think, for being so. I don't know what it was that suddenly decided Markovitch to 'make me part of his life.' I certainly did not on my side make any advances.

One evening he came to see me and stayed for hours. Then he came two or three times within the following fortnight. He gave me the effect of not caring in the least whether I were there or no, whether I replied or remained silent, whether I asked questions or simply pursued my own work. And I, on my side, had soon in my consciousness his odd, irascible, nervous, pleading, shy and boastful figure painted permanently, so that his actual physical presence seemed to be unimportant. There he was, as he liked to stand up against the white stove in my draughty room, his rather dirty nervous hands waving in front of me, his thin hair on end, his ragged beard giving his eyes an added expression of anxiety. His body was a poor affair, his legs thin and uncertain, an incipient stomach causing his waistcoat suddenly to fall inwards somewhere halfway up his chest, his feet in ill-shapen boots, and his neck absurdly small inside his high stiff collar. His stiff collar jutting sharply into his weak chin was perhaps his most striking feature. Most Russians of his careless habits wore soft collars or students' shirts that fastened tight about the neck, but this high white collar was with Markovitch a sign and a symbol, the banner of his early ambitions; it was the first and last of him. He changed it every day, it was always high and sharp, gleaming and clean, and it must have hurt him very much. He wore with it a shabby black tie that ran as far up the collar as it could go, and there was a sense of pathos and struggle about this tie as though it were a wild animal trying to escape over an imprisoning wall. He would stand clutching my stove as though it assured his safety in a dangerous country; then suddenly he would break away from it and start careering up and down my room, stopping for an instant to gaze through my window at the sea and the ships, then off again, swinging his arms, his anxious eyes searching everywhere for confirmation of the ambitions that still inflamed him.

For the root and soul of him was that he was greatly ambitious. He had been born, I learnt, in some small town in the Moscow province, and his father had been a schoolmaster in the place – a kind of Perodonov, I should imagine, from the things that Markovitch told me about him. The father, at any rate, was a mean, malicious, and grossly sensual creature, and he finally lost his post through his improper behaviour towards some of his own small pupils. The family then came to evil days, and at a very early age young Markovitch was sent to Petrograd to earn what he could with his wits. He managed to secure the post of a secretary to an old fellow who was engaged in writing the life of his grandfather – a difficult book, as the grandfather had been a voluminous letter-writer, and this correspondence had to be collected and tabulated. For months, and even years, young Markovitch laboriously endeavoured to arrange these old yellow letters, dull, pathetic, incoherent. His patron grew slowly imbecile, but through the fogs that increasingly besieged him saw only this one thing clearly, that the letters must be arranged. He kept Markovitch relentlessly at his table, allowing him no pleasures, feeding him miserably and watching him personally undress every evening lest he should have secreted certain letters somewhere on his body. There was something almost sadist apparently in the old gentleman's observation of Markovitch's labours.

It was during these years that Markovitch's ambitions took flame. He was always as he told me having 'amazing ideas.' I asked him – What kind of ideas? 'Ideas by which the world would be transformed. . . . Those letters were all old, you know, and dusty, and yellow, and eaten, some of them, by rats, and they'd lie on the floor and I'd try to arrange them in little piles according to their dates. . . . There'd be rows of little packets all across the floor . . ., and then somehow, when one's back was turned, they'd move, all of their own wicked purpose – and one would have to begin all over again, bending with one's back aching, and seeing always the stupid handwriting. . . . I hated it, Ivan Andreievitch, of course I hated it, but I had to do it for the money. And I lived in his house, too, and as he got madder it wasn't pleasant. He wanted me to sleep with him because he saw things in the middle of the night, and he'd catch hold of me and scream and twist his fat legs round me . . . no, it wasn't agreeable. *On souszem ne sympatichny.* He wasn't a nice man at all. But while I was sorting the letters these ideas would come to me and I would be on fire. . . . It seemed to me that I was to save the world, and that it would not be difficult if only one might be resolute enough. That was the trouble – to be resolute. One might say to oneself, "On Friday October 13th I will do so and so, and then on Saturday November 3rd I will do so and so, and then on December 24th it will be finished." But then on October 13th one is, may be, in quite another mood – one is even ill possibly – and so nothing is done and the whole plan is ruined. I would think all day as to how I would make myself resolute, and I would say when old Feodor Stepanovitch would pinch my ear and deny me more soup, "Ah ha, you wait, you old pig-face – you wait until I've mastered my resolution – and then I'll show you!" I fancied, for instance, that if I could command myself sufficiently I could just go to people and say, "You must have bath-houses like this and this " – I had all the plans ready, you know, and in the hottest room you have couches like this, and you have a machine that beats your back – so, so, so – not those dirty old things that leave bits of green stuff all over you – and so on, and so on. But better ideas than that, ideas about poverty and wealth, no more kings, you know, nor police, but not your cheap Socialism that fellows like Boris Nicolaievitch shout about; no, real happiness, so that no one need work as I did for an old beast who didn't give you enough soup, and have to keep quiet all the same and say nothing. Ideas came like flocks of birds, so many that I couldn't gather them all but had sometimes to let the best ones go. And I had no one to talk to about them – only the old cook and the girl in the kitchen, who had a child by old Feodor that he wouldn't own, – but she swore it was his, and told every one the time when it happened and where it was and all. . . . Then the old man fell downstairs and broke his neck, and he'd left me some money to go on with the letters. . . .'

At this point Markovitch's face would become suddenly triumphantly malevolent, like the face of a schoolboy who remembers a trick that he played on a hated master. 'Do you think I went on with them, Ivan Andreievitch? no, not I . . . but I kept the money.'

'That was wrong of you,' I would say gravely.

'Yes – wrong of course. But hadn't he been wrong always? And after all, isn't everybody wrong? We Russians have no conscience, you know, about anything, and that's simply because we can't make up our minds as to what's wrong and what's right, and even if we do make up our minds it seems a pity not to let yourself go when you may be dead tomorrow. Wrong and right. . . . What words! . . . Who knows? Perhaps it would have been the greatest wrong in the world to go on with the letters, wasting everybody's time, and for myself, too, who had so many ideas, that life simply would never be long enough to think them all out.'

It seemed that shortly after this he had luck with a little invention, and this piece of luck was, I should imagine, the ruin of his career, as pieces of luck so often are the ruin of careers. I could never understand what precisely his invention was; it had something to do with the closing of doors, something that you pulled at the bottom of the door, so that it shut softly and didn't creak with the wind. A Jew bought the invention, and gave Markovitch enough money to lead him confidently to believe that his fortune was made. Of course it was not, he never had luck with an invention again, but he was bursting with pride and happiness, set up house for himself in a little flat on the Vassily Ostrov – and met Vera Michailovna. I wish I could give some true idea of the change that came over him when he reached this part of his story. When he had spoken of his childhood, his father, his first struggles to live, his life with his old patron, he had not attempted to hide the evil, the malice, the envy that there was in his soul. He had even emphasised it, I might fancy, for my own especial benefit, so that I might see that he was not such a weak, romantic, sentimental creature as I had supposed – although God knows I had never fancied him romantic. Now when he spoke of his wife his whole body changed.

'She married me out of pity,' he told me. 'I hated her for that, and I loved her for that, and I hate and love her for it still.'

Here I interrupted him and told him that perhaps it was better that he should not confide in me the inner history of his marriage.

'Why not?' he asked me suspiciously.

'Because I'm only an acquaintance, you scarcely know me. You may regret it afterwards when you're in another mood.'

'Oh, you English!' he said contemptuously; 'you're always to be trusted. As a nation you're not, but as one man to another you're not interested enough in human nature to give away secrets.'

'Well, tell me what you like,' I said. 'Only I make no promises about anything.'

'I don't want you to,' he retorted; 'I'm only telling you what every one knows. Wasn't I aware from the first moment that she married me out of pity, and didn't they all know it, and laugh and tell her she was a fool? She knew that she was a fool too, but she was very young, and thought it fine to sacrifice herself for an idea. I was ill and I talked to her about my future. She believed in it, she thought I could do wonderful things if only some one looked after me. And at the same time despised me for wanting to be looked after. . . . And then I wasn't so ugly as I am now. She had some money of her own, and we took in lodgers, and I loved her, as I love her now, so that I could kiss her feet and then hate her because she was kind to me. She only cares for her sister, Nina; and because I was jealous of the girl and hated to see Vera good to her I had her to live with us, just to torture myself and show that I was stronger than all of them if I liked. . . . And so I am, than her beastly uncle the doctor and all the rest of them – let him do what he likes. . . .'

It was the first time that he had mentioned Semyonov.

'He's coming back,' I said.

'Oh, is he?' snarled Markovitch. 'Well, he'd better look out.' Then his voice, his face, even the shape of his body, changed once again. 'I'm not a bad man, Ivan Andreievitch. No, I'm not. . . . You think so of course, and I don't mind if you do. But I love Vera, and if she loved me I could do great things. I could astonish them all. I hear them say, "Ah, that Nicholas Markovitch, he's no good . . . with his inventions. What did a fine woman like that marry such a man for?" I know what they say. But I'm strong if I like. I gave up drink when I wished. I can give up anything. And when I succeed they'll see – and then we'll have enough money not to need these people staying with us and despising us. . . .'

'No one despises you, Nicolai Leontievitch,' I interrupted.

'And what does it matter if they do?' he fiercely retorted. 'I despise them – all of them. It's easy for them when everything goes well with them, but with me everything goes wrong. Everything! . . . But I'm strong enough to make everything go right – and I will.'

This was, for the time, the end of his confidences. He had, I was sure, something further to tell me, some plan, some purpose, but he decided suddenly that he would keep it to himself, although I am convinced that he had only told me his earlier story in order that I might understand this new idea of his. But I did not urge him to tell me. My interest in life had not yet sufficiently revived; it was, after all, none of my business.

For the rest, it seemed that he had been wildly enthusiastic about the war at its commencement. He had had great ideas about Russia, but now he had given up all hope. Russia was doomed; and Germany, whom he hated and admired, would eat her up. And what did it matter? Perhaps Germany would 'run Russia,' and then there would be order and less thieving, and this horrible war would stop. How foolish it had been to suppose that any one in Russia would ever do anything. They were all fools and knaves and idle in Russia – like himself.

And so he left me.

XI

On Christmas Eve, late in the evening, I went into a church. It was my favourite church in Petrograd, rising at the English Prospect end of the Quay, with its white rounded towers pure and quiet and modest.

I had been depressed all day. I had not been well, and the weather was harsh, a bitterly cold driving wind beating down the streets and stroking the ice of the canal into a dull grey colour. Christmas seemed to lift into sharper, bitterer irony the ghastly horrors of this endless war. Last Christmas I had been too ill to care, and the Christmas before I had been at the Front when the war had been young and full of hope, and I had seen enough nobility and self-sacrifice to be reassured about the true stuff of the human soul. Now all that seemed to be utterly gone. On the one side my mind was filled with my friends, John Trenchard and Marie Ivanovna. The sacrifice that they had made seemed to be wicked and useless. I had lost altogether that conviction of the continuance and persistence of their souls that I had, for so long, carried with me. They were dead, dead . . . simply dead. There at the Front one had believed in many things. Here in this frozen and starving town, with every ghost working against every human, there was assurance of nothing – only deep foreboding and an ominous silence. The murder of Rasputin still hung over every head. The first sense of liberty had passed, and now his dirty malicious soul seemed to be watching us all, reminding us that he had not left us, but was waiting for the striking of some vast catastrophe that the friends whom he had left behind him to carry on his work were preparing. It was this sense of moving so desperately and so hopelessly in the dark that was with me. Any chance that there had seemed to be of Russia rising from the war with a free soul appeared now to be utterly gone. Before our eyes the powers that ruled us were betraying us, laughing at us, selling us. And we did not know who was our enemy, who our friend, whom to believe, of whom to take counsel. Peculation and lying and the basest intrigue were on every side of us, hunger for which there was no necessity, want in a land packed with everything. I believe that there may have been very well another side to the picture, but at that time we could not see; we did not wish to see, we were blindfolded men. . . .

I entered the church and found that the service was over. I passed through the aisle into the little rounded cup of dark and gold where the altars were. Here there were still collected a company of people, kneeling, some of them, in front of the candles, others standing there, motionless like statues, their hands folded, gazing before them. The candles flung a mist of dim embroidery upon the walls and within the mist the dark figures of the priests moved to and fro. An old priest with long white hair was standing behind a desk close to me, and reading a long prayer in an unswerving monotonous voice. There was the scent of candles and cold stone and hot human breath in the little place. The tawdry gilt of the Ikons glittered in the candle-light, and an echo of the cold wind creeping up the long dark aisle blew the light about so that the gilt was like flashing piercing eyes. I wrapped my Shuba closely about me, and stood there lost in a hazy, indefinite dream.

I was comforted and touched by the placid, mild, kindly faces of those standing near me. 'No evil here . . .' I thought. 'Only ignorance, and for that others are responsible.'

I was lost in my dream and I did not know of what I was dreaming. The priest's voice went on, and the lights flickered, and it was as though some one, a long way off, were trying to give me a message that it was important that I should hear, important for myself and for others. There came over me, whence I know not, a sudden conviction of the fearful power of Evil, a sudden realisation, as though I had been shown something, a scene or a picture or writing which had brought this home to me. . . . The lights seemed to darken, the priest's figure faded, and I felt as though the message that some one had been trying to deliver to me had been withdrawn. I waited a moment, looking about me in a bewildered fashion, as though I had in reality just woken from sleep. Then I left the church.

Outside the cold air was intense. I walked to the end of the Quay and leaned on the stone parapet. The Neva seemed vast like a huge, white, impending shadow; it swept in a colossal wave of frozen ice out to the far horizon, where tiny, twinkling lights met it and closed it in. The bridges that crossed it held forth their lights, and there were the gleams, like travelling stars, of the passing trams, but all these were utterly insignificant against the vast body of the contemptuous ice. On the farther shore the buildings rose in a thin, tapering line, looking as though they had been made of black tissue-paper, against the solid weight of the cold, stony sky. The Peter and Paul Fortress, the towers of the Mohammedan Mosque were thin, immaterial, ghostly, and the whole line of the town was simply a black pencilled shadow against the ice, smoke that might be scattered with one heave of the force of the river. The Neva was silent, but beneath that silence beat what force and power, what contempt and scorn, what silent purposes?

I saw then, near me, and gazing, like myself, on to the river the tall, broad figure of a peasant, standing, without movement, black against the sky.

He seemed to dominate the scene, to be stronger and more contemptuous than the ice itself, but also to be in sympathy with it.

I made some movement, and he turned and looked at me. He was a fine man, with a black beard and noble carriage. He passed down the Quay and I turned towards home.

XII

About four o'clock on Christmas afternoon I took some flowers to Vera Michailovna. I found that the long sitting-room had been cleared of all furniture save the big table and the chairs round it.

About a dozen middle-aged ladies were sitting about the table and solemnly playing 'Lotto.' So serious were they that they scarcely looked up when I came in. Vera Michailovna said my name and they smiled and some of them bowed, but their eyes never left the numbered cards. '*Dvar . . . Peedecat . . . Cheteeriy . . . Zurock Tree . . . Semdecet Voisim*' . . . came from a stout and good-natured lady reading the numbers as she took them from the box. Most of the ladies were healthy, perspiring, and of a most amiable appearance. They might, many of them, have been the wives of English country clergymen, so domestic and unalarmed were they. I recognised two Markovitch aunts and a Semyonov cousin.

There was a hush and a solemnity about the proceedings. Vera Michailovna was very busy in the kitchen, her face flushed and her sleeves rolled up; Sacha, the servant, malevolently assisting her and scolding continually the stout and agitated country girl who had been called in for the occasion.

'All goes well,' Vera smilingly assured me. 'Half-past six it is – don't be late.'

'I will be in time,' I said.

'Do you know, I've asked your English friend. The big one.'

'Lawrence? . . . Is he coming?'

'Yes. At least I understood so on the telephone, but he sounded confused. Do you think he will want to come?'

'I'm sure he will,' I answered.

'Afterwards I wasn't sure. I thought he might think it impertinent when we know him so little. But he could easily have said if he didn't want to come, couldn't he?'

There seemed to me something unusual in the way that she asked me these questions. She did not usually care whether people were offended or no. She had not time to consider that, and in any case she despised people who took offence easily.

I would perhaps have said something, but the country girl dropped a plate and Sacha leapt upon the opportunity. 'Drunk! . . . What did I say, having such a girl? Is it not better to do things for yourself? But no – of course no one cares for my advice, as though last year the same thing . . .' And so on.

I left them and went home to prepare for the feast.

I returned punctually at half-past six and found every one there. Many of the ladies had gone, but the aunts remained, and there were other uncles and some cousins. We must have been in all between twenty and thirty people. The table was now magnificently spread. There was a fine glittering Father Christmas in the middle, a Father Christmas of German make, I am afraid. Ribbons and frosted strips of coloured paper ran in lines up and down the cloth. The 'Zakuska' were on a side-table near the door – herrings and ham and smoked fish and radishes and mushrooms and tongue and caviare and, most unusual of all in those days, a decanter of vodka.

No one had begun yet; every one stood about, a little uneasy and awkward, with continuous glances flung at the 'Zakuska' table. Of the company Markovitch first caught my eye. I had never seen him so clean and smart before. His high, piercing collar was of course the first thing that one saw; then one perceived that his hair was brushed, his beard trimmed, and that he wore a very decent suit of rather shiny black. This washing and scouring of him gave him a curiously subdued and imprisoned air; I felt sympathetic towards him; I could see that he was anxious to please, happy at the prospect of being a successful host, and, to-night, most desperately in love with his wife. That last stood out and beyond all else. His eyes continually sought her face; he had the eyes of a dog watching and waiting for its master's appreciative word.

I had never before seen Vera Michailovna so fine and independent and, at the same time, so kind and gracious. She was dressed in white, very plain and simple, her shining black hair piled high on her head, her kind, good eyes watching every one and everything to see that all were pleased. She, too, was happy to-night, but happy also in a strange, subdued, quiescent way, and I felt, as I always did about her, that her soul was still asleep and untouched, and that much of her reliance and independence came from that. Uncle Ivan was in his smart clothes, his round face very red, and he wore his air of rather ladylike but inoffensive superiority. He stood near the table with the 'Zakuska,' and his eyes rested there. I do not now remember many of the Markovitch and Semyonov relations. There was a tall thin young man, rather bald, with a short black moustache; he was nervous and self-assertive, and he had a high, shrill voice. He talked incessantly. There were several delightful, middle-aged women, quiet and ready to be pleased with everything – the best Russian type of all perhaps, women who knew life, who were generously tolerant, kind-hearted, with a quiet sense of humour and no nonsense about them. There was one fat red-faced man in a very tight black coat, who gave his opinion always about food and drink. He was from Moscow – his name Paul

Leontievitch Rozanov – and I met him on a later occasion of which I shall have to tell in its place. Then there were two young girls who giggled a great deal and whispered together. They hung around Nina and stroked her hair and admired her dress, and laughed at Boris Grogoff and any one else who was near them.

Nina was immensely happy. She loved parties of course, and especially parties in which she was the hostess. She was like a young kitten or puppy in a white frock, with her hair tumbling over her eyes. She was greatly excited, and as joyous as though there were no war, and no afflicted Russia, and nothing serious in all the world. This was the first occasion on which I suspected that Grogoff cared for her. Outwardly he did nothing but chaff and tease her, and she responded in that quick, rather sharp, and very often crudely personal way at which foreigners for the first time in Russian company so often wonder. Badinage with Russians so quickly passes to lively and noisy quarrelling, which in its turn so suddenly fades into quiet contented amiability that it is little wonder that the observer feels rather breathless at it all. Grogoff was a striking figure, with his fine height and handsome head and bold eyes, but there was something about him that I did not like. Immensely self-confident, he nevertheless seldom opened his mouth without betraying great ignorance about almost everything. He was hopelessly ill-educated, and was the more able therefore from the very little knowledge that he had to construct a very simple Socialist creed in which the main statutes were that everything should be taken from the rich and given to the poor, the peasants should have all the land, and the rulers of the world be beheaded. He had no knowledge of other countries, although he talked very freely of what he called his 'International Principles.' I could not respect him as I could many Russian revolutionaries, because he had never on any occasion put himself out or suffered any inconvenience for his principles, living as he did, comfortably, with all the food and clothes that he needed. At the same time he was, on the other hand, kindly and warm-hearted, and professed friendship for me, although he despised what he called my 'Capitalistic tendencies.' Had he only known, he was far richer and more autocratic than I!

In the midst of this company Henry Bohun was rather shy and uncomfortable. He was suspicious always that they would laugh at his Russian (what mattered it if they did?), and he was distressed by the noise and boisterous friendliness of every one. I could not help smiling to myself as I watched him. He was learning very fast.

He would not tell any one now that 'he really thought that he did understand Russia,' nor would he offer to put his friends right about Russian characteristics and behaviour. He watched the young giggling girls, and the fat Rozanov, and the shrill young man with ill-concealed distress. Very far these from the Lizas and Natachas of his literary imagination – and yet not so far either, had he only known.

He pinned all his faith, as I could see, to Vera Michailovna, who did gloriously fulfil his self-instituted standards. And yet he did not know her at all! He was to suffer pain there too.

At dinner he was unfortunately seated between one of the giggling girls and a very deaf old lady who was the great-aunt of Nina and Vera. This old lady trembled like an aspen leaf, and was continually dropping beneath the table a little black bag that she carried. She could make nothing of Bohun's Russian, even if she heard it, and was under the impression that he was a Frenchman. She began a long quivering story about Paris to which she had once been, how she had lost herself, and how a delightful Frenchman had put her on her right path again. . . . 'A chivalrous people, your countrymen' . . . she repeated, nodding her head so that her long silver ear-rings rattled again – 'gay and chivalrous!' Bohun was not, I am afraid, as chivalrous as he might have been, because he knew that the girl on his other side was laughing at his attempts to explain that he was not a Frenchman. 'Stupid old woman!' he said to me afterwards. 'She dropped her bag under the table at least twenty times!'

Meanwhile the astonishing fact was that the success of the dinner was Jerry Lawrence. He was placed on Vera Michailovna's left hand, Rozanov, the Moscow merchant, near to him, and I did not hear him say anything very bright or illuminating, but every one felt, I think, that he was a cheerful and dependable person. I always felt, when I observed him, that he understood the Russian character far better than any of us. He had none of the self-assertion of the average Englishman and, at the same time, he had his opinions and his preferences. He took every kind of chaff with good-humoured indifference, but I think it was above everything else his tolerance that pleased the Russians. Nothing shocked him, which did not at all mean that he had no code of honour or morals. His code was severe and stern, but his sense of human fallibility, and the fight that human nature was always making against stupendous odds stirred him to a fine and comprehending charity. He had many faults. He was obstinate, often dull and lethargic, in many ways grossly ill-educated and sometimes wilfully obtuse – but he was a fine friend, a noble enemy, and a chivalrous lover. There was nothing mean or petty in him, and his views of life and the human soul were wider and more all-embracing than in any Englishman I have ever known. You may say of course that it is sentimental nonsense to suppose at all that the human soul is making a fine fight against odds. Even I, at this period, was tempted to think that it might be nonsense, but it is a view as good as another, after all, and so ignorant are all of us that no one has a right to say that anything is impossible!

After drinking the vodka and eating the 'Zakuska,' we sat down to table and devoured crayfish soup. Every one became lively. Politics of course were discussed.

I heard Rozanov say, 'Ah, you in Petrograd! What do you know of things? Don't let me hurt any one's feelings, pray. . . . Most excellent soup, Vera Michailovna – I congratulate you. . . . But you just wait until Moscow takes things in hand. Why only the other day Maklakoff said to a friend of mine – "It's all nonsense," he said.'

And the shrill-voiced young man told a story – 'But it wasn't the same man at all. She was so confused when she saw what she'd done, that I give you my word she was on the point of crying. I could see tears . . . just trembling – on the edge. "Oh, I beg your pardon," she said, and the man was such a fool. . . .'

Markovitch was busy about the drinks. There was some sherry and some light red wine. Markovitch was proud of having been able to secure it. He was beaming with pride. He explained to everybody how it had been done. He walked round the table and stood, for an instant, with his hand on Vera Michailovna's shoulder. The pies with fish and cabbage in them were handed round. He jested with the old great-aunt. He shouted in her ear:

'Now, Aunt Isabella . . . some wine. Good for you, you know – keep you young. . . .'

'No, no, no . .' she protested, laughing and shaking her ear-rings, with tears in her eyes. But he filled her glass and she drank it and coughed, still protesting.

'Thank you, thank you,' she chattered as Bohun dived under the table and found her bag for her. I saw that he did not like the crayfish soup, and was distressed because he had so large a helping.

He blushed and looked at his plate, then began again to eat and stopped.

'Don't you like it?' one of the giggling girls asked him. 'But it's very good. Have another pie!'

The meal continued. There were little sucking-pigs with 'Kasha,' a kind of brown buckwheat. Every one was gayer and gayer. Now all talked at once, and no one listened to anything that any one else said. Of them all, Nina was by far the gayest. She had drunk no wine – she always said that she could not bear the nasty stuff, and although every one tried to persuade her, telling her that now when you could not get it anywhere, it was wicked not to drink it, she would not change her mind. It was simply youth and happiness that radiated from her, and also perhaps some other excitement for which I could not account. Grogoff tried to make her drink. She defied him. He came over to her chair, but she pushed him away, and then lightly slapped his cheek. Every one laughed. Then he whispered something to her. For an instant the gaiety left her eyes. 'You shouldn't say that!' she answered almost angrily. He went back to his seat. I was sitting next to her, and she was very charming to me, seeing that I had all that I needed and showing that she liked me. 'You mustn't be gloomy and ill and miserable,' she whispered to me. 'Oh! I've seen you! There's no need. Come to us and we'll make you as happy as we can – Vera and I. . . . We both love you.'

'My dear, I'm much too old and stupid for you to bother about!'

She put her hand on my arm. 'I know that I'm wicked and care only for pleasure. . . . Vera's always saying so. But I can be better if you want me to be.'

This was flattering, but I knew that it was only her general happiness that made her talk like that. And at once she was after something else. 'Your Englishman,' she said, looking across the table at Lawrence, 'I like his face. I should be frightened of him, though.'

'Oh no, you wouldn't,' I answered. 'He wouldn't hurt any one.'

She continued to look at him and, he glancing up, their eyes met. She smiled and he smiled. Then he raised his glass and drank.

'I mustn't drink,' she called across the table. 'It's only water and that's bad luck.'

'Oh, you can challenge any amount of bad luck – I'm sure,' he called back to her.

I fancied that Grogoff did not like this. He was drinking a great deal. He roughly called Nina's attention.

'Nina . . . Ah – Nina!'

But she, although I am certain that she heard him, paid no attention.

He called again more loudly:

'Nina . . . Nina!'

'Well?' She turned towards him, her eyes laughing at him.

'Drink my health.'

'I can't. I have only water.'

'Then you must drink wine.'

'I won't. I detest it.'

'But you must.'

He came over to her and poured a little red wine into her water. She turned and emptied the glass over his hand. For an instant his face was dark with rage.

'I'll pay you for that,' I heard him whisper.

She shrugged her shoulders. 'He's tiresome, Boris . . .' she said, 'I like your Englishman better.'

We were ever gayer and gayer. There were now of course no cakes nor biscuits, but there was jam with our tea, and there were even some chocolates. I noticed that Vera and Lawrence were getting on together famously. They talked and laughed, and her eyes were full of pleasure.

Markovitch came up and stood behind them, watching them. His eyes devoured his wife.

'Vera!' he said suddenly.

'Yes!' she cried. She had not known that he was behind her; she was startled. She turned round and he came forward and kissed her hand. She let him do this, as she let him do everything, with the indulgence that one allows a child. He stood, afterwards, half in the shadow, watching her.

And now the moment for the event of the evening had arrived. The doors of Markovitch's little work-room were suddenly opened, and there – instead of the shabby, untidy dark little hole – there was a splendid Christmas Tree blazing with a hundred candles. Coloured balls and frosted silver and wooden figures of red and blue hung all about the tree – it was most beautifully done. On a table close at hand were presents. We all clapped our hands. We were childishly delighted. The old great-aunt cried with pleasure. Boris Grogoff suddenly looked like a happy boy of ten. Happiest and proudest of them all was Markovitch. He stood there, a large pair of scissors in his hand, waiting to cut the string round the parcels. We said again and again, 'Marvellous!' 'Wonderful!' 'Splendid!' . . . 'But this year – however did you find it, Vera Michailovna?' 'To take such trouble! . . .' 'Splendid! splendid!' Then we were given our presents. Vera, it was obvious, had chosen them, for there was taste and discrimination in the choice of every one. Mine was a little old religious figure in beaten silver – Lawrence had a silver snuff-box. . . . Every one was delighted. We clapped our hands. We shouted. Some one cried, 'Cheers for our host and hostess!'

We gave them, and in no half measure. We shouted. Boris Grogoff cried, 'More cheers!'

It was then that I saw Markovitch's face, that had been puckered with pleasure like the face of a delighted child, suddenly stiffen; his hand moved forward, then dropped. I turned and found, standing in the doorway, quietly watching us, Alexei Petrovitch Semyonov.

XIII

I stared at him. I could not take my eyes away. I instantly forgot every one else, the room, the tree, the lights. . . . With a force, with a poignancy and pathos and brutality that were more cruel than I could have believed possible, that other world came back to me. Ah! I could see now that all these months I had been running away from this very thing, seeking to pretend that it did not exist, that it had never existed. All in vain – utterly in vain. I saw Semyonov as I had just seen him, sitting on his horse outside the shining white house at O———. Then Semyonov operating in a stinking room, under a red light, his arms bathed in blood; then Semyonov and Trenchard; then Semyonov speaking to Marie Ivanovna, her eyes searching his face; then that day when I woke from my dream in the orchard to find his eyes staring at me through the bright green trees, and afterwards when we went in to look at her dead; then worst of all that ride back to the 'Stab' with my hand on his thick, throbbing arm. . . . Semyonov in the Forest, working, sneering, hating us, despising us, carrying his tragedy in his eyes and defying us to care; Semyonov that last time of all, vanishing into the darkness with his 'Nothing!' – that lingering echo of a defiant desperate soul that had stayed with me, against my bidding, ever since I had heard it.

What a fool had I been to know these people! I had felt from the first to what it must lead, and I might have avoided it and I would not. I looked at him, I faced him, I smiled. He was the same as he had been. A little stouter, perhaps, his pale hair and square-cut beard looking as though it had been carved from some pale honey-coloured wood, the thick stolidity of his long body and short legs, the squareness of his head, the coldness of his eyes and the violent red of his lips, all were just as they had been – the same man, save that now he was in civilian clothes, in a black suit with a black bow tie. There was a smile on his lips, that same smile half sneer half friendliness that I knew so well. His eyes were veiled. . . .

He was, I believe, as violently surprised to see me as I had been to see him, but he held himself in complete control!

He said, 'Why, Durward! . . . Ivan Andreievitch!' Then he greeted the others.

I was able, now, to notice the general effect of his arrival. It was as though a cold wind had suddenly burst through the windows, blown out all the candles upon the tree and plunged the place into darkness. Those who did not know him felt that, with his entrance, the gaiety was gone. Markovitch's face was pale, he was looking at Vera who, for an instant, had stood, quite silently, staring at her uncle, then, recovering herself, moved forward.

'Why, Uncle Alexei!' she cried, holding out her hand. 'You're too late for the tree! Why didn't you tell us? Then you could have come to dinner . . . and now it is all over. Why didn't you tell us?'

He took her hand, and, very solemnly, bent down and kissed it.

'I didn't know myself, dear Vera Michailovna. I only arrived in Petrograd yesterday; and then in my house everything was wrong, and I've been busy all day. But I felt that I must run in and give you the greetings of the season. . . . Ah, Nicholas, how are you? And you, Ivan? . . . I telephoned to you. . . . Nina, my dear. . . .' And so on. He went round and shook hands with them all. He was introduced to Bohun and Lawrence. He was very genial, praising the tree, laughing, shouting in the ears of the great-aunt. But no one responded. As so frequently happens in Russia the atmosphere was suddenly changed. No one had anything to say. The candles on the tree were blown out. Of course, the evening was not nearly ended. There would be tea and games, perhaps – at any rate every one would sit and sit until three or four, if for no other reason, simply because it demanded too much energy to rise and make farewells. But the spirit of the party was utterly dead. . . .

The samovar hissed at the end of the table. Vera Michailovna sat there making tea for every one. Semyonov (I should now, in the heart of his relations, have thought of him as Alexei Petrovitch, but so long had he been Semyonov to me that Semyonov he must remain) was next to her, and I saw that he took trouble, talking to her, smiling, his stiff strong white fingers now and then stroking his thick beard, his red lips parting a little, then closing so firmly that it seemed that they would never open again.

I noticed that his eyes often wandered towards me. He was uneasy about my presence there, I thought, and that disturbed me. I felt as I looked at him the same confusion as I had always felt. I did not hate him. His strength of character, his fearlessness, these things in a country famous for neither quality I was driven to admire and to respect. And I could not hate what I admired.

And yet my fear gathered and gathered in volume as I watched him. What would he do with these people? What plans had he? What purpose? What secret, selfish ambitions was he out now to secure?

Markovitch was silent, drinking his tea, watching his wife, watching us all with his nervous frowning expression.

I rose to go and then, when I had said farewell to every one and went towards the door, Semyonov joined me.

'Well, Ivan Andreievitch,' he said. 'So we have not finished with one another yet.'

He looked at me with his steady unswerving eyes; he smiled.

I also smiled as I found my coat and hat in the little hall. Sacha helped me into my Shuba. He stood, his lips a little apart, watching me.

'What have you been doing all this time?' he asked me.

'I've been ill,' I answered.

'Not bad, I hope.'

'No, not bad. But enough to keep me very idle.'

'As much of an optimist as ever?'

'Was I an optimist?'

'Why, surely. A charming one. Do you love Russia as truly as ever?'

I laughed, my hand on the door. 'That's my affair, Alexei Petrovitch,' I answered.

'Certainly,' he said, smiling. 'You're looking older, you know.'

'You too,' I said.

'Yes, perhaps. . . . Would I still think you sentimental, do you suppose?'

'It is of no importance, Alexei Petrovitch,' I said. 'I'm sure you have other better things to do. Are you remaining in Petrograd?'

He looked at me then very seriously, his eyes staring straight into mine.

'I hope so.'

'You will work at your practice?'

'Perhaps.' He nodded to me. 'Strange to find you here . . .' he said. 'We shall meet again. Good-night.'

He closed the door behind me.

XIV

Next day I fell ill. I had felt unwell for several weeks, and now I woke up to a bad feverish cold, my body one vast ache, and at the same time impersonal, away from me, floating over above me, sinking under me, tied to me only by pain. . . .

I was too utterly apathetic to care. The old woman who looked after my rooms telephoned to my doctor, a stout, red-faced jolly man, who came and laughed at me, ordered me some medicine, said that I was in a high fever, and left me. After that, I was, for several days, caught into a world of dreams and nightmares. No one, I think, came near me, save my old woman, Marfa, and a new acquaintance of mine, the Rat.

The Rat I had met some weeks before outside my house. I had been returning one evening, through the dark, with a heavy bag of books which I had fetched from an English friend of mine who lodged in the Millionnaya. I had had a cab for most of the distance, but that had stopped on the other side of the bridge – it could not drive amongst the rubbish pebbles and spars of my island. As I staggered along with my bag a figure had risen, as it seemed to me, out of the ground and asked huskily whether he could help me. I had only a few steps to go, but he seized my burden and went in front of me. I submitted. I told him my door and he entered the dark passage, climbed the rickety stairs and entered my room. Here we were both astonished. He, when I had lighted my lamp, was staggered by the splendour and luxury of my life, I, as I looked at him, by the wildness and uncouthness of his appearance. He was as a savage from the centre of Africa, thick ragged hair and beard, a powerful body in rags, and his whole attitude to the world primeval and utterly primitive. His mouth was cruel; his eyes, as almost always with the Russian peasant, mild and kindly. I do not intend to take up much space here with an account of him, but he did, after this first meeting, in some sort attach himself to me. I never learned his name nor where he lived; he was, I should suppose, an absolutely abominable plunderer and pirate and ruffian. He would appear suddenly in my room, stand by the door and talk – but talk with the ignorance, naïveté, brutal simplicity of an utterly abandoned baby. Nothing mystical or beautiful about the Rat. He did not disguise from me in the least that there was no crime that he had not committed – murder, rape, arson, immorality of the most hideous, sacrilege, the basest betrayal of his best friends – he was not only savage and outlaw, he was deliberate anarchist and murderer. He had no redeeming point that I could anywhere discover. I did not in the least mind his entering my room when he pleased. I had there nothing of any value; he could take my life even, had he a mind to that. . . . The naïve abysmal depths of his depravity interested me. He formed a kind of attachment to me. He told me that he would do anything for me. He had a strange tact which prevented him from intruding upon me when I was occupied. He was as quick as any cultured civilised cosmopolitan to see if he was not wanted. He developed a certain cleanliness; he told me, with an air of disdainful superiority, that he had been to the public baths. I gave him an old suit of mine and a pair of boots. He very seldom asked for anything; once and again he would point to something and say that he would like to have it; if I said that he could not he expressed no disappointment; sometimes he stole it, but he always acknowledged that he had done so if I asked him, although he would lie stupendously on other occasions for no reason at all.

'Now you must bring that back,' I would say sternly.

'Oh no, Barin. . . . Why? You have so many things. Surely you will not object. Perhaps I will bring it – and perhaps not.'

'You must certainly bring it,' I would say.

'We will see,' he would say, smiling at me in the friendliest fashion.

He was the only absolutely happy Russian I have ever known. He had no passages of despair. He had been in prison, he would be in prison again. He had spasms of the most absolute ferocity. On one occasion I thought that I should be his next victim, and for a moment my fate hung, I think, in the balance. But he changed his mind. He had a real liking for me, I think. When he could get it, he drank a kind of furniture polish, the only substitute in these days for vodka. This was an absolutely killing drink, and I tried to prove to him that frequent indulgence in it meant an early decease. That did not affect him in the least. Death had no horror for him, although I foresaw, with justice as after events proved, that if he were faced with it he would be a very desperate coward. He liked very much my cigarettes, and I gave him these on condition that he did not spit sunflower seeds over my floor. He kept his word about this.

He chatted incessantly, and sometimes I listened and sometimes not. He had no politics and was indeed comfortably ignorant of any sort of geography or party division. There were for him only the rich and the poor. He knew nothing about the war, but he hoped, he frankly told me, that there would be anarchy in Petrograd, so that he might rob and plunder.

'I will look after you then, Barin,' he answered me, 'so that no one shall touch you.' I thanked him. He was greatly amused by my Russian accent, although he had no interest in the fact that I was English, nor did he want to hear in the least about London or any foreign town. Marfa, my old servant, was, of course, horrified at this acquaintanceship of mine, and warned me that it would mean both my death and hers. He liked to tease and frighten her, but he was never rude to her and offered sometimes to help her with her work, an offer that she always indignantly refused. He had some children, he told me, but he did not know where they were. He tried to respect my hospitality, never bringing any friends of his with him, and only once coming when he was the worse for drink. On that occasion he cried and endeavoured to embrace me. He apologised for this the next day.

They would try to take him soon, he supposed, for a soldier, but he thought that he would be able to escape. He hated the Police, and would murder them all if he could. He told me great tales of their cruelty, and he cursed thom most bitterly. I pointed out to him that society must be protected, but he did not see why this need be so. It was, he thought, wrong that some people had so much and others so little, but this was as far as his social investigations penetrated.

He was really distressed by my illness. Marfa told me that one day when I was delirious he cried. At the same time he pointed out to her that, if I died, certain things in my rooms would be his. He liked a silver cigarette case of mine, and my watch-chain, and a signet ring that I wore. I saw him vaguely, an uncertain shadow in the mists of the first days of my fever. I was not, I suppose, in actual fact, seriously ill, and yet I abandoned myself to my fate, allowing myself to slip without the slightest attempt at resistance, along the easiest way, towards death or idiocy or paralysis, towards anything that meant the indifferent passivity of inaction. I had bad, confused dreams. The silence irritated me. I fancied to myself that the sea ought to make some sound, that it was holding itself deliberately quiescent in preparation for some event. I remember that Marfa and the doctor prevented me from rising to look from my window that I might see why the sea was not roaring. Some one said to me in my dreams something about 'Ice,' and again and again I repeated the word to myself as though it were intensely significant. 'Ice! Ice! Ice! . . . Yes, that was what I wanted to know!' My idea from this was that the floor upon which I rested was exceedingly thin, made only of paper in fact, and that at any moment it might give way and precipitate me upon the ice. This terrified me, and the way that the cold blew up through the cracks in the floor was disturbing enough. I knew that my doctor thought me mad to remain in such a place. But above all I was overwhelmed by the figure of Semyonov. He haunted me in all my dreams, his presence never left me for a single instant. I could not be sure whether he were in the room or no, but certainly he was close to me . . . watching me, sneering at me as he had so often done before.

I was conscious also of Petrograd, of the town itself, in every one of its amazingly various manifestations. I saw it all laid out as though I were a great height above it – the fashionable streets, the Nevski and the Morskaia with the carriages and the motor-cars and trams, the kiosks and the bazaars, the women with their baskets of apples, the boys with the newspapers, the smart cinematographs, the shop in the Morskaia with the coloured stones in the window, the oculist and the pastry-cooks and the hairdressers and the large 'English Shop' at the corner of the Nevski, and Pivato's the restaurant, and close beside it the art shop with popular post cards and books on Serov and Vrubel, and the Astoria Hotel with its shining windows staring on to S. Isaac's Square. And I saw the Nevski, that straight and proud street, filled with every kind of vehicle and black masses of people, rolling like thick clouds up and down, here and there, the hum of their talk rising like mist from the snow. And there was the Kazan Cathedral, haughty and proud, and the book shop with the French books and complete sets of Tchekov and Merejkowsky in the window, and the bridges and the palaces and the square before the Alexander Theatre, and Elisseieff's the provision shop, and all the banks, and the shops with gloves and shirts, all looking ill-fitting as though they were never meant to be worn, and then the little dirty shops poked in between the grand ones, the shop with rubber goods and the shop with an Aquarium, gold-fish and snails and a tortoise, and the shop with oranges and bananas. Then, too, there was the Arcade with the theatre where they acted *Romance* and *Potash and Perlmutter* (almost as they do in London), and on the other side of the street, at the corner of the Sadovia, the bazaar with all its shops and its trembling mist of people. I watched the Nevski, and saw how it slipped into the Neva with the Red Square on one side of it, and S. Isaac's Square on the other, and the great station at the far end of it, and about these two lines, the Neva and the Nevski, the whole town sprawled and crept, ebbed and flowed. Away from the splendour it stretched, dirty and decrepit and untended, here piles of evil flats, there old wooden buildings with cobbled courts, and the canals twisting and creeping up and down through it all. It was all bathed, as I looked down upon it, in coloured mist. The air was purple and gold and light blue, fading into the snow and ice and transforming it. Everywhere there were the masts of ships and the smell of the sea and rough deserted places – and shadows moved behind the shadows, and yet more shadows behind *them*, so that it was all uncertain and unstable, and only the river knew what it was about.

Over the whole town Semyonov and I moved together, and the ice and snow silenced our steps, and no one in the whole place spoke a word, so that we had to lower our voices and whispered....

XV

Suddenly I was better. I quite recovered from my fever and only lay still on my bed, weak, and very hungry. I was happy, happy as I had not been since I came to Petrograd. I felt all the luxury of convalescence creeping into my bones. All that I need do was to lie there and let people feed me and read a little if it did not make my head ache. I had a water-colour painted by Alexander Benois on the wall opposite me, a night in the Caucasus, with a heavy sweep of black hill, a deep blue steady sky, and a thin grey road running into endless distance. A pleasing picture, with no finality in its appeal – intimate too, so that it was one's own road and one's own hill. I had bought it extravagantly, at last year's '*Mir Eskoustva*,' and now I was pleased at my extravagance.

Marfa was very good to me, feeding me, and being cross with me to make me take an interest in things, and acting with wonderful judgement about my visitors. Numbers of people, English and Russian, came to see me – I had not known that I had so many friends. I felt amiable to all the world, and hopeful about it, too. I looked back on the period before my illness as a bad dream.

People told me I was foolish to live out in this wretched place of mine, where it was cold and wild and lonely. And then when they came again they were not so sure, and they looked out on the ice that shone in waves and shadows of light under the sun, and thought that perhaps they too would try. But, of course, I knew well that they would not. . . .

As I grew stronger I felt an intense and burning interest in the history that had been developing when I fell ill. I heard that Vera Michailovna and Nina had called many times. Markovitch had been, and Henry Bohun and Lawrence.

Then, one sunny afternoon, Henry Bohun came in and I was surprised at my pleasure at the sight of him. He was shocked at the change in me, and was too young to conceal it.

'Oh, you do look bad!' were his first words as he sat down by my bed. 'I say, are you comfortable here? Wouldn't you rather be somewhere with conveniences – telephone and lifts and things?'

'Not at all!' I answered. 'I've got a telephone. I'm very happy where I am.'

'It is a queer place,' he said. 'Isn't it awfully unhealthy?'

'Quite the reverse – with the sea in front of it! About the healthiest spot in Petrograd!'

'But I should get the blues here. So lonely and quiet. Petrograd is a strange town! Most people don't dream there's a queer place like this.'

'That's why I like it,' I said. 'I expect there are lots of queer places in Petrograd if you only knew.'

He wandered about the room, looking at my few pictures and my books and my writing-table. At last he sat down again by my bed.

'Now tell me all the news,' I said.

'News?' he asked. He looked uncomfortable, and I saw at once that he had come to confide something in me. 'What sort of news? Political?'

'Anything.'

'Well, politics are about the same. They say there's going to be an awful row in February when the Duma meets – but then other people say there won't be a row at all until the war is over.'

'What eise do they say?'

'They say Protopopoff is up to all sorts of tricks. That he says prayers with the Empress and they summon Rasputin's ghost. . . . That's all rot of course. But he does just what the Empress tells him, and they're going to enslave the whole country and hand it over to Germany.'

'What will they do that for?' I asked.

'Why, then, the Czarevitch will have it – under Germany. They say that none of the munitions are going to the Front, and Protopopoff's keeping them all to blow up the people here with.'

'What else?' I asked sarcastically.

'No, but really, there's something in it, I expect.' Henry looked serious and important. 'Then on the other hand, Clutton-Davies says the Czar's absolutely all right, dead keen on the war and hates Germany . . . I don't know – but Clutton-Davies sees him nearly every day.'

'Anything eise?' I asked.

'Oh, food's worse than ever! Going up every day, and the bread queues are longer and longer. The Germans have spies in the queues, women who go up and down telling people it's all England's fault.'

'And people are just the same?'

'Just the same; Donons' and the Bear are crowded every day. You can't get a table. So are the cinematographs and the theatres. I went to the Ballet last night.'

'What was it?'

'"La fille mal gardée" – Karsavina dancing divinely. Every one was there.'

This closed the strain of public information. I led him further.

'Well, Bohun, what about our friends the Markovitches?' I asked. 'How are you getting on there?'

He blushed and looked at his boots.

'All right,' he said. 'They're very decent.'

Then he burst out with: 'I say, Durward, what do you think of this uncle that's turned up, the doctor chap?'

'Nothing particular. Why?'

'You were with him at the Front, weren't you?'

'I was.'

'Was he a good doctor?'

'Excellent.'

'He had a love affair at the Front, hadn't he?'

'Yes.'

'And she was killed?'

'Yes.'

'Poor devil. . . .' Then he added: 'Did he mind very much?'

'Very much.'

'Funny thing, you wouldn't think he would.'

'Why not,' I asked.

'Oh, he looks a hard sort of fellow – as though he'd stand anything. I wouldn't like to have a row with him.'

'Has he been to the Markovitches much lately?'

'Yes – almost every evening.'

'What does he do there?'

'Oh, just sits and talks. Markovitch can't bear him. You can see that easily enough. He teases him.'

'How do you mean?' I asked.

'Oh, he laughs at him all the time, at his inventions and that kind of thing. Markovitch gets awfully wild. He *is* a bit of an ass, isn't he?'

'Do you like Semyonov?' I asked.

'I do rather,' said Henry. 'He's very decent to me. I had a walk with him one afternoon. He said you were awfully brave at the Front.'

'Thank him for nothing,' I said.

'And he said you didn't like him – don't you?'

'Ah, that's too old a story,' I answered. 'We know what we feel about one another.'

'Well, Lawrence simply hates him,' continued Bohun. 'He says he's the most thundering cad, and as bad as you make them. I don't see how he can tell.'

This interested me extremely. 'When did he tell you this?' I asked.

'Yesterday. I asked him what he had to judge by, and he said instinct. I said he'd no right to go only by that.'

'Has Lawrence been much to the Markovitches?'

'Yes – once or twice. He just sits there and never opens his mouth.'

'Very wise of him if he hasn't got anything to say.'

'No, but really – do you think so? It doesn't make him popular.'

'Why, who doesn't like him?'

'Nobody,' answered Henry ungrammatically. 'None of the English anyway. They can't stand him at the Embassy or the Mission. They say he's fearfully stuck up and thinks about nothing but himself. . . . I don't agree, of course – all the same, he might make himself more agreeable to people.'

'What nonsense!' I answered hotly. 'Lawrence is one of the best fellows that ever breathed. The Markovitches don't dislike him, do they?'

'No, he's quite different with them. Vera Michailovna likes him, I know.'

It was the first time that he had mentioned her name to me. He turned towards me now, his face crimson. 'I say – that's really what

I came to talk about, Durward. I care for her madly! . . . I'd die for her. I would really. I love her, Durward. I see now I've never loved anybody before.'

'Well, what will you do about it?'

'Do about it? . . . Why, nothing, of course. It's all perfectly hopeless. In the first place, there's Markovitch.'

'Yes. There's Markovitch,' I agreed.

'She doesn't care for him – does she? You know that–' He waited, eagerly staring into my face.

I had a temptation to laugh. He was so very young, so very helpless, and yet – that sense of his youth had pathos in it too, and I suddenly liked young Bohun – for the first time.

'Look here, Bohun,' I said, trying to speak with a proper solemnity. 'Don't be a young ass. You know that it's hopeless, any feeling of that kind. She *does* care for her husband. She could never care for you in that way, and you'd only make trouble for them all if you went on with it. . . . On the other hand, she needs a friend badly. You can do that for her. Be her pal. See that things are all right in the house. Make a friend of Markovitch himself. Look after *him*!'

'Look after Markovitch!' Bohun exclaimed.

'Yes . . . I don't want to be melodramatic, but there's trouble coming there; and if you're the friend of them all, you can help – more than you know. Only none of the other business——'

Bohun flushed. 'She doesn't know – she never will. I only want to be a friend of hers, as you put it. Anything eise is hopeless, of course. I'm not the kind of fellow she'd ever look at, even if Markovitch wasn't there. But if I can do anything . . . I'd be awfully glad. What kind of trouble do you mean?' he asked.

'Probably nothing,' I said; 'only she wants a friend. And Markovitch wants one too.'

There was a pause – then Bohun said, 'I say, Durward – what an awful ass I was.'

'What about?' I asked.

'About my poetry – and all that, – thinking it so important.'

'Yes,' I said, 'you were.'

'I've written some poetry to her and I tore it up,' he ended.

'That's a good thing,' said I.

'I'm glad I told you,' he said. He got up to go. 'I say, Durward——'

'Well,' I asked.

'You're an awfully funny chap. Not a bit what you look——'

'That's all right,' I said; 'I know what you mean.'
'Well, good-night,' he said, and went.

XVI

I thought that night, as I lay cosily in my dusky room, of those old stories by Wilkie Collins that had once upon a time so deeply engrossed my interest – stories in which, because some one has disappeared on a snowy night, or painted his face blue, or locked up a room and lost the key, or broken down in his carriage on a windy night at the cross-roads, dozens of people are involved, diaries are written, confessions are made, and all the characters move along different roads towards the same lighted, comfortable Inn. That is the kind of story that intrigues me, whether it be written about outside mysteries by Wilkie Collins or inside mysteries by the great creator of' The Golden Bowl,' or mysteries of both kinds, such as Henry Galleon has given us. I remember a friend of mine, James Maradick, once saying to me, 'It's no use trying to keep out of things. As soon as they want to put you in – you're in. The moment you're born, you're done for.'

It's just that spectacle of some poor innocent being suddenly caught into some affair, against his will, without his knowledge, but to the most serious alteration of his character and fortunes, that one watches with a delight almost malicious – whether it be *The Woman in White*, *The Wings of the Dove*, or *The Roads* that offer it us. Well, I had now to face the fact that something of this kind had happened to myself.

I was drawn in – and I was glad. I luxuriated in my gladness, lying there in my room under the wavering, uncertain light of two candles, hearing the church bells clanging and echoing mysteriously beyond the wall. I lay there with a consciousness of being on the very verge of some adventure, with the assurance, too, that I was to be of use once more, to play my part, to fling aside, thank God, that old cloak of apathetic disappointment, of selfish betrayal, of cynical disbelief. Semyonov had brought the old life back to me and I had shrunk from the impact of it; but he had brought back to me, too, the presences of my absent friends who, during these weary months, had been lost to me. It seemed to me that, in the flickering twilight, John and Marie were bringing forward to me Vera and Nina and Jerry and asking me to look after them. . . . I would do my best.

And while I was thinking of these things Vera Michailovna came in. She was suddenly in the room, standing there, her furs up to her throat, her body in shadow, but her large, grave eyes shining through the candlelight, her mouth smiling.

'Is it all right?' she said, Coming forward. 'I'm not in the way? You're not sleeping?'

I told her that I was delighted to see her.

'I've been almost every day, but Marfa told me you were not well enough. She *does* guard you – like a dragon. But to-night Nina and I are going to Rozanov's, to a party, and she said she'd meet me here. . . . Shan't I worry you?'

'Worry me! You're the most restful friend I have——' I felt so glad to see her that I was surprised at my own happiness. She sat down near to me, very quietly, moving, as she always did, softly and surely.

I could see that she was distressed because I looked ill, but she asked me no tiresome questions, said nothing about my madness in living as I did (always so irritating, as though I were a stupid child), praised the room, admired the Benois picture, and then talked in her soft, kindly voice.

'We've missed you so much, Nina and I,' she said. 'I told Nina that if she came to-night she wasn't to make a noise and disturb you.'

'She can make as much noise as she likes,' I said. 'I like the right kind of noise.'

We talked a little about politics and England and anything that came into our minds. We both felt, I know, a delightful, easy intimacy and friendliness and trust. I had never with any other woman felt such a sense of friendship, something almost masculine in its comradeship and honesty. And to-night this bond between us strengthened wonderfully. I blessed my luck. I saw that there were dark lines under her eyes and that she was pale.

'You're tired,' I said.

'Yes, I am,' she acknowledged. 'And I don't know why. At least, I do know. I'm going to use you selfishly, Durdles. I'm going to tell you all my troubles and ask your help in every possible way. I'm going to let you off nothing.'

I took her hand.

'I'm proud,' I said, 'now and always.'

'Do you know that I've never asked any one's help before? I was rather conceited that I could get on always without it. When I was very small I wouldn't take a word of advice from any one, and mother and father, when I was tiny, used to consult me about everything. Then they were killed and I *had* to go on alone. . . . And after that, when I married Nicholas, it was! again who decided everything. And my mistakes taught me nothing. I didn't want them to teach me.'

She spoke that last word fiercely, and through the note that came into her voice I saw suddenly the potentialities that were in her, the other creature that she might be if she were ever awakened.

She talked then for a long time. She didn't move at all; her head rested on her hand and her eyes watched me. As I listened I thought of my other friend Marie, who now was dead, and how restless she was when she spoke, moving about the room, stopping to demand my approval, protesting against my criticism, laughing, crying out. . . . Vera was so still, so wise, too, in comparison with Marie, braver too – and yet the same heart, the same charity, the same nobility.

But she was my friend, and Marie I had loved. . . . The difference in that! And how much easier now to help than it had been then, simply because one's own soul *was* one's own and one stood by oneself!

How happy a thing freedom is – and how lonely!

She told me many things that I need not repeat here, but, as she talked, I saw how, far more deeply than I had imagined, Nina had been the heart of the whole of her life. She had watched over her, protected her, advised her, warned her, and loved her, passionately, jealously, almost madly all the time.

'When I married Nicholas,' she said, 'I thought of Nina more than any one else. That was wrong. . . . I ought to have thought most of Nicholas; but I knew that I could give her a home, that she could have everything she wanted. And still she would be with me. Nicholas was only too ready for that. I thought I would care for her until some one came who was worthy of her, and who would look after her far better than I ever could.

'But the only person who had come was Boris Grogoff. He loved Nina from the first moment, in his own careless, conceited, opinionated way.'

'Why did you let him come so often to the house if you didn't approve of him?' I asked.

'How could I prevent it?' she asked me. 'We Russians are not like the English. In England I know you just shut the door and say, "Not at home."

'Here, if any one wants to come, he comes. Very often we hate him for coming, but still there it is. It is too much trouble to turn him out, besides it wouldn't be kind – and anyway they wouldn't go. You can be as rude as you like here and nobody cares. For a long while Nina paid no attention to Boris. She doesn't like him. She will never like him, I'm sure. But now, these last weeks, I've begun to be afraid. In some way he has power over her – not much power, but a little – and she is so young, so ignorant – she knows nothing.

'Until lately she always told me everything. Now she tells me nothing. She's strange with me; angry for nothing. Then sorry and sweet again – then suddenly angry. . . . She's excited and wild, going out all the time, but unhappy too. . . I *know* she's unhappy. I can feel it as though it were myself.'

'You're imagining things,' I said. 'Now when the war's reached this period we're all nervous and overstrung. The atmosphere of this town is enough to make any one fancy that they see anything. Nina's all right.'

'I'm losing her! I'm losing her!' Vera cried, suddenly stretching out her hand as though in a gesture of appeal. 'She must stay with me. I don't know what's happening to her. Ah, and I'm so lonely without her!'

There was silence between us for a little, and then she went on.

'Durdles, I did wrong to marry Nicholas – wrong to Nina, wrong to Nicholas, wrong to myself. I thought it was right. I didn't love Nicholas – I never loved him and I never pretended to. He knew that I did not. But I thought then that I was above love, that knowledge was what mattered. Ideas – saving the world – and he had *such* ideas! Wonderful! There was, I thought, nothing that he would not be able to do if only he were helped enough. He wanted help in every way. He was such a child, so unhappy, so lonely, I thought that I could give him everything that he needed. Don't fancy that I thought that I sacrificed myself. I felt that I was the luckiest girl in all the world – and still, now when I see that he is not strong enough for his ideas, I care for him as I did then, and I would never let any trouble touch him if I could help it. But if – if——'

She paused, turned away from me, looking towards the window.

'If, after all, I was wrong. If, after all, I was meant to love. If love were to come now . . . real love . . . now. . . .'

She broke off, suddenly stood up, and very low, almost whispering, said:

'I have fancied lately that it might come. And then, what should I do? Oh, what should I do? With Nicholas and Nina and all the trouble there is now in the world – and Russia – I'm afraid of myself – and ashamed. . . .'

I could not speak. I was utterly astonished. Could it be Bohun of whom she was speaking? No, I saw at once that the idea was ludicrous. But if not——

I took her hand.

'Vera,' I said. 'Believe me. I'm much older than you, and I know. Love's always selfish, always cruel to others, always means trouble, sorrow, and disappointment. But it's worth it, even when it brings complete disaster. Life isn't life without it.'

I felt her hand tremble in mine.

'I don't know,' she said, 'I know nothing of it, except my love for Nina. It isn't that now there's anybody. Don't think that. There is no one – no one. Only my self-confidence is gone. I can't see clearly any more. My duty is to Nina and Nicholas. And if they are happy nothing else matters – nothing. And I'm afraid that I'm going to do them harm.'

She paused as though she were listening. 'There's no one there, is there?' she asked me – 'there by the door?'

'No – no one.'

'There are so many noises in this house. Don't they disturb you?'

'I don't think of them now. I'm used to them – and in fact I like them.'

She went on: 'It's Uncle Alexei of course. He comes to see us nearly every day. He's very pleasant, more pleasant than he has ever been before, but he has a dreadful effect on Nicholas——'

'I know the effect he can have,' I said.

'I know that Nicholas has been feeling for a long time that his inventions are no use. He will never own it to me or to any one – but I can tell. I know it so well. The war came and his new feeling about Russia carried him along. He put everything into that. Now that has failed him, and he despises himself for having expected it to do otherwise. He's raging about, trying to find something that he can believe in, and Uncle Alexei knows that and plays on that. . . . He teases him; he drives him wild and then makes him happy again. He can do anything with him he pleases. He always could. But now he has some plan. I used to think that he simply laughed at people because it amused him to see how weak they can be. But now there's more than that. He's been hurt himself at last, and that has hurt his pride, and he wants to hurt back. . . . It's all in the dark. The war's in the dark . . . everything. . . .' Then she smiled and put her hand on my arm. That's why I've come to you, because I trust you and believe you and know you say what you mean.'

Once before Marie had said those same words to me. It was as though I heard her voice again.

'I won't fail you,' I said.

There was a knock on the door; it was flung open as though by the wind, and Nina was with us. Her face was rosy with the cold; her eyes laughed under her little round fur cap. She came running across the room, pulled herself up with a little cry beside the bed, and then flung herself upon me, throwing her arms around my neck and kissing me.

'My dear Nina!' cried Vera.

She looked up, laughing.

'Why not? Poor Durdles. Are you better? *Biédnie* . . . give me your hands. But – how cold they are! And there are draughts everywhere. I've brought you some chocolates – and a book.'

'My dear! . . .' Vera cried again. 'He won't like *that*,' pointing to a work of fiction by a modern Russian literary lady whose heart and brain are of the succulent variety.

'Why not? She's very good. It's lovely! All about impossible people! Durdles, *dear*! I'll give up the party. We won't go. We'll sit here and entertain you. I'll send Boris away. We'll tell him we don't want him.'

'Boris!' cried Vera.

'Yes.' Nina laughed a little uneasily, I thought. 'I know you said he wasn't to come. He'll quarrel with Rozanov of course. But he said he would. And so how was one to prevent him? You're always so tiresome, Vera . . . I'm not a baby now, nor is Boris. If he wants to come he shall come.'

Vera stood away from us both. I could see that she was very angry. I had never seen her angry before.

'You know that it's impossible, Nina,' she said, 'You know that Rozanov hates him. And besides – there are other reasons. You know them perfectly well, Nina.'

Nina stood there pouting, tears were in her eyes.

'You're unfair,' she said. 'You don't let me do anything. You give me no freedom, I don't care for Boris, but if he wants to go he shall go. I'm grown up now. You have your Lawrence. Let me have my Boris.'

'My Lawrence?' asked Vera.

'Yes. You know that you're always wanting him to come – always looking for him. I like him, too. I like him very much. But you never let me talk to him. You never——'

'Quiet, Nina.' Vera's voice was trembling. Her face was sterner than I'd ever seen it. 'You're making me angry.'

'I don't care how angry I make you. It's true. You're impossible now. Why shouldn't I have my friends? I've nobody now. You never let me have anybody. And I like Mr. Lawrence——'

She began to sob, looking the most desolate figure.

Vera turned.

'You don't know what you've said, Nina, nor how you've hurt. . . . You can go to your party as you please——'

And before I could stop her she was gone.

Nina turned to me a breathless, tearful face. She waited; we heard the door below closed.

'Oh, Durdles, what have I done?'

'Go after her! Stop her!' I said.

Nina vanished and I was alone. My room was intensely quiet.

XVII

They didn't come to see me again together. Vera came twice, kind and good as always, but with no more confidences; and Nina once with flowers and fruit and a wild chattering tongue about the cinemas and Smyrnov, who was delighting the world at the Narodny Dom, and the wonderful performance of Lermontov's 'Masquerade' that was shortly to take place at the Alexandra Theatre.

'Are you and Vera friends again?' I asked her.

'Oh yes! Why not?' And she went on, snapping a chocolate almond between her teeth – 'The one at the "Piccadilly" is the best. It's an Italian one, and there's a giant in it who throws people all over the place, out of Windows and everywhere. Ah! how lovely! . . . I wish I could go every night.'

'You ought to be helping with the war,' I said severely.

'Oh, I hate the war!' she answered. 'We're all terribly tired of it. Tanya's given up going to the English hospital now, and is just meaning to be as gay as she can be; and Zinaida Fyodorovna has just come back from her Otriad on the Galician front, and she says it's shocking there now – no food or dancing or anything. Why doesn't every one make peace?'

'Do you want the Germans to rule Russia?' I asked.

'Why not? 'she said, laughing. 'We can't do it ourselves. We don't care who does it. The English can do it if they like, only they're too lazy to bother. The Germans aren't lazy, and if they were here we'd have lots of theatres and cinematographs.'

'Don't you love your country?' I asked.

'This isn't our country,' she answered. 'It just belongs to the Empress and Protopopoff'

'Supposing it became your country and the Emperor went?'

'Oh, then it would belong to a million different people, and in the end no one would have anything. Can't you see how they'd fight?' . . . She burst out laughing: 'Boris and Nicholas and Uncle Alexei and all the others!'

Then she was suddenly serious.

'I know, Durdles, you consider that I'm so young and frivolous that I don't think of anything serious. But I can see things like any one else. Can't you see that we're all so disappointed with ourselves that nothing matters? We thought the war was going to be so fine – but now it's just like the Japanese one, all robbery and lies – and we can't do anything to stop it.'

'Perhaps some day some one will,' I said.

'Oh yes!' she answered scornfully, 'men like Boris.'

After that she refused to be grave for a moment, danced about the room, singing, and finally vanished, a whirlwind of blue silk.

A week later I was out in the world again. That curious sense of excitement that had first come to me during the early days of my illness burnt now more fiercely than ever. I cannot say what it was exactly that I thought was going to happen. I have often looked back, as many other people must have done, to those days in February and wondered whether I foresaw anything of what was to come, and what were the things that might have seemed to me significant if I had noticed them. And here I am deliberately speaking of both public and private affairs. I cannot quite frankly dissever the two. At the Front, a year and a half before, I had discovered how intermingled the souls of individuals and the souls of countries were, and how permanent private history seemed to me and how transient public events; but whether that was true or no before, it was now most certain that it was the story of certain individuals that I was to record, – the history that was being made behind them could at its best be only a background.

I seemed to step into a city ablaze with a sinister glory. If that appears melodramatic I can only say that the dazzling winter weather of those weeks was melodramatic. Never before had I seen the huge buildings tower so high, never before felt the shadows so vast, the squares and streets so limitless in their capacity for swallowing light and colour. The sky was a bitter changeless blue; the buildings black; the snow and ice, glittering with purple and gold, swept by vast swinging shadows as though huge doors opened and shut in heaven, or monstrous birds hovered, their wings spread, motionless in the limitless space.

And all this had, as ever, nothing to do with human life. The little courtyards with their wood-stacks and their coloured houses, carts and the cobbled squares and the little stumpy trees that bordered the canals and the little wooden huts beside the bridges with their candles and fruit – these were human and friendly and good, but they had their precarious condition like the rest of us.

On the first afternoon of my new liberty I found myself in the Nevski Prospect, bewildered by the crowds and the talk and teams and motors and carts that passed in unending sequence up and down the long street. Standing at the corner of the Sadovia and the Nevski one was carried straight to the point of the golden spire that guarded the farther end of the great street. All was gold, the surface of the road was like a golden stream, the canal was gold, the thin spire caught into its piercing line all the colour of the swiftly fading afternoon; the wheels of the carriages gleamed, the flower-baskets of the women glittered like shining foam, the snow flung its crystal colour into the air like thin fire dim before the sun. The street seemed to have gathered on to its pavements the citizens of every country under the sun. Tartars, Mongols, Little Russians, Chinamen, Japanese, French officers, British officers, peasants and fashionable women, schoolboys, officials, actors and artists and business men and priests and sailors and beggars and hawkers and, guarding them all, friendly, Urbane, filled with a pleasant self-importance that seemed at that hour the simplest and easiest of attitudes, the Police. 'Rum – rum – rum – whirr – whirr – whirr – whirr – like the regular beat of a shuttle the hum rose and fell, as the sun faded into rosy mist and white vapours stole above the still canals.

I turned to go home and felt some one touch my elbow.

I swung round and there, his broad face ruddy with the cold, was Jerry Lawrence.

I was delighted to see him and told him so.

'Well, I'm damned glad,' he said gruffly. 'I thought you might have a grudge against me.'

'A grudge?' I said. 'Why?'

'Haven't been to see you. Heard you were ill, but didn't think you'd want me hanging round.'

'Why this modesty?' I asked.

'No – well – you know what I mean.' He shuffled his feet. 'No good in a sick-room.'

'Mine wasn't exactly a sick-room,' I said. 'But I heard that you did come.'

'Yes. I came twice,' he answered, looking at me shyly. 'Your old woman wouldn't let me see you.'

'Never mind that,' I said; 'let's have an evening together soon.'

'Yes – as soon as you like.' He looked up and down the street. 'There are some things I'd like to ask your advice about.'

'Certainly,' I said.

'What do you say to Coming and dining at my place? Ever met Wilderling?'

'Wilderling?' I could not remember for the moment the name.

'Yes – the old josser I live with. Fine old man – got a point of view of his own!'

'Delighted,' I said.

'Tomorrow. Eight o'clock. Don't dress.'

He was just going off when he turned again.

'Awfully glad you're better,' he said. He cleared his throat, looked at me in a very friendly way, then smiled.

'*Awfully* glad you're better,' he repeated, then went off, rolling his broad figure into the evening mist.

I turned towards home.

XVIII

I arrived at the Baron's punctually at eight o'clock. His flat was in a small side street off the English Quay. I paused for a moment, before turning into its dark recesses, to gather in the vast expanse of the frozen river and the long white quay. It was as though I had found my way behind a towering wall that now closed me in with a smile of contemptuous derision. There was no sound in the shining air and the only figure was a guard who moved monotonously up and down outside the Winter Palace.

I rang the bell and the 'Schwitzer,' bowing very ceremoniously, told me the flat was on the second floor. I went up a broad stone staircase and found a heavy oak door with brass nails confronting me. When this slowly swung open I discovered a very old man with white hair bowing before me. He was a splendid figure in a uniform of dark blue, his tall thin figure straight and slim, his white moustaches so neat and fierce that they seemed to keep guard over the rest of his face as though they warned him that they would stand no nonsense. There was an air of hushed splendour behind him, and I could hear the heavy, solemn ticking of a clock keeping guard over all the austere sanctities of the place. When I had taken off my Shuba and goloshes I was ushered into a magnificent room with a high gold clock on the mantelpiece, gilt chairs, heavy dark carpets and large portraits frowning from the grey walls. The whole room was bitterly silent, save for the tick of the clock. There was no fire in the fireplace, but a large gleaming white stove flung out a close scented heat from the further corner of the room. There were two long glass bookcases, some little tables with gilt legs, and a fine Japanese screen of dull gold. The only other piece of furniture was a huge grand piano near the window.

I sat down and was instantly caught into the solemn silence. There was something threatening in the hush of it all. 'We do what we're told,' the clock seemed to say, 'and so must you.' I thought of the ice and snow beyond the windows, and, in spite of myself, shivered.

Then the door opened and the Baron came in. He stood for a moment by the door, staring in front of him as though he could not penetrate the heavy and dusky air, and seen thus, under the height and space of the room, he seemed so small as to be almost ridiculous. But he was not ridiculous for long. As he approached one was struck at once by the immaculate efficiency that followed him like a protecting shadow. In himself he was a scrupulously neat old man with weary and dissipated eyes, but behind the weariness, the neatness, and dissipation was a spirit of indomitable determination and resolution. He wore a little white Imperial and a long white moustache. His hair was brushed back and his forehead shone like marble. He wore a black suit, white spats, and long, pointed, black patent-leather shoes. He had the smallest feet I have ever seen on any man.

He greeted me with great courtesy. His voice was soft, and he spoke perfect English, save for a very slight accent that was rather charming; this gave his words a certain naïveté. He rubbed his hands and smiled in a gentle but determined way, as though he meant no harm by it, but had decided that it was a necessary thing to do. I forget of what we talked, but I know that I surrendered myself at once to an atmosphere that had been strange to me for so long that I had almost forgotten its character – an atmosphere of discipline, order, comfort, and, above all, of security. My mind flew to the Markovitches, and I smiled to myself at the thought of the contrast.

Then, strangely, when I had once thought of the Markovitch flat the picture haunted me for the rest of the evening. I could see the Baron's gilt chairs and gold clock, his little Imperial and shining shoes only through the cloudy disorder of the Markovitch tables and chairs. There was poor Markovitch in his dark little room perched on his chair with his boots, with his hands, with his hair . . . and there was poor Uncle and there poor Vera. . . . Why was I pitying them? I gloried in them. That is Russia . . . This is. . . .

'Allow me to introduce you to my wife,' the Baron said, bending forward, the very points of his toes expressing amiability.

The Baroness was a large solid lady with a fine white bosom and strong white arms. Her face was homely and kind; I saw at once that she adored her husband; her placid smile carried beneath its placidity a tremulous anxiety that he should be pleased, and her mild eyes swam in the light of his encouragement. I was sure, however, that the calm and discipline that I felt in the things around me came as much from her domesticity as from his discipline. She was a fortunate woman in that she had attained the ambition of her life – to govern the household of a man whom she could both love and fear.

Lawrence came in, and we went through high folding doors into the dining-room. This room had dark-blue wall-paper, electric lights heavily shaded, and soft heavy carpets. The table itself was flooded with light – the rest of the room was dusk. I wondered as I looked about me why the Wilderlings had taken Lawrence as a paying guest. Before my visit I had imagined that they were poor, as so many of the better-class Russians were, but here were no signs of poverty. I decided that.

Our dinner was good, and the wine was excellent. We talked, of course, politics, and the Baron was admirably frank.

'I won't disguise from you, M. Durward,' he said, 'that some of us watch your English effort at winning the heart of this country with sympathy, but also, if I am not offending you, with some humour. I'm not speaking only of your propaganda efforts. You've got, I know, one or two literary gentlemen here – a novelist, I think, and a professor and a journalist. Well, soon you'll find them inefficient, and decide that you must have some commercial gentlemen, and then, disappointed with them, you'll decide for the military . . . and still the great heart of Russia will remain untouched.'

'Yes,' I said, 'because your class are determined that the peasant shall remain uneducated, and until he is educated he will be unable to approach any of us.'

'Quite so,' said the Baron, smiling at me very cheerfully. 'I perceive, M. Durward, that you are a democrat. So are we all, these days. . . . You look surprised, but I assure you that the good of the people in the interests of the people is the only thing for which any of us care. Only some of us know Russia pretty well, and we know that the Russian peasant is not ready for liberty, and if you were to give him liberty to-night you would plunge his country into the most desperate torture of anarchy and carnage known in history. A little more soup? – we are offering you only a slight dinner.'

'Yes, but, Baron,' I said, 'would you tell me when it is intended that the Russian peasant shall begin his upward course towards light and learning? If that day is to be for ever postponed?'

'It will not be for ever postponed,' said the Baron gently. 'Let us finish the war, and education shall be given slowly, under wise direction, to every man, woman, and child in the country. Our Czar is the most liberal ruler in Europe – and he knows what is good for his children.'

'And Protopopoff and Stürmer?' I asked.

'Protopopoff is a zealous, loyal liberal, but he has been made to see during these last months that Russia is not at this moment ready for freedom. Stürmer – well, M. Stürmer is gone.'

'So you, yourself, Baron,' I asked, 'would oppose at this moment all reform?'

'With every drop of blood in my body,' he answered, and his hand flat against the tablecloth quivered. 'At this crisis admit one change and your dyke is burst, your land flooded. Every Russian is asked at this moment to believe in simple things – his religion, his Czar, his country. Grant your reforms, and in a week every babbler in the country will be off his head, talking, screaming, fighting. The Germans will occupy Russia at their own good time, you will be beaten on the West and civilisation will be set back two hundred years. The only hope for Russia is unity, and for unity you must have discipline, and for discipline, in Russia at any rate, you must have an autocracy.'

As he spoke the furniture, the grey walls, the heavy carpets, seemed to whisper an echo of his words: 'Unity ... Discipline ... Discipline ... Autocracy ... Autocracy ... Autocracy ..."

'Then tell me, Baron,' I said, 'if it isn't an impertinent question, do you feel so secure in your position that you have no fears at all? Does such a crisis, as for instance Milyukoff's protest last November, mean nothing? You know the discontent. . . . Is there no fear . . .?'

'Fear!' He interrupted me, his voice swift and soft and triumphant. 'M. Durward, are you so ignorant of Russia that you consider the outpourings of a few idealistic Intelligentzia, professors and teachers and poets, as important? What about the people, M. Durward? You ask any peasant in the Moscow Government, or Little Russia, or the Ukraine whether he will remain loyal to his Little Father or no! Ask – and the question you suggested to me will be answered.'

'Then you feel both secure and justified?' I said.

'We feel both secure and justified,' he answered me, smiling.

After that our conversation was personal and social. Lawrence was very quiet. I observed that the Baroness had a motherly affection for him, that she saw that he had everything that he wanted, and that she gave him every now and then little friendly confidential smiles. As the meal proceeded, as I drank the most excellent wine and the warm austerity of my surroundings gathered ever more closely around me, I wondered whether after all my apprehensions and forebodings of the last weeks had not been the merest sick man's cowardice. Surely if any kingdom in the world was secure, it was this official Russia. I could see it stretching through the space and silence of that vast land, its servants in every village, its paths and roads all leading back to the central citadel, its whispered orders flying through the air from district to district, its judgements, its rewards, its sins, its virtues, resting upon a basis of superstition and ignorance and apathy, the three sure friends .of autocracy through history!

And on the other side – who? The Rat, Boris Grogoff, Markovitch. Yes, the Baron had reason for his confidence. . . . I thought for a moment of that figure that I had seen on Christmas Eve by the river – the strong grave bearded peasant whose gaze had seemed to go so far beyond the bounds of my own vision. But no! Russia's mystical peasant – that was an old tale. Once, on the Front, when I had seen him facing the enemy with bare hands, I had, myself, believed it. Now I thought once more of the Rat – *that* was the type whom I must now confront.

I had a most agreeable evening. I do not know how long it had been since I had tasted luxury and comfort and the true fruits of civilisation. The Baron was a most admirable teller of stories, with a capital sense of humour. After dinner the Baroness left us for half an hour, and the Baron became very pleasantly Rabelaisian, speaking of his experiences in Paris and London, Vienna and Berlin so easily and with so ready a wit that the evening flew. The Baroness returned and, seeing that it was after eleven, I made my farewells. Lawrence said that he would walk with me down the quay before turning into bed. My host and hostess pressed me to come as often as possible. The Baron's last words to me were:

'Have no fears, M. Durward. There is much talk in this country, but we are a lazy people.'

The 'we' rang strangely in my ears.

'He's of course no more a Russian than you or I,' I said to Lawrence, as we started down the quay.

'Oh yes, he is!' Lawrence said. 'Quite genuine – not a drop of German blood in spite of the name. But he's a Prussian at heart – a Prussian of the Prussians. By that I don't mean in the least that he wants Germany to win the war. He doesn't – his interests are all here, and you mayn't believe me, but I assure you he's a Patriot. He loves Russia, and he wants what's best for her – and believes that to be Autocracy.'

After that Lawrence shut up. He would not say another word. We walked for a long time in silence. The evening was most beautiful. A golden moon flung the snow into dazzling relief against the deep black of the palaces. Across the Neva the line of towers and minarets and chimneys ran like a huge fissure in the golden light from sky to sky.

'You said there was something you wanted to ask my advice about?' I broke the silence.

He looked at me with his long slow considering stare. He mumbled something; then, with a sudden gesture, he gripped my arm, and, his heavy body quivering with the urgency of his words, he said:

'It's Vera Markovitch. . . . I'd give my body and soul and spirit for her happiness and safety. . . . God forgive me, I'd give my country and my honour. . . . I ache and long for her, so that I'm afraid for my sanity. I've never loved a woman, nor lusted for one, nor touched one in my whole life, Durward – and now . . . and now . . . I've gone right in. I've spoken no word to any one; but I couldn't stand my own silence. . . . Durward, you've got to help me!'

I walked on, seeing the golden light and the curving arc of snow and the little figures moving like dolls from light to shadow. Lawrence! I had never thought of him as an urgent lover; even now, although I could still feel his hand quivering on my arm, I could have laughed at the ludicrous incongruity of romance and that stolid thick-set figure. And at the same time I was afraid. Lawrence in love was no boy on the threshold of life like Bohun . . . here was no trivial passion. I realised even in that first astonished moment the trouble that might be in store for all of us.

'Look here, Lawrence!' I said at last. 'The first thing that you may as well realise is that it is hopeless. Vera Michailovna has confided in me a good deal lately, and she is devoted to her husband, thinks of nothing else. She's simple, naïve, with all her sense and wisdom. . . .'

'Hopeless!' he interrupted, and he gave a kind of grim chuckle of derision. 'My dear Durward, what do you suppose I'm after? . . . rape and adultery and Markovitch after us with a pistol? I tell you –' and here he spoke fiercely, as though he were challenging the whole ice-bound world around us – 'that I want nothing but her happiness, her safety, her comfort! Do you suppose that I'm such an ass as not to recognise the kind of thing that my loving her would lead to? I tell you I'm after nothing for myself, and that not because I'm a fine unselfish character, but simply because the thing's too big to let anything into it but herself. She shall never know that I care twopence about her, but she's got to be happy and she's got to be safe. . . . Just now, she's neither of those things, and that's why I've spoken to you. . . . She's unhappy and she's afraid, and that's got to change. I wouldn't have spoken of this to you if I thought you'd be so short-sighted. . . .'

'All right! All right!' I said testily. 'You may be a kind of Galahad, Lawrence, outside all natural law. I don't know, but you'll forgive me if I go for a moment on my own experience – and that experience is, that you can start on as highbrow an elevation as you like, but love doesn't stand still, and the body's the body, and tomorrow isn't yesterday – not by no means. Moreover, Markovitch is a Russian and a peculiar one at that. Finally, remember that I want Vera Michailovna to be happy quite as much as you do!'

He was suddenly grave and almost boyish in his next words.

'I know that – you're a decent chap, Durward – I know it's hard to believe me, but I just ask you to wait and test me. No one knows of this – that I'd swear – and no one shall; but what's the matter with her, Durward, what's she afraid of? That's why I spoke to you. You know her, and I'll throttle you here where we stand if you don't tell me just what the trouble is. I don't care for confidences or anything of the sort. You must break them all and tell me——'

His hand was on my arm again, his big ugly face, now grim and obstinate, close against mine.

'I'll tell you,' I said slowly, 'all I know, which is almost nothing. The trouble is Semyonov, the doctor. Why or how I can't say, although I've seen enough of him in the past to know the trouble he *can* be. She's afraid of him, and Markovitch is afraid of him. He likes playing on people's nerves. He's a bitter, disappointed man, who loved desperately once, as only real sensualists can . . . and now he's in love with a ghost. That's why real life maddens him.'

'Semyonov!' Lawrence whispered the name.

We had come to the end of the quay. My dear church with its round grey wall stood glistening in the moonlight, the shadows from the snow rippling up its sides, as though it lay under water. We stood and looked across the river.

'I've always hated that fellow,' Lawrence said. 'I've only seen him about twice, but I believe I hated him before I saw him. . . . All right, Durward, that's what I wanted to know. Thank you. Good-night.'

And before I could speak he had gripped my hand, had turned back, and was walking swiftly away, across the golden-lighted quay.

XIX

From the moment that Lawrence left me, vanishing into the heart of the snow and ice, I was obsessed by a conviction of approaching danger and peril. It has been one of the most disastrous weaknesses of my life that I have always shrunk from precipitate action. Before the war it had seemed to many of us that life could be jockeyed into decisions by words and theories and speculations. The swift, and, as it were, revengeful precipitancy of the last three years had driven me into a self-distrust and cowardice which had grown and grown until life had seemed veiled and distant and mysteriously obscure. From my own obscurity, against my will, against my courage, against my own knowledge of myself, circumstances were demanding that I should advance and act. It was of no avail to myself that I should act unwisely, that I should perhaps only precipitate a crisis that I could not help. I was forced to act when I would have given my soul to hold aloof, and in this town, whose darkness and light, intrigue and display, words and action, seemed to derive some mysterious force from the very soil, from the very air, the smallest action achieved monstrous proportions. When you have lived for some years in Russia you do not wonder that its Citizens prefer inaction to demonstration – the soil is so much stronger than the men who live upon it.

Nevertheless, for a fortnight I did nothing. Private affairs of an especially tiresome kind filled my days – I saw neither Lawrence nor Vera, and, during that period, I scarcely left my rooms.

There was much expectation in the town that February 14th, when the Duma was appointed to meet, would be a critical day. Fine things were said of the challenging speeches that would be made, of the firm stand that the Cadet party intended to take, of the crisis with which the Court party would be faced.

Of course nothing occurred. It may be safely said that, in Russian affairs, no crisis occurs, either in the place or at the time or in the manner in which it is expected. Time with us here refuses to be caught by the throat. That is the revenge that it takes on the scorn with which, in Russia, it is always covered.

On the 20th of February I received an invitation to Nina's birthday party. She would be eighteen on the 28th. She scribbled at the bottom of Vera's note:

DEAR DURDLES –
If you don't come I will never forgive you. – Your loving

NINA.

The immediate problem was a present. I knew that Nina adored presents, but Petrograd was now no easy place for purchases, and I wished, I suppose as a kind of tribute to her youth and freshness and colour, to give her something for which she would really care. I sallied out on a wonderful afternoon when the town was a blaze of colour, the walls dark red, dark brown, violet, pink, and the snow a dazzling glitter of crystal. The bells were ringing for some festival, echoing as do no other bells in the world from wall to wall, roof to roof, canal to canal. Everybody moved as though they were inspired with a gay sense of adventure, men and women laughing, the Isvostchiks surveying possible fares with an eye less patronising and lugubrious than usual, the flower women and the beggars and the little Chinese boys and the wicked old men who stare at you as though they were dreaming of Eastern debauches, shared in the sun and tang of the air and high colour of the sky and snow.

I pushed my way into the shop in the Morskaia that had the coloured stones – the blue and azure and purple stones – in the window. Inside the shop, which had a fine gleaming floor, and an old man with a tired eye, there were stones of every colour, but there was nothing there for Nina – all was too elaborate and grand.

Near the Nevski is a fine shop of pictures with snow scenes and blue rivers and Italian landscapes, and copies of Repin and Verestchagin, and portraits of the Czar. I searched here, but all were too sophisticated in their bright brown frames, and their air of being the latest thing from Paris and London. Then I crossed the road, threading my way through the carriages and motor cars, past the old white-bearded sweeper with the broom held aloft, gazing at the sky, and plunged into the English Shop to see whether I might buy something warm for Nina. Here, indeed, I could fancy that I was in the High Street in Chester, or Leicester, or Truro, or Canterbury. A demure English provincialism was over everything, and a young man in a high white collar and a shiny black coat washed his hands as he told me that 'they hadn't any in stock at the moment, but they were expecting a delivery of goods at any minute.' Russian shopmen, it is almost needless to say, do not care whether they have goods in stock or no. They have other things to think about. The air was filled with the chatter of English governesses, and an English clergyman and his wife were earnestly turning over a selection of woollen comforters.

Nothing here for Nina – nothing at all. I hurried away. With a sudden flash of inspiration I realised that it was in the Jews' Market that I would find what I wanted. I snatched at the bulging neck of a sleeping coachman, and before he was fully awake was in his sledge, and had told him my destination. He grumbled and wished to know how much I intended to pay him, and when I said one and a half roubles, answered that he would not take me for less than three. I threatened him then with the fat and good-natured policeman who always guarded the confused junction of the Morskaia and Nevski, and he was frightened and moved on. I sighed as I remembered the days not so long before, when that same coachman would have thought it an honour to drive me for half a rouble. Down the Sadovaya we slipped, bumping over the uneven surface of the snow, and the shops grew smaller and the cinemas more strident, and the women and men with their barrows of fruit and coloured notepaper and toys more frequent. Then through the market with the booths and the church with its golden towers, until we stood before the hooded entrance to the Jews' Paradise. I paid him, and without listening to his discontented cries pushed my way in. The Jews' Market is a series of covered arcades with a square in the middle of it, and in the middle of the square a little church with some doll-like trees. These arcades are Western in their hideous covering of glass and the ugliness of the exterior of the wooden shops that line them, but the crowd that throngs them is Eastern, so that in the strange eyes and voices, the wild gestures, the laughs, the cries, the singing, and the dancing that meet one here it is as though a new world was suddenly born – a world offensive, dirty, voluble, blackguardly perhaps, but intriguing, tempting, and ironical. The arcades are generally so crowded that one can move only at a slow pace, and on every side one is pestered by the equivalents of the old English cry: 'What do you lack? What do you lack?'

Every mixture of blood and race that the world contains is to be seen here, but they are all – Tartars, Jews, Chinese, Japanese, Indians, Arabs, Moslem, and Christian – formed by some subtle colour of atmosphere, so that they seem all alike to be Citizens of some secret little town, sprung to life, just for a day, in the heart of this other city. Perhaps it is the dull pale mist that the glass flings down, perhaps it is the uncleanly dust-clogged air; whatever it be, there is a stain of grey shadowy smoke upon all this world, and Ikons and shabby jewels, and piles of Eastern clothes, and old brass pots, and silver-hilted swords, and golden-tasselled Tartar coats gleam through the shadow and wink and stare.

Today the arcades were so crowded that I could scarcely move, and the noise was deafening.

Many soldiers were there, looking with indulgent amusement upon the scene, and the Jews with their skull-caps and the fat, huge-breasted Jewish women screamed and shrieked and waved their arms like boughs in a storm. I stopped at many shops and fingered the cheap silver toys, the little blue and green Ikons, the buckles and beads and rosaries that thronged the trays, but I could not find anything for Nina. Then suddenly I saw a square box of mother-of-pearl and silver, so charming and simple, the figures on the silver lid so gracefully carved that I decided at once.

The Jew in charge of it wanted twice as much as I was ready to give, and we argued for ten minutes before a kindly and appreciative crowd. At last we arranged a compromise, and I moved away, pleased and satisfied. I stepped out of the arcade and faced the little Square. It was, at that instant, fantastic and oddly coloured; the sun, about to set, hung in the misty sky a perfect round crimson globe, and it was perched, almost maliciously, just above the tower of the little church.

The rest of the world was grey. The Square was a thick mass of human beings so tightly wedged together that it seemed to move backwards and forwards like a floor of black wood pushed by a lever. One lamp burnt behind the window of the church, the old houses leaned forward as though listening to the babel below their eaves.

But it was the sun that seemed to me then so evil and secret and cunning. Its deep red was aloof and menacing, and its outline so sharp that it was detached from the sky as though it were human, and would presently move and advance towards us. I don't know what there was in that crowd of struggling human beings and that detached red sun. ... The air was cruel, and through all the arcades that seemed to run like veins to this heart of the place I could feel the cold and the dark and the smoky dusk creeping forward to veil us all with deepest night.

I turned away and then saw, advancing towards me, as though he had just come from the church, pushing his way, and waving a friendly hand to me, Semyonov.

XX

His greeting was most amiable. He was wearing a rather short fur coat that only reached to a little below his knees, and the fur of the coat was of a deep rich brown, so that his pale square yellow beard contrasted with this so abruptly as to seem false. His body was as ever thick and self-confident, and the round fur cap that he wore was cocked ever so slightly to one side. I did not want to see him, but I was caught. I fancied that he knew very well that I wanted to escape, and that now, for sheer perversity, he would see that I did not. Indeed, he caught my arm and drew me out of the Market. We passed into the dusky streets.

'Now, Ivan Andreievitch,' he said, 'this is very pleasant ... very. ... You elude me, you know, which is unkind with two so old acquaintances. Of course I know that you dislike me, and I don't suppose that I have the highest opinion of *you*, but, nevertheless, we should be interested in one another. Our common experience. ...' He broke off with a little shiver, and pulled his fur coat closer around him.

I knew that all that I wanted was to break away. We had passed quickly on leaving the Market into some of the meanest streets of Petrograd. This was the Petrograd of Dostoeffsky, the Petrograd of

'Poor Folk' and 'Crime and Punishment' and 'The Despised and Rejected.' . . . Monstrous groups of flats towered above us, and in the gathering dusk the figures that slipped in and out of the doors were furtive shadows and ghosts. No one seemed to speak; you could see no faces under the spare pale-flamed lamps, only hear whispers and smell rotten stinks and feel the snow, foul and soiled under one's feet. . . .

'Look here, Semyonov,' I said, slipping from the control of his hand, 'it's just as you say. We don't like one another, and we know one another well enough to say so. Neither you nor I wish to revive the past, and there's nothing in the present that we have in common.'

'Nothing!' He laughed. 'What about my delightful nieces and their home circle? You were always one to shrink from the truth, Ivan Andreievitch. You fancy that you can sink into the bosom of a charming family and escape the disadvantages. . . . Not at all. There are always disadvantages in a Russian family. *I* am the disadvantage in this one.' He laughed again, and insisted on taking my arm once more. 'If you feel so strongly about me, Durward' (when he used my surname he always accented the second syllable very strongly) 'all you have to do is to cut my niece Vera out of your visiting list. That, I imagine, is the last thing that you wish. Well, then——'

'Vera Michailovna is my friend,' I said hotly – it was foolish of me to be so easily provoked, but I could not endure his sneering tone. 'If you imply——'

'Nonsense,' he answered sharply, 'I imply nothing. Do you suppose that I have been more than a month here without discovering the facts? It's your English friend Lawrence who is in love with Vera – and Vera with him.'

'That is a lie!' I cried.

He laughed. 'You English,' he said, 'are not so unobservant as you seem, but you hate facts. Vera and your friend Lawrence have been in love with one another since their first meeting, and my dear nephew-in-law Markovitch knows it.'

'That's impossible,' I cried. 'He——'

'No,' Semyonov replied, 'I was wrong. He does not know it – he suspects. And my nephew-in-law in a state of suspicion is a delightful study.'

By now we were in a narrow street, so dark that we stumbled at every step. We seemed to be quite alone.

It was I who now caught his arm. 'Semyonov!' I said, and my urgency stopped him so that he stood where he was. 'Leave them alone!

Leave them alone! They've done no harm to you, they can offer you nothing, they are not intelligent enough for you nor amusing enough. Even if it is true what you say it will pass – Lawrence will go away. I will see that he does. Only leave them alone! For God's sake, let them be!'

His face was very close to mine, and, looking at it in the gathering dark, it was as though it were a face of glass behind which other faces passed and repassed. I cannot hope to give any idea of the strange mingling of regret, malice, pride, pain, scorn, and humour that those eyes showed. His lips parted as though he would speak, for a moment he turned away from me and looked down the black tunnel of the street, then he walked forward again.

'You are wrong, my friend,' he said, 'if you imagine that there is no amusement for me in the study of my family. It *is* my family, you know. I have none other. Perhaps it has never occurred to you, Durward, that possibly I am a lonely man.'

As he spoke I heard again the echo of that voice as it vanished into the darkness . . . 'No one?' and the answer: 'No one.' . . .

'Don't imagine,' he continued, 'that I am asking for your pity. That indeed would be humorous. I pity no one, and I despise the men who have it to bestow . . ., but there are situations in life that are intolerable, Ivan Andreievitch, and any man who *is* a man will see that he escapes from such a thing. May I not find in the bosom of my family such an escape?' He laughed.

'I know nothing about that,' I began hotly. 'All I know is——'

But he went on as though he had not heard me.

'Have you ever thought about death since you came away from the Front, Durward? It used to occupy your mind a good deal while you were there, I remember – in a foolish, romantic, sentimental way of course. You'll forgive my saying that your views of death were those of a second-hand novelist – all the same I'll do you the justice of acknowledging that you had studied it at first hand. You're not a coward, you know.'

I was Struck most vividly with a sense of his uneasiness. During those other days uneasy was the very last thing that I ever would have said that he was – even after his catastrophe his grip of his soul did not loosen. It was just that loosening that I felt now; he had less control of the beasts that dwelt beneath the ground of his house, and he could hear them snarl and whine, and could feel the floor quiver with the echo of their movements.

I suddenly knew that I was afraid of him no longer.

'Now, see, Alexei Petrovitch,' I said, 'it isn't death that we want to talk about now. It is a much simpler thing. It is, that you shouldn't for your own amusement simply go in and spoil the lives of some of my friends for nothing at all except your own stupid pride. If that's your plan I'm going to prevent it.'

'Why, Ivan Andreievitch,' he cried, laughing, 'this is a challenge.'

'You can take it as what you please,' I answered gravely.

'But, incorrigible sentimentalist,' he went on, 'tell me – are you, English and moralist and believer in a good and righteous God as you are, are you really going to encourage this abominable adultery, this open, ruthless wrecking of a good man's home? You surprise me; this is a new light on your otherwise rather uninteresting character.'

'Never mind my character,' I answered him; 'all you've got to do is to leave Vera Michailovna alone. There'll be no wrecking of homes, unless you are the wrecker.'

He put his hand on my arm again.

'Listen, Durward,' he said, 'I'll tell you a little Story. I'm a doctor you know, and many curious things occur within my province. Well, some years ago I knew a man who was very miserable and very proud. His pride resented that he should be miserable, and he was always suspecting that people saw his weakness, and as he despised human nature, and thought his companions fools and deserving of all that they got, and more, he couldn't bear the thought that they should perceive that he allowed himself to be unhappy. He coveted death. If it meant extinction he could imagine nothing pleasanter than so restful an aloofness, quiet and apart and alone, whilst others hurried and scrambled and pursued the future. . . .

'And if death did not mean extinction then he thought that he might snatch and secure for himself something which in life had eluded him. So he coveted death. But he was too proud to reach it by suicide. That seemed to him a contemptible and cowardly evasion, and such an easy solution would have denied the purpose of all his life. So he looked about him and discovered amongst his friends a man whose character he knew well, a man idealistic and foolish and romantic, like yourself, Ivan Andreievitch, only caring more for ideas, more impulsive and more reckless. He found this man and made him his friend. He played with him as a cat does with a mouse. He enjoyed life for about a year and then he was murdered. . . .'

'Murdered!' I exclaimed.

'Yes – shot by his idealistic friend. I envy him that year. He must have experienced many breathless sensations. When the murderer was tried his only explanation was that he had been irritated and disappointed.

'"Disappointed of what?" asked the judge.

'"Of everything in which he believed . . ." said the man.

'It seemed a poor excuse for a murder; he is still, I have no doubt, in Siberia.

'But I envy my friend. That was a delightful death to die. . . . Good-night, Ivan Andreievitch.'

He waved his hand at me and was gone. I was quite alone in the long black street, engulfed by the high, overhanging flats.

XXI

Late on the afternoon of Nina's birthday, when I was on the point of setting out for the English Prospect, the Rat appeared. I had not seen him for several weeks; but there he was, stepping suddenly out of the shadows of my room, dirty and disreputable and cheerful. He had been, I perceived, drinking furniture polish.

'Good evening, Barin.'

'Good evening,' I said sternly. 'I told you not to come here when you were drunk.'

'I'm not drunk,' he said, offended, 'only a little. It's not much that you can get these days. I want some money, Barin.'

'I've none for you,' I answered.

'It's only a little – God knows that I wouldn't ask you for much, but I'm going to be very busy these next days, and it's work that won't bring pay quickly. There'll be pay later, and then I will return it to you.'

'There's nothing for you to-night,' I said.

He laughed. 'You're a fine man, Barin. A foreigner is fine – that's where the poor Russian is unhappy. I love you, Barin, and I will look after you, and if, as you say, there isn't any money here, one must pray to God and he will show one the way.'

'What's this work you're going to do?' I asked him.

'There's going to be trouble the other side of the river in a day or two,' he answered, 'and I'm going to help.'

'Help what?' I asked.

'Help the trouble,' he answered, smiling.

'Behave like a blackguard, in fact.'

'Ah, blackguard, Barin!' he protested, using a Russian word that is worse than blackguard. 'Why these names? . . . I'm not a good man, God have mercy on my soul, but then I pretend nothing. I am what you see. . . . If there's going to be trouble in the town I may as well be there. Why not I as well as another? And it is to your advantage, Barin, that I should be.'

'Why to my advantage?' I asked him.

'Because I am your friend, and we'll protect you,' he answered.

'I wouldn't trust you a yard,' I told him.

'Well, perhaps you're right,' he said. 'We are as God made us – I am no better than the rest.'

'No, indeed you're not,' I answered him. 'Why do you think there'll be trouble?'

'I know. . . . Perhaps a lot of trouble, perhaps only a little. But it will be a fine time for those of us who have nothing to lose. . . . So you have no money for me?'

'Nothing.'

'A mere rouble or so?'

'Nothing.'

'Well, I must be off. . . . I am your friend. Don't forget,' and he was gone.

It had been arranged that Nina and Vera, Lawrence and Bohun and I should meet outside the Giniselli at five minutes to eight. I left my little silver box at the flat, paid some other calls, and just as eight o'clock was striking arrived outside the Giniselli. This is Petrograd's apology for a music-hall – in other words, it is nothing but the good old-fashioned circus.

Then, again, it is not quite the circus of one's English youth, because it has a very distinct Russian atmosphere of its own. The point really is the enthusiasm of the audience, because it is an enthusiasm that in these sophisticated, twentieth-century days is simply not to be found in any other country in Europe. I am an old-fashioned man and, quite frankly, I adore a circus; and when I can find one with the right sawdust smell, the right clown, and the right enthusiasm, I am happy. The smart night is a Saturday, and then, if you go, you will see, in the little horse-boxes close to the arena, beautiful women in jewellery and powder, and young officers, and fat merchants in priceless Shubas. But to-night was not a Saturday, and therefore the audience was very democratic, screaming cat-calls from the misty distances of the gallery, and showering sunflower seeds upon the heads of the bourgeoisie, who were, for the most part, of the smaller shopkeeper kind.

Nina, to-night, was looking very pretty and excited. She was wearing a white silk dress with blue bows, and all her hair was piled on the top of her head in imitation of Vera – but this only had the effect of making her seem incredibly young and naïve, as though she had put her hair up just for the evening because there was to be a party. It was explained that Markovitch was working but would be present at supper. Vera was quiet, but looked happier, I thought, than I had seen her for a long time. Bohun was looking after her, and Lawrence was with Nina. I sat behind the four of them, in the back of the little box, like a presiding Benevolence.

Mostly I thought of how lovely Vera was to-night, and why it was, too, that more people did not care for her. I knew that she was not popular, that she was considered proud and reserved and cold. As she sat there now, motionless, her hands on her lap, her whole being seemed to me to radiate goodness and gentleness and a loving heart. I knew that she could be impatient with stupid people, and irritated by sentimentality, and infuriated by meanness and cruelty, but the whole size and grandeur of her nobility seemed to me to shine all about her and set her apart from the rest of human beings. She was not a woman whom I ever could have loved – she had not the weaknesses and naïveties and appealing helplessness that drew love from one's. heart. Nor could I have ever dared to face the depth and splendour of the passion that there was in her – I was not built on that heroic scale. God forgive me if, as I watched them, I felt a sudden glow of almost eager triumph at the thought of Lawrence as her lover! I checked it. My heart was suddenly heavy.

Such a development could only mean tragedy, and I knew it. I had even sworn to Semyonov that I would prevent it. I looked at them and felt my helpless weakness. Who was I to prevent anything? And who was there now, in the whole world, who would be guided by my opinion? They might have me as a confidant because they trusted me, but after that . . . no, I had no illusions. I was pushed off the edge of the world, hanging on still with one quivering hand – soon my grip would loosen – and, God help me, I did not want to go.

Nina turned back to me and, with a little excited clap of her hands, drew my attention to the gallant Madame Giniselli, who, although by no means a chicken, arrayed in silver tights and a large black picture-hat, stood on one foot on the back of her white horse and bowed to the already hysterical gallery. Mr. Giniselli cracked his whip, and the white horse ambled along and the sawdust flew up into our eyes, and Madame bent her knees first in and then out, and the bourgeoisie clapped their hands and the gallery shouted 'Brava.' Giniselli cracked his whip and there was the clown 'Jackomeno, beloved of his Russian public,' as it was put on the programme; and indeed so he seemed to be, for he was greeted with roars of applause. There was nothing very especially Russian about him, however, and when he had taken his coat off and brushed a place on which to put it and then flung it on the ground and stamped on it, I felt quite at home with him and ready for anything.

He called up one of the attendants and asked him whether he had ever played the guitar. I don't know what it was that the attendant answered, because something else suddenly transfixed my attention – the vision of Nina's little white-gloved hand resting on Lawrence's broad knee. I saw at once, as though she had told me, that she had committed herself to a most desperate venture. I could fancy the resolution that she had summoned to take the step, the way that now her heart would be furiously beating, and the excited chatter with which she would try to cover up her action. Vera and Bohun could not, from where they were sitting, see what she had done; Lawrence did not move, his back was set like a rock; he stared steadfastly at the arena. Nina never ceased talking, her ribbons fluttering and her other hand gesticulating.

I could not take my eyes from that little white hand. I should have been, I suppose, ashamed of her, indignant for her, but I could only feel that she was, poor child, in for the most desperate rebuff. I could see from where I sat her cheek, hot and crimson, and her shrill voice never stopped.

The interval arrived, to my intense relief, and we all went out into the dark passage that smelt of sawdust and horses. Almost at once Nina detached me from the others and walked off with me towards the lighted hall.

'You saw,' she said.

'Saw what?' I asked.

'Saw what I was doing.'

I felt that she was quivering all over, and she looked so ridiculously young, with her trembling lip and blue hat on one side and burning cheeks, that I felt that I wanted to take her into my arms and kiss and pet her.

'I saw that you had your hand on his knee,' I said. 'That was silly of you, Nina.'

'Why shouldn't I?' she answered furiously. 'Why shouldn't I enjoy life like every one else? Why should Vera have everything?'

'Vera!' I cried. 'What has it to do with Vera?'

She didn't answer my question. She put her hand on my arm, pressing close up to me as though she wanted my protection.

'Durdles, I want him for my friend. I do – I do. When I look at him and think of Boris and the others I don't want to speak to any one of them again. I only want him for my friend. I'm getting old now, and they can't treat me as a child any longer. I'll show them. I know what I'll do if I can't have the friends I want and if Vera is always managing me – I'll go off to Boris.'

'My dear Nina,' I said, 'you mustn't do that. You don't care for him.'

'No, I know I don't – but I will go if everybody thinks me a baby. And Durdles – Durdles, please – make him like me – your Mr. Lawrence.'

She said his name with the funniest little accent.

'Nina, dear,' I said, 'will you take a little piece of advice from me?'

'What is it?' she asked doubtfully.

'Well, this. . . . Don't you make any move yourself. Just wait and you'll see he'll like you. You'll make him shy if you——'

But she interrupted me furiously in one of her famous tempers.

'Oh, you Englishmen with your shyness and your waiting and your coldness! I hate you all, and I wish we were fighting with the Germans against you. Yes, I do – and I hope the Germans win. You never have any blood. You're all cold as ice. . . . And what do you mean spying on me? Yes, you were – sitting behind and spying! You're always finding out what we're doing, and putting it all down in a book. I hate you, and I won't ever ask your advice again.'

She rushed off, and I was following her when the bell rang for the beginning of the second part. We all went in, Nina chattering and laughing with Bohun just as though she had never been in a temper in her life.

Then a dreadful thing happened. We arrived at the box, and Vera, Bohun, and Nina sat in the seats they had occupied before. I waited for Lawrence to sit down, but he turned round to me.

'I say, Durward – you sit next to Nina Michailovna this time. She'll be bored having me all the while.'

'No, no!' I began to protest, but Nina, her voice shaking, cried:

'Yes, Durdles, you sit down next to me – please.'

I don't think that Lawrence perceived anything. He said very cheerfully, 'That's right – and I'll sit behind and see that you all behave.'

I sat down and the second part began. The second part was wrestling. The bell rang, the curtains parted, and instead of the splendid horses and dogs there appeared a procession of some of the most obese and monstrous types of humanity. Almost naked, they wandered round the arena, mountains of flesh glistening in the electric light. A little man, all puffed up like a poulter pigeon, then advanced into the middle of the arena, and was greeted with wild applause from the gallery. To this he bowed and then announced in a terrific voice, 'Gentlemen, you are about to see some of the most magnificent wrestling in the world. Allow me to introduce to you the combatants.' He then shouted out the names: 'Ivan Strogoff of Kiev – Paul Rosing of Odessa – Jacob Smyerioff of Petrograd – John Meriss from Africa (this the most hideous of negroes) – Karl Tubiloff of Helsingfors . . .' and so on. The gentlemen named smirked and bowed. They all marched off, and then, in a moment, one couple returned, shook hands, and, under the breathless attention of the whole house, began to wrestle.

They did not, however, command my attention. I could think of nothing but the little crushed figure next to me. I stole a look at her and saw that a large tear was hanging on one eyelash ready to fall. I looked hurriedly away. Poor child! And her birthday! I cursed Lawrence for his clumsiness. What did it matter if she had put her hand on his knee? He ought to have taken it and patted it. But it was more than likely, as I knew very well, that he had never even noticed her action. He was marvellously unaware of all kinds of things, and it was only too possible that Nina scarcely existed for him. I longed to comfort her, and I did then a foolish thing. I put out my hand and let it rest for a moment on her dress.

Instantly she moved away with a sharp little gesture.

Five minutes later I heard a little whisper: 'Durdles, it's so hot here – and I hate these naked men. Shall we go? Ask Vera ——'

The first bout had just come to an end. The little man with the swelling chest was alone, strutting up and down, and answering questions hurled at him from the gallery.

'Uncle Vanya, where's Michael of Odessa?'

'Ah, he's a soldier in the army now.'

'Uncle Vanya . . . Uncle Vanya . . . Uncle Vanya . . .'

'Well, well, what is it?'

'Why isn't *Chornaya Maska* wrestling to-night?'

'Ah, he's busy.'

'What's he busy with?'

'Never mind, he's busy.'

'What's he busy with? ... Uncle Vanya ... Uncle Vanya ...'

'*Shto?*'

'Isn't it true that Michael's dead now?'

'So they say.'

'Is it true?'

'Uncle Vanya ... Uncle Vanya ...'

The message had passed along that Nina was tired and wanted to go. We all moved out through the passage and into the cold fresh air.

'It was quite time,' said Vera. 'I was going to suggest it myself.'

'I hope you liked it,' said Lawrence politely to Nina.

'No, I hated it,' she answered furiously, and turned her back on him.

It could not be said that the birthday party was promising very well.

XXII

And yet for the first half-hour it really seemed that it would 'go' very well indeed. It had been agreed that it was to be absolutely a 'family' party, and Uncle Ivan, Semyonov, and Boris Grogoff were the only additions to our number. Markovitch was there of course, and I saw at once that he was eager to be agreeable and to be the best possible host. As I had often noticed before, there was something pathetic about Markovitch when he wished to be agreeable. He had neither the figure nor the presence with which to be fascinating, and he did not know in the least how to bring out his best points.

Especially when he tried, as he was sometimes ill-advised enough to do, to flirt with young girls, he was a dismal failure. He was intended, by nature, to be mysterious and malevolent, and had he only had a malevolent spirit there would have been no tragedy; but in the confused welter that he called his soul, malevolence was the least of the elements, and other things – love, sympathy, twisted self-pity, ambition, courage, and cowardice – drowned it. He was on his best behaviour to-night, and over the points of his high white collar his peaked, ugly, anxious face peered, appealing to the Fates for generosity.

But the Fates despise those who appeal.

I very soon saw that he was on excellent terms with Semyonov, and this could only be, I was sure, because Semyonov had been flattering him. Very soon I learnt the truth. I was standing near the table, watching the company, when I found Markovitch at my side.

'Very glad you've come, Ivan Andreievitch,' he said. 'I've been meaning to come and see you, only I've been too busy.'

'How's the ink getting along?' I asked him.

'Oh, the ink!' He brushed my words scornfully aside. 'No, that's nothing. We must postpone that to a more propitious time. Meanwhile – meanwhile, Ivan Andreievitch, I've hit it at last!'

'What is it this time?' I asked.

He could hardly speak for his excitement. 'It's wood – the bark – the bark of the tree, you know – a new kind of fibre for cloth. If I hadn't got to look after these people here, I'd take you and show you now. You're a clever fellow – you'd understand at once. I've been showing it to Alexei'(he nodded in the direction of Semyonov), 'and he entirely agrees with me that there's every kind of possibility in it. The thing will be to get the labour – that's the trouble nowadays – but I'll find somebody – one of these timber men . . .'

So that was it, was it? I looked across at Semyonov, who was now seated on Vera's right hand just opposite Boris Grogoff. He was very quiet, very still, looking about him, his square pale beard a kind of symbol of the secret immobility of his soul. I fancied that I detected behind his placidity an almost relieved self-satisfaction, as though things were going very much better than he had expected.

'So Alexei Petrovitch thinks well of it, does he?' I asked.

'Most enthusiastic,' answered Markovitch eagerly. 'He's gone into the thing thoroughly with me, and has made some admirable suggestions. . . . Ivan Andreievitch, I think I should tell you – I misjudged him. I wasn't fair in what I said to you the other day about him. Or perhaps it is that being at the Front has changed him, softened him a bit. His love affair there, you know, made him more sympathetic and kindly. I believe he means well to us all. Vera won't agree with me. She's more cynical than she used to be. I don't like that in her. She never had a suspicious nature before, but now she doesn't trust one.'

'You don't tell her enough,' I interrupted.

'Tell her?' he looked at me doubtfully. 'What is there I should tell her?'

'Everything!' I answered.

'Everything?' His eyes suddenly narrowed, his face was sharp and suspicious. 'Does she tell me everything? Answer me that, Ivan Andreievitch. There was a time once – but now – I give my confidences where I'm trusted. If she treated me fairly——'

There was no chance to say more; they called us to the table. I took my place between Nina and Ivan.

As I have said, the supper began very merrily. Boris Grogoff was, I think, a little drunk when he arrived; at any rate he was noisy from the very beginning. I have wondered often since whether he had any private knowledge that night which elated and excited him, and was responsible in part, perhaps, for what presently occurred. It may well have been so, although at the time, of course, nothing of the kind occurred to me. Nina appeared to have recovered her spirits. She was sitting next to Lawrence, and chattered and laughed with him in her ordinary fashion.

And now, stupidly enough, when I try to recall exactly the steps that led up to the catastrophe, I find it difficult to see things clearly. I remember that very quickly I was conscious that there was danger in the air. I was conscious of it first in the eyes of Semyonov, those steady, watching, relentless eyes so aloof as to be inhuman. He was on the other side of the table, and suddenly I said to myself, 'He's expecting something to happen.' Then, directly after that I caught Vera's eye, and I saw that she too was anxious. She looked pale and tired and sad.

I caught myself in the next instant saying to myself, 'Well, she's got Lawrence to look after her now' – so readily does the spirit that is beyond one's grasp act above and outside one's poor human will.

I saw then that the trouble was once again, as it had often been before, Grogoff. He was drinking heavily the rather poor claret which Markovitch had managed to secure from somewhere. He addressed the world in general.

'I tell you that we're going to stop this filthy war,' he cried. 'And if our Government won't do it, we'll take things into our own hands. . . .'

'Well,' said Semyonov, smiling, 'that's a thing that no Russian has ever said before, for certain.'

Every one laughed, and Grogoff flushed. 'Oh, it's easy to sneer!' he said. 'Just because there've been miserable cowards in Russian history, you think it will always be so. I tell you it is not so. The time is coming when tyranny will topple from its throne, and we'll show Europe the way to liberty.'

'By which you mean,' said Semyonov, 'that you'll involve Russia in at least three more wars in addition to the one she's at present so magnificently losing.'

'I tell you,' screamed Grogoff, now so excited that he was standing on his feet and waving his glass in the air, 'that this time you have not cowards to deal with. This will not be as it was in 1905; I know of what I'm speaking.'

Semyonov leant over the table and whispered something in Markovitch's ear. I had seen that Markovitch had already been longing to speak. He jumped up on to his feet, fiercely excited, his eyes flaming.

'It's nonsense that you are talking, sheer nonsense!' he cried. 'Russia's lost the war, and all we who believed in her have our hearts broken. Russia won't be mended by a few vapouring idiots who talk and talk without taking action.'

'What do you call me?' screamed Grogoff.

'I mention no names,' said Markovitch, his little eyes dancing with anger. 'Take it or no as you please. But I say that we have had enough of all this vapouring talk, all this pretence of courage. Let us admit that freedom has failed in Russia, that she must now submit herself to the yoke.'

'Coward! Coward!' screamed Grogoff.

'It's you who are the coward!' cried Markovitch.

'Call me that and I'll show you!'

'I do call you it!'

There was an instant's pause, during which we all of us had, I suppose, some idea of trying to intervene.

But it was too late. Grogoff raised his hand and, with all his force, flung his glass at Markovitch. Markovitch ducked his head, and the glass smashed with a shattering tinkle on the wall behind him.

We all cried out, but the only thing of which I was conscious was that Lawrence had sprung from his seat, had crossed to where Vera was standing, and had put his hand on her arm. She glanced up at him. That look which they exchanged, a look of revelation, of happiness, of sudden marvellous security, was so significant that I could have cried out to them both, 'Look out! Look out!'

But if I had cried they would not have heard me.

My next instinct was to turn to Markovitch. He was frowning, coughing a little, and feeling the top of his collar. His face was turned towards Grogoff and he was speaking – I could catch some words: 'No right . . . in my own house . . . Boris . . . I apologise . . . please don't think of it.' But his eyes were not looking at Boris at all; they were turned towards Vera, staring at her, begging her, beseeching her. . . . What had he seen? How much had he understood? And Nina? And Semyonov?

But at once, in a way most truly Russian, the atmosphere had changed. It was Nina who controlled the situation. 'Boris,' she cried, 'come here!'

We all waited in silence. He looked at her, a little sulkily, his head hanging, but his eyes glancing up at her.

He seemed nothing then but a boy caught in some misdemeanour, obstinate, sulky, but ready to make peace if a chance were offered him.

'Boris, come here!'

He moved across to her, looking her full in the face, his mouth sulky, but his eyes rebelliously smiling.

'Well . . . well . . .'

She stood away from the table, drawn to her full height, her eyes commanding him: 'How dare you! Boris, how dare you! My birthday – *mine* – and you've spoilt it, spoilt it all. Come here – up close!'

He came to her until his hands were almost on her body; he hung his head, standing over her.

She stood back as though she were going to strike him, then suddenly with a laugh she sprang upon the chair beside her, flung her arms round his neck and kissed him; then, still standing on the chair, turned and faced us all.

'Now, that's enough – all of you. Michael, Uncle Ivan, Uncle Alexei, Durdles – how dare you, all of you? You're all as bad – every one of you. I'll punish all of you if we have any more politics. Beastly politics! What do they matter? It's my birthday. My *birthday*, I tell you. It *shan't* be spoilt.'

She seemed to me so excited as not to know what she was saying. What had she seen? What did she know? . . . Meanwhile Grogoff was elated, wildly pleased like a boy who, contrary to all his expectations, had won a prize.

He went up to Markovitch with his hand out:

'Nicholas – forgive me – *Prasteete* – I forgot myself. I'm ashamed – my abominable temper. We are friends. You were right, too. We talk here in Russia too much, far too much, and when the moment comes for action we shrink back. We see too far perhaps. Who knows? But you were right and I am a fool. You've taught me a lesson by your nobility. Thank you, Nicholas. And all of you – I apologise to all of you.'

We moved away from the table. Vera came over to us, and then sat on the sofa with her arm around Nina's neck. Nina was very quiet now, sitting there, her cheeks flushed, smiling, but as though she were thinking of something quite different.

Some one proposed that we should play 'Petits Chevaux.' We gathered around the table, and soon every one was laughing and gambling.

Only once I looked up and saw that Markovitch was gazing at Vera; and once again I looked at Vera and saw that she was staring before her, seeing nothing, lost in some vision – but it was not of Markovitch that she was thinking. . . .

I was the first to leave – I said good-night to every one. I could hear their laughter as I waited at the bottom of the stairs for the Dvornik to let me out.

But when I was in the street the world was breathlessly still. I walked up the Prospect – no soul was in sight, only the scattered lamps, the pale snow, and the houses. At the end of the Canal I stopped. The silence was intense.

It seemed to me then that in the very centre of the Canal the ice suddenly cracked, slowly pulled apart, leaving a still pool of black water. The water slowly stirred, rippled, then a long, horned, and scaly head pushed up. I could see the shining scales on its thick side and the ribbed horn on the back of the neck. Beneath it the water stirred and heaved. With dead glazed eyes it stared upon the world, then slowly, as though it were drawn from below, it sank. The water rippled in narrowing circles – then all was still. . . .

The moon came out from behind filmy shadow. The world was intensely light, and I saw that the ice of the canal had never been broken, and that no pool of black water caught the moon's rays.

It was fiercely cold and I hurried home, pulling my Shuba more closely about me.

Part II

Lawrence

Lawrence

I

Of some of the events that I am now about to relate it is obvious that I could not have been an eye-witness – and yet, looking back from the strange isolation that is now my world I find it incredibly difficult to realise what I saw and what I did not. Was I with Nina and Vera on that Tuesday night when they stood face to face with one another for the first time? Was I with Markovitch during his walk through that marvellous new world that he seemed himself to have created? I know that I shared none of these things, . . . and yet it seems to me that I was at the heart of them all. I may have been told many things by the actors in those events – I may not. I cannot now in retrospect see any of it save as my own personal experience, and as my own personal experience I must relate it; but, as I have already said at the beginning of this book, no one is compelled to believe either my tale or my interpretation. Every man would, I suppose, like to tell his story in the manner of some other man. I can conceive the events of this part of my narration being interpreted in the spirit of the wildest farce, of the genteelest comedy, of the most humorous satire – 'Other men, other gifts.' I am a dull and pompous fellow, as Semyonov often tells me; and I hope that I never allowed him to see how deeply I felt the truth of his words.

Meanwhile I will begin with a small adventure of Henry Bohun's. Apparently, one evening soon after Nina's party, he found himself about half-past ten in the evening, lonely and unhappy, walking down the Nevski. Gay and happy crowds wandered by him, brushing him aside, refusing to look at him, showing in fact no kind of interest in his existence. He was suddenly frightened, the distances seemed terrific, and the Nevski was so hard and bright and shining that it had no use at all for any lonely young man. He decided suddenly that he would go and see me. He found an Isvostchik, but when they reached the Ekateringofsky Canal the surly coachman refused to drive further, saying that his horse had gone lame, and that this was as far as he had bargained to go.

Henry was forced to leave the cab, and then found himself outside the little people's cinema, where he had once been with Vera and myself.

He knew that my rooms were not far away, and he started off beside the white and silent canal, wondering why he had come, and wishing he were back in bed.

There was still a great deal of the baby in Henry, and ghosts and giants and scaly-headed monsters were not incredibilities to his young imagination. As he left the main thoroughfare and turned down past the widening docks, he suddenly knew that he was terrified. There had been stories of wild attacks on rich strangers, sand-bagging and the rest, often enough, but it was not of that kind of thing that he was afraid. He told me afterwards that he expected to see 'long thick crawling creatures' creeping towards him over the ice. He continually turned round to see whether some one were following him. When he crossed the tumbledown bridge that led to my island it seemed that he was absolutely alone in the whole world. The masts of the ships dim through the cold mist were like tangled spiders' webs. A strange hard red moon peered over the towers and chimneys of the distant dockyard. The ice was limitless, and of a dirty grey pallor, with black shadows streaking it. My island must have looked desolate enough, with its dirty snow-heaps, old boards and scrap-iron and tumbledown cottages.

Again, as on his first arrival in Petrograd, Henry was faced by the solemn fact that events are so often romantic in retrospect, but grimly realistic in experience. He reached my lodging and found the door open. He climbed the dark rickety stairs and entered my sitting-room. The blinds were not drawn, and the red moon peered through on to the grey shadows that the ice beyond always flung. The stove was not burning, the room was cold and deserted. Henry called my name and there was no answer. He went into my bedroom and there was no one there. He came back and stood there listening.

He could hear the creaking of some bar beyond the window and the melancholy whistle of a distant train.

He was held there, as though spellbound. Suddenly he thought that he heard some one climbing the stairs. He gave a cry, and that was answered by a movement so close to him that it was almost at his elbow.

'Who's there?' he cried. He saw a shadow pass between the moon and himself. In a panic of terror he cried out, and at the same time struck a match. Some one came towards him, and he saw that it was Markovitch.

He was so relieved to find that it was a friend that he did not stop to wonder what Markovitch should be doing hiding in my room. It afterwards struck him that Markovitch looked odd. 'Like a kind of conspirator, in an old shabby Shuba with the collar turned up. He looked jolly ill and dirty, as though he hadn't slept or washed. He didn't seem a bit surprised at seeing me there, and I think he scarcely realised that it *was* me. He was thinking of something else so hard that he couldn't take me in.'

'Oh, Bohun!' he said in a confused way.

'Hullo, Nicolai Leontievitch,' Bohun said, trying to be unconcerned. 'What are you doing here?'

'Came to see Ivan Andreievitch,' he said. 'Wasn't here; I was going to write to him.'

Bohun then lit a candle and discovered that the place was in a very considerable mess. Some one had been sifting my desk, and papers and letters were lying about the floor. The drawers of my table were open, and one chair was overturned. Markovitch stood back near the window, looking at Bohun suspiciously. They must have been a curious couple for such a position. There was an awkward pause, and then Bohun, trying to speak easily, said:

'Well, it seems that Durward isn't coming. He's out dining somewhere, I expect.'

'Probably,' said Markovitch drily.

There was another pause, then Markovitch broke out with: 'I suppose you think I've been here trying to steal something.'

'Oh no – oh no – no –' stammered Bohun.

'But I have,' said Markovitch. 'You can look round and see. There it is on every side of you. I've been trying to find a letter.'

'Oh yes,' said Bohun nervously.

'Well, that seems to you terrible,' went on Markovitch, growing ever fiercer. 'Of course it seems to you perfect Englishmen a dreadful thing. But why heed it? . . . You all do things just as bad, only you are hypocrites.'

'Oh yes, certainly,' said Bohun.

'And now,' said Markovitch with a snarl, 'I'm sure you will not think me a proper person for you to lodge with any longer – and you will be right. I am not a proper person. I have no sense of decency, thank God, and no Russian has any sense of decency, and that is why we are beaten and despised by the whole world, and yet are finer than them all – so you'd better not lodge with us any more.'

'But of course,' said Bohun, disliking more and more this uncomfortable scene – 'of course I shall continue to stay with you. You are my friends, and one doesn't mind what one's friends do. One's friends are one's friends.'

Suddenly, then, Markovitch jerked himself forward, 'just as though,' Bohun afterwards described it to me, 'he had shot himself out of a catapult.'

'Tell me,' he said, 'is your English friend in love with my wife?'

What Bohun wanted to do then was to run out of the room, down the dark stairs, and away as fast as his legs would carry him. He had not been in Russia so long that he had lost his English dislike of scenes, and he was seriously afraid that Markovitch was, as he put it, 'bang off his head.'

But at this critical moment he remembered, it seems, my injunction to him, 'to be kind to Markovitch – to make a friend of him.' That had always seemed to him before impossible enough, but now, at the very moment when Markovitch was at his queerest, he was also at his most pathetic, looking there in the mist and shadows too untidy and dirty and miserable to be really alarming. Henry then took courage. 'That's all nonsense, Markovitch,' he said. 'I suppose by "your English friend" you mean Lawrence. He thinks the world of your wife, of course, as we all do, but he's not the fellow to be in love. I don't suppose he's ever been really in love with a woman in his life. He's a kindly good-hearted chap, Lawrence, and he wouldn't do harm to a fly.'

Markovitch peered into Bohun's face. 'What did you come here for, any of you?' he asked. 'What's Russia overrun with foreigners for? We'll clear the lot of you out, all of you . . .' Then he broke off, with a pathetic little gesture, his hand up to his head. 'But I don't know what I'm saying – I don't mean it, really. Only things are so difficult, and they slip away from one so.

'I love Russia and I love my wife, Mr. Bohun – and they've both left me. But you aren't interested in that. Why should you be? Only remember when you're inclined to laugh at me that

I'm like a man in a cockle-shell boat – and it isn't my fault. I was put in it.'

'But I'm never inclined to laugh,' said Bohun eagerly. 'I may be young and only an Englishman – but I shouldn't wonder if I don't understand better than you think. You try and see.... And I'll tell you another thing, Nicolai Leontievitch, I loved your wife myself – loved her madly – and she was so good to me and so far above me, that I saw that it was like loving one of the angels. That's what we all feel, Nicolai Leontievitch, so that you needn't have any fear – she's too far above all of us. And I only want to be your friend and hers, and to help you in any way I can.'

(I can see Bohun saying this, very sincere, his cheeks flushed, eager.)

Markovitch held out both his hands.

'You're right,' he cried. 'She's above us all. It's true that she's an angel, and we are all her servants. You have helped me by saying what you have, and I won't forget it. You are right; I am wasting my time with ridiculous suspicions when I ought to be working. Concentration, that's what I want, and perhaps you will give it me.'

He suddenly came forward and kissed Bohun on both cheeks. He smelt, Bohun thought, of vodka. Bohun didn't like the embrace, of course, but he accepted it gracefully.

'Now we'll go away,' said Markovitch.

'We ought to put things straight,' said Bohun.

'No; I shall leave things as they are,' said Markovitch, 'so that he shall see exactly what I've done. I'll write a note.'

He scribbled a note to me in pencil. I have it still. It ran:

DEAR IVAN ANDREIEVITCH –

I looked for a letter from my wife to you. In doing so I was I suppose contemptible. But no matter. At least you see me as I am. I clasp your hand.

N. MARKOVITCH.

They went away together.

II

I was greatly surprised to receive, a few days later, an invitation from Baron Wilderling; he asked me to go with him on one of the first evenings in March to a performance of Lermontov's 'Masquerade' at the Alexandra Theatre. I say Lermontov, but heaven knows that that great Russian poet was not supposed to be going to have much to say in the affair. This performance had been in preparation for at least ten years, and when such delights as Gordon Craig's setting of 'Hamlet,' or Benois' dresses for 'La Locandiera' were discussed, the Wise Ones said:

'Ah, – all very well – just wait until you see " Masquerade." '

These manifestations of the artistic spirit had not been very numerous of late in Petrograd. At the beginning of the war there had been many cabarets – 'The Cow,' 'The Calf,' 'The Dog,' 'The Striped Cat' – and these had been underground cellars, lighted by Chinese lanterns, and the halls decorated with Futurist paintings by Yakkolyeff or some other still more advanced spirit. It seemed strange to me as I dressed that evening. I do not know how long it was since I had put on a dinner-jacket. With the exception of that one other visit to Baron Wilderling this seemed to be my one link with the old world, and it was curious to feel its fascination, its air of comfort and order and cleanliness, its courtesy and discipline. 'I think I'll leave these rooms,' I thought as I looked about me, 'and take a decent flat somewhere.'

It is a strange fact, behind which there lies, I believe, some odd sort of moral significance, that I cannot now recall the events of that evening in any kind of clear detail. I remember that it was bitterly cold, with a sky that was flooded with stars. The snow had a queer metallic sheen upon it as though it were coloured ice, and I can see now the Nevski like a slab of some fiercely painted metal rising out of the very smack of our horses' hoofs as my sleigh sped along – as though, silkworm-like, I spun it out of the entrails of the sledge. It was all light and fire and colour that night, with towers of gold and frosted green, and even the black crowds that thronged the Nevski pavements shot with colour.

Somewhere in one of Shorthouse's stories – in *The Little Schoolmaster Mark,* I think – he gives a curious impression of a whirling fantastic crowd of revellers who evoke by their movements some evil pattern in the air around them, and the boy who is standing in their midst sees this dark twisted sinister picture forming against the gorgeous walls and the coloured figures until it blots out the whole scene and plunges him into darkness. I will not pretend that on this evening I discerned anything sinister or ominous in the gay scene that the Alexandra Theatre offered me, but I was nevertheless weighed down by some quite unaccountable depression that would not let me alone. For this

I can see now that Lawrence was very largely responsible. When I met him and the Wilderlings in the foyer of the theatre I saw at once that he was greatly changed.

The clear open expression of his eyes was gone; his mind was far away from his company – and it was as though I could see into his brain and watch the repetition of the old argument occurring again and again and again with always the same questions and answers, the same reproaches, the same defiances, the same obstinacies. He was caught by what was perhaps the first crisis of his life. He had never been a man for much contact with his fellow-beings, he had been aloof and reserved, generous in his judgements of others, severe and narrow in his judgement of himself. Above all, he had been proud of his strength. . . .

Now he was threatened by something stronger than himself. He could have managed it so long as he was aware only of his love for Vera. . . . Now, when, since Nina's party, he knew that also Vera loved him, he had to meet the tussle of his life.

That, at any rate, is the kind of figure that I give to his mood that evening. He has told me much of what happened to him afterwards, but nothing of that particular night, except once. 'Do you remember that "Masquerade" evening? . . . I was in hell that night . . .' which, for Lawrence, was expressive enough.

Both the Baron and his wife were in great spirits. The Baron was more than ever the evocation of the genius of elegance and order; he seemed carved out of some coloured ivory, behind whose white perfection burnt a shining resolute flame.

His clothes were so perfect that they would have expressed the whole of him even though his body had not been there. He was happy. His eyes danced appreciatively; he waved his white gloves at the scene as though blessing it.

'Of course, Mr. Durward,' he said to me, 'this is nothing compared with what we could do before the war – nevertheless here you see, for a moment, a fragment of the old Petersburg – Petersburg as it shall be, please God, again one day. . . .'

I do not in the least remember who was present that evening, but it was, I believe, a very distinguished company. The lights blazed, the jewels flashed, and the chatter was tremendous. The horseshoe-shaped seats behind the stalls clustered in knots and bunches of colour under the great glitter of electricity about the Royal Box. Artists – Somoff and Benois and Dobujinsky; novelists like Sologub and Merejkowsky; dancers like Karsavina – actors from all over Petrograd – they were there, I expect, to add criticism and argument to the adulation of friends and of the carelessly observant rich Jews and merchants who had come simply to display their jewellery. Petrograd, like every other city in the world, is artistic only by the persistence of its minority.

I'm sure that there were Princesses and Grand Dukes and Grand Duchesses for any one who needed them, and it was only in the gallery where the students and their girl-friends were gathered that the name of Lermontov was mentioned. The name of the evening was 'Meyerhold,' the gentleman responsible for the production. At last the Event that had been brewing ceaselessly for the last ten years – ever since the last Revolution in fact – was to reach creation. The moment of M. Meyerhold's life had arrived – the moment, had we known it, of many other lives also; but we did not know it. We buzzed and we hummed, we gasped and we gaped, we yawned and we applauded; and the rustle of gold tissue, the scent of gold leaf, the thick sticky substance of gold paint, filled the air, flooded the arena, washed past us into the street outside. Meanwhile M. Meyerhold, white, perspiring, in his shirt-sleeves with his collar loosened and his hair damp, is in labour behind the gold tissue to produce the child of his life . . . and Behold, the Child is produced!

And such a child! It was not I am sure so fantastic an affair in reality as in my remembrance of it. I have, since then, read Lermontov's play, and I must confess that it does not seem, in cold truth, to be one of his finest works. It is long and old-fashioned, melodramatic and clumsy – but then it was not on this occasion Lermontov's play that was the thing. But it was a masquerade, and that in a sense far from the author's intention. As I watched I remember that I forgot the bad acting (the hero was quite atrocious), forgot the lapses of taste in the colour and arrangement of the play, forgot the artifices and elaborate originalities and false sincerities; there were, I have no doubt, many things in it all that were bad and meretricious – I was dreaming. I saw, against my will and outside my own agency, mingled with the gold screens, the purple curtains, the fantasies and extravagances of the costumes, the sudden flashes of unexpected colour through light or dress or backcloth – pictures from those Galician days that had been, until Semyonov's return, as I fancied, forgotten.

A crowd of revellers ran down the stage, and a shimmering cloud of gold shot with red and purple was flung from one end of the hall to the other, and behind it, through it, between it, I saw the chill light of the early morning, and Nikitin and I sitting on the bench outside the stinking hut that we had used as an operating theatre, watching the first rays of the sun warm the cold mountain's rim. I could hear voices, and the murmurs of the sleeping men and the groans of the wounded. The scene closed. There was space and light, and a gorgeous figure, stiff with the splendour of his robes, talked in a dark garden with his lady. Their voices murmured, a lute was played, some one sang, and through the thread of it all I saw that moment when, packed together on our cart, we hung for an instant on the top of the hill and looked back to a country that had suddenly crackled into flame. There was that terrific crash as of the smashing of a world of china, the fierce crackle of the machine-guns, and then the boom of the cannon from under our very feet . . . the garden was filled with revellers, laughing, dancing, singing, the air was filled again with the smell of gold paint, the tenor's voice rose higher and higher, the golden screens closed – the act was ended.

It was as though I had received, in some dim, bewildered fashion, a warning. When the lights went up, it was some moments before I realised that the Baron was speaking to me, that a babel of chatter, like a sudden rain-storm on a glass roof, had burst on every side of us, and that a huge Jewess, all bare back and sham pearls, was trying to pass me on her way to the corridor. The Baron talked away: 'Very amusing, don't you think? After Reinhardt, of course, although they say now that Reinhardt got all his ideas from your man Craig. I'm sure I don't know whether that's so. . . . I hope you're more reassured to-night, Mr. Durward. You were full of alarms the other evening. Look around you and you'll see the true Russia. . . .'

'I can't believe this to be the true Russia,' I said. 'Petrograd is not the true Russia. I don't believe that there *is* a true Russia.'

'Well, there you are,' he continued eagerly. 'No true Russia! Quite so. Very observant. But we have to pretend there is, and that's what you foreigners are always forgetting. The Russian is an individualist – give him freedom and he'll lose all sense of his companions. He will pursue his own idea. Myself and my party are here to prevent him from pursuing his own idea, for the good of himself and his country. He may be discontented, he may grumble, but he doesn't realise his luck. Give him his freedom, and in six months you'll see Russia back in the Middle Ages.'

'And another six months?' I asked.

'The Stone Age.'

'And then?'

'Ah,' he said, smiling, 'you ask me too much, Mr. Durward. We are speaking of our own generation.'

The curtain was up again and I was back in my other world. I cannot tell you anything of the rest of the play – I remember nothing. Only I know that I was actually living over again those awful days in the forest – the heat, the flies, the smells, the glassy sheen of the trees, the perpetual rumble of the guns, the desolate whine of the shells – and then Marie's death, Trenchard's sorrow, Trenchard's death, that last view of Semyonov . . . and I felt that I was being made to remember it all for a purpose, as though my old friend, rich now with his wiser knowledge, was whispering to me, 'All life is bound up. You cannot leave anything behind you; the past, the present, the future are one. You had pushed us away from you, but we are with you always for ever. I am your friend for ever, and Marie is your friend, and now, once more, you have to take your part in a battle, and we have come to you to share it with you. Do not be confused by history or public events or class struggle or any big names; it is the individual and the soul of the individual alone that matters. I and Marie and Vera and Nina and Markovitch – our love for you, your love for us, our courage, our self-sacrifice, our weakness, our defeat, our progress – these are the things for which life exists; it exists as a training-ground for the immortal soul. . . .'

With a sweep of colour the stage broke into a mist of movement. Masked and hooded figures in purple and gold and blue and red danced madly off into a forest of stinking, sodden leaves and trees as thin as tissue-paper burnt by the sun. 'Oh – aye! oh – aye! oh – aye!' came from the wounded, and the dancers answered, 'Tra-la-la-la! Tra-la-la-*la*!' The golden screens were drawn forward, the lights were up again, and the whole theatre was stirring like a coloured paper ant-heap.

Outside in the foyer I found Lawrence at my elbow.

'Go and see her,' he whispered to me, 'as soon as possible! Tell her – tell her – no, tell her nothing. But see that she's all right and let me know. See her tomorrow – early!'

I could say nothing to him, for the Baron had joined us.

'Good-night! Good-night! A most delightful evening! . . . Most amusing! . . . No, thank you, I shall walk! '

'Come and see us,' said the Baroness, smiling.

'Very soon,' I answered. I little knew that I should never see either of them again.

III

I awoke that night with a sudden panic that I must instantly see Vera. I even, in the way that one does when one is only half awake, struggled out of bed and felt for my clothes. Then I remembered and climbed back again, but sleep would not return to me. The self-criticism and self-distrust that were always attacking me and paralysing my action sprang upon me now and gripped me. What was I to do? How was I to act? I saw Vera and Nina and Lawrence and, behind them, smiling at me, Semyonov. They were asking for my help, but they were, in some strange, intangible way, most desperately remote. When I read now in our papers shrill criticisms on our officials, our Cabinet, our generals, our propagandists, our merchants, for their failure to deal adequately with Russia, I say: Deal adequately? First you must catch your bird . . . and no Western snare has ever caught the Russian bird of paradise, and I dare prophesy that no Western snare ever will. Had I not broken my heart in the pursuit, and was I not as far as ever from attainment? The secret of the mystery of life is the isolation that separates every man from his fellow – the secret of dissatisfaction too; and the only purpose in life is to realise that isolation, and to love one's fellow-man because of it, and to show one's own courage, like a flag to which the other travellers may wave their answer; but we, Westerners have at least the waiting comfort of our discipline, of our materialism, of our indifference to ideas. The Russian, I believe, lives in a world of loneliness peopled only by ideas. His impulses towards self-confession, towards brotherhood, towards vice, towards cynicism, towards his belief in God and his scorn of Him, come out of this world; and beyond it he sees his fellow-men as trees walking, and the Mountain of God as a distant peak, placed there only to emphasise his irony.

I had wanted to be friends with Nina and Vera – I had even longed for it – and now at the crisis when I must rise and act they were so far away from me that I could only see them, like coloured ghosts, vanishing into mist.

I would go at once and see Vera and there do what I could. Lawrence must return to England – then all would be well. Markovitch must be persuaded. . . . Nina must be told. . . . I slept and tumbled into a nightmare of a pursuit, down endless streets, of flying figures.

Next day I went to Vera. I found her, to my joy, alone. I realised at once that our talk would be difficult. She was grave and severe, sitting back in her chair, her head up, not looking at me at all, but beyond through the window to the tops of the trees feathery with snow against the sky of egg-shell blue. I am always beaten by a hostile atmosphere. Today I was at my worst, and soon we were talking like a couple of the merest strangers.

She asked me whether I had heard that there were very serious disturbances on the other side of the river.

'I was on the Nevski early this afternoon,' I said, 'and I saw about twenty Cossacks go galloping down towards the Neva. I asked somebody and was told that some women had broken into the bakers' shops on Vassily Ostrov . . .'

'It will end as they always end,' said Vera. 'Some arrests and a few people beaten, and a policeman will get a medal.'

There was a long pause. 'I went to "Masquerade" the other night,' I said.

'I hear it's very good. . . .'

'Pretentious and rather vulgar – but amusing, all the same.'

'Every one's talking about it and trying to get seats. . . .'

'Yes. Meyerhold must be pleased.'

'They discuss it much more than they do the war, or even politics. Every one's tired of the war.'

I said nothing. She continued:

'So I suppose we shall just go on for years and years. . . . And then the Empress herself will be tired one day and it will suddenly stop.' She showed a flash of interest, turning to me and looking at me for the first time since I had come in.

'Ivan Andreievitch, what do you stay in Russia for? Why don't you go back to England?'

I was taken by surprise. I stammered, 'Why do I stay? Why, because – because I like it.'

'You can't like it. There's *nothing* to like in Russia.'

'There's *everything*!' I answered. 'And I have friends here,' I added. But she didn't answer that, and continued to sit staring out at the trees. We talked a little more about nothing at all, and then there was another long pause. At last I could endure it no longer, I jumped to my feet.

'Vera Michailovna,' I cried, 'what have I done?'

'Done?' she asked me with a look of self-conscious surprise. 'What do you mean?'

'You know what I mean well enough,' I answered. I tried to speak firmly, but my voice trembled a little. 'You told me I was your friend. When I was ill the other day you came to me and said that you needed help and that you wanted me to help you. I said that I would——'

I paused.

'Well?' she said, in a hard, unrelenting voice.

'Well——' I hesitated and stammered, cursing myself for my miserable cowardice. 'You are in trouble now, Vera – great trouble – I came here because I am ready to do anything for you – anything – and you treat me like a stranger, almost like an enemy.'

I saw then her lip tremble – only for an instant. She said nothing.

'If you've got anything against me since you saw me last,' I went on, 'tell me and I'll go away. But I had to see you and also Lawrence——'

At the mention of his name her whole body quivered, but again only for an instant.

'Lawrence asked me to come and see you.'

She looked up at me then gravely and coldly, and without the sign of any emotion either in her face or voice.

'Thank you, Ivan Andreievitch, but I want no help – I am in no trouble. It was very kind of Mr. Lawrence, but really——'

Then I could endure it no longer. I broke out:

'Vera, what's the matter? You know all this isn't true. . . . I don't know what idea you have now in your head, but you must let me speak to you. I've got to tell you this – that Lawrence must go back to England, and as soon as possible – and I will see that he does——'

That did its work. In an instant she was upon me like a wild beast, springing from her chair, standing close to me, her head flung back, her eyes furious.

'You wouldn't dare!' she cried. 'It's none of your business, Ivan Andreievitch. You say you're my friend. You're not. You're my enemy – my enemy. I don't care for him, not in the very least – he is nothing to me – nothing to me at all. But he mustn't go back to England. It will ruin his career. You will ruin him for life, Ivan Andreievitch. What business is it of yours? You imagine – because of what you fancied you saw at Nina's party. There was nothing at Nina's party – nothing. I love my husband, Ivan Andreievitch, and you are my enemy if you say anything else. And you pretend to be his friend,

but you are his enemy if you try to have him sent back to England. . . .
He must not go. For the matter of that, I will never see him again –
never – if that is what you want. See, I promise you never – never——'
She suddenly broke down – she, Vera Michailovna, the proudest
woman I had ever known, turning from me, her head in her hands,
sobbing, her shoulders bent.

I was most deeply moved. I could say nothing at first, then, when
the sound of her sobbing became unbearable to me, I murmured:

'Vera, please. I have no power. I can't make him go. I will only do
what you wish. Vera, please, please——'

Then, with her back still turned to me, I heard her say:

'Please, go. I didn't mean – I didn't . . . but go now . . . and come
back – later.'

I waited a minute, and then, miserable, terrified of the future, I went.

IV

Next night (it was Friday evening) Semyonov paid me a visit. I was
just dropping to sleep in my chair. I had been reading that story
of De la Mare's, *The Return* – one of the most beautiful books in
our language, whether for its spirit, its prose, or its poetry – and
something of the moon-lit colour of its pages had crept into my
soul, so that the material world was spun into threads of the finest
silk behind which other worlds were more and more plainly visible.
I had not drawn my blind, and a wonderful moon shone clear on to
the bare boards of my room, bringing with its rays the mother-of-
pearl reflections of the limitless ice, and these floated on my wall in
trembling waves of opaque light. In the middle of this splendour I
dropped slowly into slumber, the book falling from my hands, and
I, on my part, seeming to float lazily backwards and forwards, as
though, truly, one were at the bottom of some crystal sea, idly and
happily drowned.

From all of this I was roused by a sharp knock on my door, and
I started up, still bewildered and bemused, but saying to myself
aloud, 'There's some one there! there's some one there! . . .' I stood
for quite a while, listening, on the middle of my shining floor, then
the knock was almost fiercely repeated. I opened the door and, to
my surprise, found Semyonov standing there. He came in, smiling,
very polite of course.

'You'll forgive me, Ivan Andreievitch,' he said. 'This is terribly unceremonious. But I had an urgent desire to see you, and you wouldn't wish me, in the circumstances, to have waited.'

'Please,' I said. I went to the window and drew the blinds. I lit the lamp. He took off his Shuba and we sat down. The room was very dim now, and I could only see his mouth and square beard behind the lamp.

'I've no Samovar, I'm afraid,' I said. 'If I'd known you were coming I'd have told her to have it ready. But it's too late now. She's gone to bed.'

'Nonsense,' he said brusquely. 'You know that I don't care about that. Now we'll waste no time. Let us come straight to the point at once. I've come to give you some advice, Ivan Andreievitch – very simple advice. Go home to England.' Before he had finished the sentence I had felt the hostility in his voice; I knew that it was to be a fight between us, and, strangely, at once the self-distrust and cowardice from which I had been suffering all those weeks left me. I felt warm and happy. I felt that with Semyonov I knew how to deal. I was afraid of Vera and Nina, perhaps, because I loved them, but of Semyonov, thank God, I was not afraid.

'Well, now, that's very kind of you,' I said, 'to take so much interest in my movements. I didn't know that it mattered to you so much where I was. Why must I go?'

'Because you are doing no good here. You are interfering in things of which you have no knowledge. When we met before you interfered, and you must honestly admit that you did not improve things. Now it is even more serious. I must ask you to leave my family alone, Ivan Andreievitch,'

'Your family!' I retorted, laughing. 'Upon my word, you do them great honour. I wonder whether they'd be very proud and pleased if they knew of your adoption of them. I haven't noticed on their side any very great signs of devotion.'

He laughed. 'No, you haven't noticed, Ivan Andreievitch. But there, you don't really notice very much. You think you see the devil of a lot and are a mighty clever fellow; but we're Russians, you know, and it takes more than sentimental mysticism to understand us. But even if you did understand us – which you don't – the real point is that we don't want you, any of you, patronising, patting us on the shoulder, explaining us to ourselves, talking about our souls, our unpunctuality, and our capacity for drink. However, that's merely in a general way.

In a personal, direct, and individual way, I beg you not to visit my family again. Stick to your own countrymen.'

Although he spoke obstinately, and with a show of assurance, I realised, behind his words, his own uncertainty.

'See here, Semyonov,' I said. 'It's just my own Englishmen that I am going to stick to. What about Lawrence? And what about Bohun? Will you prevent me from continuing my friendship with them?'

'Lawrence . . . Lawrence,' he said slowly, in a voice quite other than his earlier one, and as though he were talking aloud to himself. 'Now, that's strange . . . there's a funny thing. A heavy, dull, silent Englishman, as ugly as only an Englishman can be, and the two of them are mad about him – nothing in him – nothing – and yet there it is. It's the fidelity in the man, that's what it is, Durward. . . .' He suddenly called out the word aloud, as though he'd made a discovery. 'Fidelity . . . fidelity . . . that's what we Russians admire, and there's a man with not enough imagination to make him unfaithful. Fidelity! – lack of imagination, lack of freedom – that's all fidelity is. . . . But I'm faithful. . . . God knows, I'm faithful – always! always!'

He stared past me. I swear that he did not see me, that I had vanished utterly from his vision. I waited. He was leaning forward, pressing both his thick white hands on the table. His gaze must have pierced the ice beyond the walls, and the worlds beyond the ice.

Then quite suddenly he came back to me and said very quietly:

'Well, there it is, Ivan Andreievitch. . . . You must leave Vera and Nina alone. It isn't your affair.'

We continued the discussion then in a strange and friendly way. 'I believe it to be my affair,' I answered quietly, 'simply because they care for me and have asked me to help them if they were in trouble. I still deny that Vera cares for Lawrence. . . . Nina has had some girl's romantic idea perhaps . . . but that is the extent of the trouble. You are trying to make things worse, Alexei Petrovitch, for your own purposes – and God only knows what they are.'

He now spoke so quietly that I could scarcely hear his words. He was leaning forward on the table, resting his head on his hands and looking gravely at me.

'What I can't understand, Ivan Andreievitch,' he said, 'is why you're always getting in my way. You did so in Galicia, and now here you are again. It is not as though you were strong or wise – no, it is because you are persistent. I admire you in a way, you know, but now, this time, I assure you that you are making a great mistake in remaining. You will be able to influence neither Vera Michailovna nor your bullock of an Englishman when the moment comes. At the crisis they will never think of you at all, and the end of it simply will be that all parties concerned will hate you. I don't wish you any harm, and I assure you that you will suffer terribly if you stay. . . . By the way, Ivan Andreievitch,' his voice suddenly dropped, 'you haven't ever had – by chance – just by chance – any photograph of Marie Ivanovna with you, have you? Just by chance, you know. . . .'

'No,' I said shortly, 'I never had one.'

'No – of course – not. I only thought. . . . But of course you wouldn't – no – no. . . . Well, as I was saying, you'd better leave us all to our fate. You can't prevent things – you can't indeed.' I looked at him without speaking. He returned my gaze.

'Tell me one thing,' I said, 'before I answer you. What are you doing to Markovitch, Alexei Petrovitch?'

'Markovitch!' He repeated the name with an air of surprise as though he had never heard it before. 'What do you mean?'

'You have some plan with regard to him,' I said 'What is it?'

He laughed then. 'I a plan! My dear Durward, how romantic you always insist on being! I a plan! Your plunges into Russian psychology are as naïve as the girl who pays her ten kopecks to see the Fat Woman at the Fair! Markovitch and I understand one another. We trust one another. He is a simple fellow, but I trust him.'

'Do you remember,' I said, 'that the other day at the Jews' Market you told me the story of the man who tortured his friend, until the man shot him – simply because he was tired of life and too proud to commit suicide? Why did you tell me that story?'

'Did I tell it you?' he asked indifferently 'I had forgotten. But it is of no importance. You know, Ivan Andreievitch, that what I told you before is true. . . . We don't want you here any more. I tell you in a perfectly friendly way. I bear you no malice. But we're tired of your sentimentality. I'm not speaking only for myself – I'm not indeed. We feel that you avoid life to a ridiculous extent, and that you have no right to talk to us Russians on such a subject. What, for instance, do you know about women? For years I slept with a different woman every night of the week – old and young, beautiful and ugly, some women like men, some like God, some like the gutter. That teaches you something about women – but only something. Afterwards I found that there was only one woman – I left all the others like dirty washing – I was supremely faithful . . . so I learnt the rest. Now you have never been faithful nor unfaithful – I'm sure that you have not. Then about God? When have you ever thought about Him? Why, you are ashamed to mention His name. If an Englishman speaks of God when other men are present every one laughs – and yet why? It is a very serious and interesting question. God exists undoubtedly, and so we must make up our minds about Him. We must establish some relationship – what it is does not matter – that is our individual "case" – but only the English establish no relationship and then call it a religion. . . . And so in this affair of my family. What does it matter what they do? That is the only thing of which you think, that they should die or disgrace their name or be unhappy or quarrel. . . . Pooh! What are all those things compared with the idea behind them? If they wish to sacrifice happiness for an idea, that is their good luck, and no Russian would think of preventing them. But you come in with your English morality and sentiment, and scream and cry. . . . No, Ivan Andreievitch, go home! go home!'

I waited to be quite sure that he had finished, and then I said:

'That's all as it may be, Alexei Petrovitch. It may be as you say. The point is, that I remain here.'

He got up from his chair. 'You are determined on that?'

'I am determined,' I answered.

'Nothing will change you?'

'Nothing.'

'Then it is a battle between us?'

'If you like.'

'So be it'

I helped him on with his Shuba. He said, in an ordinary conversational tone:

'There may be trouble tomorrow. There's been shooting by the Nicholas Station this afternoon, I hear. I should avoid the Nevski tomorrow.'

I laughed. 'I'm not afraid of that kind of death, Alexei Petrovitch,' I said.

'No,' he said, looking at me. 'I will do you justice. You are not.'

He pulled his Shuba close about him.

'Good-night, Ivan Andreievitch,' he said. 'It's been a very pleasant talk.'

'Very,' I answered. 'Good-night.'

After he had gone I drew back the blinds and let the moonlight flood the room.

V

I feel conscious, as I approach the centre of my story, that there is an appearance of uncertainty in the way that I pass from one character to another. I do not defend that uncertainty.

What I think I really feel now, on looking back, is that each of us – myself, Semyonov, Vera, Nina, Lawrence, Bohun, Grogoff, yes, and the Rat himself – was a part of a mysterious figure who was beyond us, outside us, and above us all. The heart, the lungs, the mouth, the eyes . . . used against our own human agency, and yet free within that domination for the exercise of our own free will. Have you never felt when you have been swept into the interaction of some group of persons that you were being employed as a part of a figure that without you would be incomplete? The figure is formed. . . . For an instant it remains, gigantic, splendid, towering above mankind, as a symbol, a warning, a judgement, an ideal, a threat. Dimly you recognise that you have played some part in the creation of that figure, and that living for a moment, as you have done, in some force outside your individuality, you have yet expressed that same individuality more nobly than any poor assertion of your own small lonely figure could afford. You have been used and now you are alone again. . . . You were caught up and united to your fellow-men. God appeared to you – not, as you had expected, in a vision cut off from the rest of the world, but in a revelation that you shared and that was only revealed because you were uniting with others. And yet your individuality was still there, strengthened, heightened, purified.

And the vision of the figure remains. . . .

When I woke on Saturday morning, after my evening with Semyonov, I was conscious that I was relieved as though I had finally settled some affair whose uncertainty had worried me. I lay in bed chuckling as though I had won a triumph over Semyonov, as though I said to myself, 'Well, I needn't be afraid of him any longer.' It was a most beautiful day, crystal clear, with a stainless blue sky and the snow like a carpet of jewels, and I thought I would go and see how the world was behaving. I walked down the Morskaia, finding it quiet enough, although I fancied that the faces of the passers-by were anxious and nervous. Nevertheless, the brilliant sunshine and the clear peaceful beauty of the snow reassured me – the world was too beautiful and well-ordered a place to allow disturbance. Then at the corner of the English shop where the Morskaia joins the Nevski Prospect, I realised that something had occurred. It was as though the world that I had known so long, and with whom I felt upon such intimate terms, had suddenly screwed round its face and showed me a new grin.

The broad space of the Nevski was swallowed up by a vast crowd, very quiet, very amiable, moving easily, almost slothfully, in a slowly stirring stream.

As I looked up the Nevski I realised what it was that had given me the first positive shock of an altered world. The trams had stopped. I had never seen the Nevski without its trams; I had always been forced to stand on the brink, waiting whilst the stream of Isvostchiks galloped past and the heavy, lumbering, coloured elephants tottered along, amiable and slow and good-natured like everything else in that country. Now the elephants were gone; the Isvostchiks were gone. So far as my eye could see, the black stream flooded the shining way.

I mingled with the crowd and found myself slowly propelled in an amiable, aimless manner up the street.

'What's the matter?' I asked a cheerful, fat little 'Chinovnik,' who seemed to be tethered to me by some outside invincible force.

'I don't know . . .' he said. 'They're saying there's been some shooting up by the Nicholas Station – but that was last night. Some women had a procession about food. . . . *Tak oni gavoryat* – so they say. . . . But I don't know. People have just come out to see what they can see. . . .'

And so they had – women, boys, old men, little children. I could see no signs of ill-temper anywhere, only a rather open-mouthed wonder and sense of expectation.

A large woman near me, with a shawl over her head and carrying a large basket, laughed a great deal. 'No, I wouldn't go,' she said. 'You go and get it for yourself – I'm not coming. Not I, I was too clever for that.' Then she would turn, shrilly calling for some child who was apparently lost in the crowd. 'Sacha! . . . Ah! Sacha!' she cried – and turning again, 'Eh! look at the Cossack! . . . There's a fine Cossack!'

It was then that I noticed the Cossacks. They were lined up along the side of the pavement, and sometimes they would suddenly wheel and clatter along the pavement itself, to the great confusion of the crowd, who would scatter in every direction.

They were fine-looking men, and their faces expressed childish and rather worried amiability. The crowd obviously feared them not at all, and I saw a woman standing with her hand on the neck of one of the horses, talking in a very friendly fashion to the soldier who rode it. 'That's strange,' I thought to myself; 'there's something queer here.' It was then, just at the entrance of the 'Malaia Koniu-shennaia,' that a strange little incident occurred. Some fellow – I could just see his shaggy head, his pale face, and black beard – had been shouting something, and suddenly a little group of Cossacks moved towards him and he was surrounded. They turned off with him towards a yard close at hand. I could hear his voice shrilly protesting; the crowd also moved behind, murmuring. Suddenly a Cossack, laughing, said something. I could not hear his words, but every one near me laughed. The little Chinovnik at my side said to me, 'That's right. They're not going to shoot, whatever happens – not on their brothers, they say. They'll let the fellow go in a moment. It's only just for discipline's sake. That's right. That's the spirit!'

'But what about the police?' I asked.

'Ah, the police!' His cheery, good-natured face was suddenly dark and scowling. 'Let them try, that's all. It's Protopopoff who's our enemy – not the Cossacks.'

And a woman near him repeated:

'Yes, yes, it's Protopopoff. Hurrah for the Cossacks!'

I was squeezed now into a corner, and the crowd swirled and eddied about me in a tangled stream, slow, smiling, confused, and excited. I pushed my way along, and at last tumbled down the dark stone steps into the 'Cave de la Grave,' a little restaurant patronised by the foreigners and certain middle-class Russians. It was full, and every one was eating his or her meal very comfortably as though nothing at all were the matter. I sat down with a young American, an acquaintance of mine attached to the American Embassy.

'There's a tremendous crowd in the Nevski,' I said.

'Guess I'm too hungry to trouble about it,' he answered.

'Do you think there's going to be any trouble?' I asked.

'Course not. These folks are always wandering round. M. Protopopoff has it in hand all right.'

'Yes, I suppose he has,' I answered with a sigh.

'You seem to want trouble,' he said, suddenly looking up at me.

'No, I don't want trouble,' I answered. 'But I'm sick of this mess, this mismanagement, thievery, lying – one's tempted to think that anything would be better——'

'Don't you believe it,' he said brusquely. 'Excuse me, Durward, I've been in this country five years. A revolution would mean God's own upset, and you've got a war on, haven't you?'

'They might fight better than ever,' I argued.

'Fight!' he laughed. 'They're dam sick of it all, that's what they are. And a revolution would leave 'em like a lot of silly sheep wandering on to a precipice. But there won't be no revolution. Take my word.'

It was at that moment that I saw Boris Grogoff come in. He stood in the doorway looking about him, and he had the strangest air of a man walking in his sleep, so bewildered, so rapt, so removed was he. He stared about him looked straight at me, but did not recognise me; finally, when a waiter showed him a table, he sat down still gazing in front of him. The waiter had to speak to him twice before he ordered his meal, and then he spoke so strangely that the fellow looked at him in astonishment. 'Guess that chap's seen the Millennium,' remarked my American. 'Or he's drunk, maybe.'

This appearance had the oddest effect on me. It was as though I had been given a sudden conviction that after all there was something behind this disturbance. I saw, during the whole of the rest of that day, Grogoff's strange face with the exalted, bewildered eyes, the excited mouth, the body tense and strained as though waiting for a blow. And now, always when I look back I see Boris Grogoff standing in the doorway of the 'Cave de la Grave' like a ghost from another world warning me.

In the afternoon I had a piece of business that took me across the river. I did my business and turned homewards. It was almost dark, and the ice of the Neva was coloured a faint green under the grey sky; the buildings rose out of it like black bubbles poised over a swamp. I was in that strange quarter of Petrograd where the river seems, like some sluggish octopus, to possess a thousand coils. Always you are turning upon a new bend of the ice, secretly stretching into darkness; strange bridges suddenly meet you, and then, where you had expected to find a solid mass of hideous flats, there will be a cluster of masts and the smell of tar, and little fierce red lights like the eyes of waiting beasts.

I seemed to stand with ice on every side of me, and so frail was my trembling wooden bridge that it seemed an easy thing for the ice, that appeared to press with tremendous weight against its banks, to grind the supports to fragments. There was complete silence on every side of me. The street to my left was utterly deserted. I heard no cries nor calls – only the ice seemed once and again to quiver as though some submerged creature was moving beneath it. That vast crowd on the Nevski seemed to be a dream. I was in a world that had fallen into decay and desolation, and I could smell rotting wood, and could fancy that frozen blades of grass were pressing up through the very pavement stones. Suddenly an Isvostchik stumbled along past me, down the empty street, and the bumping rattle of the sledge on the snow woke me from my laziness. I started off homewards. When I had gone a little way and was approaching the bridge over the Neva some man passed me, looked back, stopped and waited for me. When I came up to him I saw to my surprise that it was the Rat. He had his coat-collar turned over his ears and his dirty fur cap pulled down over his forehead. His nose was very red, and his thin hollow cheeks a dirty yellow colour.

'Good evening, Barin,' he said, grinning.

'Good evening,' I said. 'Where are you slipping off to so secretly?'

'Slipping off?' He did not seem to understand my word. I repeated it.

'Oh, I'm not slipping off,' he said almost indignantly. 'No, indeed. I'm just out for a walk like your Honour, to see the town.'

'What have they been doing this afternoon?' I asked. 'There's been a fine fuss on the Nevski.'

'Yes, there has . . .' he said, chuckling. 'But it's nothing to the fuss there will be.'

'Nonsense,' I said. 'The police have got it all in control already. You'll see tomorrow. . . .'

'And the soldiers, Barin?'

'Oh, the soldiers won't do anything. Talk's one thing – action's another.'

He laughed to himself and seemed greatly amused. This irritated me.

'Well, what do you know?' I asked.

'I know nothing,' he chuckled. 'But remember, Barin, in a week's time, if you want me I'm your friend. Who knows? In a week I may be a rich man.'

'Some one else's riches,' I answered.

'Certainly,' he said. 'And why not? Why should he have things? Is he a better man than I? Possibly – but then it is easy for a rich man to keep within the law. And then Russia's meant for the poor man. However,' he continued, with great contempt in his voice, 'that's politics – dull stuff. While the others talk I act.'

'And what about the Germans?' I asked him. 'Does it occur to you that when you've collected your spoils the Germans will come in and take them?'

'Ah, you don't understand us, Barin,' he said, laughing. 'You're a good man and a kind man, but you don't understand us. What can the Germans do? They can't take the whole of Russia. Russia's big country. . . . No, if the Germans come here'll be more for us to take.'

We stood for a moment under a lamp-post. He put his hand on my arm and looked up at me with his queer ugly face, his sentimental dreary eyes, his red nose, and his hard, cruel little mouth.

'But no one shall touch you – unless it's myself if I'm very drunk. But you, knowing me, will understand afterwards that I was at least not malicious——'

I laughed. 'And this mysticism that they tell us about in England. Are you mystical, Rat? Have you a beautiful soul?'

He sniffed and blew his nose with his hand.

'I don't know what you're talking about, Barin – I suppose you haven't a rouble or two on you?'

'No, I haven't,' I answered. He looked up and down the bridge as though he were wondering whether an attack on me was worth while. He saw a policeman and decided that it wasn't.

'Well, good-night, Barin,' he said cheerfully. He shuffled off. I looked at the vast Neva, pale green and dim grey, so silent under the bridges. The policeman, enormous under his high coat, the sure and confident guardian of that silent world, came slowly towards me, and I turned away home.

VI

The next day, Sunday, I have always called in my mind Nina's day, and so I propose to deal with it here, describing it as far as possible from her point of view and placing her in the centre of the picture.

The great fact about Nina, at the end, when everything has been said, must always be her youth. That Russian youthfulness is something that no Western people can ever know, because no Western people are accustomed, from their very babyhood, to bathe in an atmosphere that deals only with ideas.

In no Russian family is the attempt to prevent children from knowing what life really is maintained for long; the spontaneous impetuosity of the parents breaks it down. Nevertheless the Russian boy and girl, when they come to the awkward age, have not the least idea of what life really is. Dear me, no! They possess simply a bundle of incoherent ideas, untested, ill-digested, but a wonderful basis for incessant conversation. Experience comes, of course, and for the most part it is unhappy experience.

Life is a tragedy to every Russian simply because the daily round is forgotten by him in his pursuit of an ultimate meaning. We in the West have learnt to despise ultimate meanings as unpractical and rather priggish things.

Nina had thought so much and tested so little. She loved so vehemently that her betrayal was the more inevitable. For instance, she did not love Boris Grogoff in the least, but he was in some way connected with the idea of freedom. She was, I am afraid, beginning to love Lawrence desperately – the first love of her life – and he too was connected with the idea of freedom because he was English. We English do not understand sufficiently how the Russians love us for our easy victory over tyranny, and despise us for the small use we have made of our victory – and then, after all, there is something to be said for tyranny too. . . .

But Nina did not see why she should not capture Lawrence. She felt her vitality, her health, her dominant will beat so strongly within her that it seemed to her that nothing could stop her. She loved him for his strength, his silence, his good-nature, yes, and his stupidity. This last gave her a sense of power over him, and of motherly tenderness too. She loved his stiff and halting Russian – it was as though he were but ten years old.

I am convinced, too, that she did not consider that she was doing any wrong to Vera. In the first place she was not as yet really sure that Vera cared for him. Vera, who had been to her always a mother rather than a sister, seemed an infinite age. It was ridiculous that Vera should fall in love – Vera so stately and stern and removed from passion. Those days were over for Vera, and, with her strong sense of duty and the fitness of things, she would realise that. Moreover Nina could not believe that Lawrence cared for Vera. Vera was not the figure to be loved in that way. Vera's romance had been with Markovitch years and years ago, and now, whenever Nina looked at Markovitch, it made it at once impossible to imagine Vera in any new romantic situation.

Then had come the night of the birthday party, and suspicion had at once flamed up again. She was torn that night and for days afterwards with a raging jealousy.

She hated Vera, she hated Lawrence, she hated herself. Then again her mood had changed. It was, after all, natural that he should have gone to protect Vera; she was his hostess; he was English, and did not know how trivial a Russian scene of temper was. He had meant nothing, and poor Vera, touched that at her matronly age any one should show her attention, had looked at him gratefully.

That was all. She loved Vera; she would not hurt her with such ridiculous suspicions, and, on that Friday evening when Semyonov had come to see me, she had been her old self again, behaving to Vera with all the tenderness and charm and affection that were her most delightful gifts.

On this Sunday morning she was reassured; she was gay and happy and pleased with the whole world. The excitement of the disturbances of the last two days provided an emotional background, not too thrilling to be painful, because, after all, these riots would, as usual, come to nothing, but it was pleasant to feel that the world was buzzing, and that without paying a penny one might see a real cinematograph show simply by walking down the Nevski.

I do not know, of course, what exactly happened that morning until Semyonov came in, but I can see the Markovitch family, like ten thousand other Petrograd families, assembling somewhere about eleven o'clock round the Samovar, all in various stages of undress, all sleepy and pale-faced, and a little befogged, as all good Russians are when, through the exigencies of sleep, they've been compelled to allow their ideas to escape from them for a considerable period. They discussed, of course, the disturbances, and I can imagine Markovitch portentously announcing that 'It was all over, he had the best of reasons for knowing. . . .'

As he once explained to me, he was at his worst on Sunday, because he was then so inevitably reminded of his lost youth.

'It's a gloomy day, Ivan Andreievitch, for all those who have not quite done what they expected. The bells ring, and you feel that they ought to mean something to you, but of course one's gone past all that. . . . But it's a pity. . . .'

Nina's only thought that morning was that Lawrence was coming in the afternoon to take her for a walk. She had arranged it all. After a very evident hint from her he had suggested it. Vera had refused, because some aunts were coming to call, and finally it had been arranged that after the walk Lawrence should bring Nina home, stay to half-past six dinner, and that then they should all go to the

French theatre. I also was asked to dinner and the theatre. Nina was sure that something must happen that afternoon. It would be a crisis. . . . She felt within her such vitality, such power, such domination, that she believed that today she could command anything. . . . She was, poor child, supremely confident, and that not through conceit or vanity, but simply because she was a fatalist and believed that destiny had brought Lawrence to her feet. . . .

It was the final proof of her youth that she saw the whole universe working to fulfil her desire.

The other proof of her youth was that she began, for the first time, to suffer desperately. The most casual mention of Lawrence's name would make her heart beat furiously, suffocating her, her throat dry, her cheeks hot, her hands cold. Then, as the minute of his arrival approached, she would sit as though she were the centre of a leaping fire that gradually inch by inch was approaching nearer to her, the flames staring like little eyes on the watch, the heat advancing and receding in waves like hands. She hoped that no one would notice her agitation. She talked nonsense to whomsoever was near to her with little nervous laughs; she seemed to herself to be terribly unreal, with a fierce hostile creature inside her who took her heart in his hot hands and pressed it, laughing at her.

And then the misery! That little episode at the circus of which I had been a witness was only the first of many dreadful ventures. She confessed to me afterwards that she did not herself know what she was doing. And the final result of these adventures was to encourage her because he had not repelled her. He *must* have noticed, she thought, the times when her hand had touched his, when his mouth had been so close to hers that their very thoughts had mingled, when she had felt the stuff of his coat, and even for an instant stroked it. He *must* have noticed these things, and still he had never rebuffed her. He was always so kind to her; she fancied that his voice had a special note of tenderness in it when he spoke to her, and when she looked at his ugly, quiet, solid face, she could not believe that they were not meant for one another. He *must* want her, her gaiety, happiness, youth – it would be wrong for him *not* to! There could be no girls in that stupid, practical, far-away England who would be the wife to him that she would be!

Then the cursed misery of that waiting! They could hear in their sitting-room the steps coming up the stone stairs outside their flat, and every step seemed to be his. Ah, he had come earlier than he had fixed. Vera had stupidly forgotten, perhaps, or he had found waiting any longer impossible. Yes, surely that was his footfall; she knew it so well. There, now he was turning towards the door; there was a pause; soon there would be the tinkle of the bell! . . .

No, he had mounted higher; it was not Lawrence – only some stupid, ridiculous creature who was impertinently daring to put her into this misery of disappointment. And then she would wonder suddenly whether she had been looking too fixedly at the door, whether they had noticed her, and she would start and look about her self-consciously, blushing a little, her eyes hot and suspicious.

I can see her in all these moods; it was her babyhood that was leaving her at last. She was never to be quite so spontaneously gay again, never quite so careless, so audacious, so casual, so happy. In Russia the awkward age is very short, very dramatic, often enough very tragic. Nina was as helpless as the rest of the world.

At any rate, upon this Sunday, she was sure of her afternoon. Her eyes were wild with excitement. Any one who looked at her closely must have noticed her strangeness, but they were all discussing the events of the last two days; there were a thousand stories, nearly all of them false and a few true facts.

No one in reality knew anything except that there had been some demonstrations, a little shooting, and a number of excited speeches. The town on that lovely winter morning seemed absolutely quiet.

Somewhere about mid-day Semyonov came in, and without thinking about it Nina suddenly found herself sitting in the window talking to him. This conversation, which was in its results to have an important influence on her whole life, continued the development which that eventful Sunday was to effect in her. Its importance lay very largely in the fact that her uncle had never spoken to her seriously like a grown-up woman before. Semyonov was, of course, quite clever enough to realise the change which was transforming her, and he seized it, at once, for his own advantage. She, on her side, had always, ever since she could remember, been intrigued by him. She told me once that almost her earliest memory was being lifted into the air by her uncle and feeling the thick solid strength of his grasp, so that she was like a feather in the air, poised on one of his stubborn fingers; when he kissed her each hair of his beard seemed like a pale, taut wire, so stiff and resolute was it. Her Uncle Ivan was a flabby, effeminate creature in comparison. Then, as she had grown older, she had realised that he was a dangerous man, dangerous to women, who loved and feared and hated him. Vera said that he had great power over them and made them miserable, and that he was, therefore, a bad, wicked man. But this only served to make him, in Nina's eyes, the more a romantic figure.

However, he had never treated her in the least seriously, had tossed her in the air spiritually just as he had done physically when she was a baby, had given her chocolates, taken her once or twice to the cinema, laughed at her, and, she felt, deeply despised her. Then came the war and he had gone to the Front, and she had almost forgotten him. Then came the romantic story of his being deeply in love with a nurse who had been killed, that he was heartbroken and inconsolable and a changed man. Was it wonderful that on his return to Petrograd she should feel again that old Byronic (every Russian is still brought up on Byron) romance? She did not like him, but – well – Vera was a staid old-fashioned thing. . . . Perhaps they all misjudged him; perhaps he really needed comfort and consolation. He certainly seemed kinder than he used to be. But, until today, he had never talked to her seriously.

How her heart leapt into her throat when he began, at once, in his quiet soft voice:

'Well, Nina dear, tell me all about it. I know, so you needn't be frightened. I know and I understand.'

She flung a terrified glance around her, but Uncle Ivan was reading the paper at the other end of the room, her brother-in-law was cutting up little pieces of wood in his workshop, and Vera was in the kitchen.

'What do you mean?' she said in a whisper. 'I don't understand.'

'Yes, you do,' he answered, smiling at her. 'You know, Nina, you're in love with the Englishman, and have been for a long time. Well, why not? Don't be so frightened about it. It is quite time that you should be in love with some one, and he's a fine strong young man – not over-blessed with brains, but you can supply that part of it. No, I think it's a very good match. I like it. Believe me, I'm your friend, Nina.' He put his hand on hers.

He looked so kind, she told me afterwards, that she felt as though she had never known him before; her eyes were filled with tears, so overwhelming a relief was it to find some one at last who sympathised and understood and wanted her to succeed. I remember that she was wearing that day a thin black velvet necklet with a very small diamond in front of it. She had been given it by Uncle Ivan on her last birthday, and instead of making her look grown-up it gave her a ridiculously childish appearance as though she had stolen into Vera's bedroom and dressed up in her things. Then, with her fair tousled hair and large blue eyes, open as a rule with a startled expression as though she had only just awakened into an astonishingly exciting world, she was altogether as unprotected and as guileless and as honest as any human being alive. I don't know whether Semyonov felt her innocence and youth – I expect he considered very little beside the plans that he had then in view . . . and innocence had never been very interesting to him. He spoke to her just as a kind, wise, thoughtful uncle ought to speak to a niece caught up into her first love-affair. From the moment of that half-hour's conversation in the window Nina adored him, and believed every word that came from his mouth.

'You see, Nina dear,' he went on, 'I've not spoken to you before because you neither liked me nor trusted me. Quite rightly you listened to what others said about me——'

'Oh no,' interrupted Nina. 'I never listen to anybody.'

'Well then,' said Semyonov, 'we'll say that you were very naturally influenced by them. And quite right – perfectly right. You were only a girl then – you are a woman now. I had nothing to say to you then – now I can help you, give you a little advice perhaps——'

I don't know what Nina replied. She was breathlessly pleased and excited.

'What I want,' he went on, 'is the happiness of you all. I was sorry when I came back to find that Nicholas and Vera weren't such friends as they used to be. I don't mean that there's anything wrong at all, but they must be brought closer together – and that's what you and I, who know them and love them, can do——'

'Yes, yes,' said Nina eagerly. Semyonov then explained that the thing that really was, it seemed to him, keeping them apart was Nicholas's inventions. Of course Vera had long ago seen that these inventions were never going to come to anything, that they were simply wasting Nicholas's time when he might, by taking an honest clerkship or something of the kind, be maintaining the whole household, and the very thought of him sitting in his workshop irritated her. The thing to do, Semyonov explained, was to laugh Nicholas out of his inventions, to show him that it was selfish nonsense his pursuing them, to persuade him to make an honest living.

'But I thought,' said Nina, 'you approved of them. I heard you only the other day telling him that it was a good idea, and that he must go on——'

'Ah!' said Semyonov. 'That was my weakness, I'm afraid. I couldn't bear to disappoint him. But it was wrong of me – and I knew it at the time.'

Now Nina had always rather admired her brother-in-law's inventions. She had thought it very clever of him to think of such things, and she had wondered why other people did not applaud him more.

Now suddenly she saw that it was very selfish of him to go on with these things when they never brought in a penny, and Vera had to do all the drudgery. She was suddenly indignant with him. In how clear a light her uncle placed things!

'One thing to do,' said Semyonov, 'is to laugh at him about them. Not very much, not unkindly, but enough to make him see the folly of it.'

'I think he does see that already, poor Nicholas,' said Nina with wisdom beyond her years.

'To bring Nicholas and Vera together,' said Semyonov, 'that's what we have to do, you and I. And believe me, dear Nina, I on my side will do all I can to help you. We are friends, aren't we? – not only uncle and niece.'

'Yes,' said Nina breathlessly. That was all that there was to the conversation, but it was quite enough to make Nina feel as though she had already won her heart's desire. If any one as clever as her uncle believed in this, then it *must* be true. It had not been only her own silly imagination – Lawrence cared for her. Her uncle had seen it, otherwise he would never have encouraged her – Lawrence cared for her. . . .

Suddenly, in the happy spontaneity of the moment she did what she very seldom did – bent forward and kissed him.

She told me afterwards that that kiss seemed to displease him.

He got up and walked away.

VII

I do not know exactly what occurred during that afternoon. Neither Lawrence nor Nina spoke about it to me. I only know that Nina returned subdued and restrained. I can imagine them going out into that quiet town and walking along the deserted quay; the quiet that afternoon was, I remember, marvellous. The whole world was holding its breath. Great events were occurring, but we were removed from them all. The ice quivered under the sun and the snow-clouds rose higher and higher into the blue, and once and again a bell chimed and jangled. . . . There was an amazing peace. Through this peaceful world Nina and Lawrence walked. His mind must, I know, have been very far away from Nina; probably he saw nothing of her little attempts at friendship; her gasping sentences that seemed to her so daring and significant he scarcely heard. His only concern was to endure the walk as politely as possible and return to Vera.

Perhaps if she had not had that conversation with her uncle she would have realised more clearly how slight a response was made to her, but she thought only that this was his English shyness and gaucherie – she must go slowly and carefully. He was not like a Russian. She must not frighten him. Ah, how she loved him as she walked beside him, seeing and not seeing the lovely frozen colours of the winter day, the quickly flooding saffron sky, the first bright star, the great pearl-grey cloud of the Neva as it was swept into the dark. In the dark she put, I am sure, her hand on his arm, and felt his strength and took her small hurried steps beside his long ones. He did not, I expect, feel her hand on his sleeve at all. It was Vera whom he saw through the dusk – Vera watching the door for his return, knowing that his eyes would rush to hers, that every beat of his heart was for her. . . .

I found them all seated at dinner when I entered. I brought them the news of the shooting up at the Nicholas Station.

'Perhaps we had better not go to the theatre,' I said. 'A number of people were killed this afternoon, and all the trams are stopped.'

Still it was all remote from us. They laughed at the idea of not going to the theatre. The tickets had been bought two weeks ago, and the walk would be pleasant. Of course we would go. It would be fun, too, to see whether anything were happening.

With how strange a clarity I remember the events of that evening. It is detached and hangs by itself among the other events of that amazing time, as though it had been framed and separated for some especial purpose. My impression of the colour of it now is of a scene intensely quiet.

I saw at once on my arrival that Vera was not yet prepared to receive me back into her friendship. And I saw, too, that she included Lawrence in this ostracism. She sat there, stiff and cold, smiling and talking simply because she was compelled, for politeness' sake, to do so. She would scarcely speak to me at all, and when I saw this I turned and devoted myself to Uncle Ivan, who was always delighted to make me a testing-ground for his English.

But poor Jerry! Had I not been so anxious lest a scene should burst upon us all I could have laughed at the humour of it. Vera's attitude was a complete surprise to him. He had not seen her during the preceding week, and that absence from her had heightened his desire until it burnt his very throat with its flame. One glance from her, when he came in, would have contented him. He could have rested then, happily, quietly; but instead of that glance she had avoided his eye, her hand was cold and touched his only for an instant. She had not spoken to him again after the first greeting. I am sure that he had never known a time when his feelings threatened to be too much for him. His hold on himself and his emotions had been complete. 'These fellers,' he once said to me about some Russians, 'are always letting their feelings overwhelm them – like women. And they like it. Funny thing!' Well, funny or no, he realised it now; his true education, like Nina's, like Vera's, like Bohun's, like Markovitch's, perhaps like my own, was only now beginning. Funny and pathetic, too, to watch his broad, red, genial face struggling to express a polite interest in the conversation, to show nothing but friendliness and courtesy. His eyes were as restless as minnows; they darted for an instant towards Vera, then darted off again, then flashed back. His hand moved for a plate, and I saw that it was shaking. Poor Jerry! He had learnt what suffering was during those last weeks. But the most silent of us all that evening was Markovitch. He sat huddled over his food and never said a word. If he looked up at all he glowered, and so soon as he had finished eating he returned to his workshop, closing the door behind him. I caught Semyonov looking at him with a pleasant, speculative smile. . . .

At last Vera, Nina, Lawrence, and I started for the theatre. I can't say that I was expecting a very pleasant evening, but the deathlike stillness, both of ourselves and the town did, I confess, startle me. Scarcely a word was exchanged by us between the English Prospect and Saint Isaac's Square. The square looked lovely in the bright moonlight, and I said something about it. It was indeed very fine, the cathedral like a hovering purple cloud, the old sentry in his high peaked hat, the black statue, and the blue shadows over the snow. It was then that Lawrence, with an air of determined strength, detached Vera from us and walked ahead with her. I saw that he was talking eagerly to her.

Nina said, with a little shudder, 'Isn't it quiet, Durdles? As though there were ghosts round every corner.'

'Hope you enjoyed your walk this afternoon,' I said.

'No, it was quiet then. But not like it is now. Let's walk faster and catch the others up. Do you believe in ghosts, Durdles?'

'Yes, I think I do.'

'So do I. Was it true, do you think, about the people being shot at the Nicholas Station today?'

'I daresay.'

'Perhaps all the dead people are crowding round here now. Why isn't any one out walking?'

'I suppose they are all frightened by what they've heard, and think it better to stay at home.'

We were walking down the Morskaia, and our feet gave out a ringing echo.

'Let's keep up with them,' Nina said. When we had joined the others I found that they were both silent – Lawrence very red, Vera pale. We were all feeling rather weary. A woman met us. 'You aren't allowed to cross the Nevski,' she said; 'the Cossacks are stopping everybody.' I can see her now, a stout, red-faced woman, a shawl over her head, and carrying a basket. Another woman, a prostitute I should think, came up and joined us.

'What is it?' she asked us.

The stout woman repeated in a trembling, agitated voice, 'You aren't allowed to cross the Nevski. The Cossacks are stopping everybody.'

The prostitute shook her head in her alarm, and little flakes of powder detached themselves from her nose. '*Bozhe moi – Bozhe moi!*' she said, 'and I promised not to be late.'

Vera then, very calmly and quietly, took command of the situation. 'We'll go and see,' she said, 'what is really the truth.'

We turned up the side street to the Moika Canal, which lay like powdered crystal under the moon. Not a soul was in sight.

There arrived then one of the most wonderful moments of my life. The Nevski Prospect, that broad and mighty thoroughfare, stretched before us like a great silver river. It was utterly triumphantly bare and naked. Under the moon it flowed, with proud tranquillity, so far as the eye could see between its high black banks of silent houses.

At intervals of about a hundred yards the Cossack pickets, like ebony statues on their horses, guarded the way. Down the whole silver expanse not one figure was to be seen; so beautiful was it under the high moon, so still, so quiet, so proud, that it was revealing now for the first time its real splendour. At no time of the night or day is the Nevski deserted. How happy it must have been that night! ...

For us, it was as though we hesitated on the banks of a river. I felt a strange superstition, as though something said to me, 'You cross that and you are plunged irrevocably into a new order of events. Go home, and you will avoid danger.' Nina must have had something of the same feeling, because she said:

'Let's go home. They won't let us cross. I don't want to cross. Let's go home.'

But Vera said firmly, 'Nonsense! We've gone do far. We've got the tickets. I'm going on.'

I felt the note in her voice, superstitiously, as a kind of desperate challenge, as though she had said:

'Well, you see nothing worse can happen to me than has happened.'

Lawrence said roughly, 'Of course, we're going on.'

The prostitute began, in a trembling voice, as though we must all of necessity understand her case:

'I don't want to be late this time, because I've been late so often before. . . . It always is that way with me . . . always unfortunate. . . .'

We started across, and when we stepped into the shining silver surface we all stopped for an instant, as though held by an invisible force.

'That's it,' said Vera, speaking it seemed to herself. 'So it always is with us. All revolutions in Russia end this way——'

An unmounted Cossack came forward to us.

'No hanging about there,' he said. 'Cross quickly. No one is to delay.'

We moved to the other side of the Moika bridge. I thought of the Cossacks yesterday who had assured the people that they would not fire – well, that impulse had passed. Protopopoff and his men had triumphed.

We were all now in the shadows on the other bank of the canal. The prostitute, who was still at our side, hesitated for a moment, as though she were going to speak. I think she wanted to ask whether she might walk with, us a little way. Suddenly she vanished without sound, into the black shadows.

'Come along,' said Vera. 'We shall be dreadfully late.' She seemed to be mastered by an overpowering desire not to be left alone with Lawrence. She hurried forward with Nina, and Lawrence and I came more slowly behind. We were now in a labyrinth of little streets and black overhanging flats. Not a soul anywhere – only the moonlight in great broad flashes of light – once or twice a woman hurried by keeping in the shadow. Sometimes, at the far end of the street, we saw the shining, naked Nevski.

Lawrence was silent; then, just as we were turning into the square where the Michailovsky Theatre was, he began:

'What's the matter? ... What's the matter with her, Durward? What have I done?'

'I don't know that you've done anything,' I answered.

'But don't you see?' he went on. 'She won't speak to me. She won't look at me. I won't stand this long. I tell you I won't stand it long. I'll make her come off with me in spite of them all. I'll have her to myself. I'll make her happy, Durward, as she's never been in all her life. But I must have her. . . . I can't live close to her like this, and yet never be with her. Never alone, never alone. Why is she behaving like this to me?'

He spoke really like a man in agony, the words coming from him in little tortured sentences as though they were squeezed from him desperately, with pain at every breath that he drew.

'She's afraid of herself, I expect, not of you.' I put my hand on his sleeve. 'Lawrence,' I said, 'go home. Go back to England. This is becoming too much for both of you. Nothing can come of it, but unhappiness for everybody.'

'No!' he said. 'It's too late for any of your Platonic advice, Durward. I'm going to have her, even though the earth turns upside down.'

We went up the steps and into the theatre. There was, of course, scarcely any one there. The Michailovsky is not a large theatre, but the stalls looked extraordinarily desolate, every seat watching one with a kind of insolent wink as though; like the Nevski ten minutes before, it said, 'Well, now you humans are getting frightened, you're all stopping away. We're coming back to our own!'

There was some such malicious air about the whole theatre. Above, in the circle, the little empty boxes were dim and shadowy, and one fancied figures moved there, and then saw that there was no one. Some one up in the gallery laughed, and the laugh went echoing up and down the empty spaces. A few people came in and sat nervously about, and no one spoke except in a low whisper, because voices sounded so loud and impertinent.

Then again the man in the gallery laughed, and every one looked up frowning. The play began. It was, I think, *Les Idées de Françoise,* but of that I cannot be sure. It was a farce of the regular French type, with a bedroom off, and marionettes who continually separated into couples and giggled together. The giggling to-night was of a sadly hollow sort. I pitied and admired the actors, spontaneous as a rule, but now bravely stuffing any kind of sawdust into the figures in their hands, but the leakage was terrible, and the sawdust lay scattered all about the stage. The four of us sat as solemn as statues – I don't think one of us smiled. It was during the second Act that I suddenly laughed. I don't know that anything very comic was happening on the stage, but I was aware, with a kind of ironic subconsciousness, that some of the superior spirits in their superior Heaven must be deriving a great deal of fun from our situation. There was Vera thinking, I suppose, of nothing but Lawrence, and Lawrence thinking of nothing but Vera, and Nina thinking of nothing but Lawrence, and the audience thinking of their safety, and the players thinking of their salaries, and Protopopoff at home thinking of his victory, and the Czar in Tsarskoe thinking of his God-sent autocracy, and Europe thinking of its ideals, and Germany thinking of its militarism – all self-justified, all mistaken, and all fulfilling some deeper plan at whose purpose they could not begin to guess. And how intermingled we all were! – Vera and Nina, M. Robert and Mdlle. Flori on the other side of the footlights, Trenchard and Marie killed in Galicia, the Kaiser and Hindenburg, the Archbishop of Canterbury and the postmaster of my village in Glebeshire.

The curtain is coming down, the fat husband is deceived once again, the lovers are in the bedroom listening behind the door, the comic waiter is winking at the chamber-maid. . . .

The lights are up and we are alone again in the deserted theatre.

Towards the end of the last interval I went out into the passage behind the stalls to escape from the chastened whispering that went trembling up and down like the hissing of terrified snakes. I leaned against the wall in the deserted passage and watched the melancholy figure of the cloak-room attendant huddled up on a chair, his head between his hands.

Suddenly I saw Vera. She came up to me as though she were going to walk past me, and then she stopped and spoke. She talked fast, not looking at me, but beyond, down the passage.

'I'm sorry, Ivan Andreievitch,' she said. 'I was cross the other day. I hurt you. I oughtn't to have done that.'

'You know,' I said, 'that I never thought of it for a minute.'

'No, I was wrong. But I've been terribly worried during these last weeks. I've thought it all out today and I've decided –' there was a catch in her breath and she paused; she went on – 'decided that there mustn't be any more weakness. I'm much weaker than I thought. I would be ashamed if I didn't think that shame was a silly thing to have. But now I am quite clear; I must make Nicholas and Nina happy. Whatever else comes I must do that. It has been terrible, these last weeks. We've all been angry and miserable, and now I must put it right. I can if I try. I've been forgetting that I chose my own life myself, and now I mustn't be cowardly because it's difficult. I will make it right myself. . . .'

She paused again; then she said, looking me straight in the face:

'Ivan Andreievitch, does Nina care for Mr. Lawrence?'

She was looking at me with large black eyes so simply, with such trust in me, that I could only tell her the truth.

'Yes,' I said, 'she does.'

Her eyes fell, then she looked up at me again.

'I thought so,' she said. 'And does he care for her?'

'No,' I said, 'he does not.'

'He must,' she said. 'It would be a very happy thing for them to marry.'

She spoke very low, so that I could scarcely hear her words.

'Wait, Vera,' I said. 'Let it alone. Nina's very young. The mood will pass. Lawrence, perhaps, will go back to England.'

She drew in her breath and I saw her hand tremble, but she still looked at me, only now her eyes were not so clear. Then she laughed. 'I'm getting an old woman, Ivan Andreievitch. It's ridiculous. . . .' She broke off. Then held out her hand.

'But we'll always be friends now, won't we? I'll never be cross with you again.'

I took her hand. 'I'm getting old too,' I said. 'And I'm useless at everything. I only make a bungle of everything I try. But I'll be your true friend to the end of my time——'

The bell rang and we went back into the theatre.

VIII

And yet, strangely enough, when I lay awake that night in my room on my deserted island, it was of Markovitch that I was thinking. Of all the memories of the preceding evening that of Markovitch huddled over his food, sullen and glowering, with Semyonov watching him, was predominant.

Markovitch was, so to speak, the dark horse of them all, and he was also when one came to look at it all the way round the centre of the story. And yet it was Markovitch with his inconsistencies, his mysteries, his impulses, and purposes, whom I understood least of them all. He makes, indeed, a very good symbol of my present difficulties.

In that earlier experience of Marie in the forests of Galicia the matter had been comparatively easy. I had then been concerned with the outward manifestation of war – cannon, cholera, shell, and the green glittering trees of the forest itself. But the war had made progress since then. It had advanced out of material things into the very souls of men. It was no longer the forest of bark and tinder with which the chiefs of this world had to deal, but, to adapt the Russian proverb itself, 'with the dark forest of the hearts of men.'

How much more baffling and intangible this new forest, and how deeply serious a business now for those who were still thoughtlessly and selfishly juggling with human affairs.

'There is no ammunition,' I remember crying desperately in Galicia. We had moved further than the question of ammunition now.

I had a strange dream that night. I saw my old forest of two years before – the very woods of Buchatch with the hot painted leaves, the purple slanting sunlight, the smell, the cries, the whirr of the shell. But in my dream the only inhabitant of that forest was Markovitch. He was pursued by some animal. What beast it was I could not see, always the actual vision was denied to me, but I could hear it plunging through the thickets, and once I caught a glimpse of a dark crouching body like a shadow against the light.

But Markovitch I saw all the time, sweating with heat and terror, his clothes torn, his eyes inflamed, his breath coming in desperate pants, turning once and again as though he would stop and offer defiance, then hasting on, his face and hands scratched and bleeding. I wanted to offer him help and assistance, but something prevented me; I could not get to him. Finally he vanished from my sight and I was left alone in the painted forest. . . .

All the next morning I sat and wondered what I had better do, and at last I decided that I would go and see Henry Bohun.

I had not seen Bohun for several weeks. I myself had been, of late, less to the flat in the English Prospect, but I knew that he had taken my advice that he should be kind to Nicholas Markovitch with due British seriousness, and that he had been trying to bring some kind of relationship about. He had even asked Markovitch to dine alone with him, and Markovitch, although he declined the invitation, was, I believe, greatly touched.

So, about half-past one, I started off for Bohun's office on the Fontanka. I've said somewhere before, I think, that Bohun's work was in connection with the noble but uphill task of enlightening the Russian public as to the righteousness of the war, the British character, and the Anglo-Russian alliance. I say 'uphill,' because only a few of the *real* population of Russia showed the slightest desire to know anything whatever about any country outside their own. Their interest is in ideas, not in boundaries – and what I mean by 'real' will be made patent by the events of this very day. However, Bohun did his best, and it was not his fault that the British Government could only spare enough men and money to cover about one inch of the whole of Russia – and I hasten to add that if that same British Government had plastered the whole vast country from Archangel to Vladivostock with pamphlets, orators, and photographs it would not have altered, in the slightest degree, after events.

To make any effect in Russia, England needed not only men and money but a hundred years' experience of the country. That same experience was possessed by the Germans alone of all the Western peoples – and they have not neglected to use it.

I went by tram to the Fontanka, and the streets seemed absolutely quiet. That strange shining Nevski of the night before was a dream. Some one in the tram said something about rifle-shots in the Summer Garden, but no one listened. As Vera had said last night, we had, none of us, much faith in Russian revolutions.

I went up in the lift to the Propaganda office and found it a very nice airy place, clean and smart, with coloured advertisements by Shepperson and others on the walls, pictures of Hampstead and St. Albans and Kew Gardens that looked strangely satisfactory and homely to me, and rather touching and innocent. There were several young women clicking away at typewriters, and maps of the Western front, and a colossal toy map of the London Tube, and a nice English library with all the best books from Chaucer to D. H. Lawrence and from the *Religio Medici* to E. V. Lucas' *London*.

Everything seemed clean and simple and a little deserted, as though the heart of the Russian public had not, as yet, quite found its way there. I think 'guileless' was the adjective that came to my mind, and certainly Burrows, the head of the place – a large, red-faced, smiling man with glasses – seemed to me altogether too cheerful and pleased with life to penetrate the wicked recesses of Russian pessimism.

I went into Bohun's room and found him very hard at work in a serious, emphatic way which only made me feel that he was playing at it. He had a little bookcase over his table, and I noticed the *Georgian Book of Verse*, Conrad's *Nostromo*, and a translation of Ropshin's *Pale Horse*.

'Altogether too pretty and literary,' I said to him; 'you ought to be getting at the peasant with a pitchfork and a hammer – not admiring the Intelligentzia.'

'I daresay you're right,' he said, blushing. 'But whatever we do we're wrong. We have fellows in here cursing us all day. If we're simple we're told we're not clever enough; if we're clever we're told we're too complicated. If we're militant we're told we ought to be tender-hearted, and if we're tender-hearted we're told we're sentimental – and at the end of it all the Russians don't care a damn.'

'Well, I daresay you're doing some good somewhere,' I said indulgently.

'Come and look at my view,' he said, 'and see whether it isn't splendid.'

He spoke no more than the truth. We looked across the Canal over the roofs of the city – domes and towers and turrets, grey and white and blue, with the dark red walls of many of the older houses stretched like an Arabian carpet beneath white bubbles of clouds that here and there marked the blue sky. It was a scene of intense peace, the smoke rising from the chimneys, Isvostchiks stumbling along on the farther banks of the Canal, and the people sauntering in their usual lazy fashion up and down the Nevski. Immediately below our window was a skating-rink that stretched straight across the Canal. There were some figures, like little dolls, skating up and down, and they looked rather desolate beside the deserted band-stands and the empty seats. On the road outside our door a cart loaded with wood slowly moved along, the high hoop over the horse's back gleaming with red and blue.

'Yes, it *is* a view!' I said. 'Splendid! – and all as quiet as though there'd been no disturbances at all. Have you heard any news?'

'No,' said Bohun. 'To tell the truth I've been so busy that I haven't had time to ring up the Embassy. And we've had no one in this morning. Monday morning, you know,' he added; 'always very few people on Monday morning' – as though he didn't wish me to think that the office was always deserted.

I watched the little doll-like men circling placidly round and round the rink. One bubble cloud rose and slowly swallowed up the sun. Suddenly I heard a sharp crack like the breaking of a twig. 'What's that?' I said, stepping forward on to the balcony. 'It sounded like a shot.'

'I didn't hear anything,' said Bohun. 'You get funny echoes up here sometimes.' We stepped back into Bohun's room and, if I had had any anxieties, they would at once, I think, have been reassured by the unemotional figure of Bohun's typist, a gay young woman with peroxide hair, who was typing away as though for her very life.

'Look here, Bohun, can I talk to you alone for a minute?' I asked.

The peroxide lady left us.

'It's just about Markovitch I wanted to ask you,' I went on. 'I'm infernally worried, and I want your help. It may seem ridiculous of me to interfere in another family like this, with people with whom I have, after all, nothing to do. But there are two reasons why it isn't ridiculous. One is the deep affection I have for Nina and Vera. I promised them my friendship, and now I've got to back that promise. And the other is that you and I are really responsible for bringing Lawrence into the family. They never would have known him if it hadn't been for us. There's danger and trouble of every sort brewing, and Semyonov, as you know, is helping it on wherever he can. Well, now, what I want to know is, how much have you seen of Markovitch lately, and has he talked to you?'

Bohun considered. 'I've seen very little of him,' he said at last. 'I think he avoids me now. He's such a weird bird that it's impossible to tell of what he's really thinking. I know he was pleased when I asked him to dine with me at the Bear the other night. He looked *most awfully* pleased. But he wouldn't come. It was as though he suspected that I was laying a trap for him.'

'But what have you noticed about him otherwise?'

'Well, I've seen very little of him. He's sulky just now. He suspected Lawrence, of course – always after that night of Nina's party. But I think that he's reassured again. And of course it's all so ridiculous, because there's nothing to suspect, absolutely nothing – is there?'

'Absolutely nothing,' I answered firmly.

He sighed with relief. 'Oh, you don't know how glad I am to hear that,' he said. 'Because, although I've *known* that it was all right,

Vera's been so odd lately that I've wondered – you know how I care about Vera and——'

'How do you mean – odd?' I sharply interrupted.

'Well – for instance – of course I've told nobody – and you won't tell any one either – but the other night I found her crying in the flat, sitting up near the table, sobbing her heart out. She thought every one was out – I'd been in my room and she hadn't known. But Vera, Durward – Vera of all people! I didn't let her see me – she doesn't know now that I heard her. But when you care for any one as I care for Vera, it's awful to think that she can suffer like that and one can do nothing. Oh, Durward, I wish to God I wasn't so helpless! You know before I came out to Russia I felt so old; I thought there was nothing I couldn't do, that I was good enough for anybody. And now I'm the most awful ass. Fancy, Durward! Those poems of mine – I thought they were wonderful. I thought——'

He was interrupted by a sudden sharp crackle like a fire bursting into a blaze quite close at hand. We both sprang to the windows, threw them open (they were not sealed, for some unknown reason), and rushed out on to the balcony. The scene in front of us was just what it had been before – the bubble clouds were still sailing lazily before the blue, the skaters were still hovering on the ice, the cart of wood that I had noticed was vanishing slowly into the distance. But from the Liteiny – just over the bridge – came a confused jumble of shouts, cries, and then the sharp, unmistakable rattle of a machine-gun. It was funny to see the casual life in front of one suddenly pause at that sound. The doll-like skaters seemed to spin for a moment and then freeze; one figure began to run across the ice. A small boy came racing down our street shouting. Several men ran out from doorways and stood looking up into the sky, as though they thought the noise had come from there. The sun was just setting; the bubble clouds were pink, and windows flashed fire. The rattle of the machine-gun suddenly stopped, and there was a moment's silence when the only sound in the whole world was the clatter of the wood-cart turning the corner. I could see to the right of me the crowds in the Nevski, that had looked like the continual unwinding of a ragged skein of black silk, break their regular movement and split up like flies falling away from an opening door.

We were all on the balcony by now – the stout Burrows, Peroxide, and another lady typist, Watson, the thin and most admirable secretary (he held the place together by his diligence and order), two Russian clerks, Henry, and I.

We all leaned over the railings and looked down into the street beneath us. To our left the Fontanka Bridge was quite deserted – then, suddenly, an extraordinary procession poured across it. At that same moment (at any rate it seems so now to me on looking back) the sun disappeared, leaving a world of pale grey mist shot with gold and purple. The stars were, many of them, already out, piercing with their sharp cold brilliance the winter sky.

We could not at first see of what exactly the crowd now pouring over the bridge was composed. Then, as it turned and came down our street, it revealed itself as something so theatrical and melodramatic as to be incredible. Incredible, I say, because the rest of the world was not theatrical with it. That was always to be the amazing feature of the new scene into which, without knowing it, I was at that moment stepping. In Galicia the stage had been set – ruined villages, plague-stricken peasants, shell-holes, trenches, roads cut to pieces, huge trees levelled to the ground, historic chateaux pillaged and robbed. But here the world was still the good old jog-trot world that one had always known; the shops and hotels and theatres remained as they had always been. There would remain, I believe, for ever those dull Jaeger undergarments in the windows of the bazaar, and the bound edition of Tchekov in the book-shop just above the Moika, and the turtle and the gold-fish in the aquarium near Elisseieff; and whilst those things were there I could not believe in melodrama.

And we did not believe. We dug our feet into the snow, and leaned over the balcony railings absorbed with amused interest. The procession consisted of a number of motor lorries, and on these lorries soldiers were heaped. I can use no other word because, indeed, they seemed to be all piled upon one another, some kneeling forward, some standing, some sitting, and all with their rifles pointing outwards until the lorries looked like hedgehogs. Many of the rifles had pieces of red cloth attached to them, and one lorry displayed proudly a huge red flag that waved high in air with a sort of flaunting arrogance of its own. On either side of the lorries, filling the street, was the strangest mob of men, women, and children. There seemed to be little sign of order or discipline amongst them, as they were all shouting different cries: 'Down the Fontanka!' 'No, the Duma!' 'To the Nevski!' 'No, no, *Tovaristchi* (comrades), to the Nicholas Station!'

Such a rabble was it that I remember that my first thought was of pitying indulgence. So this was the grand outcome of Boris Grogoff's eloquence, and the Rat's plots for plunder! – a fitting climax to such vain dreams. I saw the Cossack, that ebony figure of Sunday night. Ten such men, and this rabble was dispersed for ever! I felt inclined to lean over and whisper to them, 'Quick! quick! Go home! . . . They'll be here in a moment and catch you!'

And yet, after all, there seemed to be some show of discipline. I noticed that, as the crowd moved forward, men dropped out and remained picketing the doorways of the street. Women seemed to be playing a large part in the affair, peasants with shawls over their heads, many of them leading by the hand small children.

Burrows treated it all as a huge joke. 'By Jove,' he cried, speaking across to me, 'Durward, it's like that play Martin Harvey used to do – what was it? – about the French Revolution, you know.'

'"The Only Way,"' said Peroxide, in a prim, strangled voice.

'That's it – "The Only Way" – with their red flags and all. Don't they look ruffians, some of them?'

There was a great discussion going on under our windows. All the lorries had drawn up together, and the screaming, chattering, and shouting was like the noise of a parrots' aviary. The cold blue light had climbed now into the sky, which was thick with stars; the snow on the myriad roofs stretched like a filmy cloud as far as the eye could see. The moving, shouting crowd grew with every moment mistier.

'Oh, dear! Mr. Burrows,' said the little typist, who was not Peroxide, 'do you think I shall ever be able to get home? We're on the other side of the river, you know. Do you think the bridges will be up? My mother will be so terribly anxious.'

'Oh, you'll get home all right,' answered Burrows cheerfully. 'Just wait until this crowd has gone by. I don't expect there's any fuss down by the river. . . .'

His words were cut short by some order from one of the fellows below. Others shouted in response, and the lorries again began to move forward.

'I believe he was shouting to us,' said Bohun. 'It sounded like "Get off" or "Get away."'

'Not he!' said Burrows; 'they're too busy with their own affairs.'

Then things happened quickly. There was a sudden strange silence below; I saw a quick flame from some fire that had apparently been lit on the Fontanka Bridge; I heard the same voice call out once more sharply, and a second later I felt rather than heard a whizz like the swift flight of a bee past my ear; I was conscious that a bullet had struck the brick behind me. That bullet swung me into the Revolution. . . .

IX

. . . We were all gathered together in the office. I heard one of the Russians say in an agitated whisper, 'Don't turn on the light! . . . Don't turn on the light! They can see!'

We were all in half-darkness, our faces mistily white. I could hear Peroxide breathing in a tremulous manner, as though in a moment she would break into hysteria.

'We'll go into the inside room. We can turn the light on there,' said Burrows. We all passed into the reception-room of the office, a nice airy place, with the library along one wall and bright coloured maps on the other. We stood together and considered the matter.

'It's real!' said Burrows, his red, cheery face perplexed and strained. 'Who'd have thought it?'

'Of course it's real!' cried Bohun impatiently. (Burrows' optimism had been often difficult to bear with indulgence.)

'Now you see! What about your beautiful Russian mystic now?'

'Oh dear!' cried the little Russian typist. 'And my mother! . . . What ever shall I do? She'll hear reports and think that I'm being murdered. I shall never get across.'

'You'd better stay with me to-night, Miss Peredonov,' said Peroxide firmly. 'My flat's quite close here in Gagarinsky. We shall be delighted to have you.'

'You can telephone to your mother, Miss Peredonov,' said Burrows. 'No difficulty at all.'

It was then that Bohun took me aside.

'Look here!' he said. 'I'm worried. Vera and Nina were going to the Astoria to have tea with Semyonov this afternoon. I should think the Astoria might be rather a hot spot if this spreads. And I wouldn't trust Semyonov. Will you come down with me there now?'

'Yes,' I said, 'of course I'll come.'

We said a word to Burrows, put on our Shubas and goloshes, and started down the stairs. At every door there were anxious faces. Out of one flat came a very fat Jew.

'Gentlemen, what is this all about?'

'Riots,' said Bohun.

'Is there shooting?'

'Yes,' said Bohun.

'*Bozhe moi! Bozhe moi!* And I live over on Vassily Ostrov! What do you advise, *Gaspoda?* Will the bridges be up?'

'Very likely,' I answered. 'I should stay here.'

'And they are shooting?' he asked again.

'They are,' I answered.

'Gentlemen, gentlemen – stay for a moment. Perhaps together we could think. . . . I am all alone here except for a lady . . . most unfortunate. . . .'

But we could not stay.

The world into which we stepped was wonderful. The background of snow under the star-blazing sky made it even more fantastic than it naturally was. We slipped into the crowd and, becoming part of it, were at once, as one so often is, sympathetic with it. It seemed such a childish, helpless, and good-natured throng. No one seemed to know anything of arms or directions. There were, as I have already said, many women and little children, and some of the civilians who had rifles looked quite helpless. I saw one boy holding his gun upside down. No one paid any attention to us. There was as yet no class note in the demonstration, and the only hostile cries I heard were against Protopopoff and the police. We moved back into the street behind the Fontanka, and here I saw a wonderful sight. Some one had lighted a large bonfire in the middle of the street and the flames tossed higher and higher into the air, bringing down the stars in flights of gold, flinging up the snow until it seemed to radiate in lines and circles of white light high over the very roofs of the houses. In front of the fire a soldier, mounted on a horse, addressed a small crowd of women and boys. On the end of his rifle was a ragged red cloth.

I could not see his face. I saw his arms wave, and the fire behind him exaggerated his figure and then dropped it into a straggling silhouette against the snow. The street seemed deserted except for this group, although now I could hear distant shouting on every side of me, and the monotonous clap-clap-clap-clap of a machine-gun.

I heard him say: '*Tovaristchi!* now is your time! Don't hesitate in the sacred cause of freedom! As our brethren did in the famous days of the French Revolution, so must we do now. All the Army is coming over to our side. The Preobrojenski have come over to us and have arrested their officers and taken their arms. We must finish with Protopopoff and our other tyrants, and see that we have a just rule. *Tovaristchi!* there will never be such a chance again, and you will repent for ever if you have not played your part in the great fight for freedom!'

So it went on. It did not seem that his audience was greatly impressed. It was bewildered and dazed. But the fire leapt up behind him, giving him a legendary splendour, and the whole picture was romantic and unreal like a gaudy painting on a coloured screen.

We hurried through into the Nevski, and this we found nearly deserted. The trams of course had stopped, a few figures hurried along, and once an Isvostchik went racing down towards the river.

'Well, now, we seem to be out of it,' said Bohun, with a sigh of relief. 'I must say I'm not sorry. I don't mind France, where you can tell which is the front and which the back, but this kind of thing does get on one's nerves. I daresay it's only local. We shall find them all as easy as anything at the Astoria, and wondering what we're making a fuss about.'

At that moment we were joined by an English merchant whom we both knew, a stout elderly man who had lived all his life in Russia. I was surprised to find him in a state, of extreme terror. I had always known him as a calm, conceited, stupid fellow, with a great liking for Russian ladies. This pastime he was able as a bachelor to enjoy to the full. Now, however, instead of the ruddy, coarse, self-confident merchant there was a pallid, trembling jelly-fish.

'I say, you fellows,' he asked, catching my arm. 'Where are you off to?'

'We're off to the Astoria,' I answered.

'Let me come with you. I'm not frightened, not at all – all the same I don't want to be left alone. I was in the 1905 affair. That was enough for me. Where are they firing – do you know?'

'All over the place,' said Bohun, enjoying himself. 'They'll be down here in a minute.'

'Good God! Do you really think so? It's terrible – these fellows – once they get loose they stick at nothing. . . . I remember in 1905. . . . Good heavens! Where had we better go? It's very exposed here, isn't it?'

'It's very exposed everywhere,' said Bohun. 'I doubt whether any of us are alive in the morning.'

'Good heavens! You don't say so! Why should they interfere with us?'

'Oh, rich, you know, and that kind of thing. And then we're Englishmen. They'll clear out all the English.'

'Oh, I'm not really English. My mother was Russian. I could show them my papers. . . .'

Bohun laughed. 'I'm only kidding you, Watchett,' he said. 'We're safe enough. Look, there's not a soul about!' We were at the corner of the Moika now; all was absolutely quiet. Two women and a man were standing on the bridge talking together. A few stars clustered above the bend of the Canal seemed to shift and waver ever so slightly through a gathering mist, like the smoke of blowing candles.

'It seems all right,' said the merchant, sniffing the air suspiciously as though he expected to smell blood. We turned towards the Morskaia. One of the women detached herself from the group and came to us.

'Don't go down the Morskaia,' she said, whispering, as though some hostile figure were leaning over her shoulder. 'They're firing round the Telephone Exchange.' Even as she spoke I heard the sharp clatter of the machine-gun break out again, but now very close, and with an intimate note as though it were the same gun that I had heard before, which had been tracking me down round the town.

'Do you hear that?' said the merchant.

'Come on,' said Bohun. 'We'll go down the Moika. That seems safe enough!'

How strangely in the flick of a bullet the town had changed! Yesterday every street had been friendly, obvious, and open; they were now no longer streets, but secret blind avenues with strange trees, fantastic doors, shuttered windows, a grinning moon, malicious stars, and snow that lay there simply to prevent every sound. It was a town truly beleaguered as towns are in dreams. The uncanny awe with which I moved across the bridge was increased when the man with the women turned towards me, and I saw that he was – or seemed to be – that same grave bearded peasant whom I had seen by the river, whom Henry had seen in the Cathedral, who remained with one, as passing strangers sometimes do, like a symbol or a message or a threat.

He stood, with the Nevski behind him, calm and grave, and even, it seemed, a little amused, watching me as I crossed. I said to Bohun, 'Did you ever see that fellow before?'

Bohun turned and looked.

'No,' he said.

'Don't you remember? The man that first day in the Kazan?'

'They're all alike,' Bohun said. 'One can't tell. . . .'

'Oh, come on,' said the merchant. 'Let's get to the Astoria.'

We started down the Moika, past that faded picture-shop where there are always large moth-eaten canvases of corn-fields under the moon and Russian weddings and Italian lakes. We had got very nearly to the little street with the wooden hoardings when the merchant gripped my arm.

'What's that?' he gulped. The silence now was intense. We could not hear the machine-gun nor any shouting. The world was like a picture smoking under a moon now red and hard. Against the wall of the street two women were huddled, one on her knees, her head pressed against the thighs of the other, who stood stretched as though crucified, her arms out, staring on to the Canal. Beside a little kiosk, on the space exactly in front of the side street, lay a man on his face. His bowler-hat had rolled towards the kiosk; his arms were stretched out so that he looked oddly like the shadow of the woman against the wall.

Instead of one hand there was a pool of blood. The other hand with all the fingers stretched was yellow against the snow.

As we came up a bullet from the Morskaia struck the kiosk.

The woman, not moving from the wall, said: 'They've shot my husband . . . he did nothing.'

The other woman, on her knees, only cried without ceasing.

The merchant said: 'I'm going back—to the Europe,' and he turned and ran.

'What's down that street?' I said to the woman, as though I expected her to say 'Hobgoblins.'

Bohun said: 'This is rather beastly. . . . We ought to move that fellow out of that. He may be alive still.'

And how silly such a sentence when only yesterday, just here, there was the beggar who sold boot-laces, and just there, where the man lay, an old muddled Isvostchik asleep on his box!

We moved forward, and instantly it was as though I were in the middle of a vast desert quite alone with all the hosts of heaven aiming at me malicious darts. As I bent down my back was so broad that it stretched across Petrograd, and my feet were tiny like frogs.

We pulled at the man. His head rolled and his face turned over, and the mouth was full of snow. It was so still that I whispered, whether to Bohun or myself, 'God, I wish somebody would shout!' Then I heard the wood of the kiosk crack, ever so slightly, like an opening door, and panic flooded me as I had never known it do during all my time at the Front.

'I've no strength,' I said to Bohun.

'Pull for God's sake!' he answered. We dragged the body a little way; my hand clutched the thigh, which was hard and cold under the stuff of his clothing. His head rolled round, and his eyes now were covered with snow. We dragged him, and he bumped grotesquely. We had him under the wall, near the two women, and the blood welled out and dripped in a spreading pool at the women's feet.

'Now,' said Bohun, 'we've got to run for it.'

'Do you know,' said I, as though I were making a sudden discovery, 'I don't think I can.' I leaned back against the wall and looked at the pool of blood near the kiosk where the man had been.

'Oh, but you've got to,' said Bohun, who seemed to feel no fear. 'We can't stay here all night.'

'No, I know,' I answered. 'But the trouble is – I'm not myself.' And I was not. That *was* the trouble. I was not John Durward at all. Some stranger was here with a new heart, poor shrivelled limbs, an enormous nose, a hot mouth with no eyes at all. This stranger had usurped my clothes and he refused to move. He was tied to the wall and he would not obey me.

Bohun looked at me. 'I say, Durward, come on, it's only a step. We must get to the Astoria.'

But the picture of the Astoria did not stir me. I should have seen Nina and Vera waiting there, and that should have at once determined me. So it would have been had I been myself. This other man was there ... Nina and Vera meant nothing to him at all. But I could not explain that to Bohun. 'I can't go . . .' I saw Bohun's eyes – I was dreadfully ashamed. 'You go on . . .' I muttered. I wanted to tell him that I did not think that I could endure to feel again that awful expansion of my back and the turning of my feet into toads.

'Of course I can't leave you,' he said.

And suddenly I sprang back into my own clothes again. I flung the charlatan out and he flumped off into air.

'Come on,' I said, and I ran. No bullets whizzed past us. I was ashamed of running, and we walked quite quietly over the rest of the open space.

'Funny thing,' I said, 'I was damned frightened for a moment.'

'It's the silence and the houses,' said Bohun.

Strangely enough I remember nothing between that moment and our arrival at the Astoria. We must have skirted the Canal, keeping in the shadow of the wall, then crossed the Saint Isaac's Square. The next thing I can recall is our standing, rather breathless, in the hall of the Astoria, and the first persons I saw there were Vera and Nina, together at the bottom of the staircase, saying nothing, waiting.

In front of them was a motley crowd of Russian officers all talking and gesticulating together. I came nearer to Vera and at once I said to myself, 'Lawrence is here somewhere.' She was standing, her head up, watching the doors, her eyes glowed with anticipation, her lips were a little parted. She never moved at all, but was so vital that the rest of the people seemed dolls beside her. As we came towards them Nina turned round and spoke to some one, and I saw that it was Semyonov who stood at the bottom of the staircase, his thick legs apart, stroking his beard with his hand.

We came forward and Nina began at once:

'Durdles – tell us! What's happened?'

'I don't know,' I answered. The lights after the dark and the snow bewildered me, and the noise and excitement of the Russian officers were deafening.

Nina went on, her face lit. 'Can't you tell us anything? We haven't heard a word, We came just in an ordinary way about four o'clock. There wasn't a sound, and then, just as we were sitting down to tea, they all came bursting in, saying that all the officers were being murdered, and that Protopopoff was killed, and that——'

'That's true anyway,' said a young Russian officer, turning round to us excitedly. 'I had it from a friend of mine who was passing just as they stuck him in the stomach. He saw it all; they dragged him out of his house and stuck him in the stomach——'

'They say the Czar's been shot,' said another officer, a fat, red-faced man with very bright red trousers, 'and that Rodziancko's formed a government....'

I heard on every side such words as 'People – Rodziancko – Protopopoff – Freedom,' and the officer telling his tale again. 'And they stuck him in the stomach, just as he was passing his house....'

Through all this tale Vera never moved. I saw, to my surprise, that Lawrence was there now, standing near her but never speaking. Semyonov stood on the stairs watching.

Suddenly I saw that she wanted me.

'Ivan Andreievitch,' she said, 'will you do something for me?' She spoke very low, and her eyes did not look at me, but beyond us all out to the door.

'Certainly,' I said.

'Will you keep Alexei Petrovitch here? Mr. Lawrence and Mr. Bohun can see us home. I don't want him to come with us. Will you ask him to wait and speak to you?'

I went up to him. 'Semyonov,' I said, 'I want a word with you, if I may——'

'Certainly,' he said, with that irritating smile of his, as though he knew exactly of what I was thinking.

We moved up the dark stairs. As we went I heard Vera's clear, calm voice:

'Will you see us home, Mr. Lawrence? . . . I think it's quite safe to go now.'

We stopped on the first floor under the electric light. There were two easy-chairs there, with a dusty palm behind them. We sat down.

'You haven't really got anything to say to me,' he began.

'Oh yes, I have,' I said.

'No. . . . You simply suggested conversation because Vera asked you to do so.'

'I suggested a conversation,' I answered, 'because I had something of some seriousness to tell you.'

'Well, she needn't have been afraid,' he went on. 'I wasn't going home with them. I want to stop and watch these ridiculous people a little longer. . . . What had you got to say, my philosophical, optimistic friend?'

He looked quite his old self, sitting stockily in the chair, his strong thighs pressing against the cane as though they'd burst it, his thick square beard more wiry than ever, and his lips red and shining. He seemed to have regained his old self-possession and confidence.

'What I wanted to say,' I began, 'is that I'm going to tell you once more to leave Markovitch alone. I know the other day – that alone——'

'Oh, *that*!' he brushed it aside impatiently. 'There are bigger things than that just now, Durward. You lack, as I have always said, two very essential things, a sense of humour and a sense of proportion. And you pretend to know Russia whilst you are without those two admirable gifts!

'However, let us forget personalities. . . . There are better things here!'

As he spoke two young Russian officers came tumbling up the stairs. They were talking excitedly, not listening to one another, red in the face and tripping over their swords. They went up to the next floor, their voices very shrill.

'So much for your sentimental Russia,' said Semyonov. He spoke very quietly. 'How I shall love to see these fools all toppled over, and then the fools who toppled them toppled in their turn.

'Durward, you're a fool too, but you're English, and at least you've got a conscience. I tell you, you'll see in these next months such cowardice, such selfishness, such meanness, such ignorance as the world has never known – and all in the name of Freedom! Why, they're chattering about Freedom already downstairs as hard as they can go!'

'As usual, Semyonov,' I answered hotly, 'you believe in the good of no one. If there's really a Revolution coming, which I still doubt, it may lead to the noblest liberation.'

'Oh, you're an ass!' he interrupted quietly. 'Nobility and the human race! I tell you, Ivan Andreievitch of the noble character, that the human race is rotten; that it is composed of selfishness, vice, and meanness; that it is hypocritical beyond the bounds of hypocrisy, and that of all mean cowardly nations on this earth the Russian nation is the meanest and most cowardly! . . . That fine talk of ours that you English slobber over! – a mere excuse for idleness, and you'll know it before another year is through. I despise mankind with a contempt that every day's fresh experience only the more justifies. Only once have I found some one who had a great soul, and she, too, if I had secured her, might have disappointed me. . . . No, my time is coming. I shall see at last my fellowmen in their true colours, and I shall even perhaps help them to display them. My worthy Markovitch, for example——'

'What about Markovitch?' I asked sharply.

He got up, smiling. He put his hand on my shoulder.

'He shall be driven by ghosts,' he answered, and turned off to the stairs.

He looked back for a moment. 'The funny thing is, I like you, Durward,' he said.

X

I remember very little of my return to my island that night. The world was horribly dark and cold, the red moon had gone, and a machine-gun pursued me all the way home like a barking dog. I crossed the bridge frankly with nerves so harassed, with so many private anxieties and so much public apprehension, with so overpowering a suspicion that every shadow held a rifle that my heart leapt in my breast, and I was suddenly sick with fear when some one stepped across the road and put his hand on my arm. You see I have nothing much to boast about myself. My relief was only slightly modified when I saw that it was the Rat. The Rat had changed! He stood, as though on purpose under the very faint grey light of the lamp at the end of the bridge, and seen thus, he did in truth seem like an apparition. He was excited of course, but there was more in his face than that. The real truth about him was, that he was filled with some determination, some purpose. He was like a child who is playing at being a burglar, his face had exactly that absorption, that obsessing pre-occupation.

'I've been waiting for you, Barin,' he said in his hoarse musical voice.

'What is it?' I asked.

'This is where I live,' he said, and he showed me a very dirty piece of paper. 'I think you ought to know.'

'Why?' I asked him.

'*Kto snaiet?* (who knows?). The Czar's gone and we are all free men. . . .'

I felt oddly that suddenly now he knew himself my master. That was now in his voice.

'What are you going to do with your freedom?' I asked.

He sighed.

'I shall have my duties now,' he said. 'I'm not a free man at all. I obey orders for the first time. The people are going to rule. I am the people.'

He paused. Then he went on very seriously. 'That is why, Barin, I give you that paper. I have friendly feelings towards you. I don't know what it is, but I am your brother. They may come and want to rob your house. Show them that paper.'

'Thank you very much,' I said. 'But I'm not afraid. There's nothing I mind them stealing. All the same I'm very grateful.'

He went on very seriously.

'There'll be no Czar now and no police. We will stop the war and all be rich.' He sighed. 'But I don't know that it will bring happiness.' He suddenly seemed to me forlorn and desolate and lonely, like a lost dog. I knew quite well that very soon, perhaps directly he had left me, he would plunder and murder and rob again.

But that night, the two of us alone on the island and everything so still, waiting for great events, I felt close to him and protective.

'Don't get knocked on the head, Rat,' I said, 'during one of your raids. Death is easily come by just now. Look after yourself.'

He shrugged his shoulders. '*Shto boodet, boodet* (what will be, will be). *Neechevo* (it's of no importance).' He had vanished into the shadows.

XI

I realise that the moment has come in my tale when the whole interest of my narrative centres in Markovitch. Markovitch is really the point of all my story as I have, throughout, subconsciously, recognised. The events of that wonderful Tuesday, when for a brief instant the sun of freedom really did seem to all of us to break through the clouds, that one day in all our lives when hopes, dreams, Utopias, fairy tales seemed to be sober and realistic fact, those events might be seen through the eyes of any of us. Vera, Nina, Grogoff, Semyonov, Lawrence, Bohun and I, all shared in them and all had our sensations and experiences. But my own were drab and ordinary enough, and from the others I had no account so full and personal and true as from Markovitch. He told me all about that great day afterwards, only a short time before that catastrophe that overwhelmed us all, and in his account there was all the growing suspicion and horror of disillusion that after-events fostered in him. But as he told me, sitting through the purple hours of the night, watching the light break in ripples and circles of colour over the sea, he regained some of the splendours of that great day, and before he had finished his tale he was right back in that fantastic world that had burst at the touch like bubbles in the sun. I will give his account, as accurately as possible in his own words. I seldom interrupted him, and I think he soon forgot that I was there. He had come to me that night in a panic, for reasons which will be given later, and I, in trying to reassure him, had reminded him of that day, when the world was suddenly Utopia.

'That *did* exist, that world,' I said. 'And once having existed it cannot now be dead. Believe, believe that it will come back.'

'Come back!' He shook his head. 'Even if it is still there I cannot go back to it. I will tell you, Ivan Andreievitch, what that day was . . . and why now I am so bitterly punished for having believed in it. Listen what happened to me. It occurred, all of it, exactly as I tell you.

You know that, just at that time, I had been worrying very much about Vera. The Revolution had come, I suppose, very suddenly to every one; but truly to myself, because I had been thinking of Vera, it was like a thunder-clap. It's always been my trouble, Ivan Andreievitch, that I can't think of more than one thing at once, and the worry of it has been that in my life there has been almost invariably more than one thing that I ought to think of . . . I would think of my invention, you know, that I ought to get on with it a little faster. Because really it was making a sort of cloth out of bark that I was working at; as every day passed, I could see more and more clearly that there was a great deal in this particular invention, and that it only needed real application to bring it properly forward. Only application as you know is my trouble. If I could only shut my brain up. . . .'

He told me then, I remember, a lot about his early childhood, and then the struggle that he had had to see one thing at once, and not two or three things that got in the way and hindered him from doing anything. He went on about Vera.

'You know that one night I had crept up into your room, and looked to see whether there were possibly a letter there. That was a disgraceful thing to do, wasn't it? But I felt then that I had to satisfy myself. I wonder whether I can make you understand. It wasn't jealousy exactly, because I had never felt that I had had any very strong right over Vera, considering the way that she had married me; but I don't think I ever loved her more than I did during those weeks, and she was unattainable. I was lonely, Ivan Andreievitch, that's the truth. Everything seemed to be slipping away from me, and in some way Alexei Petrovitch Semyonov seemed to accentuate that. He was always reminding me of one day or another when I had been happy with Vera long ago – some silly little expedition we had taken – or he was doubtful about my experiments being any good, or he would recall what I had felt about Russia at the beginning of the war. . . . All in a very kindly way, mind you. He was more friendly than he had ever been, and seemed to be altogether softer-hearted. But he made me think a great deal about Vera. He talked often so much. He thought that I ought to look after her more, and I explained that that wasn't my right.

'The truth is that ever since Nina's birthday-party I had been anxious. I knew really that everything was right. Vera is of course the soul of honour – but something had occurred then which made me. . . .

'Well, well, that doesn't matter now. The only point is that I was thinking of Vera a great deal, and wondering how I could make her happy. She wasn't happy. I don't know how it was, but during those weeks just before the Revolution we were none of us happy. We were all uneasy as though we expected something were going to happen – and we were all suspicious. . . .

'I only tell you this because then you will see why it was that the Revolution broke upon me with such surprise. I had been right inside myself, talking to nobody, wanting nobody to talk to me. I get like that sometimes, when words seem to mean so much that it seems dangerous to throw them about. . . . And perhaps it is. But silence is dangerous too. Everything is dangerous if you are unlucky by nature. . . .

'I had been indoors all that Monday working at my invention, and thinking about Vera, wondering whether I'd speak to her, then afraid of my temper (I have a bad temper), wanting to know what was the truth, thinking at one moment that if she cared for some one else I'd go away . . . and then suddenly angry and jealous, wishing to challenge him, but I am a ludicrous figure to challenge any one, as I very well know. Semyonov had been to see me that morning, and he had just sat there without saying anything. I couldn't endure that very long, so I asked him what he came for and he said, "Oh, nothing." I felt as though he were spying and I became uneasy. Why should he come so often now? And I was beginning to think of him when he wasn't there. It was as though he thought he had a right over all of us, and that irritated me. . . . Well, that was Monday. They all came late in the afternoon and told me all the news. They had been at the Astoria. The whole town seemed to be in revolt, so they said.

'But even then I didn't realise it. I was thinking of Vera just the same. I looked at her all the evening just as Semyonov had looked at me. And didn't say anything. . . . I never wanted her so badly before. I made her sleep with me all that night. She hadn't done that for a long time, and I woke up early in the morning to hear her crying softly to herself. She never used to cry. She was so proud. I put my arms round her, and she stopped crying and lay quite still. It wasn't fair what I did, but I felt as though Alexei Petrovitch had challenged me to do it. He always hated Vera I knew. I got up very early and went to my wood. You can imagine I wasn't very happy. . . .

'Then suddenly I thought I'd go out into the streets, and see what was happening. I couldn't believe really that there had been any change. So I went out.

'Do you know of recent years I've walked out very seldom? What was it? A kind of shyness. I knew when I was in my own house, and I knew whom I was with. Then I was never a man who cared greatly about exercise, and there was no one outside whom I wanted very much to see. So when I went out that morning it was as though I didn't know Petrograd at all, and had only just arrived there. I went over the Ekateringofsky Bridge, through the Square, and to the left down the Sadovaya.

'Of course the first thing that I noticed was that there were no trams, and that there were multitudes of people walking along and that they were all poor people and all happy. And I *was* glad when I saw that. Of course I'm a fool, and life can't be as I want it, but that's always what I had thought life ought to be – all the streets filled with poor people, all free and happy. And here they were! . . . with the snow crisp under their feet, and the sun shining, and the air quite still, so that all the talk came up, and up into the sky like a song. But of course they were bewildered as well as happy. They didn't know where to go, they didn't know what to do – like birds let out suddenly from their cages. I didn't know myself. That's what sudden freedom does – takes your breath away so that you go staggering along, and get caught again if you're not careful. No trams, no policemen, no carriages filled with proud people cursing you. . . . Oh, Ivan Andreievitch, I'd be proud myself if I had money, and servants to put on my clothes, and new women every night, and different food every day. . . . I don't blame them – but suddenly proud people were gone, and I was crying without knowing it – simply because that great crowd of poor people went pushing along, all talking under the sunny sky as freely as they pleased.

'I began to look about me. I saw that there were papers posted on the walls. They were those proclamations, you know, of Rodziancko's new government, saying that while everything was unsettled, Milyukoff, Rodziancko, and the others would take charge in order to keep order and discipline. It seemed to me that there was little need to talk about discipline. Had beggars appeared there in the road I believed that the crowd would have stripped off their clothes and given them, rather than that they should want.

'I stood by one proclamation and read it out to the little crowd. They repeated the names to themselves, but they did not seem to care much. "The Czar's wicked they tell me," said one man to me. "And all our troubles come from him."

'"It doesn't matter," said another. "There'll be plenty of bread now."

'And indeed what did names matter now? I couldn't believe my eyes or my ears, Ivan Andreievitch. It looked too much like Paradise and I'd been deceived so often. So I determined to be very cautious. "You've been taken in, Nicolai Leontievitch, many many times. Don't you believe this." But I couldn't help feeling that if only this world would continue, if only the people could always be free and happy and the sun could shine, perhaps the rest of the world would see its folly and the war would stop and never begin again. This thought would grow in my mind as I walked, although I refused to encourage it.

'Motor lorries covered with soldiers came dashing down the street. The soldiers had their guns pointed, but the crowd cheered and cheered, waving hands and shouting. I shouted too. The tears were streaming down my face. I couldn't help myself. I wanted to hold the sun and the snow and the people all in my arms fixed so that it should never change, and the world should see how good and innocent life could be.

'On every side people had asked what had really happened, and of course no one knew. But it did not matter. Every one was so simple. A soldier standing beside one of the placards was shouting: "*Tovaristchi!* What we must have is a splendid Republic and a good Czar to look after it."

'And they all cheered him and laughed and sang. I turned up one of the side streets on to the Fontanka, and here I saw them emptying the rooms of one of the police. That was amusing! I laugh still when I think of it. Sending everything out of the windows, – underclothes, ladies' bonnets, chairs, books, flower-pots, pictures, and then all the records, white and yellow and pink paper, all fluttering in the sun like so many butterflies. The crowd was perfectly peaceful, in an excellent temper. Isn't that wonderful when you think that for months those people had been starved and driven, waiting all night in the street for a piece of bread, and that now all discipline was removed, no more policemen except those hiding for their lives in houses, and yet they did nothing, they touched no one's property, did no man any harm? People say now that it was their apathy, that they were taken by surprise, that they were like animals who did not know where to go, but I tell you, Ivan Andreievitch, that it was not so. I tell you that it was because just for an hour the soul could come up from its dark waters and breathe the sun and the light and see that all was good. Oh, why cannot that day return? Why cannot that day return? . . .'

He broke off and looked at me like a distracted child, his brows puckered, his hands beating the air. I did not say anything. I wanted him to forget that I was there.

He went on: '... I could not be there all day, I thought that I would go on to the Duma. I flowed on with the crowd. We were a great river swinging without knowing why, in one direction and only interrupted, once and again, by the motor lorries that rattled along, the soldiers shouting to us and waving their rifles, and we replying with cheers. I heard no firing that morning at all. They said, in the crowd, that many thousands had been killed last night. It seemed that on the roof of nearly every house in Petrograd there was a policeman with a machine-gun. But we marched along, without fear, singing. And all the time the joy in my heart was rising, rising, and I was checking it, telling myself that in a moment I would be disappointed, that I would soon be tricked as I had been so often tricked before. But I couldn't help my joy, which was stronger than myself. ...

'It must have been early afternoon, so long had I been on the road, when I came at last to the Duma. You saw yourself, Ivan Andreievitch, that all that week the crowd outside the Duma was truly a sea of people with the motor lorries that bristled with rifles for sea-monsters and the gun-carriages for ships. And such a babel! Every one talking at once and nobody listening to any one.

'I don't know now how I pushed through into the Court, but at last I was inside and found myself crushed up against the doors of the Palace by a mob of soldiers and students. Here there was a kind of hush.

'When the door of the Palace opened there was a little sigh of interest. At intervals armed guards marched up with some wretched pale dirty Gorodovoi whom they had taken prisoner——'

Nicholas Markovitch paused again and again. He had been looking out to the sea over whose purple shadows the sky pale green and studded with silver stars seemed to wave magic shuttles of light, to and fro, backwards and forwards.

'You don't mind all these details, Ivan Andreievitch? I am trying to discover, for my own sake, all the details that led me to my final experience. I want to trace the chain link by link . . . nothing is unimportant. ...'

I assured him that I was absorbed by his story. And indeed I was. That little, uncouth, lost, and desolate man was the most genuine human being whom I had ever known. That quality, above all others, stood forth in him. He had his secret as all men have their secret, the key to their pursuit of their own immortality. . . . But Markovitch's secret was a real one, something that he faced with real bravery, real pride, and real dignity, and when he saw what the issue of his conduct must be he would, I knew, face it without flinching.

He went on, but looking at me now rather than the sea – looking at me with his grave, melancholy, angry eyes. '. . . After one of these convoys of prisoners the door remained for a moment open, and I seeing my chance slipped in after the guards. Here I was then in the very heart of the Revolution; but still, you know, Ivan Andreievitch, I couldn't properly seize the fact, I couldn't grasp the truth that all this was really occurring and that it wasn't just a play, a pretence, or a dream . . . yes, a dream . . . especially a dream . . . perhaps, after all, that was what it was. The Circular Hall was piled high with machine-guns, bags of flour, and provisions of all kinds. There were some armed soldiers of course and women, and beside the machine-guns the floor was strewn with cigarette ends and empty tins and papers and bags and cardboard boxes and even broken bottles. Dirt and Desolation! I remember that it was then when I looked at that floor that the first little suspicion stole into my heart – not a suspicion so much as an uneasiness. I wanted at once myself to set to work to clean up all the mess with my own hands.

'I didn't like to see it there, and no one caring whether it were there or no.

'In the Catherine Hall into which I peered there was a vast mob, and this huge mass of men stirred and coiled and uncoiled like some huge ant-heap. Many of them, as I watched, suddenly turned into the outer hall. Men jumped on to chairs and boxes and balustrades, and soon all over the place there were speakers, some shouting, some shrieking, some with tears rolling down their cheeks, some swearing, some whispering as though to themselves . . . and all the regiments came pouring in from the station, tumbling in like puppies or babies with pieces of red cloth tied to their rifles, some singing, some laughing, some dumb with amazement . . . thicker and thicker and thicker . . . standing round the speakers with their mouths open and their eyes wide, pushing and jostling, but good-naturedly, like young dogs.

'Everywhere, you know, men were forming committees, committees for social right, for a just Peace, for Women's Suffrage, for Finnish Independence, for literature and the arts, for the better treatment of prostitutes, for education, for the just division of the land. I had crept into my corner, and soon, as the soldiers came thicker and thicker, the noise grew more and more deafening, the dust floated in hazy clouds. The men had their kettles and they boiled tea, squatting down there, sometimes little processions pushed their way through, soldiers shouting and laughing with some white-faced policeman in their midst. Once I saw an old man, his Shuba about his ears, stumbling with his eyes wide open, and staring as though he were sleep-walking. That was Stürmer being brought to judgement. Once I saw a man so terrified that he couldn't move, but must be prodded along by the rifles of the soldiers. That was Pitirim. . . .

'And the shouting and screaming rose and rose like a flood. Once Rodziancko came in and began shouting, "*Tovaristchi! Tovaristchi!* . . ." but his voice soon gave away, and he went back into the Salle Catherine again. The Socialists had it their way. There were so many, and their voices were so fresh, and the soldiers liked to listen to them. "Land for everybody! "they shouted. "And Bread and Peace! Hurrah! Hurrah!" cried the soldiers.

'"That's all very well," said a huge man near me. "But Nicholas is coming, and tomorrow he will eat us all up!"

'But no one seemed to care. They were all mad, and I was mad too. It was the drunkenness of dust. It got in our heads and our brains. We all shouted. I began to shout too, although I didn't know what it was that I was shouting.

'A grimy soldier caught me round the neck and kissed me. "Land for everybody!" he cried. "Have some tea, *Tovaristch!*" and I shared his tea with him.

'Then through the dust and noise I suddenly saw Boris Grogoff! That was an astonishing thing. You see I had dissociated all this from my private life. I had even, during these last hours, forgotten Vera, perhaps for the very first moment since I met her. She had seemed to have no share in this, – and then suddenly the figure of Boris showed me that one's private life is always with one, that it is a secret city in which one must always live, and whose gates one will never pass through, whatever may be going on in the world outside. But Grogoff! What a change! You know, I had always patronised him, Ivan Andreievitch. It had seemed to me that he was only a boy with a boy's crude ideas. You know his fresh face with the way that he used to push back his hair from his forehead, and shout his ideas. He never considered any one's feelings. He was a complete egoist, and a man, it seemed to me, of no importance. But now! He stood on a bench and had around him a large crowd of soldiers. He was shouting in just his old way that he used in the English Prospect, but he seemed to have grown in the meantime, into a man. He did not seem afraid any more. I saw that he had power over the men to whom he was speaking. . . . I couldn't hear what he said, but through the dust and heat he seemed to grow and grow until it was only him whom I saw there.

'"He will carry off Nina" was my next thought – ludicrous there at such a time, in such a crowd, but it is exactly like that that life shifts and shifts until it has formed a pattern. I was frightened by Grogoff. I could not believe that the new freedom, the new Russia, the new world would be made by such men. He waved his arms, he pushed back his hair, the men shouted. Grogoff was triumphant: "The New World . . . *Novaya Jezn, Novaya Jezn!*" (New Life!) I heard him shout.

'The sun before it set flooded the hall with light. What a scene through the dust! The red flags, the women and the soldiers and the shouting!

'I was suddenly dismayed. "How can order come out of this?" I thought. "They are all mad. . . . Terrible things are going to happen." I was dirty and tired and exhausted. I fought my way through the mob, found the door. For a moment I looked back, to that sea of men lit by the last light of the sun. Then I pushed out, was thrown, it seemed to me, from man to man, and was at last in the air. . . . Quiet, fires burning in the courtyard, a sky of the palest blue, a few stars, and the people singing the "Marseillaise."

'It was like drinking great draughts of cold water after an intolerable thirst. . . .

'. . . Hasn't Tchekov said somewhere that Russians have nostalgia but no patriotism? That was never true of me – I can't remember how young I was when I remember my father talking to me about the idea of Russia. I've told you that he was by any kind of standard a bad man. He had, I think, no redeeming points at all – but he had, all the same, that sense of Russia. I don't suppose that he put it to any practical use, or that he even tried to teach it to his pupils, but it would suddenly seize him and he would let himself go, and for an hour he would be a fine master – of words. And what Russian is ever more than that at the end?

'He spoke to me and gave me a picture of a world inside a world, and this inside world was complete in itself. It had everything in it – beauty, wealth, force, power; it could be anything, it could do anything. But it was held by an evil enchantment as though a wicked magician had it in thrall, and everything slept as in Tchaikowsky's Ballet. But one day, he told me, the Prince would come and kill the Enchanter, and this great world would come into its own. I remember that I was so excited that I couldn't bear to wait, but prayed that I might be allowed to go out and find the Enchanter . . . but my father laughed and said that there were no Enchanters now, and then I cried. All the same I never lost my hope. I talked to people about Russia, but it was never Russia itself they seemed to care for – it was women or drink or perhaps freedom and socialism, or perhaps some part of Russia, Siberia, or the Caucasus – but my world they none of them believed in. It didn't exist, they said. It was simply my imagination that had painted it, and they laughed at me and said it was held together by the lashes of the knout, and when those went Russia would go too. As I grew up some of them thought that I was revolutionary, and they tried to make me join their clubs and societies. But those were no use to me. They couldn't give me what I wanted. They wanted to destroy, to assassinate some one, or to blow up a building. They had no thought beyond destruction, and that to me seemed only the first step. And they never think of Russia, our revolutionaries. You will have noticed that yourself, Ivan Andreievitch. Nothing so small and trivial as Russia! It must be the whole world or nothing at all. Democracy. . . Freedom . . . the Brotherhood of Man! Oh, the terrible harm that words have done to Russia! Had the Russians of the last fifty years been born without the gift of speech we would be now the greatest people on the earth!

'But I loved Russia from end to end. The farthest villages in Siberia, the remotest hut beyond Archangel, from the shops in the Sadovaya to the Lavra at Kieff, from the little villages on the bank of the Volga to the woods round Tarnopol – all, all one country, one people, one world within a world. The old man to whom I was secretary discovered this secret hope of mine. I talked one night when I was drunk and told him everything. I mentioned even the Enchanter and the Sleeping Beauty! How he laughed at me! He would never leave me alone. "Nicolai Leontievitch believes in Holy Russia! "he would say. "Not so much Holy, you understand, as Bewitched. A Fairy Garden, ladies, with a sleeping beauty in the middle of it. Dear me, Nicolai Leontievitch, no wonder you are heart-free!"

'How I hated him and his yellow face and his ugly stomach! I would have stamped on it with delight. But that made me shy. I was afraid to speak of it to any one, and I kept to myself. Then Vera came and she didn't laugh at me. The two ideas grew together in my head. Vera and Russia! The two things in my life by which I stood – because man must have something in life round which he may nestle as a cat curls up by the fire.

'But even Vera did not seem to care for Russia as Russia. "What can Siberia be to me?" she would say. "Why, Nicholas, it is no more than China."

'But it was more than China; when I looked at it on the map I recognised it as though it were my own country. Then the war came and I thought the desire of my heart was fulfilled. At last men talked about Russia as though she truly existed. For a moment all Russia was united, all classes, rich and poor, high and low. Men were patriotic together as though one heart beat through all the land. But only for a moment. Divisions came, and quickly things were worse than before. There came Tannenberg and afterwards Warsaw.

'All was lost. . . . Russia was betrayed, and I was a sentimental fool. You know yourself how cynical even the most sentimental Russians are – that is because if you stick to facts you know where you are, but ideas are always betraying you. Life simply isn't long enough to test them, that's all, and man is certainly not a patient animal.

'At first I watched the war going from bad to worse, and then I shut myself in and refused to look any longer. I thought only of Vera and my work. I would make a great discovery and be rich, and then Vera at last would love me. Idiot! As though I had not known that Vera would not love for that kind of reason. . . . I determined that I would think no more of Russia, that I would be a man of no country. Then during those last weeks before the Revolution I began to be suspicious of Vera and to watch her. I did things of which I was ashamed, and then I despised myself for being ashamed.

'I am a man, I can do what I wish. Even though I am imprisoned I am free. . . . I am my own master. But all the same, to be a spy is a mean thing, Ivan Andreievitch. You Englishmen, although you are stupid you are not mean. It was that day when your young friend, Bohun, found me looking in your room for letters, that in spite of myself I was ashamed.

'He looked at me in a sort of way as though, down to his very soul, he was astonished at what I had done. Well, why should I mind that he should be astonished? He was very young and all wrong in his ideas of life. Nevertheless that look of his influenced me. I thought about it afterwards. Then came Alexei Petrovitch. I've told you already. He was always hinting at something. He was always there as though he were waiting for something to happen. He hinted things about Vera. It's strange, Ivan Andreievitch, but there was a day, just a week before the Revolution, when I was very nearly jumping up and striking him. Just to get rid of him so that he shouldn't be watching me. . . . Why, even when I wasn't there he. . . .

'But what's that got to do with my walk? Nothing perhaps. All the same, it was all these little things that made me, when I walked out of the Duma that evening, so queer. You see I'd been getting desperate. All that I had left was being taken from me, and then suddenly this Revolution had come and given me back Russia again. I forgot Alexei Petrovitch and your Englishman Lawrence and the failure of my work – I remembered, once again, just as I had those first days of the war, Vera and Russia.

'There, in the clear evening air, I forgot all the talk there had been inside the Duma, the mess and the noise and the dust. I was suddenly happy again, and excited, and hopeful. . . . The Enchanter had come after all, and Russia was to awake.

'Ah, what a wonderful evening that was! You know that there have been times – very, very rare occasions in one's life – when places that one knows well, streets and houses so common and customary as to be like one's very skin – are suddenly for a wonderful half-hour places of magic, the trees are gold, the houses silver, the bricks jewelled, the pavement of amber. Or simply perhaps they are different, a new country of new colour and mystery . . . when one is just in love or has won some prize, or finished at last some difficult work. Petrograd was like that to me that night; I swear to you, Ivan Andreievitch, I did not know where I was. I seem now on looking back to have been in places that night, magical places, that by the morning had flown away. I could not tell you where I went. I know that I must have walked for miles. I walked with a great many people who were all my brothers. I had drunk nothing, not even water, and yet the effect on me was exactly as though I were drunk, drunk with happiness, Ivan Andreievitch, and with the possibility of all the things that might now be.

'We, many of us, marched along, singing the "Marseillaise," I suppose. There was firing, I think, in some of the streets, because I can remember now on looking back that once or twice I heard a machine-gun quite close to me and didn't care at all, and even laughed. . . . Not that I've ever cared for that. Bullets aren't the sort of things that frighten me. There are other terrors. . . . All the same it was curious that we should all march along as though there were no danger and the peace of the world had come. There were women with us – quite a number of them, I think – and, I believe, some children. I remember that some of the way I carried a child, fast asleep in my arms. How ludicrous it would be now if I, of all men in the world, carried a baby down the Nevski! But it was quite natural that night. The town seemed to me blazing with light. Of course that it cannot have been; there can have only been the stars and some bonfires. And perhaps we stopped at the police-courts which were crackling away. I don't remember that, but I know that somewhere there were clouds of golden sparks opening into the sky and mingling with the stars – a wonderful sight, flocks of golden birds and behind them a roar of sound like a torrent of water. . . . I know that, most of the night, I had one man especially for my companion. I can see him quite clearly now, although whether it is all my imagination or not I can't say. Certainly I've never seen him since and never will again. He was a peasant, a bigly made man, very neatly and decently dressed in a workman's blouse and black trousers. He had a long black beard and was grave and serious, speaking very little but watching everything. Kindly, our best type of peasant – perhaps the type that will one day give Russia her real freedom . . . one day . . . a thousand years from now. . . .

'I don't know why it is that I can still see him so clearly, because I can remember no one else of that night, and even this fellow may have been my imagination. But I think that, as we walked along, I talked to him about Russia and how the whole land now from Archangel to Vladivostock might be free and be one great country of peace and plenty, first in all the world.

'It seemed to me that every one was singing, men and women and children. . . .

'We must, at last, have parted from most of the company. I had come with my friend into the quieter streets of the city. Then it was that I suddenly smelt the sea. You must have noticed how Petrograd is mixed up with the sea, how suddenly, where you never would expect it, you see the masts of ships all clustered together against the sky. I smelt the sea, the wind blew fresh and strong and there we were on the banks of the Neva. Everywhere there was perfect silence. The Neva lay tranquil, bound under its ice. The black hulks of the ships lay against the white shadows like sleeping animals. The curve of the sky, with its multitude of stars, was infinite.

'My friend embraced me and left me and I stayed alone, so happy, so sure of the peace of the world that I did what I had not done for years – sent up a prayer of gratitude to God. Then with my head on my hands, looking down at the masts of the ships, feeling Petrograd behind me with its lights as though it were the City of God, I burst into tears – tears of happiness and joy and humble gratitude. . . . I have no memory of anything further.'

XII

So much for the way that one Russian saw it. There were others. For instance, Vera. . . .

I suppose that the motive of Vera's life was her pride. Quite early, I should imagine, she had adopted that as the sort of talisman that would save her from every kind of ill. She told me once that when she was a little girl, the story of the witch who lured two children into the wood and then roasted them in her oven had terrified her beyond all control, and she would lie awake and shiver for hours because of it. It became a symbol of life to her – the Forest was there and the Oven and the Witch – and so clever and subtle was the Witch that the only way to outwit her was by pride. Then there was also her maternal tenderness; it was through that that Markovitch won her. She had not of course loved him – she had never pretended to herself that she had – but she had seen that he wanted caring for, and then, having taken the decisive step, her pride had come to her aid, had shown her a glimpse of the Witch waiting in the Forest darkness, and had proved to her that here was her great opportunity. She had then, with the easy superiority of a young girl, ignorant of life, dismissed love as of something that others might care for but that would, in no case, concern herself. Did Love for a moment smile at her or beckon to her, Pride came to her and showed her Nina and Nicholas, and that was enough.

But Love knows his power. He suddenly put forth his strength and Vera was utterly helpless – far more helpless than a Western girl with her conventional code and traditional training would have been. Vera had no convention and no tradition. She had only her pride and her maternal instinct and these, for a time, fought a battle for her . . . then they suddenly deserted her.

I imagine that they really deserted her on the night of Nina's birthday-party, but she would not admit defeat so readily, and fought on for a little. On this eventful week when the world, as we knew it, was tumbling about our ears, she had told herself that the only thing to which she must give a thought was her fixed loyalty to Nina and Nicholas. She would not think of Lawrence. . . . She would not think of him. And so resolving, thought of him all the more.

By Wednesday morning her nerves were exhausted. The excitements of this week came as a climax to many months of strain. With the exception of her visit to the Astoria she had been out scarcely at all and, although the view from her flat was peaceful enough she could imagine every kind of horror beyond the boundaries of the Prospect – and in every horror Lawrence figured.

There occurred that morning a strange little conversation between Vera, Semyonov, Nicholas Markovitch, and myself. I arrived about ten o'clock to see how they were and to hear the news. I found Vera sitting quietly at the table sewing. Markovitch stood near to her, his anxious eyes and trembling mouth perched on the top of his sharp peaky collar and his hands rubbing nervously one within another. He was obviously in a state of very great excitement. Semyonov sat opposite Vera, leaning his thick body on his arms, his eyes watching his niece and every once and again his firm pale hand stroking his beard.

When I joined them he said to me:

'Well, Ivan Andreievitch, what's the latest news of your splendid Revolution?'

'Why my Revolution?' I asked. I felt an especial dislike this morning of his sneering eyes and his thick pale honey-coloured beard. 'Whose ever it was he should be proud of it. To see thousands of people who've been hungry for months wandering about as I've seen them this morning and none of them touching a thing – it's stupendous!'

Semyonov smiled but said nothing. His smile irritated me. 'Oh, of course you sneer at the whole thing, Alexei Petrovitch!' I said. 'Anything fine in human nature excites your contempt as I know of old.'

I think that that was the first time that Vera had heard me speak to him in that way, and she looked up at me with sudden surprise and I think gratitude.

Semyonov treated me with complete contempt. He answered me slowly: 'No, Ivan Andreievitch, I don't wish to deprive you of any kind of happiness. I wouldn't for worlds. But do you know our people, that's the question? You haven't been here very long; you came loaded up with romantic notions, some of which you've discarded but only that you may pick up others. . . . I don't want to insult you at all, but you simply don't know that the Christian virtues that you are admiring just now so extravagantly are simply cowardice and apathy. . . . Wait a little! Wait a little! and then tell me whether I've not been right.'

There was a moment's pause like the hush before the storm, and then Markovitch broke in upon us. I can see and hear him now, standing there behind Vera with his ridiculous collar and his anxious eyes. The words simply pouring from him in a torrent, his voice now rising into a shrill scream, now sinking into a funny broken bass like the growl of a young baby tiger. And yet he was never ridiculous. I've known other mortals, and myself one of the foremost, who, under the impulse of some sudden anger, enthusiasm, or regret, have been simply figures of fun. . . . Markovitch was never that. He was like a dying man fighting for possession of the last plank. I can't at this distance of time remember all that he said. He talked a great deal about Russia; while he spoke I noticed that he avoided Semyonov's eyes, which never for a single instant left his face.

'Oh, don't you see, don't you see?' he cried. 'Russia's chance has come back to her? We can fight now a holy, patriotic war. We can fight, not because we are told to by our masters, but because we, of our own free will, wish to defend the soil of our sacred country. *Our* country! No one has thought of Russia for the last two years – we have thought only of ourselves, our privations, our losses – but now – now. O God! The world may be set free again because Russia is at last free!'

'Yes,' said Semyonov quietly (his eyes covered Markovitch's face as a searchlight finds out the running figure of a man). 'And who has spoken of Russia during the last few days? Russia! Why, I haven't heard the word mentioned once. I may have been unlucky, I don't know. I've been out and about the streets a good deal . . . I've listened to a great many conversations. . . . Democracy, yes, and Brotherhood and Equality and Fraternity and Bread and Land and Peace and Idleness – but Russia! Not a sound . . .'

'It will come! It will come!' Markovitch urged. 'It *must* come! You didn't walk, Alexei, as I did last night, through the streets, and see the people and hear their voices and see their faces. . . . Oh! I believe that at last good has come to the world, and happiness and peace; and it is Russia who will lead the way. . . . Thank God! Thank God!' Even as he spoke some instinct in me urged me to try and prevent him. I felt that Semyonov would not forget a word of this, and would make his own use of it in the time to come. I could see the purpose in Semyonov's eyes. I almost called out to Nicholas, 'Look out! Look out!' just as though a man were standing behind him with a raised weapon. . . .

'You really mean this?' asked Semyonov.

'Of course I mean it!' cried Markovitch. 'Do I not sound as though I did?'

'I will remind you of it one day,' said Semyonov.

I saw that Markovitch was trembling with excitement from head to foot. He sat down at the table near Vera and put one hand on the tablecloth to steady himself. Vera suddenly covered his hand with hers as though she were protecting him. His excitement seemed to stream away from him, as though Semyonov were drawing it out of him.

He suddenly said:

'You'd like to take my happiness away from me if you could, Alexei. You don't want me to be happy.'

'What nonsense!' Semyonov said, laughing. 'Only I like the truth – I simply don't see the thing as you do. I have my view of us Russians. I have watched since the beginning of the war. I think our people lazy and selfish – I think you must drive them with a whip to make them do anything. I think they would be ideal under German rule, which is what they'll get if their Revolution lasts long enough . . . that's all.'

I saw that Markovitch wanted to reply, but he was trembling so that he could not.

He said at last: 'You leave me alone, Alexei; let me go my own way.'

'I have never tried to prevent you,' said Semyonov.

There was a moment's silence.

Then, in quite another tone, he remarked to me: 'By the way, Ivan Andreievitch, what about your friend Mr. Lawrence? He's in a position of very considerable danger where he is with Wilderling. They tell me Wilderling may be murdered at any moment.'

Some force stronger than my will drove me to look at Vera. I saw that Nicolai Leontievitch also was looking at her. She raised her eyes for an instant, her lips moved as though she were going to speak, then she looked down again at her sewing.

Semyonov watched us all. 'Oh, he'll be all right,' I answered. 'If any one in the world can look after himself it's Lawrence.'

'That's all very well,' said Semyonov, still looking at Markovitch. 'But to be in Wilderling's company this week is a very unhealthy thing for any one. And that type of Englishman is not noted for cowardice.'

'I tell you that Lawrence can look after himself,' I insisted angrily.

Semyonov knew and Markovitch knew that I was speaking to Vera. No one then said a word. There was a long pause. At last Semyonov saw fit to go.

'I'm off to the Duma,' he said. 'There's a split, I believe. And I want to hear whether it's true that the Czar's abdicated.'

'I believe you'd rather he hadn't, Alexei Petrovitch,' Markovitch broke in fiercely.

He laughed at us all and said, 'Whose interests am I studying? My own? . . . Holy Russia's? . . . Yours? . . . When will you learn, Nicholas, my friend, that I am a spectator, not a participator?'

Vera was alone during most of that day; and even now, after the time that has passed, I cannot bear to think of what she suffered. She realised quite definitely, and now with no chance whatever of self-deception, that she loved Lawrence with a force that no denial or sacrifice on her part could alter. She told me afterwards that she walked up and down that room for hours, telling herself again and again that she must not go and see whether he were safe. She did not dare even to leave the room. She felt that if she entered her bedroom the sight of her hat and coat there would break down her resolution, that if she went to the head of the stairs and listened she must then go farther and then farther again. She knew quite well that to go to him now would mean complete surrender. She had no illusions about that. The whole of her body was quivering with desire for his embrace, for the warm strength of his body, for the kindness in his eyes, and the compelling mastery of his hands.

She had never loved a man before; but it seemed to her now that she had known all these sensations always, and that she was now, at last, her real self, and that the earlier Vera had been a ghost. And what ghosts were Nina and Markovitch!

She told me afterwards that, on looking back, this seemed to her the most horrible part of the horrible afternoon. These two, who had been for so many years the very centre of her life, whom she had forced to hold up, as it were, the whole foundation of her existence, now simply were not real at all. She might call to them, and their voices were like far echoes or the wind. She gazed at them, and the colours of the room and the street seemed to shine through them. . . . She fought for their reality. She forced herself to recall all the many things that they had done together – Nina's little ways, the quarrels with Nicholas, the reconciliations, the times when he had been ill, the times when they had gone to the country, to the theatre . . . and through it all she heard

Semyonov's voice, 'By the way, what about your friend Lawrence? . . . He's in a position of very considerable danger . . . considerable danger . . . considerable danger . . .'

By the evening she was almost frantic. Nina had been with a girl friend in the Vassily Ostrov all day. She would perhaps stay there all night if there were any signs of trouble. No one returned. Only the clock ticked on. Old Sacha asked whether she might go out for an hour. Vera nodded her head. She was then quite alone in the flat.

Suddenly, about seven o'clock, Nina came in. She was tired, nervous, and unhappy. The Revolution had not come to *her* as anything but a sudden crumbling of all the life that she had known and believed in. She had had, that afternoon, to run down a side street to avoid a machine-gun, and afterwards on the Morskaia she had come upon a dead man huddled up in the snow like a piece of offal. These things terrified her and she did not care about the larger issues. Her life had been always intensely personal – not selfish so much as vividly egoistic through her vitality. And now she was miserable, not because she was afraid for her own safety, but because she was face to face, for the first time, with the unknown and the uncertain.

She came in, sat down at the table, put her head into her arms and burst into tears. She must have looked a very pathetic figure with her little fur hat askew, her hair tumbled – like a child whose doll is suddenly broken.

Vera was at her side in a moment. She put her arms around her.

'Nina, dear, what is it? . . . Has somebody hurt you? Has something happened? Is anybody – killed?'

'No! 'Nina sobbed. 'Nobody – nothing – only – I'm frightened. It all looks so strange. The streets are so funny, and – there was – a dead man on the Morskaia.'

'You shouldn't have gone out, dear. I oughtn't to have let you. But now we can just be cosy together. Sacha's gone out. There's no one here but ourselves. We'll have supper and make ourselves comfortable.'

Nina looked up, staring about her. 'Has Sacha gone out? Oh, I wish she hadn't! . . . Supposing somebody came.'

'No one will come. Who could? No one wants to hurt *us*! I've been here all the afternoon, and no one's come near the flat. If anybody did come we've only got to telephone to Nicholas. He's with Rozanov all the afternoon.'

'Nicholas!' Nina repeated scornfully. 'As though he could help anybody.' She looked up. Vera told me afterwards that it was at that moment, when Nina looked such a baby with her tumbled hair and her flushed cheeks stained with tears, that she realised her love for her with a fierceness that for a moment seemed to drown even her love for Lawrence. She caught her to her and hugged her, kissing her again and again.

But Nina was suspicious. There were many things that had to be settled between Vera and herself. She did not respond, and Vera let her go. She went into her room to take off her things.

Afterwards they lit the samovar and boiled some eggs and put the caviare and sausage and salt fish and jam on the table. At first they were silent, and then Nina began to recover a little.

'You know, Vera, I've had an extraordinary day. There were no trams running, of course, and I had to walk all the distance. When I got there I found Katerina Ivanovna in a terrible way because their Masha – whom they've had for years, you know – went to a Revolutionary meeting last evening, and was out all night, and she came in this morning and said she wasn't going to work for them any more, that every one was equal now, and that they must do things for themselves. Just fancy! When she's been with them for years and they've been so good to her. It upset Katerina Ivanovna terribly, because of course they couldn't get any one else, and there was no food in the house.'

'Perhaps Sacha won't come back again.'

'Oh, she must! *She's* not like that . . . and we've been so good to her. *Nu . . . Patom,* some soldiers came early in the afternoon and they said that some policeman had been firing from Katya's windows and they must search the flat. They were very polite – quite a young student was in charge of them, he was rather like Boris – and they went all over everything. They were very polite, but it wasn't nice seeing them stand there with their rifles in the middle of the dining-room. Katya offered them some wine, but they wouldn't touch it. They said they had been told not to, and they looked quite angry with her for offering it. They couldn't find the policeman anywhere, of course; but they told Katya they might have to burn the house down if they didn't find him. I think they just said it to amuse themselves. But Katya believed it, and was in a terrible way and began collecting all her china in the middle of the floor, and then Ivan came in and told her not to be silly.'

'Weren't you frightened to come home?' asked Vera.

'Ivan wanted to come with me but I wouldn't let him. I felt quite brave in the flat, as though I'd face anybody. And then every step I took outside I got more and more frightened. It was so strange, so quiet with the trams not running and the shops all shut. The streets are quite deserted except that in the distance you see crowds, and sometimes there were shots and people running. . . . Then suddenly I began to run. I felt as though there were animals in the canals and things crawling about on the ships. And then, just as I thought I was getting home, I saw a man, dead on the snow. . . . I'm not going out alone again until it's over. I'm so glad I'm back, Vera darling. We'll have a lovely evening.'

They both discovered then how hungry they were, and they had an enormous meal. It was very cosy with the curtains drawn and the wood crackling in the stove and the samovar chuckling. There was a plateful of chocolates, and Nina ate them all. She was quite happy now, and sang and danced about as they cleared away most of the supper, leaving the samovar and the bread and the jam and the sausage for Nicholas and Bohun when they came in.

At last Vera sat down in the old red arm-chair that had the holes and the places where it suddenly went flat, and Nina piled up some cushions and sat at her feet. For a time they were happy, saying very little, Vera softly stroking Nina's hair. Then, as Vera afterwards described it to me, 'Some fright or sudden dread of loneliness came into the room. It was exactly as though the door had opened and some one had joined us . . . and, do you know, I looked up and expected to see Uncle Alexei.'

However, of course, there was no one there; but Nina moved away a little, and then Vera, wanting to comfort her, tried to draw her closer, and then of course Nina (because she was like that) with a little peevish shrug of the shoulders drew even farther away. There was, after that, silence between them, an awkward ugly silence, piling up and up with discomfort until the whole room seemed to be eloquent with it.

Both their minds were, of course, occupied in the same direction, and suddenly Nina, who moved always on impulse and had no restraint, burst out:

'I must know how Andrey Stepanovitch (their name for Lawrence, because Jeremy had no Russian equivalent) 'is – I'm going to telephone.'

'You can't,' Vera said quietly. 'It isn't working – I tried an hour ago to get on to Nicholas.'

'Well then, I shall go off and find out,' said Nina, knowing very well that she would not.

'Oh, Nina, of course you mustn't. . . . You know you can't. Perhaps when Nicholas comes in he will have some news for us.'

'Why shouldn't I?'

'You know why not. What would he think? Besides, you're not going out into the town again to-night.'

'Oh, aren't I? And who's going to stop me?'

'I am,' said Vera.

Nina sprang to her feet. In her later account to me of this quarrel she said, 'You know, Durdles, I don't believe I ever loved Vera more than I did just then. In spite of her gravity she looked so helpless and as though she wanted loving so terribly. I could just have flung my arms round her and hugged her to death at the very moment that I was screaming at her. Why are we like that?'

At any rate Nina stood up there and stamped her foot, her hair hanging all about her face and her body quivering. 'Oh, you're going to keep me, are you? What right have you got over me? Can't I go and leave the flat at any moment if I wish, or am I to consider myself your prisoner? . . . *Tzuineeto, paja-lueesta* . . . I didn't know. I can only eat my meals with your permission, I suppose. I have to ask your leave before going to see my friends. . . . Thank you, I know now. But I'm not going to stand it. I shall do just as I please. I'm grown up. No one can stop me. . . .'

Vera, her eyes full of distress, looked helplessly about her. She never could deal with Nina when she was in these storms of rage, and today she felt especially helpless.

'Nina, dear . . . don't. . . . You know that it isn't so. You can go where you please, do what you please.'

'Thank you,' said Nina, tossing her head. 'I'm glad to hear it.'

'I know I'm tiresome very often. I'm slow and stupid. If I try you sometimes you must forgive me and be patient. . . . Sit down again and let's be happy. You know how I love you. Nina, darling . . . come again.'

But Nina stood there pouting. She was loving Vera so intensely that it was all that she could do to hold herself back, but her very love made her want to hurt. . . . 'It's all very well to say you love me, but you don't act as though you do. You're always trying to keep me in. I want to be free. And Andrey Stepanovitch. . . .'

They both paused at Lawrence's name. They knew that that was at the root of the matter between them, that it had been so for a long time, and that any other pretence would be false.

'You know I love him –' said Nina, 'and I'm going to marry him.'

I can see then Vera taking a tremendous pull upon herself as though she suddenly saw in front of her a gulf into whose depths, in another moment, she would fall. But my vision of the story, from this point, is Nina's.

Vera told me no more until she came to the final adventure of the evening. This part of the scene then is witnessed with Nina's eyes, and I can only fill in details which, from my knowledge of them both, I believe to have occurred. Nina knew, of course, what the effect of her announcement would be upon Vera, but she had not expected the sudden thin pallor which stole like a film over her sister's face, the withdrawal, the silence. She was frightened, so she went on recklessly. 'Oh, I know that he doesn't care for me yet. . . . I can see that of course. But he will. He must. He's seen nothing of me yet. But I am stronger than he, I can make him do as I wish. I *will* make him. You don't want me to marry him and I know why.'

She flung that out as a challenge, tossing her head scornfully, but nevertheless watching with frightened eyes her sister's face. Suddenly Vera spoke, and it was in a voice so stern that it was to Nina a new voice, as though she had suddenly to deal with some new figure whom she had never seen before.

'I can't discuss that with you, Nina. You can't marry because, as you say, he doesn't care for you – in that way. Also if he did it would be a very unhappy marriage. You would soon despise him. He is not clever in the way that you want a man to be clever. You'd think him slow and dull after a month with him. . . . And then he ought to beat you and he wouldn't. He'd be kind to you and then you'd be ruined. I can see now that I've always been too kind to you – indeed, every one has – and the result is, that you're spoilt and know nothing about life at all – or men. You are right. I've treated you as a child too long. I will do so no longer.'

Nina turned like a little fury, standing back from Vera as though she were going to spring upon her. 'That's it, is it?' she cried. 'And all because you want to keep him for yourself. I understand. I have eyes. You love him. You are hoping for an intrigue with him. . . . You love him! You love him! You love him! . . . and he doesn't love you and you are so miserable. . . .

Vera looked at Nina, then suddenly turned and burying her head in her hands sobbed, crouching in her chair. Then slipping from the chair, knelt catching Nina's knees, her head against her dress.

Nina was aghast, terrified – then in a moment overwhelmed by a surging flood of love so that she caught Vera to her, caressing her hair, calling her by her little name, kissing her again and again and again.

'Vērotchka – Vērotchka – I didn't mean anything. I didn't indeed. I love you. I love you. You know that I do. I was only angry and wicked. Oh, I'll never forgive myself. Vērotchka – get up – don't kneel to me like that . . .!'

She was interrupted by a knock on the outer hall door. To both of them that sound must have been terribly alarming. Vera said afterwards that 'at once we realised that it was the knock of some one more frightened than we were.'

In the first place, no one ever knocked; they always rang the rather rickety electric bell – and then the sound was furtive and hurried, and even frantic; 'as though,' said Vera, 'some one on the other side of the door was breathless.'

The sisters stood, close together, for quite a long time without moving. The knocking ceased and the room was doubly silent. Then suddenly it began again, very rapid and eager, but muffled, almost as though some one were knocking with a gloved hand.

Vera went then. She paused for a moment in the little hall, for again there was silence and she fancied that perhaps the intruder had given up the matter in despair. But, no – there it was again – and this third time seemed to her, perhaps because she was so close to it, the most urgent and eager of all. She went to the door and opened it. There was no light in the passage save the dim reflection from the lamp on the lower floor, and in the shadow she saw a figure cowering back into the corner behind the door.

'Who is it?' she asked. The figure pushed past her, slipping into their own little hall.

'But you can't come in like that,' she said, turning round on him.

'Shut the door!' he whispered. '*Bozhe moi! Bozhe moi. . . .* Shut the door.'

She recognised him then. He was the policeman from the corner of their street, a man whom they knew well. He had always been a pompous little man, stout and short of figure, kindly so far as they knew, although they had heard of him as cruel in the pursuit of his official duties. They had once talked to him a little and he explained: 'I wouldn't hurt a fly, God knows,' he had said, 'of myself, but a man likes to do his work efficiently – and there are so many lazy fellows about here.'

He prided himself, they saw, on a punctilious attention to duty. When he had to come there for some paper or other he was always extremely polite, and if they were going away he helped them about their passports. He told them on another occasion that 'he was pleased with life – although one never knew of course when it might come down upon one –'

Well, it had come down on him now. A more pitiful object Vera had never seen. He was dressed in a dirty black suit and wore a shabby fur cap; his padded overcoat was torn.

But the overwhelming effect of him was terror. Vera had never before seen such terror, and at once, as though the thing were an infectious disease, her own heart began to beat furiously. He was shaking so that the fur cap, which was too large for his head, waggled up and down over his eye in a ludicrous manner.

His face was dirty as though he had been crying, and a horrid pallid grey in colour.

His collar was torn, showing his neck between the folds of his overcoat.

Vera looked out down the stairs as though she expected to see something. The flat was perfectly still. There was not a sound anywhere. She turned back to the man again; he was crouching against the wall.

'You can't come in here,' she repeated. 'My sister and I are alone. What do you want? . . . What's the matter?'

'Shut the door! . . . . Shut the door! . . . Shut the door! . . ." he repeated.

She closed it. 'Now what is it?' she asked, and then, hearing a sound, turned to find that Nina was standing with wide eyes, watching.

'What is it?' Nina asked in a whisper.

'I don't know,' said Vera, also whispering. 'He won't tell me.'

He pushed past them then into the dining-room, looked about him for a moment, then sank into a chair as though his legs would no longer support him, holding on to the cloth with both hands.

The sisters followed him into the dining-room.

'Don't shiver like that!' said Vera; 'tell us why you've come in here?' . . .

His eyes looked past them, never still, wandering from wall to wall, from door to door.

'They're after me . . .' he said. 'That's it – I was hiding in our cupboard all last night and this morning. They were round there all the time breaking up our things. . . . I heard them shouting. They were going to kill me. I've done nothing – O God! what's that?'

'There's no one here,' said Vera, 'except ourselves.'

'I saw a chance to get away and I crept out. But I couldn't get far. . . . I knew you would be good-hearted . . . good-hearted. Hide me somewhere – anywhere! . . . and they won't come in here. Only until the evening. I've done no one any harm. . . . Only my duty. . . .'

He began to snivel, taking out from his coat a very dirty pocket-handkerchief and dabbing his face with it.

The odd thing that they felt, as they looked at him, was the incredible intermingling of public and private affairs. Five minutes before they had been passing through a tremendous crisis in their personal relationship. The whole history of their lives together, flowing through how many years, through how many phases, how many quarrels, and happiness and adventures had reached here a climax whose issue was so important that life between them could never be the same again.

So urgent had been the affair that during that hour they had forgotten the Revolution, Russia, the war. Moreover, always in the past, they had assumed that public life was no affair of theirs. The Russo-Japanese War, even the spasmodic revolt in 1905, had not touched them except as a wind of ideas which blew so swiftly through their private lives that they were scarcely affected by it.

Now in the person of that trembling, shaking figure at their table, the Revolution had come to them, and not only the Revolution, but the strange new secret city that Petrograd was . . . the whole ground was quaking beneath them.

And in the eyes of the fugitive they saw what terror of death really was. It was no tale read in a story-book, no recounting of an adventure by some romantic traveller, it was *here* with them in the flat and at any moment. . . .

It was then that Vera realised that there was no time to lose – something must be done at once.

'Who's pursuing you?' she asked quickly. 'Where are they?'

He got up and was moving about the room as though he was looking for a hiding-place.

'All the people. . . . Everybody!' He turned round upon them, suddenly striking, what seemed to them, a ludicrously grand attitude. 'Abominable! That's what it is. I heard them shouting that I had a machine-gun on the roof and was killing people. I had no machine-gun. Of course not. I wouldn't know what to do with one if I had one. But there they were. That's what they were shouting! And I've always done my duty. What's one to do? Obey one's superior officer? Of course, what he says one does. What's life for? . . . and then naturally one expects a reward. Things were going well with me, very well indeed – and then this comes. It's a degrading thing for a man to hide for a day and a night in a cupboard.' His teeth began to chatter then so that he could scarcely speak. He seemed to be shaking with ague.

He caught Vera's hand. 'Save me – save me!' he said. 'Put me somewhere. . . . I've done nothing disgraceful. They'll shoot me like a dog——'

The sisters consulted.

'What are we to do?' asked Nina. 'We can't let him go out to be killed.'

'No. But if we keep him here and they come in and find him, we shall all be involved. . . . It isn't fair to Nicholas or Uncle Ivan. . . .'

'We can't let him go out.'

'No, we can't,' Vera replied. She saw at once how impossible that was. Were he caught outside and shot they would feel that they had his death for ever on their souls.

'There's the linen cupboard,' she said.

She turned round to Nina. 'I'm afraid,' she said, 'if you hide here, you'll have to go into another cupboard. And it can only be for an hour or two. We couldn't keep you here all night.'

He said nothing except 'Quick. Take me.' Vera led him into her bedroom and showed him the place. Without another word he pressed in amongst the clothes. It was a deep cupboard, and, although he was a fat man, the door closed quite evenly.

It was suddenly as though he had never been. Vera went back to Nina.

They stood close to one another in the middle of the room, and talked in whispers.

'What are we going to do?'

'We can only wait!'

'They'll never dare to search your room, Vera.'

'One doesn't know now . . . everything's so different.'

'Vera, you *are* brave. Forgive me what I said just now. . . . I'll help you if you want——'

'Hush, Nina dear. Not that now. We've got to think – what's best. . . .'

They kissed very quietly, and then they sat down by the table and waited. There was simply nothing else to do.

Vera said that, during that pause, she could see the little policeman everywhere. In every part of the room she found him, with his fat legs and dirty, streaky face and open collar. The flat was heavy, portentous with his presence, as though it stood with a self-important finger on its lips saying, 'I've got a secret in here. *Such* a secret. You don't know what *I've* got. . . .'

They discussed in whispers as to who would come in first. Nicholas or Uncle Ivan or Bohun or Sacha? And supposing one of them came in while the soldiers were there? Who would be the most dangerous? Sacha? She would scream and give everything away. Suppose they had seen him enter and were simply waiting, on the cat-and-mouse plan, to catch him? That was an intolerable thought.

'I think,' said Nina, 'I must go and see whether there's any one outside.'

But there was no need for her to do that. Even as she spoke they heard the steps on the stairs; and instantly afterwards there came the loud knocking on their door. Vera pressed Nina's hand and went into the hall.

'*Kto tam* . . . Who's there?' she asked.

'Open the door! . . . The Workmen and Soldiers' Committee demand entrance in the name of the Revolution.'

She opened the door at once. During those first days of the Revolution they cherished certain melodramatic displays. Whether consciously or no they built on all the old French Revolution traditions, or perhaps it is that every Revolution produces of necessity the same clothing with which to cover its nakedness. A strange mixture of farce and terror were those detachments of so-called justice. At their head there was, as a rule, a student, often smiling and bespectacled. The soldiers themselves, from one of the Petrograd regiments, were frankly out for a good time and enjoyed themselves thoroughly, but, as is the Slavonic way, playfulness could pass with surprising suddenness to dead earnest – with, indeed, so dramatic a precipitance that the actors themselves were afterwards amazed. Of these 'little, regrettable mistakes 'there had already, during the week, been several examples. To Vera, with the knowledge of the contents of her linen-cupboard, the men seemed terrifying enough. Their leader was a fat and beaming student – quite a boy. He was very polite, saying '*Zdrastvuite,* and taking off his cap. The men behind him – hulking men from one of the Guards regiments – pushed about in the little hall like a lot of puppies, joking with one another, holding their rifles upside down, and making sudden efforts at a seriousness that they could not possibly sustain.

Only one of them, an older man with a thick black beard, was intensely grave, and looked at Vera with beseeching eyes, as though he longed to tell her the secret of his life.

'What can I do for you?' she asked the student.

'*Prosteete* . . . Forgive us.' He smiled and blinked at her, then put on his cap, clicked his heels, gave a salute, and took his cap off again. 'We wish to be in no way an inconvenience to you. We are simply obeying orders. We have instructions that a policeman is hiding in one of these flats. . . . We know, of course, that he cannot possibly be here. Nevertheless we are compelled . . . *Prosteete*. . . . What nice pictures you have!' he ended suddenly. It was then that Vera discovered that they were by this time in the dining-room, crowded together near the door and gazing at Nina with interested eyes.

'There's no one here, of course,' said Vera very quietly. 'No one at all.'

'*Tak Tochno* (quite so),' said the black-bearded soldier, for no particular reason, suddenly.

'You will allow me to sit down?' said the student very politely. 'I must, I am afraid, ask a few questions.'

'Certainly,' said Vera quietly. 'Anything you like.'

She had moved over to Nina, and they stood side by side. But she could not think of Nina, she could not think even of the policeman in the cupboard. . . . She could think only of that other house on the Quay where, perhaps even now, this same scene was being enacted. They had found Wilderling. . . . They had dragged him out. . . . Lawrence was beside him. . . . They were condemned together. . . . Oh! love had come to her at last in a wild, surging flood! Of all the steps she had been led until at last, only half an hour before in that scene with Nina, the curtains had been flung aside and the whole view revealed to her. She felt such a strength, such a pride, such a defiance, as she had not known belonged to human power. She had, for many weeks, been hesitating before the gates. Now, suddenly, she had swept through. His death now was not the terror that it had been only an hour before. Nina's accusation had shown her, as a flash of lightning flings the mountains into view, that now she could never lose him, were he with her or no, and that beside that truth nothing mattered.

Something of her bravery and grandeur and beauty must have been felt by them all at that moment. Nina realised it. . . . She told me that her own fear left her altogether when she saw how Vera was facing them. She was suddenly calm and quiet and very amused.

The student officer seemed now to be quite at home. He had taken a great many notes down in a little book, and looked very important as he did so. His chubby face expressed great self-satisfaction. He talked half to himself and half to Vera. 'Yes . . . Yes . . . quite so. Exactly. And your husband is not yet at home, Madame Markovitch. . . . *Nu da.* . . . Of course these are very troublesome times, and, as you say, things have to move in a hurry.

'You've heard perhaps that Nicholas Romanoff has abdicated entirely – and refused to allow his son to succeed. Makes things simpler. . . . Yes. . . . Very pleasant pictures you have – and Ostroffsky – six volumes. Very agreeable. I have myself acted in Ostroffsky at different times. I find his plays very enjoyable. I am sure you will forgive us, Madame, if we walk through your charming flat'

But indeed by this time the soldiers themselves had begun to roam about on their own account. Nina remembers one soldier in especial – a large dirty fellow with ragged moustache – who quite frankly terrified her. He seemed to regard her with particular satisfaction, staring at her, and, as it were, licking his lips over her. He wandered about the room fingering things, and seemed to be immensely interested in Nicholas's little den, peering through the glass window that there was in the door and rubbing the glass with his finger. He presently pushed the door open and soon they were all in there.

Then a characteristic thing occurred. Apparently Nicholas's inventions – his little pieces of wood and bark and cloth, his glass bottles, and tubes – seemed to them highly suspicious. There was laughter at first, and then sudden silence. Nina could see part of the room through the open door, and she watched them as they gathered round the little table, talking together in excited whispers. The tall, rough-looking fellow who had frightened her before picked up one of the tubes, and then, whether by accident or intention, let it fall, and the tinkling smash of the glass frightened them all so precipitately that they came tumbling out into the larger room. The big fellow whispered something to the student, who at once became more self-important than ever, and said very seriously to Vera:

'That is your husband's room, Madame, I understand?'

'Yes,' said Vera quietly, 'he does his work in there.'

'What kind of work?'

'He is an inventor.'

'An inventor of what?'

'Various things. . . . He is working at present on something to do with the making of cloth.'

Unfortunately this serious view of Nicholas's inventions suddenly seemed to Nina so ridiculous that she tittered. She could have done nothing more regrettable. The student obviously felt that his dignity was threatened. He looked at her very severely:

'This is no laughing matter,' he said. He himself then got up and went into the inner room. He was there for some time, and they could hear him fingering the tubes and treading on the broken glass. He came out again at last.

He was seriously offended.

'You should have told us your husband was an inventor.'

'I didn't think it was of importance,' said Vera.

'Everything is of importance,' he answered. The atmosphere was now entirely changed. The soldiers were angry – they had, it seemed, been deceived and treated like children. The melancholy fellow with the black beard looked at Vera with eyes of deep reproach.

'When will your husband return?' asked the student.

'I am afraid I don't know,' said Vera. She realised that the situation was now serious, but she could not keep her mind upon it. In that house on the Quay what was happening? What had, perhaps, already happened? . . .

'Where has he gone?'

'I don't know.'

'Why didn't he tell you where he was going?'

'He often does not tell me.'

'Ah, that is wrong. In these days one should always say where one is going.'

He stood up very stiff and straight. 'Search the house,' he said to his men.

Suddenly then Vera's mind concentrated. It was as though, she told me, 'I came back into the room and saw for the first time what was happening.'

'There is no one in the rest of the flat,' she said, 'and nothing that can interest you.'

'That is for me to judge,' said the little officer grimly.

'But I assure you there is nothing,' she went on eagerly. 'There is only the kitchen and the bathroom and the five bedrooms.'

'Whose bedrooms?' said the officer.

'My husband's, my own, my sister's, my uncle's, and an Englishman's,' she answered, colouring a little.

'Nevertheless we must do our duty. . . . Search the house,' he repeated.

'But you must not go into our bedrooms,' she said, her voice rising. 'There is nothing for you there. I am sure you will respect our privacy.'

'Our orders must be obeyed,' he answered angrily.

'But——' she cried.

'Silence, Madame,' he said furiously, staring at her as though she were his personal, deadly enemy.

'Very well,' said Vera proudly. 'Please do as you wish.'

The officer walked past her with his head up, and the soldiers followed him, their eyes malicious and inquisitive and excited. The sisters stood together waiting. Of course the end had come. They simply stood there fastening their resolution to the extreme moment.

'I must go with them,' said Vera. She followed them into her bedroom, It was a very little place and they filled it. They looked rather sheepish now, whispering to one another.

'What's in there?' said the officer, tapping the cupboard.

'Only some clothes,' said Vera.

'Open it!' he ordered.

Then the world did indeed stand still. The clock ceased to tick, the little rumble in the stove was silenced, the shuffling feet of one of the soldiers stayed, the movement of some rustle in the wall paper was held. The world was frozen.

'Now I suppose we shall all be shot,' was Vera's thought, repeated over and over again with a ludicrous monotony. Then she could see nothing but the little policeman, tumbling out of the cupboard, dishevelled and terrified. Terrified! what that look in his eyes would be! That at any rate she could not face and she turned her head away from them, looking out through the door into the dark little passage.

She heard as though from an infinite distance the words:

'Well, there's nobody there.'

She did not believe him, of course. He said that, whoever he was, to test her, to tempt her to give herself away. But she was too clever for them. She turned back and faced them, and then saw, to the accompaniment of an amazement that seemed like thunder in her ears, that the cupboard was indeed empty.

'There is nobody,' said the black-bearded soldier.

The student looked rather ashamed of himself. The white clothes, the skirts, and the blouses in the cupboard reproached him.

'You will of course understand, Madame,' he said stiffly, 'that the search was inevitable, – regrettable but necessary. I'm sure you will see that for your own satisfaction. . . .'

'You are assured now that there is no one here?' Vera interrupted him coldly.

'Assured,' he answered.

But where was the man? She felt as though she were in some fantastic nightmare in which nothing was as it seemed. The cupboard was not a cupboard, the policeman not a policeman. . . .

'There is the kitchen,' she said.

In the kitchen of course they found nothing. There was a large cupboard in one corner, but they did not look there. They had had enough. They returned into the dining-room, and there, looking very surprised, his head very high above his collar, was Markovitch.

'What does this mean?' he asked.

'I regret extremely,' said the officer pompously. 'I have been compelled to make a search. Duty only . . . I regret. But no one is here. Your flat is at liberty. I wish you good afternoon.'

Before Markovitch could ask further questions the room was emptied of them all. They tramped out, laughing and joking, children again, the hall door closed behind them.

Nina clutched Vera's arm.

'Vera . . . Vera, where is he?'

'I don't know,' said Vera.

'What's all this?' asked Nicholas.

They explained to him, but he scarcely seemed to hear. He was radiant – smiling in a kind of ecstasy.

'They have gone? I am safe?'

In the doorway was the little policeman, black with grime and dust, so comical a figure that, in reaction from the crisis of ten minutes before, they laughed hysterically.

'Oh, look! look! . . .' cried Nina. 'How dirty he is!'

'Where have you been?' asked Vera. 'Why weren't you in the cupboard?'

The little man's teeth were chattering, so that he could scarcely speak. . . .

'I heard them in the other room. I knew that the cupboard would be the first place. I slipped into the kitchen and hid in the fireplace.'

'You're not angry, Nicholas?' Vera asked. 'We couldn't send him out to be shot.'

'What does that matter?' he almost impatiently brushed it aside. 'There are other things more important.' He looked at the trembling dirty figure. 'Only you'd better go back and hide again until it's dark. They might come back. . . .'

He caught Vera by the arm. His eyes were flames. He drew her with him back into her little room. He closed the door.

'The Revolution has come – it has really come,' he cried.

'Yes,' she answered, 'it has come into this very house. The world has changed.'

'The Czar has abdicated. . . . The old world has gone, the old wicked world! Russia is born again!'

His eyes were the eyes of a fanatic.

Her eyes, too, were alight. She gazed past him.

'I know – I know,' she whispered as though to herself.

'Russia – Russia,' he went on, coming closer and closer, 'Russia and you. We will build a new world. We will forget our old troubles. Oh, Vera, my darling, my darling, we're going to be happy now! I love you so. And now I can hope again. All our love will be clean in this new world. We're going to be happy at last!'

But she did not hear him. She saw into space. A great exultation ran through her body. All lost for love! At last she was awakened, at last she lived; at last, at last, she knew what love was.

'I love him! I love him . . . him,' her soul whispered; 'and nothing now in this world or the next can separate us.'

'Vera – Vera,' Nicholas cried, 'we are together at last – as we have never been. And now we'll work together again – for Russia.'

She looked at the man whom she had never loved, with a great compassion and pity. She put her arms around him and kissed him, her whole maternal spirit suddenly aware of him and seeking to comfort him.

At the touch of her lips his body trembled with happiness. But he did not know that it was a kiss of farewell. . . .

XIII

I have no idea at all what Lawrence did during the early days of that week. He has never told me, and I have never asked him. He never, with the single exception of the afternoon at the Astoria, came near the Markovitches, and I know that was because he had now reached a stage where he did not dare trust himself to see Vera – just as she at that time did not trust herself to see him. . . .

I do not know what he thought of those first days of the Revolution. I can imagine that he took it all very quietly, doing his duty and making no comment. He had of course his own interest in it, but it would be, I am sure, an entirely original interest, unlike any one else's. I remember Dune once, in the long-dead days, saying to me, 'It's never any use guessing what Lawrence is thinking. When you think it's football it's Euripides, and when you think it's Euripides it's Marie Corelli.' Of all the actors in this affair he remains to me to the last as the most mysterious. I know that he loved Vera with the endurance of the rock, the heat of the flame, the ruthlessness of a torrent, but behind that love there sat the man himself, invisible, silent, patient, watching.

He may have had Semyonov's contempt for the Revolutionary idealist, he may have had Wilderling's belief in the Czar's autocracy, he may have had Boris Grogoff's enthusiasm for freedom and a general holiday. I don't know. I know nothing at all about it. I don't think that he saw much of the Wilderlings during the earlier part of the week. He himself was a great deal with the English Military Mission, and Wilderling was with *his* party whatever that might be. He could see of course that Wilderling was disturbed, or perhaps indignant is the right word. 'As though, you know,' he said, 'some dirty little boy had been pullin' snooks at him.' Nevertheless the Baroness was the human link. Lawrence could see from the first – that is, from the morning of the Sunday – that she was in an agony of horror. She confided in nobody, but went about as though she was watching for something, and at dinner her eyes never left her husband's face for a moment. Those evening meals must have been awful. I can imagine the dignity, the solemn heavy room with all the silver, the ceremonious old man-servant and Wilderling himself behaving as though nothing at all were the matter. To do him all justice he was as brave as a lion, and as proud as a gladiator, and as conceited as a Prussian. On the Wednesday evening he did not return home. He telephoned that he was kept on important business.

The Baroness and Lawrence had the long slow meal together. It was almost more than Jerry could stand, having of course his own private tortures to face. 'It was as though the old lady felt that she had been deputed to support the honour of the family during her husband's absence. She must have been wild with anxiety, but she showed no sign except that her hand trembled when she raised her glass.'

'What did you talk about?' I asked him.

'Oh, about anything! Theatres and her home, when she was a girl and England. . . . Awful, every minute of it!'

There was a moment, towards the end of the meal, when the good lady nearly broke down. The bell in the hall rang and there was a step; she thought it was her husband and half rose. It was, however, the Dvornik with a message of no importance. She gave a little sigh. 'Oh, I do wish he would come! . . . I do wish he would come!' she murmured to herself.

'Oh, he'll come,' Lawrence reassured her, but she seemed indignant with him for having overheard her. Afterwards, sitting together desolately in the magnificent drawing-room, she became affectionately maternal. I have always wondered why Lawrence confided to me the details of their very intimate conversation. It was exactly the kind of thing he was most reticent about.

She asked him about his home, his people, his ambitions. She had asked him about these things before, but to-night there was an appeal in her questions, as though she said:

'Take my mind off that other thing. Help me to forget, if it's only for a moment.'

'Have you ever been in love?' she asked.

'Yes. Once,' he said.

Was he in love now?

Yes.

With some one in Russia?

Yes.

She hoped that he would be happy. He told her that he didn't think happiness was quite the point in this particular case. There were other things more important – and anyway it was inevitable.

He had fallen in love at first sight?

Yes. The very first moment.

She sighed. So had she. It was, she thought, the only real way. She asked him whether it might not, after all, turn out better than he expected.

No, he did not think that it could. But he didn't mind how it turned out – at least he couldn't look that far. The point was that he was in it, up to the neck, and he was never going to be out of it again.

There was something boyish about that that pleased her. She put her plump hand on his knee and told him how she had first met the Baron, down in the South, at Kieff; how grand he had looked; how, seeing her across a room full of people, he had smiled at her before he had ever spoken to her or knew her name. 'I was quite pretty then,' she added. 'I have never regretted our marriage for a single moment,' she said. 'Nor, I know, has he.

'We hoped there would be children. . . .' She gave a pathetic little gesture. 'We will get away down to the South again as soon as the troubles are over,' she ended.

I don't suppose he was thinking much of her – his mind was on Vera all the time – but after he had left her and lay in bed, sleepless, his mind dwelt on her affectionately, and he thought that he would like to help her. He realised quite clearly that Wilderling was in a very dangerous position, but I don't think that it ever occurred to him for a moment that it would be wise for him to move to another flat.

On the next day, Thursday, Lawrence did not return until the middle of the afternoon. The town was, by now, comparatively quiet again. Numbers of the police had been caught and imprisoned, some had been shot and others were in hiding; most of the machine-guns shooting from the roofs had ceased. The abdication of the Czar had already produced the second phase of the Revolution – the beginning of the struggle between the Provisional Government and the Council of Workmen and Soldiers' Deputies, and this was proceeding, for the moment, inside the walls of the Duma rather than in the streets and squares of the town. Lawrence returned, therefore, that afternoon with a strange sense of quiet and security.

'It was almost, you know, as though this tommy-rot about a White Revolution might be true after all – with this jolly old Duma and their jolly old Kerensky runnin' the show. Of course I'd seen the nonsense about their not salutin' the officers and all that, but I didn't think any fellers alive would be such dam fools. . . . I might have known better.'

He let himself into the flat and found there a death-like stillness – no one about and no sound except the tickings of the large clock in the drawing-room.

He wandered into that horribly impressive place and suddenly sat down on the sofa with a realisation of extreme physical fatigue. He didn't know why he was so tired, he had felt quite 'bobbish' all the week; suddenly now his limbs were like water, he had a bad ache down his spine and his legs were as heavy as lead. He sat in a kind of trance on that sofa; he was not asleep, but he was also, quite certainly, not awake. He wondered why the place was so 'beastly still' after all the noise there had been all the week. There was no one left alive – every one dead – except himself and Vera . . . Vera . . . Vera.

Then he was conscious that some one was looking at him through the double doors. At first he didn't realise who it was, the face was so white and the figure so quiet; then, pulling himself together, he saw that it was the old servant.

'What is it, André?' he asked, sitting up.

The old man didn't answer, but came into the room, carefully closing the door behind him. Lawrence saw that he was trembling with fright, but was still endeavouring to behave with dignity.

'Barin! Barin!' he whispered, as though Lawrence were a long way from him. 'Paul Konstantinovitch! (that was Wilderling). He's mad. . . . He doesn't know what he's doing. Oh, sir, stop him, stop him, or we shall all be murdered!'

'What is he doing?' asked Lawrence, standing up.

'In the little back room,' André whispered, as though now he were confiding a terrible secret. 'Come quickly . . .!'

Lawrence followed him; when he had gone a few steps down the passage he heard suddenly a sharp, muffled report.

'What's that?'

André came close to him, his old, seamed face white like plaster.

'He has a rifle in there . . .' he said. 'He's shooting at them!' Then as Lawrence stepped up to the door of the little room that was Wilderling's dressing-room, André caught his arm –

'Be careful, Barin. . . . He doesn't know what he's about. He may not recognise you.'

'Oh, that's all right!' said Lawrence. He pushed the door open and walked in. To give for a moment his own account of it: 'You know that room was the rummiest thing. I'd never been into it before. I knew the old fellow was a bit of a dandy, but I never expected to see all the pots and jars and glasses there were. You'd have thought one wouldn't have noticed a thing at such a time, but you couldn't escape them, – his dressing-table simply covered, – white round jars with pink tops, bottles of hair-oil with ribbons round the neck, manicure things, heaps of silver things, and boxes with Chinese patterns on them, and one thing, open, with what was mighty like rouge in it. And clothes all over the place – a red silk dressing-gown with golden tassels, and red leather slippers!

'I don't remember noticing any of this at the moment, but it all comes back to me as soon as I begin to think of it – and the room stank of scent!'

But of course it was the old man in the corner who mattered. It was, I think, very significant of Lawrence's character and his unEnglish-English tradition that the first thing that he felt was the pathos of it. No other Englishman in Petrograd would have seen that at all.

Wilderling was crouched in the corner against a piece of gold Japanese embroidery. He was in the shadow, away from the window, which was pushed open sufficiently to allow the muzzle of the rifle to slip between the woodwork and the pane. The old man, his white hair disordered, his clothes dusty, and his hands grimy, crept forward just as Lawrence entered, fired down into the side-street, then moved swiftly back into his corner again. He muttered to himself without ceasing in French, 'Chiens! Chiens! . . . Chiens!' He was very hot, and he stopped for a moment to wipe the sweat from his forehead, then he saw Lawrence.

'What do you want?' he asked, as though he didn't recognise him.

Lawrence moved down the side of the room, avoiding the window. He touched the little man's arm.

'I say, you know,' he said, 'this won't do.'

Wilderling smelt of gunpowder, and he was breathing hard as though he had been running desperately. He quivered when Lawrence touched him.

'Go away!' he said, 'you mustn't come here. . . . I'll get them yet – I tell you I'll get them yet – I tell you I'll get them – Let them dare . . . Chiens . . . Chiens . . .' He jerked his rifle away from the window and began, with trembling fingers, to load it again.

Lawrence gripped his arm. 'When I did that,' he said, 'it felt as though there wasn't an arm there at all, but just a bone which I could break if I pressed a bit harder.'

'Come away!' he said. 'You damn fool – don't you see that it's hopeless?'

'And I'd always been so respectful to him . . .' he added in parenthesis.

Wilderling hissed at him, saying no words, just drawing in his breath.

'I've got two of them,' he whispered suddenly. 'I'll get them all.'

Then a bullet crashed through the window, burying itself in the opposite wall.

After that, things happened so quickly that it was impossible to say in what order they occurred. There was suddenly a tremendous noise in the flat.

'It was just as though the whole place was going to tumble about our ears. All the pots and bottles began to jump about, and then another bullet came through, landed on the dressing-table, and smashed everything. The looking-glass crashed, and the hair-oil was all over the place. I rushed out to see what was happening in the hall. . . .'

What 'was happening' was that the soldiers had broken the hall door in. Lawrence saw then a horrible thing. One of the men rushed forward and stuck André, who was standing, paralysed, by the drawing-room door, in the stomach. The old man cried out 'just like a shot rabbit,' and stood there 'for what seemed ages,' with the blood pouring out of his middle.

That finished Lawrence. He rushed forward, and they would certainly have 'stuck' him too if some one hadn't cried out, 'Look out, he's an Englishman – an *Anglichanin* – I know him.'

After that, for a time, he was uncertain of anything. He struggled; he was held. He heard noises around him – shouts or murmurs or sighs – that didn't seem to him to be connected with anything human. He could not have said where he was nor what he was doing. Then, quite suddenly, everything cleared. He came to himself with a consciousness of that utter weariness that he had felt before. He was able to visualise the scene, to take it all in, but as a distant spectator. 'It was like nothing so much as watching a cinematograph,' he told me. He could do nothing; he was held by three soldiers, who apparently wished him to be a witness of the whole affair. André's body lay there, huddled up in a pool of drying blood, that glistened under the electric light. One of his legs was bent crookedly under him, and Lawrence had a strange mad impulse to thrust his way forward and put it straight.

It was then, with a horrible sickly feeling, exactly like a blow in the stomach, that he realised that the Baroness was there. She was standing, quite alone, at the entrance of the hall, looking at the soldiers, who were about eight in number.

He heard her say, 'What's happened? Who are you? . . .' and then in a sharper, more urgent voice, 'Where's my husband?'

Then she saw André. . . . She gave a sharp little cry, moved forward towards him, and stopped.

'I don't know what she did then,' said Lawrence. 'I think she suddenly began to run down the passage. I know she was crying, "Paul! Paul! Paul!" . . . I never saw her again.'

The officer – an elderly kindly-looking man like a doctor or a lawyer (I am trying to give every possible detail, because I think it important) – then came up to Lawrence and asked him some questions:

What was his name?

Jeremy Ralph Lawrence.

He was an Englishman?

Yes.

Working at the British Embassy?

No, at the British Military Mission.

He was an officer?

Yes.

In the British Army?

Yes. He had fought for two years in France.

He had been lodging with Baron Wilderling?

Yes – ever since he came to Russia.

The officer nodded his head. They knew about him, had full information. A friend of his, a Mr. Boris Grogoff, had spoken of him.

The officer was then very polite, told him that they regretted extremely the inconvenience and discomfort to which he might be put, but that they must detain him until this affair was concluded – 'which will be very soon,' added the officer. He also added that he wished Lawrence to be a witness of what occurred, so that he should see that, under the new regime in Russia, everything was just and straightforward.

'I tried to tell him,' said Lawrence to me, 'that Wilderling was off his head. I hadn't the least hope, of course. . . . It was all quite clear, and, at such a time, quite just. Wilderling had been shooting them out of his window. . . . The officer listened very politely, but when I had finished he only shook his head. That was their affair, he said.

'It was then that I realised Wilderling. He was standing quite close to me. He had obviously been struggling a bit, because his shirt was all torn, and you could see his chest. He kept moving his hand and trying to pull his shirt over; it was his only movement. He was as straight as a dart, and, except for the motion of his hand, as still as a statue, standing between the soldiers, looking directly in front of him. He had been mad in that other room, quite dotty.

'He was as sane as anything now, grave and serious and rather ironical, just as he always looked. Well it was at that moment, when I saw him there, that I thought of Vera. I had been thinking of her all the time, of course. I had been thinking of nothing else for weeks. But that minute, there in the hall, settled me. Callous, wasn't it? I ought to have been thinking only of Wilderling and his poor old wife. After all, they'd been awfully good to me. She'd been almost like a mother all the time. . . . But there it was. It came over me like a storm. I'd been fighting for nights and days, and days and nights, not to go to her – fighting like hell, trying to play the game the sentimentalists would call it. I suppose seeing the old man there and knowing what they were going to do to him settled it. It was a sudden conviction, like a blow, that all this thing was real, that they weren't playing at it, that any one in the town was as near death as winking. . . . And so there it was! Vera! I'd got to get to her – at once – and never leave her again until she was safe. I'd got to get to her! I'd got to get to her! I'd got to get to her! . . . Nothing else mattered, – not Wilderling's death nor mine either, except that if I was dead I'd be out of it and wouldn't be able to help her. They talk about men with one idea. From that moment I had only one idea in all the world – I don't know that I've had any other one since. They talk about scruples, moralities, traditions. They're all right, but there just are moments in life when they simply don't count at all. . . . Vera was in danger – well, that was all that mattered.

'The officer said something to Wilderling. I heard Wilderling answer: "You're rebels against His Majesty. . . . I wish I'd shot more of you!" Fine old boy, you know, whatever way you look at it.

'They moved him forward then. He went quite willingly, without any kind of resistance. They motioned to me to follow. We walked out of the flat down the stairs, no one saying a word. We went out on to the Quay. There was no one there. They stood him up against the wall, facing the river. It was dark, and when he was against the wall he seemed to vanish, – only I got one kind of gesture, a sort of farewell, you know, his grey hair waving in the breeze from the river.

'There was a report, and it was as though a piece of the wall slowly unsettled itself and fell forward. No sound except the report. Oh, he was a fine old boy!

'The officer came up to me and said very politely:

'"You are free now, sir," and something about regretting incivility, and something, I think, about them perhaps wanting me again to give some sort of evidence. Very polite he was.

'I was mad, I suppose – I don't know. I believe I said something to him about Vera, which of course he didn't understand.

'I know I wanted to run like hell to Vera to see that she was safe.

'But I didn't. I walked off as slowly as anything. It was awful. They'd been so good to me, and yet I wasn't thinking of Wilderling at all. . . .'

XIV

Markovitch on that same afternoon came back to the flat early. He also, like Lawrence, felt the strange peace and tranquillity of the town, and it seemed inevitably like the confirmation of all his dearest hopes. The Czar was gone, the Old Regime was gone; the people, smiling and friendly, were maintaining their own discipline, – above all, Vera had kissed him.

He did not go deeper into his heart and see how strained all their recent relations must have been for this now to give him such joy. He left that – it simply was that at last he and Vera understood one another; she had found that she cared for him after all, and that he was necessary to her happiness. What that must mean for their future life together he simply dared not think. . . . It would change the world for him. He felt like the man in the story from whom the curse is suddenly lifted. . . .

He walked home through the quiet town, humming to himself. He fancied that there was a warmth in the air, a strange kindly omen of spring, although the snow was still thick on the ground, and the Neva a grey carpet of ice.

He came into the flat and found it empty. He went into his little room and started on his inventions. He was so happy that he hummed to himself as he worked and cut slices off his pieces of wood, and soaked flannel in bottles, and wrote funny little sentences in his abominable handwriting in a red notebook.

One need not grudge it him, poor Markovitch. It was the last happy half-hour of his life.

He did not turn on his green-shaded lamp, but sat there in the gathering dusk, chipping up the wood and sometimes stopping, idly lost in happy thoughts.

Some one came in. He peered through his little glass window and saw that it was Nina. She passed quickly through the dining-room, beyond, towards her bedroom, without stopping to switch on the light.

Nina had broken the spell. He went back to his table, but he couldn't work now, and he felt vaguely uneasy and cold. He was just going to leave his work and find the *Retch* and settle down to a comfortable read, when he heard the hall door close. He stood behind his little glass window and watched; it was Vera, perhaps . . . it must be . . . his heart began eagerly to beat.

It *was* Vera. At once he saw that she was strangely agitated. Before she had switched on the light he realised it. With a click the light was on. Markovitch had intended to open his door and go out to her, smiling. He saw at once that she was waiting for some one. . . . He stood, trembling, on tiptoe, his face pressed against the glass of the pane.

Lawrence came in. He had the face, Markovitch told me many weeks afterwards, 'of a triumphant man.'

They had obviously met outside, because Vera said, as though continuing a conversation:

'And it's only just happened?'

'I've come straight from there,' Lawrence answered.

Then he went up to her. She let herself at once go to him, and he half carried her to a chair near the table and exactly opposite Markovitch's window.

They kissed 'like people who had been starving all their lives.' Markovitch was trembling so that he was afraid lest he should tumble or make some noise. The two figures in the chair were like statues in their immobile, relentless, unswerving embrace.

Suddenly he saw that Nina was standing in the opposite doorway 'like a ghost.' She was there for so brief a moment that he could not be sure that she had been there at all. Only her white, frightened face remained with him.

One of his thoughts was:

'This is the end of my life.'

Another was:

'How could they be so careless, with the light on, and perhaps people in the flat!'

And after that:

'They need it so much that they don't care who sees, – starved people. . . .'

And after that:

'I'm starved too.'

He was so cold that his teeth were chattering, and he crept back from his window, crept into the farthest farthest corner of his little room, and crouched there on the floor, staring and staring, but seeing nothing at all.

Part III

Markovitch and Semyonov

Markovitch and Semyonov

I

On the evening of that very afternoon, Thursday, I again collapsed. I was coming home in the dusk through a whispering world. All over the streets, everywhere on the broad shining snow, under a blaze of stars so sharp and piercing that the sky seemed strangely close and intimate, the talk went on. Groups everywhere and groups irrespective of all class distinction – a well-to-do woman in rich furs, a peasant woman with a shawl over her head, a wild, bearded soldier, a stout, important officer, a maid-servant, a cab-driver, a shopman – talking, talking, talking, talking. . . . The eagerness, the ignorance, the odd fairy-tale world spun about those groups, so that the coloured domes of the churches, the silver network of the stars, the wooden booths, the mist of candles before the Ikons, the rough painted pictures on the shops advertising the goods sold within – all these things shared in that crude, idealistic, cynical ignorance, in that fairy-tale of brutality, goodness, cowardice and bravery, malice and generosity, superstition and devotion, that was so shortly to be offered to a materialistic, hard-fighting, brave, and unthinking Europe! . . .

That, however, was not now my immediate business – enough of that presently. My immediate business, as I very quickly discovered, was to pluck up enough strength to drag my wretched body home. The events of the week had, I suppose, carried me along. I was to suffer now the inevitable reaction. I felt exactly as though I had been shot from a gun and landed, suddenly, without breath, without any strength in any of my limbs, in a new and strange world. I was standing, when I first realised my weakness, beside the wooden booths in the Sadovaya. They were all closed, of course, but along the pavement women and old men had baskets containing sweets and notepaper and red paper tulips offered in memory of the glorious Revolution. Right across the Square the groups of people scattered in little dusky pools against the snow, until they touched the very doors of the church. . . . I saw all this, was conscious that the stars and the church candles mingled . . . then suddenly I had to clutch the side of the booth behind me to prevent myself from falling. My head swam, my limbs were as water, and my old so well-remembered friend struck me in the middle of the spine as though he had cut me in two with his knife. How was I ever to get home? No one noticed me – indeed they seemed to my sick eyes to have ceased to be human, – ghosts in a ghostly world, the snow gleaming through them, so that they only moved like a thin diaphanous veil against the wall of the sky. . . . I clutched my booth. In a moment I should be down. The pain in my back was agony, my legs had ceased to exist, and I was falling into a dark, dark pool of clear jet-black water, at the bottom of which lay a star. . . .

The strange thing is that I do not know who it was who rescued me. I know that some one came. I know that to my own dim surprise an Isvostchik was there and that very feebly I got into it. Some one was with me. Was it my black-bearded peasant? I fancy now that it was. I can even, on looking back, see him sitting up, very large and still, one thick arm holding me. I fancy that I can still smell the stuff of his clothes. I fancy that he talked to me, very quietly, reassuring me about something. But, upon my word, I don't know. One can so easily imagine what one wants to be true, and now I want, more than I would then ever have believed to be possible, to have had actual contact with him. It is the only conversation between us that can ever have existed: never, before or after, was there another opportunity. And in any case there can scarcely have been a conversation, because I certainly said nothing, and I cannot remember anything that he said, if indeed he said anything at all. At any rate I was there in the Sadovaya, I was in a cab, I was in my bed. The truth of the rest of it any one may decide for himself. . . .

II

That Thursday was March 15. I was conscious of my existence again on Sunday, April 1st. I opened my eyes and saw that there was a thaw. That was the first thing of which I was aware – that water was apparently dripping on every side of me. It is a strange sensation to lie on your bed very weak, and very indifferent, and to feel the world turning to moisture all about you. . . . My ramshackle habitation had never been a very strong defence against the outside world. It seemed now to have definitely decided to abandon the struggle. The water streamed down the panes of my window opposite my bed. One patch of my ceiling (just above my only bookcase, confound it!) was coloured a mouldy grey, and from this huge drops like elephant's tears splashed monotonously. (Already *The Spirit of Man* was disfigured by a long grey streak, and the green back of Galleon's *Roads* was splotched with stains.) Some one had placed a bucket near the door to catch a perpetual stream flowing from the corner of the room. Down into the bucket it pattered with a hasty, giggling, hysterical jiggle. I rather liked the companionship of it. I didn't mind it at all. I really minded nothing whatever. . . . I sighed my appreciation of my return to life. My sigh brought some one from the corner of my room and that some one was, of course, the inevitable Rat. He came up to my bed in his stealthy, furtive fashion, and looked at me reproachfully. I asked him, my voice sounding to myself strange and very far away, what he was doing there. He answered that if it had not been for him I should be dead. He had come early one morning and found me lying in my bed and no one in the place at all. No one – because the old woman had vanished. Yes, the neighbours had told him. Apparently on that very Thursday she had decided that the Revolution had given her her freedom, and that she was never going to work for anybody ever again. She had told a woman-neighbour that she heard that the land now was going to be given back to everybody, and she was returning therefore to her village somewhere in the Moscow Province. She had not been back there for twenty years. And first, to celebrate her liberty, she would get magnificently drunk on furniture polish.

'I did not see her of course,' said the Rat. 'No. When I came, early in the morning, no one was here. I thought that you were dead, Barin, and I began collecting your property, so that no one else should take it. Then you made a movement, and I saw that you were alive – so I got some cabbage soup and gave it you. That certainly saved you . . . I'm going to stay with you now.'

I did not care in the least whether he went or stayed. He chattered on. By staying with me he would inevitably neglect his public duties. Perhaps I didn't know that he had public duties? Yes, he was now an Anarchist, and I should be astonished very shortly, by the things the Anarchists would do. All the same, they had their own discipline. They had their own processions, too, like any one else. Only four days ago he had marched all over Petrograd carrying a black flag. He must confess that he was rather sick of it. But they must have processions. . . . Even the prostitutes had marched down the Nevski the other day demanding shorter hours.

But of course I cannot remember all that he said. During the next few days I slowly pulled myself out of the misty dead world in which I had been lying. Pain came back to me, leaping upon me and then receding, finally, on the third day suddenly leaving me altogether. The Rat fed me on cabbage soup and glasses of tea and caviare and biscuits. During those three days he never left me, and indeed tended me like a woman. He would sit by my bed and with his rough hand stroke my hair, while he poured into my ears ghastly stories of the many crimes that he had committed. I noticed that he was cleaner and more civilised. His beard was clipped and he smelt of cabbage and straw – a rather healthy smell. One morning he suddenly took the pail, filled it with water and washed himself in front of my windows. He scrubbed himself until I should have thought that he had no skin left.

'You're a fine big man, Rat,' I said.

He was delighted with that, and came quite near my bed, stretching his naked body, his arms and legs and chest, like a pleased animal.

'Yes, I'm a fine man, Barin,' he said; 'many women have loved me, and many will again . . .' Then he went back, and producing clean drawers and vest from somewhere (I suspect that they were mine but I was too weak to care), put them on.

On the second and third days I felt much better. The thaw was less violent, the wood crackled in my stove. On the morning of Wednesday April 14 I got up, dressed, and sat in front of my window. The ice was still there, but over it lay a faint, a very faint, filmy sheen of water. It was a day of gleams, the sun flashing in and out of the clouds. Just beneath my window a tree was pushing into bud. Pools of water lay thick on the dirty melting snow. I got the Rat to bring a little table and put some books on it. I had near me *The Spirit of Man,* Keats's *Letters, The Roads,* Beddoes, and *Pride and Prejudice.* A consciousness of the outer world crept, like warmth, through my bones.

'Rat,' I said, 'who's been to see me?'

'No one,' said he.

I felt suddenly a ridiculous affront.

'No one?' I asked, incredulous.

'No one,' he answered. 'They've all forgotten you, Barin,' he added maliciously, knowing that that would hurt me.

It was strange how deeply I cared. Here was I who, only a short while before, had declared myself done with the world for ever, and now I was almost crying because no one had been to see me! Indeed, I believe in my weakness and distress I actually did cry. No one at all? Not Vera nor Nina nor Jeremy nor Bohun? Not young Bohun even ...? And then slowly my brain realised that there was now a new world. None of the old conditions held any longer.

We had been the victims of an earthquake. Now it was – every man for himself! Quickly then there came upon me an eager desire to know what had happened in the Markovitch family. What of Jerry and Vera? What of Nicholas? What of Semyonov ...?

'Rat,' I said, 'this afternoon I am going out!'

'Very well, Barin,' he said, 'I, too, have an engagement.'

In the afternoon I crept out like an old sick man. I felt strangely shy and nervous. When I reached the corner of Ekateringofsky Canal and the English Prospect I decided not to go in and see the Markovitches. For one thing I shrank from the thought of their compassion. I had not shaved for many days. I was that dull sickly yellow colour that offends the taste of all healthy vigorous people. I did not want their pity. No. . . . I would wait until I was stronger.

My interest in life was reviving with every step that I took. I don't know what I had expected the outside world to be. This was April 14. It was nearly a month since the outburst of the Revolution, and surely there should be signs in the streets of the results of such a cataclysm. There were, on the surface, no signs. There was the same little cinema on the canal with its gaudy-coloured posters, there was the old woman sitting at the foot of the little bridge with her basket of apples and bootlaces, there was the same wooden hut with the sweets and the fruit, the same figures of peasant women, soldiers, boys hurrying across the bridge, the same slow, sleepy Isvostchik stumbling along carelessly. One sign there was. Exactly opposite the little cinema, on the other side of the canal, was a high grey block of flats. This now was starred and sprayed with the white marks of bullets. It was like a man marked for life with smallpox. That building alone was witness to me that I had not dreamt the events of that week.

The thaw made walking very difficult. The water poured down the sides of the houses and gurgled in floods through the pipes. The snow was slippery under the film of gleaming wet, and there were huge pools at every step. Across the middle of the English Prospect, near the Baths, there was quite a deep lake ...

I wandered slowly along, enjoying the chill warmth of the soft spring sun. The winter was nearly over! Thank God for that! What had happened during my month of illness? Perhaps a great Revolutionary army had been formed, and a mighty, free, and united Russia was going out to save the world! Oh, I did hope that it was so! Surely that wonderful white week was a good omen. No Revolution in history had started so well as this one ...

I found my way at last very slowly to the end of the Quay, and the sight of the round towers of my favourite church was like the reassuring smile of an old friend. The sun was dropping low over the Neva. The whole vast expanse of the river was coloured very faintly pink. Here, too, there was the film of the water above the ice; the water caught the colour, but the ice below it was grey and still. Clouds of crimson and orange and faint gold streamed away in great waves of light from the sun. The long line of buildings and towers on the farther side was jet-black; the masts of the ships clustering against the Quay were touched at their tips with bright gold. It was all utterly still, not a sound nor a movement anywhere; only one figure, that of a woman, was coming slowly towards me. I felt, as one always does at the beginning of a Russian spring, a strange sense of expectation. Spring in Russia is so sudden and so swift that it gives an overwhelming impression of a powerful organising Power behind it. Suddenly the shutters are pulled back and the sun floods the world! Upon this afternoon one could feel the urgent business of preparation pushing forward, arrogantly, ruthlessly. I don't think that I had ever before realised the power of the Neva at such close quarters. I was almost ashamed at the contrast of its struggle with my own feebleness.

I saw then that the figure coming towards me was Nina.

III

As she came nearer I saw that she was intensely preoccupied. She was looking straight in front of her but seeing nothing. It was only when she was quite close to me that I saw that she was crying. She was making no sound. Her mouth was closed; the tears were slowly, helplessly, rolling down her cheeks.

She was very near to me indeed before she saw me; then she looked at me closely before she recognised me. When she saw that it was I, she stopped, fumbled for her handkerchief, which she found, wiped her eyes, then turned away from me and looked out over the river.

'Nina, dear,' I said, 'what's the matter?'

She didn't answer; at length she turned round and said:

'You've been ill again, haven't you?'

One cheek had a dirty tear-stain on it, which made her inexpressibly young and pathetic and helpless.

'Yes,' I said, 'I have.'

She caught her breath, put out her hand, and touched my arm.

'Oh, you *do* look ill! . . . Vera went to ask, and there was a rough-looking man there who said that no one could see you, but that you were all right. . . . One of us ought to have forced a way in – M. Bohun wanted to – but we've all been thinking of ourselves.'

'What's the matter, Nina?' I asked. 'You've been crying.'

'Nothing's the matter. I'm all right.'

'No, you're not. You ought to tell me. You trusted me once.'

'I don't trust any one,' she answered fiercely. 'Especially not Englishmen.'

'What's the matter?' I asked again.

'Nothing. . . . We're just as we were. Except,' she suddenly looked up at me, 'Uncle Alexei's living with us now.'

'Semyonov!' I cried out sharply, 'living with you!'

'Yes,' she went on, 'in the room where Nicholas had his inventions is Uncle Alexei's bedroom.'

'Why, in Heaven's name?' I cried.

'Uncle Alexei wanted it. He said he was lonely, and then he just came. I don't know whether Nicholas likes it or not. Vera hates it, but she agreed at once.'

'And do you like it?' I asked.

'I like Uncle Alexei,' she answered. 'We have long talks. He shows me how silly I've been.'

'Oh!' I said . . . 'and what about Nicholas's inventions?'

'He's given them up for ever.' She looked at me doubtfully, as though she were wondering whether she could trust me. 'He's so funny now – Nicholas, I mean. You know he was so happy when the Revolution came. Now he's in a different mood every minute. Something's happened to him that we don't know about.'

'What kind of thing?' I asked.

'I don't know. He's seen something or heard something. It's some secret he's got. But Uncle Alexei knows.'

'How can you tell?'

'Because he's always saying things that make Nicholas angry, and we can't see anything in them at all. . . . Uncle Alexei's very clever.'

'Yes, he is,' I agreed. 'But you haven't told me why you were crying just now.'

She looked at me. She gave a little shiver. 'Oh, you do look ill! . . . Everything's going wrong together, isn't it?'

And with that she suddenly left me, hurrying away from me, leaving me miserable and apprehensive of some great trouble in store for all of us.

IV

It is impossible to explain how disturbed I was by Nina's news. Semyonov living in the flat! He must have some very strong reason for this, to leave his big comfortable flat for the pokiness of the Markovitches'!

And then that the Markovitches should have him! There were already inhabitants enough – Nicholas, Vera, Nina, Uncle Ivan, Bohun. Then the inconvenience and discomfort of Nicholas's little hole as a bedroom! How Semyonov must loathe it!

From that moment the Markovitches' flat became for me the centre of my drama. Looking back I could see now how all the growing development of the story had centred round those rooms. I did not of course know at this time of that final drama of the Thursday afternoon, but I knew of the adventure with the policeman, and it seemed to me that the flat was a cup into which the ingredients were being poured one after another until at last the preparation would be complete, and then . . .

Oh, but I cared for Nina and Vera and Nicholas – yes, and Jerry too! I wanted to see them happy and at peace before I left them – in especial Nicholas.

And Semyonov came closer to them and closer, following some plan of his own and yet, after all, finally like a man driven by a power, constructed it might be, out of his own very irony.

I made a kind of bet with fate that by Easter Day every one should be happy.

Next day, the 15th of April, was the great funeral for the victims of the Revolution. I believe, although of course at that time I had heard nothing, that there had been great speculation about the day, many people thinking that it would be an excuse for further trouble, the Monarchists rising, or the 'Soviet' attacking the Provisional Government, or Milyukoff and his followers attacking the Soviet. They need not have been alarmed. No one had as yet realised the lengths that Slavonic apathy may permit itself. . . .

I went down about half-past ten to the Square at the end of the Sadovaya and found it filled with a vast concourse of peasants, not only the Square was filled, but the Sadovaya as far as the eye could see. They were arranged in perfect order, about eight in a row, arm in arm. Every group carried its banner, and far away into the distance one could see the words 'Freedom,' 'Brotherhood,' 'The Land for All,' 'Peace of the World,' floating on the breeze. Nevertheless, in spite of these fine words, it was not a very cheering sight. The day was wretched – no actual rain, but a cold damp wind blowing and the dirty snow, half ice and half water; the people themselves were not inspiring. They were all, it seemed, peasants. I saw very few workmen, although I believe that multitudes were actually in the procession. Those strange, pale, Eastern faces, passive, apathetic, ignorant, childish, unreasoning, stretched in a great cloud under the grey overhanging canopy of the sky. They raised once and again a melancholy little tune that was more wail than anything else. They had stood there, I was told, in pools of frozen water for hours, and were perfectly ready to stand thus for many hours more if they were ordered to do so. As I regarded their ignorance and apathy I realised for the first time something of what the Revolution had already done.

A hundred million of these children – ignorant, greedy, pathetic, helpless, revengeful – let loose upon the world! Where were their leaders? Who, indeed, would their leaders be? The sun sometimes broke through for a moment, but the light that it threw on their faces only made them more pallid, more death-like. They did not laugh nor joke as our people at home would have done. . . . I believe that very few of them had any idea why they were there. . . .

Suddenly the word came down the lines to move forward. Very slowly, wailing their little tune, they advanced.

But the morning was growing old and I must at once see Vera. I had made up my mind, during the night, to do anything that lay in my power to persuade Vera and Nina to leave their flat. The flat was the root of all their trouble, there was something in its atmosphere, something gloomy and ominous. They would be better at the other end of the town, or, perhaps, over on the Vassily Ostrov. I would show Vera that it was a fatal plan to have Semyonov to live with them (as in all probability she herself knew well enough), and their leaving the flat was a very good excuse for getting rid of him. I had all this in my head as I went along. I was still feeling ill and feeble, and my half-hour's stand in the market-place had seriously exhausted me. I had to lean against the walls of the houses every now and then; it seemed to me that, in the pale watery air, the whole world was a dream, the high forbidding flats looking down on to the dirty ice of the canals, the water dripping, dripping, dripping. . . . No one was about. Every one had gone to join in the procession. I could see it, with my mind's eye, unwinding its huge tail through the watery-oozing channels of the town, like some pale-coloured snake, crawling through the misty labyrinths of a marsh.

In the flat I found only Uncle Ivan sitting very happily by himself at the table playing patience. He was dressed very smartly in his English black suit and a black bow tie. He behaved with his usual elaborate courtesy to me but, to my relief, on this occasion, he spoke Russian.

It appeared that the Revolution had not upset him in the least. He took, he assured me, no interest whatever in politics. The great thing was 'to live inside oneself,' and by living inside oneself he meant, I gathered, that one should be entirely selfish. Clothes were important, and food and courteous manners, but he must say that he could not see that one would be very much worse off even though one were ruled by the Germans – one might, indeed, be a great deal more comfortable. And as to this Revolution he couldn't really understand why people made such a fuss. One class or another class, what did it matter? (As to this he was, I fear, to be sadly undeceived. He little knew that, before the year was out, he would be shovelling snow in the Morskaia for a rouble an hour.) So centred was he upon himself that he did not notice that I looked ill. He offered me a chair, indeed, but that was simply his courteous manners. Very ridiculous, he thought, the fuss that Nicholas made about the Revolution – very ridiculous the fuss that he made about everything. . . .

Alexei had been showing Nicholas how ridiculous he was.

'Oh, has he?' said I. 'How's he been doing that?'

Laughing at him, apparently. They all laughed at him. It was his own fault.

'Alexei's living with us now, you know.'

'Yes, I know,' I said. 'What's he doing that for?'

'He wanted to,' said Uncle Ivan simply. 'He's always done what he's wanted to, all his life.'

'It makes it a great many of you in one small flat.'

'Yes, doesn't it?' said Uncle Ivan amiably. 'Very pleasant – although, Ivan Andreievitch, I will admit to you quite frankly that I've always been frightened of Alexei. He has such a very sharp tongue. He discovers one's weak spots in a marvellous manner. . . . We all have weak spots, you know,' he added apologetically.

'Yes, we have,' I said.

Then, to my relief, Vera came in. She was very sweet to me, expressing much concern about my illness, asking me to stay and have my meal with them. . . . She suddenly broke off. There was a letter lying on the table addressed to her. I saw at once that it was in Nina's handwriting.

'Nina! Writing to *me*!' She picked it up, stood back looking at the envelope before she opened it. She read it, then turned on me with a cry.

'Nina! . . . She's gone!'

'Gone!' I repeated, starting at once.

'Yes. . . . Read!' She thrust it into my hand.

In Nina's sprawling schoolgirl hand I read:

DEAR VERA –

I've left you and Nicholas for ever. . . . I have been thinking of this for a long time, and now Uncle Alexei has shown me how foolish I've been, wanting something I can't have. But I'm not a child any longer. I must lead my own life. . . . I'm going to live with Boris who will take care of me. It's no use you or any one trying to prevent me. I will not come back. I must lead my own life now.

NINA.

Vera was beside herself.

'Quick! Quick! Some one must go after her. She must be brought back at once. Quick! *Scora! Scora!* . . . I must go. No, she is angry with me. She won't listen to me. Ivan Andreievitch, you must go. At once! You must bring her back with you. Darling, darling Nina! . . . Oh, my God, what shall I do if anything happens to her!'

She clutched my arm. Even as she spoke she had got my hat and stick.

'This is Alexei Petrovitch,' I said.

'Never mind who it is,' she answered. 'She must be brought back at once. She is so young. She doesn't know. . . . Boris —— Oh! it's impossible. Don't leave without bringing her back with you.'

Even old Uncle Ivan seemed distressed.

'Dear, dear . . .' he kept repeating, 'dear, dear. . . . Poor little Nina. Poor little Nina——'

'Where does Grogoff live?' I asked

'16 Gagarinskaya . . . Flat 3. Quick. You must bring her back with you. Promise me.'

'I will do my best,' I said.

I found by a miracle of good fortune an Isvostchik in the street outside. We plunged along through the pools of water in the direction of the Gagarinskaya. That was a horrible drive. In the Sadovaya we met the slow, winding funeral procession.

On they went, arm in arm, the same little wailing tune, monotonously repeating, but sounding like nothing human, rather exuding from the very cobbles of the road and the waters of the stagnant canals.

The march of the peasants upon Petrograd! I could see them from all the quarters of the town, converging upon the Marsovoie Pole, stubborn, silent, wraiths of earlier civilisation, omens of later dominations. I thought of Boris Grogoff. What did he, with all his vehemence and conceit, intend to do with these? First he would flatter them – I saw that clearly enough. But then when his flatteries failed, what then? Could he control them? Would they obey him? Would they obey anybody until education had shown them the necessities for co-ordination and self-discipline? The river at last was overflowing its banks – would not the savage force of its power be greater than any one could calculate? The stream flowed on. . . . My Isvostchik took his cab down a side street, and then again met the strange sorrowful company. From this point I could see several further bridges and streets, and over them all I saw the same stream flowing, the same banners blowing – and all so still, so dumb, so patient.

The delay was maddening. My thoughts were all now on Nina. I saw her always before me as I had beheld her yesterday, walking slowly along, her eyes fixed on space, the tears trickling down her face. 'Life,' Nikitin once said to me, 'I sometimes think is like a dark room, the door closed, the windows bolted and your enemy shut in with you. Whether your enemy or yourself is the stronger who knows? . . . Nor does it matter, as the issue is always decided outside . . . Knowing that, you can at least afford to despise him.'

I felt something of that impotence now. I cursed the Isvostchik, but wherever he went this slow endless stream seemed to impede our way. Poor Nina! Such a baby! What was it that had driven her to this? She did not love the man, and she knew quite well that she did not. No, it was an act of defiance. But defiance to whom – to Vera? to Lawrence? ... and what had Semyonov said to her?

Then, thank Heaven, we crossed the Nevski, and our way was clear. The old cabman whipped up his horse, and in a minute or two we were outside 16 Gagarinskaya. I will confess to very real fears and hesitations as I climbed the dark stairs (the lift was, of course, not working). I was not the kind of man for this kind of job. In the first place I hated quarrels, and knowing Grogoff's hot temper I had every reason to expect a tempestuous interview. Then I was ill, aching in every limb and seeing everything, as I always did when I was unwell, mistily and with uncertainty. Then I had a very shrewd suspicion that there was considerable truth in what Semyonov had said, that I was interfering in what only remotely concerned me. At any rate, that was certainly the view that Grogoff would take, and Nina perhaps also. I felt, as I rang the bell of No. 3, that unpleasant pain in the pit of the stomach that tells you that you're going to make a fool of yourself.

Well, it would not be for the first time.

'Boris Nicolaievitch *doma*?' I asked the cross-looking old woman who opened the door.

'*Doma*,' she answered, holding it open to let me pass.

I was shown into a dark, untidy sitting-room. It seemed at first sight to be littered with papers, newspapers, Revolutionary sheets and proclamations, the *Pravda,* the *Novaya Jezn,* the *Soldatskaya Mwyssl.* ... On the dirty wall-paper there were enormous dark photographs, in faded gilt frames, of family groups; on one wall there was a large garishly coloured picture of Grogoff himself in student's dress. The stove was unlighted and the room was very cold. My heart ached for Nina.

A moment after Grogoff came in. He came forward to me very amiably, holding out his hand.

'Nu, Ivan Andreievitch ... What can I do for you?' he asked, smiling.

And how he had changed! He was positively swollen with self-satisfaction. He had never been famous for personal modesty, but he seemed now to be physically twice his normal size. He was fat, his cheeks puffed, his stomach swelling beneath the belt that bound it. His fair hair was long, and rolled in large curls on one side of his head and over his forehead. He spoke in a loud, overbearing voice.

'Nu, Ivan Andreievitch, what can I do for you?' he repeated.

'Can I see Nina?' I asked.

'Nina? . . .' he repeated as though surprised. 'Certainly – but what do you want to say to her?'

'I don't see that that's your business,' I answered. 'I have a message for her from her family.'

'But of course it's my business,' he answered. 'I'm looking after her now.'

'Since when?' I asked.

'What does that matter? . . . She is going to live with me.'

'We'll see about that,' I said.

I knew that it was foolish to take this kind of tone. It could do no good, and I was not the sort of man to carry it through.

But he was not at all annoyed.

'See, Ivan Andreievitch,' he said, smiling, 'what is there to discuss? Nina and I have long considered living together. She is a grown-up woman. It's no one's affair but her own.'

'Are you going to marry her?' I asked.

'Certainly not,' he answered; 'that would not suit either of us. It's no good your bringing your English ideas here, Ivan Andreievitch. We belong to the new world, Nina and I.'

'Well, I want to speak to her,' I answered.

'So you shall, certainly. But if you hope to influence her at all you are wasting your time, I assure you. Nina has acted very rightly. She found the home life impossible. I'm sure I don't wonder. She will assist me in my work. The most important work, perhaps, that man has ever been called on to perform. . . .'

He raised his voice here as though he were going to begin a speech. But at that moment Nina came in. She stood in the doorway looking across at me with a childish mixture of hesitation and boldness, of anger and goodwill in her face. Her cheeks were pale, her eyes heavy. Her hair was done in two long plaits. She looked about fourteen.

She came up to me, but she didn't offer me her hand. Boris said:

'Nina dear, Ivan Andreievitch has come to give you a message from your family.' There was a note of scorn in his voice as he repeated my earlier sentence.

'What is it?' she asked, looking at me defiantly.

'I'd like to give it you alone,' I said.

'Whatever you say to me it is right that Boris should hear,' she answered.

I tried to forget that Grogoff was there. I went on:

'Well then, Nina, you must know what I want to say. They are heartbroken at your leaving them. You know of course that they are. They beg you to come back. . . . Vera and Nicholas too. They simply won't know what to do without you. Vera says that you have been angry with her. She doesn't know why, but she says that she will do her very best if you come back, so that you won't be angry any more. . . . Nina, dear, you know that it is they whom you really love. You never can be happy here. You know that you cannot. . . . Come back to them! Come back! I don't know what it was that Alexei Petrovitch said to you, but whatever it was you should not listen to it. He is a bad man and only means harm to your family. He does indeed. . . .'

I paused. She had never moved whilst I was speaking. Now she only said, shaking her head, 'It's no good, Ivan Andreievitch. . . . It's no good.'

'But why? Why?' I asked. 'Give me your reasons, Nina.'

She answered proudly, 'I don't see why I should give you any reasons, Ivan Andreievitch. I am free. I can do as I wish.'

'There's something behind this that I don't know,' I said. 'I ought to know. . . . It isn't fair not to tell me. What did Alexei Petrovitch say to you?'

But she only shook her head.

'He had nothing to do with this. It is my affair, Ivan Andreievitch. I couldn't live with Vera and Nicholas any longer.'

Grogoff then interfered.

'I think this is about enough, . . .' he said. 'I have given you your opportunity. Nina has been quite clear in what she has said. She does not wish to return. There is your answer.' He cleared his voice and went on in rather a higher tone: 'I think you forget, Ivan Andreievitch, another aspect of this affair. It is not only a question of our private family disputes. Nina has come here to assist me in my national work. As a member of the Soviet I may, without exaggeration, claim to have an opportunity in my hands that has been offered in the past to few human beings. You are an Englishman, and so hidebound with prejudices and conventions. You may not be aware that there has opened this week the greatest war the world has ever seen – the war of the proletariats against the bourgeoisies and capitalists of the world.' I tried to interrupt him, but he went on, his voice ever rising and rising: 'What is your wretched German war? What but a struggle between the capitalists of the different countries to secure greater robberies and extortions, to set their feet more firmly than ever on the broad necks of the wretched People! Yes, you English, with your natural hypocrisy, pretend that you are fighting for the freedom of the world. What about Ireland? What about India? What about South Africa? . . . No, you are all alike. Germany, England, Italy, France, and our own wretched Government that has, at last, been destroyed by the brave will of the People. We declare a People's War! . . . We cry aloud to the People to throw down their arms! And the People will hear us!'

He paused for breath. His arms were raised, his eyes on fire, his cheeks crimson.

'Yes,' I said, 'that is all very well. But suppose the German people are the only ones who refuse to listen to you. Suppose that all the other nations, save Germany, have thrown down their arms – a nice chance then for German militarism!'

'But the German people will listen!' he screamed, almost frothing at the mouth. 'They are ready at any moment to follow our example. William and your George and the rest of them – they are doomed, I tell you!'

'Nevertheless,' I went on, 'if you desert us now by making peace and Germany wins this war you will have played only a traitor's part, and all the world will judge you.'

'Traitor! Traitor!' The word seemed to madden him. 'Traitor to whom, pray? Traitor to our Czar and your English king? Yes, and thank God for it! Did the Russian people make the war? They were led like lambs to the slaughter. Like lambs, I tell you. But now they will have their revenge. On all the Bourgeoisie of the world. The Bourgeoisie of the world! . . .'

He suddenly broke off, flinging himself down on the dirty sofa. 'Pheugh. Talking makes one hot! . . . Have a drink, Ivan Andreievitch. . . . Nina, fetch a drink.'

Through all this my eyes had never left her for a moment. I had hoped that this empty tubthumping to which we had been listening would have affected her. But she had not moved nor stirred.

'Nina!' I said softly. 'Nina. Come with me!'

But she only shook her head. Grogoff, quite silent now, lolled on the sofa, watching us. I went up to her and put my hand on her sleeve.

'Dear Nina,' I said, 'come back to us.'

I saw her lip tremble. There were unshed tears in her eyes. But again she shook her head.

'What have they done,' I asked, 'to make you take this step?'

'Something has happened . . .' she said slowly. 'I can't tell you.'

'Just come and talk to Vera.'

'No, it's hopeless . . . I can't see her again. But, Durdles . . . tell her it's not her fault.'

At the sound of my pet name I took courage again.

'But tell me, Nina . . . Do you love this man?'

She turned round and looked at Grogoff as though she were seeing him for the first time.

'Love? . . . Oh no, not love! But he will be kind to me, I think. And I must be myself, be a woman, not a child any longer.'

Then, suddenly clearing her voice, speaking very firmly, looking me full in the face, she said:

'Tell Vera . . . that I saw . . . what happened that Thursday afternoon – the Thursday of the Revolution week. Tell her that – when you're alone with her. Tell her that – then she'll understand.'

She turned and almost ran out of the room.

'Well, you see,' said Grogoff, smiling lazily from the sofa, 'that settles it.'

'It doesn't settle it,' I answered. 'We shall never rest until we have got her back.'

But I had to go. There was nothing more just then to be done.

V

On my return I found Vera alone waiting for me with restless impatience.

'Well?' she said eagerly. Then when she saw that I was alone her face clouded.

'I trusted you –' she began.

'It's no good,' I said at once. 'Not for the moment. She's made up her mind. It's not because she loved him nor, I think, for anything very much that her uncle said. She's got some idea in her head. Perhaps you can explain it.'

'I?' said Vera, looking at me.

'Yes. She gave me a message for you.'

'What was it?' But even as she asked the question she seemed to fear the answer, because she turned away from me.

'She told me to tell you that she saw what happened on the afternoon of the Thursday in Revolution week. She said that then you would understand.'

Vera looked at me with the strangest expression of defiance, fear, triumph.

'What did she see?'

'I don't know. That's what she told me.'

Vera did a strange thing. She laughed.

'They can all know. I don't care. I want them to know. Nina can tell them all.'

'Tell them what?'

'Oh, you'll hear with the rest. Uncle Alexei has done this. He told Nina because he hates me. He won't rest until he ruins us all. But I don't care. He can't take from me what I've got. He can't take from me what I've got.... But we must get her back, Ivan Andreievitch. She *must* come back——'

Nicholas came in and then Semyonov and then Bohun.

Bohun, drawing me aside, whispered to me: 'Can I come and see you? I must ask your advice——'

'Tomorrow evening,' I told him, and left.

Next day I was ill again. I had I suppose done too much the day before. I was in bed alone all day. My old woman had suddenly returned without a word of explanation or excuse. She had not, I am sure, even got so far as the Moscow Province. I doubt whether she had even left Petrograd. I asked her no questions. I could tell of course that she had been drinking. She was a funny old creature, wrinkled and yellow and hideous, very little different in any way from a native in the wilds of Central Africa. The savage in her liked gay colours and trinkets, and she would stick flowers in her hair and wear a tinkling necklace of bright red and blue beads. She had a mangy dog, hairless in places and rheumy at the eyes, who was all her passion, and this creature she would adore, taking it to sleep with her, talking to it by the hour together, pulling its tail and twisting its neck so that it growled with rage – and then, when it growled, she, too, would make strange noises as though sympathising with it.

She returned to me from no sort of sense of duty, but simply because, I think, she did not know where else to go. She scowled on me and informed me that now that there had been the Revolution everything was different; nevertheless the sight of my sick yellow face moved her as sickness and misfortune always move every Russian, however old and debased he may be.

'You shouldn't have gone out walking,' she said crossly. 'That man's been here again?' referring to the Rat, whom she hated.

'If it hadn't been for him,' I said, 'I would have died.'

But she made the flat as cheerful as she could, lighting the stove, putting some yellow flowers into a glass, dusting the Benois watercolour, putting my favourite books beside my bed.

When Henry Bohun came in he was surprised at the brightness of everything.

'Why, how cosy you are!' he cried.

'Ah, ha,' I said, 'I told you it wasn't so bad here.'

He picked up my books, looked at Galleon's *Roads* and then *Pride and Prejudice*.

'It's the simplest things that last,' he said. 'Galleon's jolly good, but he's not simple enough. *Tess* is the thing, you know, and *Tono-Bungay*, and *The Nigger of the Narcissus* . . . I usen't to think so. I've grown older, haven't I?'

He had.

'What do you think of *Discipline* now?' I asked.

'Oh, Lord!' he blushed, 'I was a young cuckoo.'

'And what about knowing all about Russia after a week?'

'No – and that reminds me!' He drew his chair closer to my bed. 'That's what I've come to talk about. Do you mind if I gas a lot?'

'Gas as much as you like,' I said.

'Well, I can't explain things unless I do. . . . You're sure you're not too seedy to listen?'

'Not a bit. It does me good,' I told him.

'You see in a way you're really responsible. You remember, long ago, telling me to look after Markovitch when I talked all that rot about caring for Vera?'

'Yes – I remember very well indeed.'

'In a way it all started from that. You put me on to seeing Markovitch in quite a different light. I'd always thought of him as an awfully dull dog with very little to say for himself, and a bit loose in the topstory too. I thought it a terrible shame a ripping woman like Vera having married him, and I used to feel sick with him about it. Then sometimes he'd look like the devil himself, as wicked as sin, poring over his inventions, and you'd fancy that to stick a knife in his back might be perhaps the best thing for everybody.

'Well, you explained him to me and I saw him different – not that I've ever got very much out of him. I don't think that he either likes me or trusts me, and anyway he thinks me too young and foolish to be of any importance – which I daresay I am. He told me, by the way, the other day, that the only Englishman he thought anything of was yourself——'

'Very nice of him,' I murmured.

'Yes, but not very flattering to me when I've spent months trying to be fascinating to him. Anyhow, although I may be said to have failed in one way, I've got rather keen on the pursuit. If I can't make him like me I can at least study him and learn something. That's a leaf out of your book, Durward. You're always studying people, aren't you?'

'Oh, I don't know,' I said.

'Yes, of course you are. Well, I'll tell you frankly I've got fond of the old bird. I don't believe you could live at close quarters with any Russian, however nasty, and not get a kind of affection for him. They're so damned childish.'

'Oh yes, you could,' I said. 'Try Semyonov.'

'I'm coming to him in a minute,' said Bohun. 'Well, Markovitch was most awfully unhappy. That's one thing one saw about him at once – unhappy of course because Vera didn't love him and he adored her. But there was more in it than that. He let himself go one night to me – the only time he's ever talked to me really. He was drunk a bit, and he wanted to borrow money off me. But there was more in it than that. He talked to me about Russia. That seemed to have been his great idea when the war began that it was going to lead to the most marvellous patriotism all through Russia. It seemed to begin like that, and do you know, Durward, as he talked I saw that patriotism *was* at the bottom of everything, that you could talk about Internationalism until you were blue in the face, and that it only began to mean anything when you'd learnt first what nationality was – that you couldn't really love all mankind until you'd first learnt to love one or two people close to you. And that you couldn't love the world as a vast democratic state until you'd learnt to love your own little bit of ground, your own fields, your own river, your own church tower. Markovitch had it all as plain as plain. "Make your own house secure and beautiful. Then it is ready to take its place in the general scheme. We Russians always begin at the wrong end. We jump all the intermediate stages. I'm as bad as the rest." I know you'll say I'm so easily impressed, Durward, but he was wonderful that night – and so *right*. So that as he talked I just longed to rush back and see that my village – Topright in Wiltshire – was safe and sound with the highgate at the end of the village street, and the village stores with the lollipop windows, and the green with the sheep on it, and the ruddy stream with the small trout and the high Down beyond. . . . Oh well, you know what I mean——'

'I know,' said I.

'I saw that the point of Markovitch was that he must have some ideal to live up to. If he couldn't have Vera he'd have Russia, and if he couldn't have Russia he'd have his inventions. When we first came along a month or two ago he'd lost Russia, he was losing Vera, and he wasn't very sure about his inventions. A bad time for the old boy, and you were quite right to tell me to look after him. Then came the Revolution, and he thought that everything was saved. Vera and Russia and everything. Wasn't he wonderful that week? Like a child who has suddenly found Paradise. . . . Could any Englishman ever be cheated like that by anything? Why, a fellow would be locked up for a loony if he looked as happy as Markovitch looked that week. It wouldn't be decent. . . . Well, then . . .' He paused dramatically. 'What's happened to him since, Durward?'

'How do you mean? What's happened to him since?' I asked.

'I mean just what I say. Something happened to him at the end of that week. I can put my finger almost exactly on the day – the Thursday of that week. What was it? That's one of the things I've come to ask you about?'

'I don't know. I was ill,' I said.

'No, but has nobody told you anything?'

'I haven't heard a word,' I said.

His face fell. 'I felt sure you'd help me,' he said.

'Tell me the rest and perhaps I can put things together,' I suggested.

'The rest is really Semyonov. The queerest things have been happening. Of course, the thing is to get rid of all one's English ideas, isn't it? and that's so damned difficult. It's no use saying an English fellow wouldn't do this or that. Of course he wouldn't. . . . Oh, they *are* queer!'

He sighed, poor boy, with the difficulty of the whole affair.

'Giving them up in despair, Bohun, is as bad as thinking you understand them completely. Just take what comes.'

'Well, "what came" was this. On that Thursday evening Markovitch was as though he'd been struck in the face. You never saw such a change. Of course we all noticed it. White and sickly, saying nothing to anybody. Next morning, quite early, Semyonov came over and proposed lodging with us.

'It absolutely took my breath away, but no one else seemed very astonished. What on earth did he want to leave his comfortable flat and come to us for? We were packed tight enough as it was. I never liked the feller, but upon my word I simply hated him as he sat there, so quiet, stroking his beard and smiling at us in his sarcastic way.

'To my amazement Markovitch seemed quite keen about it. Not only agreed, but offered his own room as a bedroom. "What about your inventions?" some one asked him.

'"I've given them up," he said, looking at us all just like a caged animal – "for ever."

'I would have offered to retire myself if I hadn't been so interested, but this was all so curious that I was determined to see it out to the end. And you'd told me to look after Markovitch. If ever he'd wanted looking after it was now! I could see that Vera hated the idea of Semyonov coming, but after Markovitch had spoken she never said a word. So then it was all settled.'

'What did Nina do?' I asked.

'Nina? She never said anything either. At the end she went up to Semyonov and took his hand and said, "I'm so glad you're coming, Uncle Alexei," and looked at Vera. Oh! they're all as queer as they can be, I tell you! '

'What happened next?' I asked eagerly.

'Everything's happened and nothing's happened,' he replied. 'Nina's run away. Of course you know that. What she did it for I can't imagine. Fancy going to a fellow like Grogoff! Lawrence has been coming every day and just sitting there, not saying anything. Semyonov's amiable to everybody – especially amiable to Markovitch. But he's laughing at him all the time, I think. Anyway he makes him mad sometimes, so that I think Markovitch is going to strike him. But of course he never does. . . . Now here's a funny thing. This is really what I want to ask you most about.'

He drew his chair closer to my bed and dropped his voice as though he were going to whisper a secret to me.

'The other night I was awake – about two in the morning it was – and wanted a book – so I went into the dining-room. I'd only got bedroom slippers on and I was stopped at the door by a sound. It was Semyonov sitting over by the farther window, in his shirt and trousers, his beard in his hands, and sobbing as though his heart would break. I'd never heard a man cry like that. I hate hearing a man cry anyway. I've heard fellers at the Front when they're off their heads or something . . . but Semyonov was worse than that. It was a strong man crying, with all his wits about him. . . . Then I heard some words. He kept repeating again and again. "Oh, my dear, my dear, my dear! . . . Wait for me! . . . Wait for me! Wait for me! . . ." over and over again – awful! I crept back to my room frightened out of my life. I've never known anything so awful. And Semyonov of all people!

'It was like that man in *Wuthering Heights*. What's his name? Heathcliffe! I always thought that was a bit of an exaggeration when he dashed his head against a tree and all that. But, by Jove, you never know! . . . Now, Durward, you've got to tell me. You've known Semyonov for years. You can explain. What's it all about, and what's he trying to do to Markovitch?'

'I can scarcely think what to tell you,' I said at last. 'I don't really know much about Semyonov, and my guesses will probably strike you as insane.'

'No, they won't,' said Bohun. 'I've learnt a bit lately.'

'Semyonov,' I said, 'is a deep-dyed sensualist. All his life he's thought about nothing but gratifying his appetites. That's simple enough – there are plenty of that type everywhere. But unfortunately for him he's a very clever man, and like every Russian both a cynic and an idealist – a cynic in facts *because* he's an idealist – He got everything so easily all through his life that his cynicism grew and grew. He had wealth and women and position. He was as strong as a horse. Every one gave way to him, and he despised everybody. He went to the Front, and one day came across a woman different from any other whom he had ever known.'

'How different?' asked Bohun, because I paused.

'Different in that she was simpler and naïver and honester and better and more beautiful.'

'Better than Vera?' Bohun asked.

'Different,' I said. 'She was younger, less strong-willed, less clever, less passionate perhaps. But alone – alone, in all the world. Every one must love her – no one could help it . . . .'

I broke off again. Bohun waited.

I went on. 'Semyonov saw her and snatched her from the Englishman to whom she was engaged. I don't think she ever really loved the Englishman, but she loved Semyonov.'

'Well?' said Bohun.

'She was killed. A stray shot, when she was giving tea to the men in the trenches. . . . It meant a lot . . . to all of us. The Englishman was killed too, so he was all right. I think Semyonov would have liked that same end; but he didn't get it, so he's remained desolate. Really desolate, in a way that only your thorough sensualist can be. A beautiful fruit just within his grasp, something at last that can tempt his jaded appetite. He's just going to taste it, when whisk! it's gone, and gone, perhaps, into some one else's hands. How does he know? How does he know anything? There may be another life – who can really prove there isn't? and when you've seen something in the very thick and glow of existence, something more alive than life itself, and, click! it's gone – well, it *must* have gone somewhere, mustn't it? Not the body only, but that soul, that spirit, that individual personal expression of beauty and purity and loveliness? Oh, it must be somewhere yet! . . . It *must be!* . . . At any rate *he* didn't know. And he didn't know either that she might not have proved his idealism right after all. Ah! to your cynic there's nothing more maddening! Do you think your cynic loves his cynicism? Not a bit of it! Not he! But he won't be taken in by sham any more. That he swears. . . .

'So it was with Semyonov. This girl might have proved the one real exception; she might have lasted, she might have grown even more beautiful and more wonderful, and so proved his idealism true after all. He doesn't know, and I don't know. But there it is. He's haunted by the possibility of it all his days. He's a man now ruled by an obsession. He thinks of one thing and one thing only, day and night. His sensuality has fallen away from him because women are dull – sterile to him beside that perfect picture of the woman lost. Lost! he may recover her! He doesn't know. The thought of death obsesses him. What is there in it? Is she behind there or no? Is she behind there, maddening thought, with her Englishman?

'He must know. He *must* know. He calls to her – she won't come to him. What is he to do? Suicide? No, to a proud man like Semyonov that's a miserable confession of weakness. How they'd laugh at him, these other despicable human beings, if he did that! He'd prove himself as weak as they. No, that's not for him. What then?

'This is a fantastic world, Bohun, and nothing is impossible for it. Suppose he were to select some one, some weak and irritable and sentimental and disappointed man, some one whose every foible and weakness he knew, suppose he were to place himself near him and so irritate and confuse and madden him that at last one day, in a fury of rage and despair, that man were to do for him what he is too proud to do for himself! Think of the excitement, the interest, the food for his cynicism, the food for his conceit such a game would be to Semyonov. Is this going to do it? Or this? Or this? Now I've got him far enough? Another five minutes! . . . Think of the hairbreadth escapes, the check and counter check, the sense, above all, that to a man like Semyonov is almost everything, that he is master of human emotions, that he can direct wretched, weak human beings whither he will.

'And the other – the weak, disappointed, excitable man – can't you see that Semyonov has him close to his hand, that he has only to stretch a finger——?'

'Markovitch!' cried Bohun.

'Now you know,' I said, 'why you've got to stay on in that flat.'

VI

I have said already, I think, that the instinctive motive of Vera's life was her independent pride. Cling to that, and however the world might rock and toss around her she could not be wrecked. Imagine, then, what she must have suffered during the weeks that followed her surrender to Lawrence. Not that for a moment she intended to go back on her surrender, which was, indeed, the proudest moment of her whole life. She never looked back for one second after that embrace, she never doubted herself or him or the supreme importance of love itself; but the rest of her – her tenderness, her fidelity, her loyalty, her self-respect – this was all tortured now by the things that she seemed compelled to do. It must have appeared to her as though Fate, having watched that complete abandonment, intended to deprive her of everything upon which she had depended. She was, I think, a woman of very simple instincts. The things that had been in her life – her love for Nina, her maternal tenderness for Nicholas, her sense of duty – remained with her as strongly after that tremendous Thursday afternoon as they had been before it. She did not see why they need be changed. She did not love Nina any the less because she loved Lawrence; indeed, she had never loved Nina so intensely as on the night when she had realised her love for Lawrence to the full, that night when they had sheltered the policeman. And she had never pretended to love Nicholas. She had always told him that she did not love him. She had been absolutely honest with him always, and he had often said to her, 'If ever real love comes into your life, Vera, you will leave me,' and she had always answered him, 'No, Nicholas, why should I? I will never change. Why should I?'

She honestly thought that her love for Lawrence need not alter things. She would tell Nicholas, of course, and then she would act as he wished. If she were not to see Lawrence she would not see him – that would make no difference to her love for him. What she did not realise – and that was strange after living with him for so long – was that he was always hoping that her tender kindliness towards him would, one day, change into something more passionate. I think that, subconsciously, she did realise it, and that was why she was, during those weeks before the Revolution, so often uneasy and unhappy. But I am sure that definitely she never admitted it.

The great fact was that, as soon as possible, she must tell Nicholas all about it. And the days went by, and she did not. She did not, partly because she had now some one else as well as herself to consider. I believe that in those weeks between that Thursday and Easter Day she never had one moment alone with Lawrence. He came, as Bohun had told me, to see them; he sat there and looked at her, and listened and waited. She herself, I expect, prevented their being alone. She was waiting for something to happen. Then Nina's flight overwhelmed every-thing. That must have been the most awful thing. She never liked Grogoff, never trusted him, and had a very clear idea of his character. But more awful to her than his weakness was her knowledge that Nina did not love him. What could have driven her to do such a thing? She knew of her affection for Lawrence, but she had, perhaps, never taken that seriously. How could Nina really love Lawrence when he, so obviously, cared nothing at all for her? She reasoned then, as every one always does, on the lines of her own character. She herself could never have cared seriously for any one had there been no return. Her pride would not have allowed her. . . .

But Nina had been the charge of her life. Before Nicholas, before her own life, before everything. Nina was her duty, her sacred cause – and now she was betraying her trust! Something must be done – but what? but what? She knew Nina well enough to realise that a false step would only plunge her farther than ever into the business. It must have seemed to her indeed that because of her own initial disloyalty the whole world was falling away from her.

Then there came Semyonov; I did not at this time at all sufficiently realise that her hatred of her uncle – for it *was* hatred, more, much more than mere dislike – had been with her all her life. Many months afterwards she told me that she could never remember a time when she had not hated him. He had teased her when she was a very little girl, laughing at her naïve honesty, throwing doubts on her independence, cynically ridiculing her loyalty. There had been one horrible winter month when she (then ten or eleven years of age) had been sent to stay with him in Moscow.

He had a fine house near the Arbat, and he was living (although she did not of course know anything about that at the time) with one of his gaudiest mistresses. Her mother and father being dead, she had no protection. She was defenceless. I don't think that he in any way perverted her innocence. I expect that he was especially careful to shield her from his own manner of life (he had always his own queer tradition of honour which he affected indeed to despise), but she felt more than she perceived. The house was garish, over-scented and over-lighted. There were many gilt chairs and large pictures of naked women and numbers of coloured cushions. She was desperately lonely. She hated the woman of the house, who tried, I have no doubt, to be kind to her, and after the first week she was left to herself.

One night, long after she had gone to bed, there was a row downstairs, one of the scenes common enough between Semyonov and his women. Terrified, she went to the head of the stairs and heard the smash of falling glass and her uncle's voice raised in a scream of rage and vituperation. A great naked woman in a gold frame swung and leered at her in the lighted passage. She fled back to her dark room and lay, for the rest of that night, trembling and quivering with her head beneath the bed-clothes.

From that moment she feared her uncle as much as she hated him. Long afterwards came his influence over Nicholas. No one had so much influence over Nicholas as he. Nicholas himself admitted it. He was alternately charmed and frightened, beguiled and disgusted, attracted and repulsed. Before the war Semyonov had, for a time, seen a good deal of them, and Nicholas steadily degenerated. Then Semyonov was bored with it all and went off after other game more worthy of his doughty spear. Then came the war, and Vera devoutly hoped that her dear uncle would meet his death at the hands of some patriotic Austrian. He did indeed for a time disappear from their lives, and it seemed that he might never come back again. Then on that fateful Christmas Day he did return, and Vera's worst fears were realised. She hated him all the more because of her impotence. She could do nothing against him at all. She was never very subtle in her dealings with people, and her own natural honesty made her often stupid about men's motives. But the thing for which she feared her uncle most was his, as it seemed to her, supernatural penetration into the thoughts of others.

She of course greatly exaggerated his gifts in that direction simply because they were in no way her gifts, and he, equally of course, discovered very early in their acquaintance that this was the way to impress her. He played tricks with her exactly as a conjurer produces a rabbit out of a hat. . . .

When he announced his intention of coming to live in the flat she was literally paralysed with fright. Had it been any one else she would have fought, but in her uncle's drawing gradually nearer and nearer to the centre of all their lives, coming as it seemed to her so silently and mysteriously, without obvious motive, and yet with so stealthy a plan, against this man she could do nothing. . . .

Nevertheless she determined to fight for Nicholas to the last – to fight for Nicholas, to bring back Nina, these were now the two great aims of her life; and whilst they were being realised her love for Lawrence must be passive, passive as a deep passionate flame beats with unwavering force in the heart of the lamp. . . .

They had made me promise long before that I would spend Easter Eve with them and go with them to our church on the Quay. I wondered now whether all the troubles of the last weeks would not negative that invitation, and I had privately determined that if I did not hear from them again I would slip off with Lawrence somewhere. But on Good Friday Markovitch, meeting me in the Morskaia, reminded me that I was coming.

It is very difficult to give any clear picture of the atmosphere of the town between Revolution week and this Easter Eve, and yet all the seeds of the later crop of horrors were sown during that period. Its spiritual mentality corresponded almost exactly with the physical thaw that accompanied it – mist, then vapour dripping of rain, the fading away of one clear world into another that was indistinct, ghostly, ominous. I find written in my Diary of Easter Day – exactly five weeks after the outbreak of the Revolution – these words: 'From long talks with K. and others I see quite clearly that Russians have gone mad for the time being. It's heartbreaking to see them holding meetings everywhere, arguing at every street corner as to how they intend to arrange a democratic peace for Europe, when meanwhile the Germans are gathering every moment force upon the frontiers.'

Pretty quick, isn't it, to change from Utopia to threatenings of the worst sort of Communism? But the great point for us in all this – the great point for our private personal histories as well as the public one – was that it was during these weeks that the real gulf between Russia and the Western world showed itself! Yes, for more than three years we had been pretending that a week's sentiment and a hurriedly proclaimed Idealism could bridge a separation which centuries of magic and blood and bones had gone to build. For three years we tricked ourselves (I am not sure that the Russians were ever really deceived) . . . but we liked the Ballet, we liked Tolstoi and Dostoieffsky (we translated their inborn mysticism into the weakest kind of sentimentality), we liked the theory of inexhaustible numbers, we liked the picture of their pounding, steam-roller like, to Berlin . . . we tricked ourselves, and in the space of a night our trick was exposed.

Plain enough the reasons for these mistakes that we in England have made over that same Revolution, mistakes made by none more emphatically than by our own Social Democrats. Those who hailed the Revolution as the fulfilment of all their dearest hopes, those who cursed it as the beginning of the damnation of the world – all equally in the wrong. The Revolution had no thought for *them.* Russian extremists might shout as they pleased about their leading the fight for the democracies of the world – they never even began to understand the other democracies. Whatever Russia may do, through repercussion, for the rest of the world, she remains finally alone – isolated in her Government, in her ideals, in her ambitions, in her abnegations. For a moment the world-politics of her foreign rulers seemed to draw her into the Western Whirlpool. For a moment only she remained there. She has slipped back again behind her veil of mist and shadow. We may trade with her, plunge into her politics, steal from her Art, emphasise her religion – she remains alone, apart, mysterious. . . .

I think it was with a kind of gulping surprise, as after a sudden plunge into icy cold water, that we English became conscious of this. It came to us first in the form that to us the war was everything – to the Russian, by the side of an idea the war was nothing at all. How was I, for instance, to recognise the men who took a leading part in the events of this extraordinary year as the same men who fought with bare hands, with fanatical bravery through all the Galician campaign of two years before?

Had I not realised sufficiently at that time that Russia moves always according to the Idea that governs her – and that when that Idea changes the world, *his* world changes with it? . . .

Well, to return to Markovitch. . . .

VII

I was on the point of setting out for the English Prospect on Saturday evening when there was a knock on my door, and to my surprise Nicholas Markovitch came in. He was in evening dress – rather quaint it seemed to me, with his pointed collar so high, his tail-coat so much too small, and his large-brimmed bowler hat. He explained to me confusedly that he wished to walk with me alone to the church . . . that he had things to tell me . . . that we should meet the others there. I saw at once two things, that he was very miserable, that he was a little drunk. His misery showed itself in his strange, pathetic, gleaming eyes, that looked so often as though they held unshed tears (this gave him an unfortunate ridiculous aspect), in his hollow pale cheeks and the droop of his mouth, not petulant nor peevish, simply unhappy in the way that animals or very young children express unhappiness. His drunkenness showed itself in quite another way. He was unsteady a little on his feet, and his hands trembled, his forehead was flushed, and he spoke thickly, sometimes running his words together. At the same time he was not very drunk, and was quite in control of his thoughts and intentions.

We went out together. It could not have been called a fine night – it was too cold, and there was a hint of rain in the air – and yet there is beauty, I believe, in every Russian Easter Eve. The day comes so wonderfully at the end of the long heavy winter. The white nights with their incredible, almost terrifying beauty are at hand, the ice is broken, the new world of sun and flowers is ready, at an instant's magic word, to be born. Nevertheless this year there was an incredible pathos in the wind. The soul of Petrograd was indeed stirring, but mournfully, ominously. There were not, for one thing, the rows of little fairy lamps that on this night always make the streets so gay. They hang in chains and Clusters of light from street to street, blazing in the square, reflected star-like in the canals, misty and golden-veiled in distance. To-night only the churches had their lights; for the rest, the streets were black chasms of windy desolation, the canals burdened with the breaking ice which moved restlessly against the dead barges. Very strong in the air was the smell of the sea; the heavy clouds that moved in a strange kind of ordered procession over-head seemed to carry that scent with them, and in the dim pale shadows of the evening glow one seemed to see at the end of every street mysterious Clusters of masts, and to hear the clank of chains and the creak of restless boards. There were few people about and a great silence everywhere. The air was damp and thick, and smelt of rotten soil, as though dank grass was everywhere pushing its way up through the cobbles and paving-stones.

As we walked Markovitch talked incessantly. It was only a very little the talk of a drunken man, scarcely disconnected at all, but every now and again running into sudden little wildnesses and extravagances. I cannot remember nearly all that he said. He came suddenly, as I expected him to do, to the subject of Semyonov.

'You know of course that Alexei Petrovitch is living with us now?'

'Yes. I know that.'

'You can understand, Ivan Andreievitch, that when he came first and proposed it to me I was startled. I had other things – veiy serious things – to think of just then. We weren't – we aren't – very happy at home just now . . . you know that. . . . I didn't think he'd be very gay with us. I told him that. He said he didn't expect to be gay anywhere at this time, but that he was lonely in his flat all by himself, and he thought for a week or two he'd like company. He didn't expect it would be for very long. No. . . . He said he was expecting "something to happen." Something to himself, he said, that would alter his affairs. So, as it was only for a little time, well, it didn't seem to matter. Besides, he's a powerful man. He's difEcult to resist – very difficult to resist. . . .'

'Why have you given up your inventions, Nicolai Leontievitch?' I said to him, suddenly turning round upon him.

'My inventions?' he repeated, seeming very startled at that.

'Yes, your inventions.'

'No, no. . . . Understand, I have no more use for them. There are other things now to think about – more important things.'

'But you were getting on with them so well?'

'No – not really. I was deceiving myself as I have often deceived myself before. Alexei showed me that. He told me that they were no good——'

'But I thought that he encouraged you?'

'Yes – at first – only at first. Afterwards he saw into them more clearly; he changed his mind. I think he was only intending to be kind. A strange man . . . a strange man. . . .'

'A very strange man. Don't you let him influence you, Nicholas Markovitch.'

'Influence me? Do you think he does that?' He suddenly came close to me, catching my arm.

'I don't know. I haven' t seen you often together.'

'Perhaps he does . . . *Mojet bweet* . . . You may be right. I don't know – I don't know what I feel about him at all. Sometimes he seems to me very kind; sometimes I'm frightened of him, sometimes' – here he dropped his voice – 'he makes me very angry, so angry that I lose control of myself – a despicable thing . . . a despicable thing . . . just as I used to feel about the old man to whom I was secretary. I nearly murdered him once. In the middle of the night I thought suddenly of his stomach, all round and white and shining. It was an irresistible temptation to plunge a knife into it. I was awake for hours thinking of it. Every man has such hours. . . . At the same time Alexei can be very kind.'

'How do you mean – kind?' I asked.

'For instance he has some very good wine – fifty bottles at least – he has given it all to us. Then he insists on paying us for his food. He is a generous-spirited man. Money is nothing to us——'

'Don't you drink his wine,' I said.

Nicholas was instantly offended.

'What do you mean, Ivan Andreievitch? Not drink his wine? Am I an infant? Can I not look after myself? – *Blagadaryoo Vas.* . . . I am more than ten years old.' He took his hand away from my arm.

'No, I didn't mean that at all,' I assured him. 'Of course not – only you told me not long ago that you had given up wine altogether. That's why I said what I did.'

'So I have! So I have!' he eagerly assured me. 'But Easter's a time for rejoicing. . . . Rejoicing!' – his voice rose suddenly shrill and scornful – 'rejoicing with the world in the State that it is. Truly, Ivan Andreievitch, I don't wonder at Alexei's cynicism. I don't indeed. The world is a sad spectacle for an observant man.' He suddenly put his hand through my arm, so close to me now that I could feel his beating heart. 'But you believe, don't you, Ivan Andreievitch, that Russia now has found herself?' His voice became desperately urgent and beseeching. 'You must believe that. You don't agree with those fools who don't believe that she will make the best of all this? Fools? Scoundrels! Scoundrels! That's what they are. I must believe in Russia now or I shall die. And so with all of us. If she does not rise now as one great country and lead the world, she will never do so. Our hearts must break. But she will . . . she will! No one who is watching events can doubt it. Only cynics like Alexei doubt – he doubts everything. And he cannot leave anything alone. He must smear everything with his dirty finger. But he must leave Russia alone . . . I tell him . . .'

He broke off. 'If Russia fails now,' he spoke very quietly, 'my life is over. I have nothing left. I will die.'

'Come, Nicolai Leontievitch,' I said, 'you mustn't let yourself go like that. Life isn't over because one is disappointed in one's country. And even though one is disappointed one does not love the less. What's friendship worth if every disappointment chills one's affection? One loves one's country because she is one's country, not because she's disappointing. . . .' And so I went on with a number of amiable platitudes, struggling to comfort him somewhere, and knowing that I was not even beginning to touch the trouble of his soul.

He drew very close to me, his fingers gripping my sleeve. 'I'll tell you, Ivan Andreievitch – but you mustn't tell anybody else. I'm afraid. Yes, I am. Afraid of myself, afraid of this town, afraid of Alexei, although that must seem strange to you. Things are very bad with me, Ivan Andreievitch. Very bad, indeed. Oh! I have been disappointed! yes, I have. Not that I expected anything else. But now it has come at last, the blow that I have always feared has fallen – a very heavy blow. My own fault, perhaps, I don't know. But I'm afraid of myself. I don't know what I may do. I have such strange dreams – Why has Alexei come to stay with us?'

'I don't know,' I said.

Then, thank God, we reached the church. It was only as we went up the Steps that I realised that he had never once mentioned Vera.

VIII

And yet with all our worries thick upon us it was quite impossible to resist the sweetness and charm and mystery of that service.

I think that perhaps it is true, as many have said, that people did not crowd to the churches on that Easter as they had on earlier ones, but our church was a small one, and it seemed to us to be crammed.

We stumbled up the dark steps, and found ourselves at the far end of the very narrow nave. At the other end there was a pool of soft golden light in which dark figures were bathed mysteriously. At the very moment of our entering, the procession was passing down the nave on its way round the outside of the church to look for the Body of Our Lord. Down the nave they came, the people Standing on either side to let them pass, and then, many of them, falling in behind. Every one carried a lighted candle. First there were the singers, then men carrying the coloured banners, then the priest in stiff gorgeous raiment, then officials and dignitaries, finally the crowd. The singing, the forest of lighted candles, the sudden opening of the black door and the blowing in of the cold night wind, the passing of the voices out into the air, the soft dying away of the singing, and then the hushed expectation of the waiting for the return – all this had in it something so elemental, so simple, and so true to the very heart of the mystery of life that all trouble and sorrow fell away and one was at peace.

How strange was that expectation! We knew so well what the word must be; we could tell exactly the moment of the knock at the door, the deep sound of the priest's voice, the embracings and dropping of wax over every one's clothes that would follow it – and yet every year it was the same! There *was* truth in it, there was some deep response to the human dependence, some whispered promise of a future good. We waited there, our hearts beating, crowded against the dark walls. It was a very democratic assembly, bourgeoisie, workmen, soldiers, officers, women in evening dress and peasant women with shawls over their heads. No one spoke or whispered.

Suddenly there was a knock. The door was opened. The priest stood there, in his crimson and gold. 'Christ is risen!' he cried, his voice vibrating as though he had indeed but just now, out there in the dark and wind, made the great discovery.

'He is risen indeed!' came the reply from us all. Markovitch embraced me. 'Let us go,' he whispered, 'I can't bear it somehow to-night.'

We went out. Everywhere the bells were ringing – the wonderful deep boom of St. Isaac's, and then all the other bells, jangling, singing, crying, chattering, answering from all over Petrograd. From the other side of the Neva came the report of the guns and the fainter, more distant echo of the guns near the sea. I could hear behind it all the incessant 'chuck-chuck, chuck-chuck,' of the ice colliding on the river.

It was very cold, and we hurried back to Anglisky Prospect. Markovitch was quite silent all the way.

When we arrived we found Vera and Uncle Ivan and Semyonov waiting for us (Bohun was with friends). On the table was the *paskha*, a sweet paste made of eggs and cream, curds and sugar, a huge ham, a large cake or rather sweet bread called *kulich*, and a big bowl full of Easter eggs, as many-coloured as the rainbow. This would be the fare during the whole week, as there was to be no cooking until the following Saturday – and very tired of the ham and the eggs one became before that day. There was also wine – some of Semyonov's gift, I supposed – and a tiny bottle of vodka.

We were not a very cheerful Company. Uncle Ivan, who was really distinguished by his complete inability to perceive what was going on under his nose, was happy, and ate a great deal of the ham and certainly more of the *paskha* than was good for him.

I do not know who was responsible for the final incident – Semyonov perhaps – but I have often wondered whether some word or other of mine precipitated it. We had finished our meal and were sitting quietly together, each occupied with his own thoughts. I had noticed that Markovitch had been drinking a great deal.

I was just thinking it was time for me to go when I heard Semyonov say:

'Well, what do you think of your Revolution now, Nicholas?'

'What do you mean – my Revolution?' he asked.

(The strange thing on looking back is that the whole of this scene seems to me to have passed in a whisper, as though we were all terrified of somebody.)

'Well – do you remember how you talked to me? . . . about the saving of the world and all the rest of it that this was going to be? Doesn't seem to be quite turning out that way, does it, from all one hears? A good deal of quarrelling, isn't there? And what about the army – breaking up a bit, isn't it?'

'Don't, Uncle Alexei,' I heard Vera whisper.

'What I said I still believe,' Nicholas answered very quietly. 'Leave Russia alone, Alexei – and leave me alone, too.'

'I'm not touching you, Nicholas,' Semyonov answered, laughing softly.

'Yes you are – you know that you are. I'm not angry – not yet. But it's unwise of you – unwise. . . . '

'Unwise – how?'

'Never mind. "Below the silent pools there lie hidden many devils." Leave me alone. You are our guest.'

'Indeed, Nicholas,' said Semyonov, still laughing, 'I mean you no harm. Ask our friend Durward here whether I ever mean any one any harm. He will, I'm sure, give me the best of characters.'

'No – no harm perhaps – but still you tease me. . . . I'm a fool to mind. . . . But then I am a fool – every one knows it.'

All the time he was looking with his pathetic eyes and his pale face at Vera.

Vera said again, very low, almost in a whisper: 'Uncle Alexei . . . please.'

'But really, Nicholas,' Semyonov went on, 'you underrate yourself. You do indeed. Nobody thinks you a fool. I think you a very lucky man. With your talents——'

'Talents!' said Nicholas softly, looking at Vera. 'I have no talents.'

'– And Vera's love for you,' went on Semyonov.

'Ah! that is over!' Nicholas said, so low that I scarcely heard it. I do not know what then exactly happened. I think that Vera put out her hand to cover Nicholas'. At any rate I saw him draw his away, very gently. It lay on the table, and the only sound beside the voices was the tiny rattle of his nails as his hand trembled against the woodwork.

Vera said something that I did not catch.

'No . . .' Nicholas said. 'No . . . We must be true with one another, Vera. I have been drinking too much wine. My head is aching, and perhaps my words are not very clear. But it gives me courage to say what I have in my mind. I haven't thought out yet what we must do. Perhaps you can help me. But I must tell you that I saw everything that happened here on that Thursday afternoon in the week of the Revolution——'

Vera made a litte movement of distress.

'Yes, you didn't know – but I was in my room – where Alexei sleeps now, you know. I couldn't help seeing. I'm very sorry.'

'No, Nicholas, I'm very glad,' Vera answered quietly. 'I would have told you in any case. I should have told you before. I love him and he loves me, just as you saw. I would like Ivan Andreievitch and Uncle Ivan and every one to know. There is nothing to conceal. I have never loved any one before, and I'm not ashamed of loving some one now . . . It doesn't alter our life, Nicholas. I care for you just as I did care, and I will do just as you tell me. I will never see him again if that's what you wish, but I shall always love him.'

'Ah, Vera – you are cruel.' Nicholas gave a little cry like a hurt animal, then he went away from us, Standing for a moment looking at us.

'We'll have to consider what we must do. I don't know. I can't think to-night. . . . And you, Alexei, you leave me alone . . .'

He went stumbling away towards his bedroom.

Vera said nothing to any of us. She got up slowly, looked about her for a moment as though she were bewildered by the light, and then went after Nicholas. I turned to Semyonov.

'You'd better go back to your own place,' I said.

'Not yet, thank you,' he answered, smiling.

IX

On the afternoon of Easter Monday I was reminded by Bohun of an engagement that I had made some weeks before to go that evening to a party at the house of a rich merchant, Rozanov by name. I have, I think, mentioned him earlier in this book. I cannot conceive why I had ever made the promise, and in the afternoon, meeting Bohun at Watkins' bookshop in the Morskaia, I told him that I couldn't go.

'Oh, come along!' he said. 'It's your duty.'

'Why my duty? '

'They're all talking as hard as they can about saving the world by turning the other cheek, and so on; and a few practical facts about Germany from you will do a world of good.'

'Oh, your propaganda!' I said.

'No, it isn't my propaganda,' he answered. 'It's a matter of life and death to get these people to go on with the war, and every little helps.'

'Well, I'll come,' I said, shaking my head at the bookseller, who was anxious that I should buy the latest works of Mrs. Elinor Glyn and Miss Ethel Dell. I had in fact reflected that a short excursion into other worlds would be good for me. During these weeks I had been living in the very heart of the Markovitches, and it would be healthy to escape for a moment.

But I was not to escape.

I met Bohun at the top of the English Prospect, and we decided to walk. Rozanov lived in the street behind the Kazan Cathedral. I did not know very much about him except that he was a very wealthy merchant, who had made his money by selling cheap sweets to the peasant. He lived, I knew, an immoral and self-indulgent life, and his hobby was the quite indiscriminate collection of modern Russian paintings, his walls being plastered with innumerable works by Benois, Somoff, Dobeijinsky, Yakofflyeff, and Lançeray. He had also two Serovs, a fine Vrubel, and several Ryepins. He had also a fine private collection of indecent drawings.

'I really don't know what on earth we're going to this man for,' I said discontentedly. 'I was weak this afternoon.'

'No, you weren't,' said Bohun. 'And I'll tell you frankly that I'm jolly glad not to be having a meal at home to-night. Do you know, I don't believe I can stick that flat much longer!'

'Why, are things worse?' I asked.

'It's getting so jolly creepy,' Bohun said. 'Everything goes on normally enough outwardly, but I suppose there's been some tremendous row. Of course I don't know anything about that. After what you told me the other night though, I seem to see everything twice its natural size.'

'What do you mean?' I asked him.

'You know when something queer's going on inside a house you seem to notice the furniture of the rooms much more than you ordinarily do. I remember once a fellow's piano making me quite sick whenever I looked at it. I didn't know why; I don't know why now, but the funny thing is that another man who knew him once said exacdy the same thing to me about it. He felt it too. Of course we're none of us quite normal just now. The whole town seems to be turning upside down. I'm always imagining there are animals in the canals; and don't you notice what lots of queer fellows there are in the Nevski now, and Chinese and Japs – all sorts of wild men? And last night I had a dream that all the lumps of ice in the Nevski turned into griffins and went marching through the Red Square eating every one up on their way. . . .' Bohun laughed. 'That's because I'd eaten something of course – too much *paskha* probably.

'But, seriously, I came in this evening at five o'clock, and the first thing I noticed was that little red lacquer musical-box of Semyonov's. You know it. The one with a sportsman in a top hat and a horse and a dog on the lid. He brought it with some other little things when he moved in. It's a jolly thing to look at, but it's got two most irritating tunes. One's like "The Blue Bells of Scotland." You said yourself the other day it would drive you mad if you heard it often. Well, there it was, jangling away in its self-sufficient wheezy voice. Semyonov was sitting in the armchair reading the newspaper, Markovitch was standing behind the chair with the strangest look on his face.

Suddenly, just as I came in, he bent down and I heard him say: "Won't you stop the beastly thing?" "Certainly," said Semyonov, and he went across in his heavy plodding kind of way and stopped it. I went off to my room and then, upon my word, five minutes after I heard it begin again, thin and reedy through the walls. But when I came back into the dining-room there was no one there. You can't think how that tune irritated me, and I tried to stop it. I went up to it, but I couldn't find the hinge or the key. So on it went, over and over again. Then there's another thing. Have you ever noticed how some chairs will creak in a room, just as though some one were sitting down or getting up? It always, in ordinary times, makes you jump, but when you're strung up about something –! There's a chair in the Markovitches' dining-room just like that. It creaks more like a human being than anything you ever heard, and to-night I could have sworn Semyonov got up out of it. It was just like his heavy slow movement. However, there wasn't any one there. Do you think all this silly?' he asked.

'No, indeed I don't,' I answered.

'Then there's a picture. You know that awful painting of a mid-Victorian ancestor of Vera's – a horrible old man with bushy eyebrows and a high, rather dirty-looking stock?'

'Yes, I know it,' I said.

'It's one of those pictures with eyes that follow you all round the room. At least it has now. I usen't to notice them. Now they stare at you as though they'd eat you, and I know that Markovitch feels them because he keeps looking up at the beastly thing. Then there's – But no, I'm not going to talk any more about it. It isn't any good. One gets thinking of anything these days. One's nerves are all on edge. And that flat's too full of people any way.'

'Yes, it is,' I agreed.

We arrived at Rozanov's house, and went up in a very elegant heavily-gilt lift. Once in the flat we were enveloped in a cloud of men and women, tobacco smoke, and so many pictures that it was like tumbling into an art-dealer's. Where there weren't pictures there was gilt, and where there wasn't gilt there was naked statuary, and where there wasn't naked statuary there was Rozanov, very red and stout and smiling, gay in a tighdy fitting black tail coat, white waistcoat and black trousers. Who all the people were I haven't the least idea. There were a great many. A number of Jews and Jewesses, amiable, prosperous, and kindly, an artist or two, a novelist, a lady pianist, two or three actors. I noticed these. Then there was an old maid, a Mlle.

Finisterre, famous in Petrograd society for her bitterness and acrimony, and in appearance an exact copy of Balzac's Sophie Gamond.

I noticed several of those charming, quiet, wise women of whom Russia is so prodigal, a man or two whom I had met at different times, especially one officer, one of the finest, bravest, and truest men I have ever known; some of the inevitable giggling girls – and then suddenly, standing quite alone, Nina!

Her loneliness was the first thing that struck me. She stood back against the wall underneath the shining frames, looking about her with a nervous, timid smile. Her hair was piled up on top of her head in the old way that she used to do when she was trying to imitate Vera, and I don't know why but that seemed to me a good omen, as though she were already on her way back to us. She was wearing a very simple white frock.

In spite of her smile she looked unhappy, and I could see that during this last week experience had not been kind to her; because there was an air of shyness and uncertainty which had never been there before. I was just going over to speak to her when two of the giggling girls surrounded her and carried her off.

I carried the little picture of her in my mind all through the noisy, strident meal that followed. I couldn't see her from where I sat, nor did I once catch the tones of her voice, although I listened. Only a month ago there would have been no party at which Nina was present where her voice would not have risen above all others.

No one watching us would have believed any stories about food shortage in Petrograd. I daresay at this very moment in Berlin they are having just such meals. Until the last echo of the last Trump has died away in the fastnesses of the advancing mountains the rich will be getting from somewhere the things that they desire! I have no memory of what we had to eat that night, but I know that it was all very magnificent and noisy, kind-hearted and generous and vulgar. A great deal of wine was drunk, and by the end of the meal every one was talking as loudly as possible. I had for companion the beautiful Mlle. Finisterre. She had lived all her life in Petrograd, and she had a contempt for the citizens of that fine town worthy of Semyonov himself. Opposite us sat a stout, good-natured Jewess, who was very happily enjoying her food. She was certainly the most harmless being in creation, and was probably guilty of a thousand generosities and kindnesses in her private life. Nevertheless, Mlle. Finisterre had for her a dark and sinister hatred, and the remarks that she made about her, in her bitter and piercing voice, must have reached their victim. She also abused her host very roundly, beginning to tell me in the fullest detail the history of an especially unpleasant scandal in which he had notoriously figured. I stopped her at last.

'It seems to me,' I said, 'that it would be better not to say these things about him while you're eating his bread and salt.'

She laughed shrilly, and tapped me on the arm with a bony finger.

'Oh, you English! ... always so moral and strict about the proprieties ... and always so hypercritical too. Oh, you amuse me! I'm French, you see – not Russian at all; these poor people see through nothing – but we French!'

After dinner there was a strange scene. We all moved into the long, over-decorated drawing-room. We sat about, admired the pictures (a beautiful one by Somoff I especially remember – an autumn scene with eighteenth-century figures and colours so soft and deep that the effect was inexpressibly delicate and mysterious), talked and then fell into one of those Russian silences that haunt every Russian party. I call those silences 'Russian,' because I know nothing like them in any other part of the world. It is as though the souls of the whole company suddenly vanished through the windows, leaving only the bodies and clothes. Every one sits, eyes half closed, mouths shut, hands motionless, host and hostess, desperately abandoning every attempt at rescue, gaze about them in despair.

The mood may easily last well into the morning, when the guests, still silent, will depart, assuring everybody that they have enjoyed themselves immensely, and really believing that they have; or it may happen that some remark will suddenly be made, and instantly back through the windows the souls will come, eagerly catching up their bodies again, and a babel will arise, deafening, baffling, stupefying. Or it may happen that a Russian will speak with sudden authority, almost like a prophet, and will continue for half an hour and more, pouring out his soul, and no one will dream of thinking it an improper exhibition.

In fine, anything can happen at a Russian party. What happened on this occasion was this. The silence had lasted for some minutes, and I was wondering for how much longer I could endure it (I had one eye on Nina somewhere in the background, and the other on Bohun restlessly kicking his patent-leather shoes one against the other), when suddenly a quiet, ordinary little woman seated near me said:

'The thing for Russia to do now is to abandon all resistance and so shame the world.' She was a mild, pleasant-looking woman, with the eyes of a very gende cow, and spoke exactly as though she were still pursuing her own private thoughts. It was enough; the windows flew open, the souls came flooding in, and such a torrent of sound poured over the carpet that the naked statuary itself seemed to shiver at the threatened deluge. Every one talked; every one, even, shouted. Just as, during the last weeks, the streets had echoed to the words 'Liberty,' 'Democracy,' 'Socialism,' 'Brotherhood,' 'Anti-annexation,' 'Peace of the world,' so now the art gallery echoed. The very pictures shook in their frames.

One old man in a white beard continued to cry, over and over again, 'Firearms are not our weapons . . . bullets are not our weapons. It's the Peace of God, the Peace of God that we need.'

One lady (a handsome Jewess) jumped up from her chair, and Standing before us all recited a kind of chant, of which I only caught sentences once and again:

'Russia must redeem the world from its sin . . . this slaughter must be stayed. . . . Russia the Saviour of the world . . . this slaughter must be stayed.'

I had for some time been watching Bohun. He had travelled a long journey since that original departure from England in December; but I was not sure whether he had travelled far enough to forget his English terror of making a fool of himself. Apparendy he had. . . . He said, his voice shaking a little, blushing as he spoke:

'What about Germany?'

The lady in the middle of the floor turned upon him furiously:

'Germany! Germany will learn her lesson from us. When we lay down our arms her people, too, will lay down theirs.'

'Supposing she doesn't?'

The interest of the room was now centred on him, and every one else was silent.

'That is not our fault. We shall have made our example.'

A little hum of applause followed this reply, and that irritated Bohun. He raised his voice:

'Yes, and what about your allies, England and France, are you going to betray them?'

Several voices took him up now. A man continued:

'It is not betrayal. We are not betraying the proletariat of England and France. They are our friends. But the alliance with the French and

English Capitalistic Governments was made not by us but by our own Capitalistic Government, which is now destroyed.'

'Very well, then,' said Bohun. 'But when the war began did you not – all of you, not only your Government, but you people now sitting in this room – did you not all beg and pray England to come in? During those days before England's intervention, did you not threaten to call us cowards and traitors if we did not come in? *Pomnite?*'

There was a storm of answers to this. I could not distinguish much of what it was. I was fixed by Mlle. Finisterre's eagle eye, gleaming at the thought of the storm that was rising.

'That's not our affair. . . . That's not our affair,' I heard voices crying. 'We did support you. For years we supported you. We lost millions of men in your Service. . . . Now this terrible slaughter must cease, and Russia show the way to peace.'

Bohun's moment then came upon him. He sprang to his feet, his face crimson, his body quivering; so desperate was his voice, so urgent his distress that the whole room was held.

'What has happened to you all? Don't you see, don't you see what you are doing? What has come to you, you who were the most modest people in Europe and are now suddenly the most conceited? What do you hope to do by this surrender?

'Do you know, in the first place, what you will do? You will deliver the peoples of three-quarters of the globe into hopeless slavery; you will lose, perhaps for ever, the opportunity of democracy; you will establish the grossest kind of militarism for all time. Why do you think Germany is going to listen to you? What sign has she ever shown that she would? When have her people ever turned away or shown horror at any of the beastly things her rulers have been doing in this war? . . . What about your own Revolution? Do you believe in it? Do you treasure it? Do you want it to last? Do you suppose for a moment that, if you bow to Germany, she won't instanüy trample out your Revolution and give you back your monarchy? How can she afford to have a revolutionary republic close to her own gates? What is she doing at this moment? Piling up armies with which to invade you, and conquer you, and lead you into slavery. What have you done so far by your Revolutionary orders? What have you done by relaxing discipline in the army? What good have you done to any one or anything? Is any one the happier? Isn't there disorder everywhere – aren't all your works stopping and your industries failing? What about the eighty million peasants who have been liberated in the course of a night?

Who's going to lead them if you are not? This thing has happened by its own force, and you are sitting down under it, doing nothing. Why did it succeed? Simply because there was nothing to oppose it. Authority depended on the army, not on the Czar, and the army was the people. So it is with the other armies of the world. Do you think that the other armies couldn't do just as you did if they wished? They could, in half an hour. They hate the war as much as you do, but they have also patriotism. They see that their country must be made strong first before other countries will listen to its ideas. But where is your patriotism? Has the word Russia been mentioned once by you since the Revolution? Never once. . . . "Democracy," "Brotherhood" – but how are Democracy and Brotherhood to be secured unless other countries respect you? . . . Oh, I tell you it's absurd! . . . It's more than absurd, it's wicked, it's rotten. . . .'

Poor boy, he was very near tears. He sat down suddenly, staring blankly in front of him, his hands clenched.

Rozanov answered him, Rozanov flushed, his fat body swollen with food and drink, a little unsteady on his legs, and the light of the true mystic in his pig-like eyes. He came forward into the middle of the circle.

'That's perhaps true what you say,' he cried; 'it's very English, very honest, and, if you will forgive me, young man, very simple. You say that we Russians are conceited. No, we are not conceited, but we see farther than the rest of the world. Is that our curse? Perhaps it is, but equally, perhaps, we may save the world by it. Now look at me! Am I a fine man? No, I am not. Every one knows I am not. No man could look at my face and say that I am a fine man. I have done disgraceful things all my life. All present know some of the things I have done, and there are some worse things which nobody knows save myself. Well, then. . . . Am I going to stop doing such things? Am I now, at fifty-five, about to become instandy a saint? Indeed not. I shall continue to do the things that I have already done, and I shall drop into a beastly old age. I know it.

'So, young man, I am a fair witness. You may trust me to speak the truth as I see it. I believe in Christ. I believe in the Christ-life, the Christ-soul. If I could, I would stop my beastliness and become Christlike. I have tried on several occasions, and failed, because I have no character. But does that mean that I do not believe in it when I see it? Not at all. I believe in it more than ever. And so with Russia – you don't see far enough, young man, neither you nor any of your countrymen. It is one of your greatest failings that you do not care for ideas. How is this war going to end? By the victory of Germany? Perhaps. . . . Perhaps even it may be that Russia by her weakness will help to that victory. But is that the end? No. . . . If Russia has an Idea and because of her faith in that Idea, she will sacrifice everything, will be buffeted on both cheeks, will be led into slavery, will deliver up her land and her people, will be mocked at by all the world . . . perhaps that is her destiny. . . . She will endure all that in order that her Idea may persist. And her Idea will persist. Are not the Germans and Austrians human like ourselves? Slowly, perhaps very slowly, they will say to themselves: "There is Russia who believes in the peace of the world, in the brotherhood of man, and she will sacrifice everything for it, she will go out, as Christ did, and be tortured and be crucified – and then on the third day she will rise again." Is not that the history of every triumphant Idea? . . . You say that meanwhile Germany will triumph. Perhaps for a time she may, but our Idea will not die.

'The further Germany goes, the deeper will that Idea penetrate into her heart. At the end she will die of it, and a new Germany will be born into a new world. . . . I tell you I am an evil man, but I believe in God and in the righteousness of God.'

What do I remember after those words of Rozanov? It was like a voice speaking to me across a great gulf of waters – but that voice was honest. I do not know what happened after his speech. I think there was a lot of talk. I cannot remember.

Only just before I was going I was near Nina for a moment.

She looked up at me just as she used to do.

'Durdles – is Vera all right?'

'She's miserable, Nina, because you're not there. Come back to us.' But she shook her head.

'No, no, I can't. Give her my——' Then she stopped. 'No, tell her nothing.'

'Can I tell her you're happy?' I asked.

'Oh, I'm all right,' she answered roughly, turning away from me.

X

But the adventures of that Easter Monday night were not yet over. I had walked away with Bohun; he was very silent, depressed, poor boy, and shy with the reaction of his outburst.

'I made the most awful fool of myself,' he said.

'No, you didn't,' I answered.

'The trouble of it is,' he said slowly, 'that neither you nor I see the humorous side of it all strongly enough. We take it too seriously. It's got a funny side all right.'

'Maybe you're right,' I said. 'But you must remember that the Markovitch Situation isn't exactly funny just now – and we're both in the middle of it. Oh! if only I could find Nina back home and Semyonov away, I believe the strain would lift. But I'm frightened that something's going to happen. I've grown very fond of these people, you know, Bohun – Vera and Nina and Nicholas. Isn't it odd how one gets to love Russians – more than one's own people? The more stupid things they do the more you love them – whereas with one's own people it's quite the other way. Oh, I do *want* Vera and Nina and Nicholas to be happy!'

'Isn't the town queer to-night?' said Bohun, suddenly stopping. (We were just at the entrance to the Mariensky Square.)

'Yes,' I said. 'I think these days between the thaw and the white nights are in some ways the strangest of all. There seems to be so much going on that one can't quite see.'

'Yes – over there – at the other end of the Square – there's a kind of mist – a sort of water-mist. It comes from the Canal.'

'And do you see a figure like an old bent man with a red lantern? Do you see what I mean – that red light?'

'And those shadows on the further wall like riders passing with silver-tipped spears? Isn't it . . .? There they go – ten, eleven, twelve, thirteen. . . .'

'How still the Square is? Do you see those three windows all alight? Isn't there a dance going on? Don't you hear the music?'

'No, it's the wind.'

'No, surely. . . . That's a flute – and then violins. Listen! Those are fiddles for certain!'

'How still, how still it is!'

We stood and listened whilst the white mist gathered and grew over the cobbles. Certainly there was a strain of music, very faint and dim, threading through the air.

'Well, I must go on,' said Bohun. 'You go up to the left, don't you? Good-night.' I watched Bohun's figure cross the Square. The light was wonderful, like fold on fold of gauze, but opaque, so that buildings showed with sharp outline behind it. The moon was full and quite red. I turned to go home and ran straight into Lawrence.

'Good heavens!' I cried. 'Are you a ghost too?'

He didn't seem to feel any surprise at meeting me. He was plainly in a state of tremendous excitement. He spoke breathlessly.

'You're exactly the man. You must come back with me. My diggings now are only a yard away from here.'

'It's very late,' I began, 'and——'

'Things are desperate,' he said. 'I don't know –' he broke off. 'Oh! come and help me, Durward, for God's sake!'

I went with him, and we did not exchange another word until we Were in his rooms.

He began hurriedly taking off his clothes. 'There! Sit on the bed. Different from Wilderling's, isn't it? Poor devil. . . . I'm going to have a bath if you don't mind – I've got to clear my head.'

He dragged out a tin bath from under his bed, then a big can of water from a corner. Stripped, he looked so thick and so strong, with his short neck and his bull-dog build, that I couldn't help saying:

'You don't look a day older than the last time you played Rugger for Cambridge.'

'I am, though.' He sluiced the cold water over his head, grunting. 'Not near so fit – gettin' fat too. . . . Rugger days are over. Wish all my other days were over too.'

He got out of the bath, wiped himself, put on Pyjamas, brushed his teeth, then his hair, took out a pipe, and then sat beside me on the bed.

'Look here, Durward,' he said. 'I'm desperate, old man.' (He said 'desprite.') 'We're all in a hell of a mess.'

'I know,' I said.

He puffed furiously at his pipe.

'You know, if I'm not careful I shall go a bit queer in the head. Get so angry, you know,' he added simply.

'Angry with whom?' I asked.

'With myself mostly for bein' such a bloody fool. But not only myself – with Civilisation, Durward, old cock! – and also with that swine Semyonov.'

'Ah, I thought you'd come to him,' I said.

'Now the points are these,' he went on, counting on his thick stubby fingers. 'First, I love Vera – and when I say love I mean love. Never been in love before, you know – honest Injun, never. . . . Never had affairs with tobacconists' daughters at Cambridge – never had an affair with a woman in my life – no, never. Used to wonder what was the matter with me, why I wasn't like other chaps. Now I know. I was waitin' for Vera. Quite simple. I shall never love any one again – never. I'm not a kid, you know, like young Bohun – I love Vera once and for all, and that's that . . .'

'Yes,' I said. 'And the next point?'

'The next point is that Vera loves me. No need to go into that – but she does.'

'Yes, she does,' I said.

'Third point, she's married, and although she don't love her man she's sorry for him. Fourth point, he loves her. Fifth point, there's a damned swine hangin' round called Alexei Petrovitch Semyonov. . . . Well, then, there you have it.'

He considered, scratching his head. I waited. Then he went on:

'Now it would be simpler if she didn't want to be kind to Nicholas, if Nicholas didn't love her, if – a thousand things were different. But they must be as they are, I suppose. I've just been with her. She's nearly out of her mind with worry.'

He paused, puffing furiously at his pipe. Then he went on:

'She's worrying about me, about Nina, and about Nicholas. And especially about Nicholas. There's something wrong with him. He knows about my kissing her in the flat. Well, that's all right. I meant him to know. Everything's just got to be above-board. But Semyonov knows too, and that devil's been raggin' him about it, and Nicholas is just like a bloomin' kid. That's got to stop. I'll wring that feller's neck. But even that wouldn't help matters much. Vera says Nicholas is not to be hurt whatever happens. "Never mind us," she says, "we're strong and can stand it." But he can't. He's weak. And she says he's just goin' off his dot. And it's got to be stopped – it's just got to be stopped. There's only one way to stop it.'

He stayed. Suddenly he put his heavy hand on my knee.

'What do you mean?' I asked.

'I've got to clear out; that's what I mean. Right away out. Back to England.'

I didn't speak.

'That's it,' he went on, but now as though he were talking to himself. 'That's what you've got to do, old son. . . . She says so, and she's right. Can't alter our love, you know. Nothing changes that. We've got to hold on. . . . Ought to have cleared out before. . . .'

Suddenly he turned. He almost flung himself upon me. He gripped my arms so that I would have cried out if the agony in his eyes hadn't held me.

'Here,' he muttered, 'let me alone for a moment. I must hold on. I'm pretty well beat. I'm just about done.'

For what seemed hours we sat there. I believe it was, in reality, only a few minutes. He sat facing me, his eyes staring at me but not seeing me, his body close against me, and I could see the sweat glistening on his chest through the open pyjamas. He was rigid as though he had been struck into stone.

He suddenly relaxed.

'That's right,' he said; 'thanks, old man. I'm better now. It's a bit late, I expect, but stay on a while.'

He got into bed. I sat beside him, gripped his hand, and ten minutes later he was asleep.

XI

The next day, Tuesday, was stormy with wind and rain. It was strange to see from my window the whirlpool of ice-encumbered waters. The rain fell in slanting, hissing sheets upon the ice, and the ice, in lumps and sheets and blocks, tossed and heaved and spun. At times it was as though all the ice was driven by some strong movement in one direction, then it was like the whole pavement of the world slipping down the side of the firmament into space. Suddenly it would be checked and, with a kind of quiver, station itself and hang chattering and clutching until the sweep would begin in the opposite direction.

I could see only dimly through the mist, but it was not difficult to imagine that, in very truth, the days of the flood had returned. Nothing could be seen but the tossing, heaving welter of waters with the ice, grim and grey through the shadows, like 'ships and monsters, sea-serpents and mermaids,' to quote Galleon's *Spanish Nights*.

Of course the water came in through my own roof, and it was on that very afternoon that I decided, once and for all, to leave this abode of mine. Romantic it might be; I felt it was time for a little comfortable realism. My old woman brought me the usual cutlets, macaroni, and tea for lunch; then I wrote to a friend in England; and finally, about four o'clock, after one more look at the hissing waters, drew my curtains, lit my candles, and sat down near my stove to finish that favourite of mine, already mentioned in these pages, De la Mare's *The Return*.

I read on with absorbed attention. I did not hear the dripping on the roof, nor the patter-patter of the drops from the ceiling, nor the beating of the storm against the glass. My candles blew in the draught, and shadows crossed and recrossed the page. Do you remember the book's closing words? –

'Once, like Lawford in the darkness at Widderstone, he glanced up sharply across the lamplight at his phantasmagorical shadowy companion, heard the steady surge of multitudinous rain-drops, like the roar of Time's winged chariot hurrying near, then he too, with spectacles awry, bobbed on in his chair, a weary old sentinel on the outskirts of his friend's denuded battlefield.'

'Shadowy companion,' 'multitudinous rain-drops,' 'a weary old sentinel,' 'his friend's denuded battlefield' . . . the words echoed like little muffled bells in my brain, and it was, I suppose, to their chiming that I fell into dreamless sleep.

From this I was suddenly roused by the sharp noise of knocking, and starting up, my book clattering to the floor, I saw facing me, in the doorway, Semyonov. Twice before he had come to me just like this – out of the heart of a dreamless sleep. Once in the orchard near Buchatch, on a hot summer afternoon; once in this same room on a moonlit night. Some strange consciousness, rising, it seemed, deep out of my sleep, told me that this would be the last time that I would so receive him.

'May I come in?' he said.

'If you must, you must,' I answered. 'I am not physically strong enough to prevent you.'

He laughed. He was dripping wet. He took off his hat and overcoat, sat down near the stove, bending forward, holding his cloak in his hands and watching the steam rise from it.

I moved away and stood watching. I was not going to give him any possible illusion as to my welcoming him. He turned round and looked at me.

'Truly, Ivan Andreievitch,' he said, 'you are a fine host. This is a miserable greeting.'

'There can be no greetings between us ever again,' I answered him. 'You are a blackguard. I hope that this is our last meeting.'

'But it is,' he answered, looking at me with friendliness; 'that is precisely why I've come. I've come to say good-bye.'

'Good-bye?' I repeated with astonishment. This chimed in so strangely with my premonition. 'I never was more delighted to hear it. I hope you're going a long distance from us all.'

'That's as may be,' he answered. 'I can't tell you definitely.'

'When are you going?' I asked.

'That I can't tell you either. But I have a premonition that it will be soon.'

'Oh, a premonition,' I said, disappointed. 'Is nothing settled?'

'No, not definitely. It depends on others.'

'Have you told Vera and Nicholas?'

'No – in fact, only last night Vera begged me to go away, and I told her that I would love to do anything to oblige her, but this time I was afraid that I couldn't help her. I would be compelled, alas, to stay on indefinitely.'

'Look here, Semyonov,' I said, 'stop that eternal fooling. Tell me honestly – are you going or not?'

'Going away from where?' he asked, laughing.

'From the Markovitches, from all of us, from Petrograd?'

'Yes – I've told you already,' he answered. 'I've come to say good-bye.'

'Then what did you mean by telling Vera——'

'Never you mind, Ivan Andreievitch. Don't worry your poor old head with things that are too complicated for you – a habit of yours, I'm afraid. Just believe me when I say that I've come to say good-bye. I have an intuition that we shall never talk together again. I may be wrong. But my intuitions are generally correct.'

I noticed then that his face was haggard, his eyes dark, the light in them exhausted as though he had not slept. . . . I had never before seen him show positive physical distress. Let his soul be what it might, his body seemed always triumphant.

'Whether your intuition is right or no,' I said, 'this *is* the last time. I never intend to speak to you again if I can help it. The day that I hear that you have really left us, never to return, will be one of the happiest days of my life.'

Semyonov gave me a strange look, humorous, ironical, and, upon my word, almost affectionate: 'That's very sad what you say, Ivan Andreievitch – if you mean it. And I suppose you mean it, because you English always do mean what you say. . . . But it's sad because, truly, I have friendly feelings towards you, and you're almost the only man in the world of whom I could say that.'

'You speak as though your friendship were an honour,' I said hotly. 'It's a degradation.'

He smiled. 'Now that's melodrama, straight out of your worst English plays. *And* how bad they can be! . . . But you hadn't always this vehement hatred. What's changed your mind?'

'I don't know that I *have* changed my mind,' I answered. 'I think I've always disliked you. But there at the Front and in the Forest you were brave and extraordinarily competent. You treated Trenchard abominably, of course – but he rather asked for it in some ways. Here you've been nothing but the meanest skunk and sneak. You've set out deliberately to poison the lives of some of the best-hearted and most helpless people on this earth. . . . You deserve hanging, if any murderer ever did!'

He looked at me so mildly and with such genuine interest that I was compelled to feel my indignation a whit melodramatic.

'If you are going,' I said more calmly, 'for Heaven's sake go! It *can't* be any pleasure to you, clever and talented as you are, to bait such harmless people as Vera and Nicholas. You've done harm enough. Leave them, and I forgive you everything.'

'Ah, of course your forgiveness is of the first importance to me,' he said, with ironic gravity. 'But it's true enough. You're going to be bothered with me – I *do* seem a worry to you, don't I? – for only a few days more. And how's it going to end, do you think? Who's going to finish me off? Nicholas or Vera? Or perhaps our English Byron, Lawrence? Or even yourself? Have you your revolver with you? I shall offer no resistance, I promise you.'

Suddenly he changed. He came closer to me. His weary, exhausted eyes gazed straight into mine: 'Ivan Andreievitch, never mind about the rest – never mind whether you do or don't hate me, that matters to nobody. What I tell you is the truth. I have come to you, as I have always come to you, like the moth to the flame. Why am I always pursuing you? Is it for the charm and fascination of your society? Your wit? Your beauty? I won't flatter you – no, no, it's because you alone, of all these fools here, knew her. You knew her as no one else alive knew her. She liked you – God knows why! At least I do know why – it was because of her youth and innocence and simplicity, because she didn't know a wise man from a fool, and trusted all alike. . . . But you knew her, you knew her. You remember her and can talk of her. Ah, how I've hungered, hungered, to talk to you about her! Sometimes I've come all this way and then turned back at the door. How I've prayed that it might have been some other who knew her, some real man, not a sentimental, gloomy old woman like yourself, Ivan Andreievitch. And yet you have your points. You have in you the things that she saw – you are honest, you are brave. . . . You are like a good English clergyman. But she! . . . I should have had some one with wit, with humour, with a sense of life about her. All the things, all the little things – the way she walked, her clothes, her smile – when she was cross! Ah, she was divine when she was cross! . . . Ivan Andreievitch, be kind to me! Think for a moment less of your morals, less of your principles – and talk to me of her! Talk to me of her!'

He had drawn quite close to me; he looked like a madman – I have no doubt that, at that moment, he was one.

'I can't! . . . I won't!' I answered, drawing away. 'She is the most sacred memory I have in my life. I hate to think of her with you. And that because you smirch everything you touch. I have no feeling of jealousy. . . .'

'You? Jealousy!' he said, looking at me scornfully. 'Why should you be jealous?'

'I loved her too,' I said.

He looked at me. In spite of myself the colour flooded my face. He looked at me from head to foot – my plainness, my miserable physique, my lameness, my feeble frame – everything was comprehended in the scorn of that glance.

'No,' I said, 'you need not suppose that she ever realised. She did not. I would have died rather than have spoken of it. But I will not talk about her. I will not.'

He drew away from me. His face was grave; the mockery had left it.

'Oh, you English, how strange you are! . . . In trusting, yes. . . . But the things you miss! I understand now many things. I give up my desire. You shan't smirch your precious memories. . . . And you, too, must understand that there has been all this time a link that has bound us. . . . Well, that link has snapped. I must go. Meanwhile, after I am gone, remember that there is more in life, Ivan Andreievitch, than you will ever understand. Who am I? . . . Rather ask, what am I? I am a Desire, a Purpose, a Pursuit – what you like. If another suffer for that I cannot help it, and if human nature is so weak, so stupid, it is right that it should suffer. But perhaps I am not myself at all, Ivan Andreievitch. Perhaps this is a ghost that you see. . . . What if the town has changed in the night and strange souls have slipped into our old bodies?

'Isn't there a stir about the town? Is it I that pursue Nicholas, or is it my ghost that pursues myself? Is it Nicholas that I pursue? Is not Nicholas dead, and is it not my hope of release that I follow? . . . . Don't be so sure of your ground, Ivan Andreievitch. You know the proverb: "There's a secret city in every man's heart. It is at that city's altars that the true prayers are offered." There has been more than one Revolution in the last two months.'

He came up to me:

'Do not think too badly of me, Ivan Andreievitch, afterwards. I'm a haunted man, you know.'

He bent forward and kissed me on the lips. A moment later he was gone.

XII

That Tuesday night poor young Bohun will remember to his grave – and beyond it, I expect.

He came in from his work about six in the evening and found Markovitch and Semyonov sitting in the dining-room. Everything was ordinary enough. Semyonov was in the arm-chair reading a newspaper; Markovitch was Walking very quietly up and down the farther end of the room. He wore faded blue carpet slippers; he had taken to them lately. Everything was the same as it had always been. The storm that had raged all day had now died down, and a very pale evening sun struck little patches of colour on the big table with the fading table-cloth, on the old brown carpet, on the picture of the old gendeman with bushy eyebrows, on Semyonov's musical-box, on the old knick-knacks and the untidy shelf of books. (Bohun looked especially to see whether the musical-box were still there. It was there on a little side-table.) Bohun, tired with his long day's efforts to shove the glories of the British Empire down the reluctant throats of the indifferent Russians, dropped into the other arm-chair with a tattered copy of Turgenieff's *House of Gentlefolks*, and soon sank into a state of half-slumber.

He roused himself from this to hear Semyonov reading extracts from the newspaper. He caught, at first, only portions of sentences. I am writing this, of course, from Bohun's account of it, and I cannot therefore quote the actual words, but they were incidents of disorder at the Front.

'There!' Semyonov would say, musing. 'Now, Nicholas . . . What do you say to that? A nice state of things. The Colonel was murdered, of course, although our friend the *Retch* doesn't put it quite so bluntly. The *Novaya Jezn* of course highly approves. Here's another. . . .' This went on for some ten minutes, and the only sound beside Semyonov's voice was Markovitch's padding steps. 'Ah! here's another bit! . . . Now what about that, my fine upholder of the Russian Revolution? See what they've been doing near Riga! It says . . .'

'Can't you leave it alone, Alexei? Keep your paper to yourself!'

These words came in so strange a note, a tone so different from Markovitch's ordinary voice, that they were, to Bohun, like a warning blow on the shoulder.

'There's gratitude – when I'm trying to interest you! How childish, too, not to face the real situation! Do you think you're going to improve things by pretending that anarchy doesn't exist? So soon, too, after your beautiful Revolution! How long is it? Let me see . . . March, April . . . yes, just about six weeks. . . . Well, well!'

'Leave me alone, Alexei! . . . Leave me alone!'

Bohun had with that such a sense of a superhuman effort at control behind the words that the pain of it was almost intolerable. He wanted, there and then, to have left the room. It would have been better for him had he done so. But some force held him in his chair, and, as the scene developed, he felt as though his sudden departure would have laid too emphatic a stress on the discomfort of it.

He hoped that in a moment Vera or Uncle Ivan would come and the scene would end.

Semyonov, meanwhile, continued: 'What were those words you used to me not so long ago? Something about free Russia, I think – Russia moving like one man to save the world – Russia with an unbroken front. . . . Too optimistic, weren't you?'

The padding feet stopped. In a whisper that seemed to Bohun to fill the room with echoing sound Markovitch said:

'You have tempted me for weeks now, Alexei. . . . I don't know why you hate me so, nor why you pursue me. Go back to your own place. If I am an unfortunate man, and by my own fault, that should be nothing to you who are more fortunate.'

'Torment you! I? . . . My dear Nicholas, never! But you are so childish in your ideas – and are you unfortunate? I didn't know it. Is it about your inventions that you are speaking? Well, they were never very happy, were they?'

'You praised them to me!'

'Did I? . . . My foolish kindness of heart, I'm afraid. To tell the truth, I was thankful when you saw things as they were. . . .'

'You took them away from me.'

'I took them away? What nonsense! It was your own wish – Vera's wish too.'

'Yes, you persuaded both Vera and Nina that they were no good. They believed in them before you came.'

'You flatter me, Nicholas. I haven't such power over Vera's opinions, I'm afraid. If I tell her anything she believes at once the opposite. You must have seen that yourself.'

'You took her belief away from me. You took her love away from me.'

Semyonov laughed. That laugh seemed to rouse Markovitch to frenzy. He screamed out. 'You have taken everything from me! . . . You will not leave me alone! You must be careful. You are in danger, I tell you.'

Semyonov sprang up from his chair, and the two men, advancing towards one another, came into Bohun's vision.

Markovitch was like a madman, his hands raised, his eyes staring from his head, his body trembling. Semyonov was quiet, motionless, smiling, standing very close to the other.

'Well, what are you going to do?' he asked.

Markovitch stood for a moment, his hands raised, then his whole body seemed to collapse. He moved away, muttering something which Bohun could not hear. With shuffling feet, his head lowered, he went out of the room. Semyonov returned to his seat.

To Bohun, an innocent youth with very simple and amiable ideas about life, the whole thing seemed 'beastly beyond words.'

'I saw a man torture a dog once,' he told me. 'He didn't do much to it really. Tied it up to a tree and dug into it with a pen-knife. I went home and was sick. . . . Well, I felt sick this time, too.'

Nevertheless his own 'sickness' was not the principal affair. The point was the sense of danger that seemed now to tinge with its own faint stain every article in the room. Bohun's hatred of Semyonov was so strong that he felt as though he would never be able to speak to him again; but it was not really of Semyonov that he was thinking. His thoughts were all centred round Markovitch. You must remember that for a long time now he had considered himself Markovitch's protector. This sense of his protection had developed in him an affection for the man that he would not otherwise have felt. He did not, of course, know of any of Markovitch's deepest troubles. He could only guess at his relations with Vera, and he did not understand the passionate importance that he attached to his Russian idea. But he knew enough to be aware of his childishness, his simplicity, his *naïveté*, and his essential goodness. 'He's an awfully decent sort, really,' he used to say in a kind of apologetic defence. The very fact of Semyonov's strength made his brutality seem now the more revolting. 'Like hitting a fellow half your size.' . . .

He saw that things in that flat were approaching a climax, and he knew enough now of Russian impetuosity to realise that climaxes in that country are, very often, no ordinary affairs. It was just as though there were an evil smell in the flat, he explained to me. 'It seemed to hang over everything. Things looked the same and yet they weren't the same at all.'

His main impression that 'something would very soon happen if he didn't look out,' drove everything else from his mind – but he didn't quite see what to do. Speak to Vera? To Nicholas? To Semyonov? . . . He didn't feel qualified to do any of these things.

He went to bed that night early, about ten o'clock. He couldn't sleep. His door was not quite closed and he could hear first Vera, then Uncle Ivan, lastly Markovitch go to bed. He lay awake then, with that exaggerated sense of hearing that one has in the middle of the night, when one is compelled, as it were, against one's will, to listen for sounds. He heard the dripping of the tap in the bathroom, the creaking of some door in the wind (the storm had risen again) and all the thousand and one little uncertainties, like the agitated beating of innumerable hearts that penetrate the folds and curtains of the night. As he lay there he thought of what he would do did Markovitch really go off his head. He had a revolver, he knew. He had seen it in his hand. And then what was Semyonov after? My explanation had seemed, at first, so fantastic and impossible that Bohun had dismissed it, but now, after the conversation that he had just overheard, it did not seem impossible at all – especially in the middle of the night. His mind travelled back to his own first arrival in Petrograd, that first sleep at the 'France' with the dripping water and the crawling rats, the plunge into the Kazan Cathedral, and everything that followed.

He did not see, of course, his own progress since that day, nor the many things that Russia had already done for him, but he did feel that such situations as the one he was now sharing were, today, much more in the natural order of things than they would have been four months before. . . .

He dozed off and then was awakened, sharply, abruptly, by the sound of Markovitch's padded feet. There could be no mistaking them;

very softly they went past Bohun's door, down the passage towards the dining-room. He sat up in bed, and all the other sounds of the night seemed suddenly to be accentuated – the dripping of the tap, the blowing of the wind, and even the heavy breathing of old Sacha, who always slept in a sort of cupboard near the kitchen, with her legs hanging out into the passage. Suddenly no sound! The house was still, and, with that, the sense of danger and peril was redoubled, as though the house were holding its breath as it watched. . . .

Bohun could endure it no longer; he got up, put on his dressing-gown and bedroom slippers, and went out. When he got as far as the dining-room door he saw that Markovitch was standing in the middle of the room with a lighted candle in his hand. The glimmer of the candle flung a circle, outside which all was dusk. Within the glimmer there was Markovitch, his hair rough and strangely like a wig, his face pale yellow, and wearing an old quilted bed-jacket of a purple green colour. He was in a night-dress, and his naked legs were like sticks of tallow.

He stood there, the candle shaking in his hand, as though he were uncertain as to what he would do next. He was saying something to himself, Bohun thought.

At any rate his lips were moving. Then he put his hand into the pocket of his bed-coat and took out a revolver. Bohun saw it gleam in the candle-light. He held it up very close to his eyes as though he were short-sighted and seemed to sniff at it. Then, very clumsily, Bohun said, he opened it, to see whether it were loaded, I suppose, and closed it again. After that, very softly indeed, he shuffled off towards the door of Semyonov's room, the room that had once been the sanctuary of his inventions.

All this time young Bohun was paralysed. He said that all his life now, in spite of his having done quite decently in France, he would doubt his capacity in a crisis because, during the whole of this affair, he never stirred. But that was because it was all exactly like a dream. 'I was in the dream, you know, as well as the other fellows. You know those dreams when you're doing your very damnedest to wake up – when you struggle and sweat and know you'll die if something doesn't happen – well, it was like that, except that I didn't struggle and sweat, but just stood there, like a painted picture, watching. . . .'

Markovitch had nearly reached Semyonov's door (you remember that there was a little square window of glass in the upper part of it) when he did a funny thing. He stopped dead as though some one had rapped him on the shoulder. He stopped and looked round, then, very slowly, as though he were compelled, gazed with his nervous blinking eyes up at the portrait of the old gentleman with the bushy eyebrows. Bohun looked up too and saw (it was probably a trick of the faltering candle-light) that the old man was not looking at him at all, but steadfastly, and, of course, ironically, at Markovitch. The two regarded one another for a while, then Markovitch, still moving with the greatest caution, slipped the revolver back into his pocket, got a chair, climbed on to it and lifted the picture down from its nail. He looked at it for a moment, staring into the cracked and roughened paint, then hung it deliberately back on its nail again, but with its face to the wall. As he did this his bare, skinny legs were trembling so on the chair that, at every moment, he threatened to topple over. He climbed down at last, put the chair back in its place, and then once more turned towards Semyonov's door.

When he reached it he stopped and again took out the revolver, opened it, looked into it, and closed it. Then he put his hand on the door-knob.

It was then that Bohun had, as one has in dreams, a sudden impulse to scream: 'Look out! Look out! Look out!' although, Heaven knows, he had no desire to protect Semyonov from anything. But it was just then that the oddest conviction came over him, namely, an assurance that Semyonov was standing on the other side of the door, looking through the little window and waiting. He could not have told, any more than one can ever tell in dreams, how he was so certain of this. He could only see the little window as the dimmest and darkest square of shadow behind Markovitch's candle, but he was sure that this was so. He could even see Semyonov standing there, in his shirt, with his thick legs, his head a little raised, listening. . . .

For what seemed an endless time Markovitch did not move. He also seemed to be listening. Was it possible that he heard Semyonov's breathing? . . . But, of course, I have never had any actual knowledge that Semyonov was there. That was simply Bohun's idea. . . .

Then Markovitch began very slowly, bending a little, as though it were stiff and difficult, to turn the handle. I don't know what then Bohun would have done. He must, I think, have moved, shouted, screamed, done something or other. There was another interruption. He heard a quick, soft step behind him. He moved into the shadow.

It was Vera, in her night-dress, her hair down her back.

She came forward into the room and whispered very quietly: 'Nicholas!'

He turned at once. He did not seem to be startled or surprised; he had dropped the revolver at once back into his pocket. He came up to her, she bent down and kissed him, then put her arm round him and led him away.

When they had gone Bohun also went back to bed. The house was very still and peaceful. Suddenly he remembered the picture. It would never do, he thought, if in the morning it were found by Sacha or Uncle Ivan with its face to the wall. After hesitating he lit his own candle, got out of bed again, and went down the passage.

'The funny thing was,' he said, 'that I really expected to find it just as it always was, face outwards . . . as though the whole thing really had been a dream. But it wasn't. It had its face to the wall all right. I got a chair, turned it round, and went back to bed again.'

XIII

That night, whether as a result of my interview with Semyonov I do not know, my old enemy leapt upon me once again. I had, during the next three days, one of the worst bouts of pain that it has ever been my fortune to experience. For twenty-four hours I thought it more than any man could bear, and I hid my head and prayed for death; during the next twenty-four I slowly rose, with a dim far-away sense of deliverance; on the third day I could hear, in the veiled distance, the growls of my defeated foe. . . .

Through it all, behind the wall of pain, my thoughts knocked and thudded, urging me to do something. It was not until the Friday or the Saturday that I could think consecutively. My first thought was driven in on me by the old curmudgeon of a doctor, as his deliberate opinion that it was simply insanity to stay on in those damp rooms when I suffered from my complaint, that I was only asking for what I got, and that he, on his part, had no sympathy for me. I told him that I entirely agreed with him, that I had determined several weeks ago to leave these rooms, and that I thought that I had found some others in a different, more populated part of the town. He grunted his approval, and, forbidding me to go out for at least a week, left me. At least a week! . . . . No, I must be out long before that. Now that the pain had left me, weak though I was, I was wildly impatient to return to the Markovitches. Through all these last days' torments I had been conscious of Semyonov, seen his hair and his mouth and his beard and his square solidity and his tired, exhausted eyes, and strangely, at the end of it all, felt the touch of his lips on mine. Oddly, I did not hate Semyonov; I saw quite clearly that I had never hated him – something too impersonal about him, some sense, too, of an outside power driving him. No, I did not hate him, but God! how I feared him – feared him not for my own sake, but for the sake of those who had – was this too arrogant? – been given as it seemed to me, – into my charge.

I remembered that Monday was the 30th of April, and that, on that evening, there was to be a big Allied meeting at the Bourse, at which our Ambassador, Sir George Buchanan, the Belgian Consul, and others, were to speak. I had promised to take Vera to this. Tuesday the 1st of May was to see a great demonstration by all the workmen's and soldiers' committees. It was to correspond with the Labour demonstrations arranged to take place on that day all over Europe, and the Russian date had been altered to the new style in order to provide for this. Many people considered that the day would be the cause of much rioting, of definite hostility to the Provisional Government, of anti-foreign demonstrations, and so on; others, idealistic Russians, believed that all the soldiers, the world over, would on that day throw down their arms and proclaim a universal peace. . . .

I for my part believed that it would mark the ending of the first phase of the Revolution and the beginning of the second, and that for Russia at any rate it would mean the changing from a war of nations into a war of class – in other words, that it would mean the rising up of the Russian peasant as a definite positive factor in the world's affairs.

But all that political business was only remotely, at that moment, my concern. What I wanted to know was what was happening to Nicholas, to Vera, to Lawrence, and the others. Even whilst I was restlessly wondering what I could do to put myself into touch with them, my old woman entered with a letter which she said had been brought by hand.

The letter was from Markovitch.

I give this odd document here exactly as I received it. I do not attempt to emphasise or explain or comment in any way. I would only add that no Russian is so mad as he seems to any Englishman, and no Englishman so foolish as he seems to any Russian.

I must have received this letter, I think, late on Sunday afternoon, because I was, I remember, up and dressed, and walking about my room. It was written on flimsy grey paper in pencil, which made it difficult to read. There were sentences unfinished, words misspelt, and the whole of it in the worst of Russian handwritings. Certain passages, I am, even now, quite unable to interpret:

It ran as follows:

DEAR IVAN ANDREIEVITCH –

Vera tells me that you are ill again. She has been round to enquire, I think. I did not come because I knew that if I did I should only talk about my own troubles, the same as you've always listened to, and what kind of food is that for a sick man? All the same, that is just what I am doing now, but reading a letter is not like talking to a man; you can always stop and tear the paper when perhaps it would not be polite to ask a man to go. But I hope, nevertheless, that you won't do that with this – not because of any desire I may have to interest you in myself, but because of something of much more importance than either of us, something I want you to believe – something you must believe. . . . Don't think me mad. I am quite sane sitting here in my room writing. . . . Every one is asleep. Every one but not everything. I've been queer, now and again, lately . . . off and on. Do you know how it comes? When the inside of the world goes further and further within dragging you after it, until at last you are in the bowels of darkness choking. I've known such moods all my life. Haven't you known them? Lately, of course, I've been drinking again. I tell you, but I wouldn't own it to most people. But they all know, I suppose. . . . Alexei made me start again, but it's foolish to put everything on to him. If I weren't a weak man he wouldn't be able to do anything with me, would he? Do you believe in God, and don't you think that He intended the weak to have some compensation somewhere, because it isn't their fault that they're weak, is it? They can struggle and struggle, but it's like being in a net. Well, one must just make a hole in the net large enough to get out of, that's all. And now, ever since two days ago, when I resolved to make that hole, I've been quite calm. I'm as calm as anything now writing to you. Two days ago Vera told me that he was going back to England. . . . Oh, she was so good to me that day, Ivan Andreievitch. We sat together all alone in the flat, and she had her hand in mine, just as we used to do in the old days when I pretended to myself that she loved me. Now I know that she did not, but the warmer and more marvellous was her kindness to me, her goodness, and nobility. Do you not think, Ivan Andreievitch, that if you go deep enough in every human heart, there is this kernel of goodness, this fidelity to some ideal? Do you know we have a proverb: 'In each man's heart there is a secret town at whose altars the true prayers are offered!' Even perhaps with Alexei it is so, only there you must go very deep, and there is no time.

But I must tell you about Vera. She told me so kindly that he was going to England, and that now her whole life would be led in Nina and myself. I held her hand very close in mine and asked her, Was it really true that she loved him. And she said, yes she did, but that that she could not help. She said that she had spoken with him, and that they had decided that it would be best for him to go away. Then she begged my forgiveness for many things, because she had been harsh or cross, – I don't know what things. . . . Oh, Ivan Andreievitch, *she* to beg forgiveness of *me*!

But I held her hand closer and closer, because I knew that it was the last time that I would be able so truly to hold it. How could she not see that now everything was over – everything – quite everything! Am I one to hold her, to chain her down, to keep her when she has already escaped? Is that the way to prove my fidelity to her?

Of course I did not speak to her of this, but for the first time in all our years together, I felt older than her and wiser. But of course Alexei saw it. How he heard I do not know, but that same day he came to me and he seemed to be very kind.

I don't know what he said, but he explained that Vera would always be unhappy now, always, longing and waiting and hoping. . . 'Keep him here in Russia!' he whispered to me. 'She will get tired of him then – they will tire of one another; but if you send him away. . . .' Oh! he is a devil, Ivan Andreievitch, and why has he persecuted me so? What have I ever done to him? Nothing . . . but for weeks now he has pursued me and destroyed my inventions, and flung Russia in my face and made Nina, dear Nina, laugh at me, and now, when the other things are finished, he shows me that Vera will be unhappy so long as I am alive. What have I ever done, Ivan Andreievitch? I am so unimportant, why has he taken such a trouble? Today I gave him his last chance . . . or last night . . . it is four in the morning now, and the bells are already ringing for the early Mass. I said to him:

'Will you go away? Leave us all for ever? Will you promise never to return?'

He said in that dreadful quiet sure way of his: 'No, I will never go away until you make me.'

Vera hates him. I cannot leave her alone with him, can I? I (here there are three lines of illegible writing) ... so I will think again and again of that last time when we sat together and all the good things that she said. What greatness of soul, what goodness, what splendour! And perhaps after all I am a fortunate man to be allowed to be faithful to so fine a grandeur! Many men have poor ambitions, and God bestows His gifts with strange blindness, I often think. But I am tired, and you too will be tired. Perhaps you have not got so far. I must thank you for your friendship to me. I am very grateful for it. And you, if afterwards you ever think of me, think that I always wished to ... no, why should you think of me at all? But think of Russia! That is why I write this. You love Russia, and I believe that you will continue to love Russia whatever she will do. Never forget that it is because she cares so passionately for the good of the world that she makes so many mistakes. She sees farther than other countries, and she cares more. But she is also more ignorant. She has never been allowed to learn anything or to try to do anything for herself.

You are all too impatient, too strongly aware of your own conditions, too ignorant of hers! Of course there are wicked men here and many idle men, but every country has such. You must not judge her by that nor by all the talk you hear. We talk like blind men on a dark road. . . . Do you believe that there are no patriots here? Ah! how bitterly I have been disappointed during these last weeks! It has broken my heart . . . but do not let your heart be broken. You can wait. You are young. Believe in Russian patriotism, believe in Russian future, believe in Russian soul. . . . Try to be patient and understand that she is blindfolded, ignorant, stumbling . . . but the glory will come; I can see it shining far away! . . . It is not for me, but for you – and for Vera . . . for Vera . . . Vera. . . .

Here the letter ended; only scrawled very roughly across the paper the letters N. M. . . . .

XIV

As soon as I had finished reading the letter I went to the telephone and rang up the Markovitches' flat. Bohun spoke to me. I asked him whether Nicholas was there, he said, 'Yes, fast asleep in the arm-chair.' Was Semyonov there? No, he was dining out that night. I asked him to remind Vera that I was expecting to take her to the meeting next day, and rang off. There was nothing more to be done just then. Two minutes later there was a knock on my door and Vera came in.

'Why!' I cried, 'I've just been ringing up to tell you that, of course, I was coming on Monday.'

'That is partly what I wanted to know,' she said, smiling. 'And also I thought that you'd fancied we'd all deserted you.'

'No,' I answered. 'I don't expect you round here every time I'm ill. That would be absurd. You'll be glad to know at any rate that I've decided to give up these ridiculous rooms. I deserve all the illness I get so long as I'm here.'

'Yes, that's good,' she answered. 'How you could have stayed so long –' She dropped into a chair, closed her eyes and lay back. 'Oh, Ivan Andreievitch, but I'm tired!'

She looked, lying there, white-faced, her eyelids like grey shadows, utterly exhausted. I waited in silence. After a time she opened her eyes and said suddenly:

'We all come and talk to you, don't we? I, Nina, Nicholas, Sherry (she meant Lawrence), even Uncle Alexei. I wonder why we do, because we never take your advice, you know. . . . Perhaps it's because you seem right outside everything.'

I coloured a little at that.

'Did I hurt you? . . . I'm sorry. No, I don't know that I am. I don't mind now whether I hurt any one. You know that he's going back to England?'

I nodded my head.

'He told you himself?'

'Yes,' I said.

She lay back in her chair and was silent for a long time.

'You think I'm a noble woman, don't you? Oh yes, you do! I can see you just thirsting for my nobility. It's what Uncle Alexei always says about you, that you've learnt from Dostoieffsky how to be noble, and it's become a habit with you.'

'If you're going to believe——' I began angrily.

'Oh, I hate him! I listen to nothing that he says. All the same, Durdles, this passion for nobility on your part is very irritating. I can see you now making up the most magnificent picture of my nobility. I'm sure if you were ever to write a book about us all, you'd write of me something like this: "Vera Michailovna had won her victory. She had achieved her destiny. . . . Having surrendered her lover she was as fine as a Greek statue!" Something like that. . . . Oh, I can see you at it!'

'You don't understand——' I began.

'Oh, but I do!' she answered. 'I've watched your attitude to me from the first. You wanted to make poor Nina noble, and then Nicholas, and then, because they wouldn't either of them do, you had to fall back upon me: memories of that marvellous woman at the Front, Marie some one or other, have stirred up your romantic soul until it's all whipped cream and jam – mulberry jam, you know, so as to have the proper dark colour.'

'Why all this attack on me?' I asked. 'What have I done?'

'You've done nothing,' she cried. 'We all love you, Durdles, because you're such a baby, because you dream such dreams, see nothing as it is. . . . And perhaps after all you're right – your vision is as good as another. But this time you've made me restless. You're never to see me as a noble woman again, Ivan Andreievitch. See me as I am, just for five minutes! I haven't a drop of noble feeling in my soul!'

'You've just given him up,' I said. 'You've sent him back to England, although you adore him, because your duty's with your husband. You're breaking your heart——'

'Yes, I am breaking my heart,' she said quietly. 'I'm a dead woman without him. And it's my weakness, my cowardice, that is sending him away. What would a French woman or an English woman have done? Given up the world for their lover – given up a thousand Nicholases, sacrificed a hundred Ninas. That's real life. That's real, I tell you. What feeling is there in my soul that counts for a moment beside my feeling for Sherry? I say and I feel and I know that I would die for him, die with him, happily, gladly. Those are no empty words.

'I who have never been in love before, I am devoured by it now until there is nothing left of me – nothing. . . . And yet I remain. It is our weakness, our national idleness. I haven't the strength to leave Nicholas. I am soft, sentimental, about his unhappiness. Pah! how I despise myself. . . . I am capable of living on here for years with husband and lover, going from one to another, weeping for both of them. Already I am pleading with Sherry that he should remain here. We will see what will happen. We will see what will happen! Ah, my contempt for myself! Without bones, without energy, without character.

'But this is life, Ivan Andreievitch! I stay here; I send him away because I cannot bear to see Nicholas suffer. And I do not care for Nicholas. Do you understand that? I never loved him, and now I have a contempt for him – in spite of myself. Uncle Alexei has done that. Oh yes! He has made a fool of Nicholas for months, and although I have hated him for doing that, I have seen, also, what a fool Nicholas is! But he is a hero, too. Make *him* as noble as you like, Ivan Andreievitch. You cannot colour it too high. He is the real thing and I am the sham. . . . But oh! I do not want to live with him any more; I am tired of him, his experiments, his lamentations, his weakness, his lack of humour – tired of him, sick of him. And yet I cannot leave him, because I am soft, soft without bones, like my country, Ivan Andreievitch. . . . My lover is strong. Nothing can change his will. He will go, will leave me, until he knows that I am free. Then he will never leave me again.

'Perhaps I will get tired of his strength one day – it may be – just as now I am tired of Nicholas's weakness. Everything has its end.

'But no! he has humour, and he sees life as it is. I shall be able always to tell him the truth. With Nicholas it is always lies. . . .'

She suddenly sprang up and stood before me.

'Now, do you think me noble?' she cried.

'Yes,' I answered.

'Ah! you are incorrigible! You have drunk Dostoieffsky until you can see nothing but God and the moujik! But I am alive, Ivan Andreievitch, not a heroine in a book! Alive, alive, alive! Not one of your Lisas or Annas or Natashas. I'm alive enough to shoot Uncle Alexei and poison Nicholas – but I'm soft too, soft so that I cannot bear to see a rabbit killed . . . and yet I love Sherry so that I am blind for him and deaf for him and dead for him – when he is not there. My love – the only one of my life – the first and the last——'

She flung out her arms:

'Life! Now! Before it is too late! I want it, I want him, I want happiness!'

She stood thus for a moment, staring out to the sea. Then her arms dropped. She laughed, fastening her cloak:

'There's your nobility, Ivan Andreievitch – theatrical, all of it. I know what I am, and I know what I shall do. Nicholas will live to eighty; I also. I shall hate him, but I shall be in an agony when he cuts his finger. I shall never see Sherry again. Later, he will marry a fresh English girl like an apple. . . . I, because I am weak, soft putty – I have made it so.'

She turned away from me, staring desperately at the wall. When she looked back to me her face was grey.

She smiled. 'What a baby you are! . . . But take care of yourself. Don't come on Monday if it's bad weather. Good-bye.'

She went.

After a bad, sleepless night, and a morning during which I dozed in a nightmareish kind of way, I got up early in the afternoon, had some tea, and about six o'clock started out.

It was a lovely evening; the spring light was in the air, the tufted trees beside the canal were pink against the pale sky, and thin layers of ice, like fragments of jade, broke the soft blue of the water. How pleasant to feel the cobbles firm beneath one's feet, to know that the snow was gone for many months, and that light now would flood the streets and squares! Nevertheless, my foreboding was not raised, and the veils of colour hung from house to house and from street to street could not change the realities of the scene.

I climbed the stairs to the flat and found Vera waiting for me. She was with Uncle Ivan, who, I found to my disappointment, was coming with us.

We started off.

'We can walk across to the Bourse,' she said. 'It's such a lovely evening, and we're a little early.'

We talked of nothing but the most ordinary things; Uncle Ivan's company prevented anything else. To say that I cursed him is to put it very mildly. He had been, I believe, oblivious of all the scenes that had occurred during the last weeks. If the Last Judgement occurred under his very nose, and he had had a cosy meal in front of him, he would have noticed nothing. The Revolution had had no effect on him at all; it did not seem strange to him that Semyonov should come to live with them; he had indeed fancied that Nicholas had not 'been very well' lately, but then Nicholas had always been an odd and cantankerous fellow, and he, as he told me, never paid too much attention to his moods. His one anxiety was lest Sacha should be hindered from her usual shopping on the morrow, it being May Day, when there would be processions and other tiresome things. He hoped that there was enough food in the house.

'There will be cold cutlets and cheese,' Vera said.

He told me that he really did not know why he was going to this meeting. He took no interest in politics, and he hated speeches, but he would like to see our Ambassador. He had heard that he was always excellently dressed....

Vera said very little. Her troubles that evening must have been accumulating upon her with terrible force – I did not know, at that time, about her night-scene with Nicholas. She was very quiet, and just as we entered the building she whispered to me:

'Once over tomorrow——'

I did not catch the rest. People pressed behind us, and for a moment we were separated; we were not alone again. I have wondered since what she meant by that, whether she had a foreboding or some more definite warning, or whether she simply referred to the danger of riots and general lawlessness. I shall never know now.

I had expected a crowded meeting, but I was not prepared for the multitude that I found. We entered by a side-door, and then passed up a narrow passage, which led us to the reserved seats at the side of the platform. I had secured these some days before. In the dark passage one could realise nothing; important gentlemen in frock-coats, officers, and one or two soldiers were hurrying to and fro, with an air of having a great deal to do, and not knowing at all how to do it. Beyond the darkness there was a steady hum, like the distant whirr of a great machine. There was a very faint smell in the air of boots and human flesh. A stout gentleman with a rosette in his buttonhole showed us to our seats. Vera sat between Uncle Ivan and myself. When I looked about me I was amazed. The huge hall was packed so tightly with human beings that one could see nothing but wave on wave of faces, or, rather, the same face, repeated again and again and again, the face of a baby, of a child, of a credulous, cynical dreamer, a face the kindest, the naïvest, the cruellest, the most friendly, the most human, the most savage, the most Eastern, and the most Western in the world.

That vast presentation of that reiterated visage seemed suddenly to explain everything to me. I felt at once the stupidity of any appeal, and the instant necessity for every kind of appeal. I felt the negation, the sudden slipping into insignificant unimportance of the whole of the Western world – and, at the same time, the dismissal of the East. 'No longer, my masters' a voice seemed to cry from the very heart of that multitude. 'No longer will we halt at your command, no longer will your words be wisdom to us, no longer shall we smile with pleasure at your stories and cringe with fear at your displeasure; you may hate our defection, you may lament our disloyalty, you may bribe us and smile upon us, you may preach to us and bewail our sins. We are no longer yours – WE ARE OUR OWN. Salute a new world, for it is nothing less that you see before you! . . .'

And yet never were there forces more unconscious of their destiny – utterly unselfconscious as animals, babies, the flowers of the field. Still there to be driven, perhaps to be persuaded, to be whipped, to be cajoled, to be blinded, to be tricked and deceived, drugged and deafened – but not for long! The end of that old world had come – the new world was at hand – 'Life begins tomorrow!'

The dignitaries came upon the platform, and beyond them all in distinction, nobility, wisdom, was our own Ambassador. This is no place for a record of the discretion and tact and forbearance that he had shown during those last two years. To him had fallen perhaps the most difficult work of all in the war. It might seem that on broad grounds the Allies had failed with Russia, but the end was not yet, and in years to come, when England reaps unexpected fruit from her Russian alliance, let her remember to whom she owed it. No one could see him there that night without realising that there stood before Russia, as England's representative, not only a great courtier and statesman, but a great gentleman, who had bonds of courage and endurance that linked him to the meanest soldier there.

I have emphasised this because he gave the note to the whole meeting. Again and again one's eyes came back to him, and always that high brow, that unflinching carriage of the head, the nobility and breeding of every movement, gave one reassurance and courage. One's own troubles seemed small beside that example, and the tangled morality of that vexed time seemed to be tested by a simpler and higher standard.

It was altogether a strange affair. At first it lacked interest; some member of the Italian Embassy spoke, I think, and then some one from Serbia. The audience was apathetic. All those bodies, so tightly wedged together that arms and legs were held in an iron vice, stayed motionless, and once and again there would be a short burst of applause or a sibilant whisper, but it would be something mechanical and uninspired. I could see one soldier, in the front row behind the barrier, a stout fellow with a face of supreme good humour, down whose forehead the sweat began to trickle; he was patient for a while, then he tried to raise his hand. He could not move without sending a ripple down the whole front line. Heads were turned indignantly in his direction. He submitted; then the sweat trickled into his eyes. He made a superhuman effort and half raised his arm; the crowd pushed again and his arm fell. His face wore an expression of ludicrous despair. . . .

The hall got hotter and hotter. Soldiers seemed to be still pressing in at the back. The Italian gentleman screamed and waved his arms, but the faces turned up to his were blank and amiably expressionless.

'It is indeed terribly hot,' said Uncle Ivan.

Then came a sailor from the Black Sea Fleet who had made himself famous during these weeks by his impassioned oratory. He was a thin dark-eyed fellow, and he obviously knew his business. He threw himself at once into the thick of it all, paying no attention to the stout frock-coated gentlemen who sat on the platform, dealing out no compliments whether to the audience or the speakers, wasting no time at all. He told them all that they had debts to pay, that their honour was at stake, and that Europe was watching them. I don't know that that Face that stared at him cared very greatly for Europe, but it is certain that a breath of emotion passed across it, that there was a stir, a movement, a response. . . .

He sat down; there was a roar of applause. He regarded them contemptuously. At that moment I caught sight of Boris Grogoff. I had been on the watch for him. I had thought it very likely that he would be there. Well, there he was, at the back of the crowd, listening with a contemptuous sneer on his face, and a long golden curl poking out from under his cap.

And then something else occurred – something really strange. I was conscious, as one sometimes is in a crowd, that I was being stared at by some one deliberately. I looked about me, and then, led by the attraction of the other's gaze, I saw quite close to me, on the edge of the crowd nearest to the platform, the Rat.

He was dressed rather jauntily in a dark suit with his cap set on one side, and his hair shining and curled. His face glittered with soap, and he was smiling in his usual friendly way. He gazed at me quite steadily. My lips moved very slightly in recognition. He smiled and, I fancy, winked.

Then, as though he had actually spoken to me, I seemed to hear him say:

'Well, good-bye. . . . I'm never coming to you again.'

It was as definite a farewell as you can have from a man, more definite than you will have from most; as though, further, he said: 'I'm gone for good and all. I have other company and more profitable plunder. On the back of our glorious Revolution I rise from crime to crime. . . . Good-bye.'

I was, in sober truth, never to speak to him again. I cannot but regret that on the last occasion when I should have a real opportunity of looking him full in the face, he was to offer me a countenance of determined robbery and plunder.

In spite of this, I shall have, until I die, a feeling of tenderness. . . .

I was recalled from my observation of Grogoff and the Rat by the sensation that the waters of emotion were rising higher around me. I raised my eyes and saw that the Belgian Consul was addressing the meeting. He was a stout little man, with eyeglasses and a face of no importance, but it was quite obvious at once that he was most terribly in earnest. Because he did not know the Russian language he was under the unhappy necessity of having a translator, a thin and amiable Russian, who suffered from short sight and a nervous stammer.

He could not therefore have spoken under heavier disadvantages, and my heart ached for him. It need not have done so. He started in a low voice, and they shouted to him to speak up. At the end of his first paragraph the amiable Russian began his translation, sticking his nose into the paper, losing the place and stuttering over his sentences. There was a restless movement in the hall, and the poor Belgian Consul seemed lost. He was made, however, of no mean stuff. Before the Russian had finished his translation the little man had begun again. This time he had stepped forward, waving his glasses and his head and his hand, bending forward and backward, his voice rising and rising. At the end of his next paragraph he paused, and, because the Russian was slow and stammering once again, went forward on his own account. Soon he forgot himself, his audience, his translator, everything except his own dear Belgium. His voice rose and rose; he pleaded with a marvellous rhythm of eloquence her history, her fate, her shameful devastation. He appealed on behalf of her murdered children, her ravished women, her slaughtered men.

He appealed on behalf of her arts, her cathedrals, and libraries ruined, her towns plundered. He told a story, very quietly, of an old grandfather and grandmother murdered and their daughter ravished before the eyes of her tiny children. Here he himself began to shed tears. He tried to brush them back. He paused and wiped his eyes. . . . Finally, breaking down altogether, he turned away and hid his face. . . .

I do not suppose that there were more than a dozen persons in that hall who understood anything of the language in which he spoke. Certainly it was the merest gibberish to that whole army of listening men. Nevertheless, with every word that he uttered the emotion grew tenser. Cries – little sharp cries like the bark of a puppy – broke out here and there. '*Verrno! Verrno! Verrno!* (True! True! True!)' Movements, like the swift finger of the wind on the sea, hovered, wavered, and vanished. . . .

He turned back to them, his voice broken with sobs, and he could only cry the one word 'Belgia . . . Belgia . . . Belgia . . .' To that they responded. They began to shout, to cry aloud. The screams of '*Verrno . . . Verrno*' rose until it seemed that the roof would rise with them. The air was filled with shouts, 'Bravo for the Allies.' '*Soyousniki! Soyousniki!*' Men raised their caps and waved them, smiled upon one another as though they had suddenly heard wonderful news, shouted and shouted and shouted . . . and in the midst of it all the little rotund Belgian Consul stood bowing and wiping his eyes.

How pleased we all were! I whispered to Vera: 'You see! They do care! Their hearts are touched. We can do anything with them now!'

Even Uncle Ivan was moved, and murmured to himself: 'Poor Belgium! Poor Belgium!'

How delighted, too, were the gentlemen on the platform! Smiling, they whispered to one another, and I saw several shake hands. A great moment. The little Consul bowed finally and sat down.

Never shall I forget the applause that followed. Like one man the thousands shouted, tears raining down their cheeks – shaking hands, even embracing! A vast movement, as though the wind had caught them and driven them forward, rose, lifted them, so that they swayed like bending corn towards the platform; for an instant we were all caught up together. There was one great cry: 'Belgium!'

The sound rose, fell, sunk into a muttering whisper, died to give way to the breathless attention that awaited the next speaker.

I whispered to Vera: 'I shall never forget that. I'm going to leave on that. It's good enough for me.'

'Yes,' she said, 'we'll go.'

'What a pity,' whispered Uncle Ivan, 'that they didn't understand what they were shouting about.'

We slipped out behind the platform, turned down the dark long passage, hearing the new speaker's voice like a bell ringing beyond thick walls, and found our way into the open.

The evening was wonderfully fresh and clear. The Neva lay before us like a blue scarf, and the air faded into colourless beauty above the dark purple of the towers and domes. Vera caught my arm: 'Look!' she whispered, 'there's Boris!' I knew that she had on several occasions tried to force her way into his flat, that she had written every day to Nina (letters, as it afterwards appeared, that Boris kept from her). I was afraid that she would do something violent.

'Wait!' I whispered; 'perhaps Nina is here somewhere.'

Grogoff was standing with another man on a small improvised platform just outside the gates of the Bourse.

As the soldiers came out (many of them were leaving now on the full tide of their recent emotions), Grogoff and his friend caught them, held them, and proceeded to instruct their minds.

I caught some of Grogoff's sentences. '*Tova-ristchi!*' I heard him cry: 'Comrades! Listen to me. Don't allow your feelings to carry you away! You have serious responsibilities now, and the thing for you to do is not to permit sentiment to make you foolish. Who brought you into this war? Your leaders? No, your old masters. They bled you and robbed you and slaughtered you to fill their own pockets. Who is ruling the world now? The people to whom the world truly belongs? No, the Capitalists, the money-grubbers, the old thieves like Nicholas who is now under lock and key . . . Capitalists . . . England, France . . . Thieves, robbers. . . .

'Belgium? What is Belgium to you? Did you swear to protect her people? Does England, who pretends such loving care for Belgium – does she look after Ireland? What about her persecution of South Africa? Belgium? Have you heard what she did in the Congo? . . .'

As the men came, talking, smiling, wiping their eyes, they were caught by Grogoff's voice. They stood there and listened. Soon they began to nod their heads. I heard them muttering that good old word '*Verrno! Verrno!*' again. The crowd grew. The men began to shout their approval. 'Aye! it's true,' I heard a soldier near me mutter, 'the English are thieves;' and another, 'Belgium? . . . After all, I could not understand a word of what that little fat man said.'

I heard no more, but I did not wonder now at the floods that were rising and rising, soon to engulf the whole of this great country. The end of this stage of our story was approaching for all of us.

We three had stood back, a little in the shadow, gazing about to see whether we could hail a cab.

As we waited I took my last look at Grogoff, his stout figure against the purple sky, the masts of the ships, the pale tumbling river, the black line of the farther shore. He stood, his arms waving, his mouth open, the personification of the disease from which Russia is suffering.

A cab arrived. I turned, said, as it were, my farewell to Grogoff and everything for which he stood, and went.

We drove home almost in silence, Vera staring in front of her, her face proud and reserved, building up a wall of her own thoughts.

'Come in for a moment, won't you?' she asked me, rather reluctantly I thought. But I accepted, climbed the stairs, and followed Uncle Ivan's stubby and self-satisfied progress into the flat.

I heard Vera cry. I hurried after her, and found, standing close together, in the middle of the room, Henry Bohun and Nina!

With a little sob of joy, and shame too, Nina was locked in Vera's arms.

XV

This is obviously the place for the story, based, of course, on the very modest and slender account given me by the hero of it, of young Bohun's knightly adventure. In its inception the whole affair is still mysterious to me. Looking back from this distance of time I see that he was engaged on one knightly adventure after another – first Vera, then Markovitch, lastly Nina. The first I caught at the very beginning, the second I may be said to have inspired, but to the third I was completely blind. I was blind, I suppose, because, in the first place, Nina had, from the beginning, laughed at Bohun, and in the second, she had been entirely occupied with Lawrence.

Bohun's knight-errantry came upon her with, I am sure, as great a shock of surprise as it did upon me. And yet, when you come to think of it, it was the most natural thing. They were the only two of our party who had any claim to real youth, and they were still so young that they could believe in one ideal after another as quick as you can catch goldfish in a bowl of water. Bohun would, of course, have indignantly denied that he was out to help anybody, but that, nevertheless, was the direction in which his character led him; and once Russia had stripped from him that thin coat of self-satisfaction, he had nothing to do but mount his white charger and enter the tournament.

I've no idea when he first thought of Nina. He did not, of course, like her at the beginning, and I doubt whether she caused him any real concern, too, until her flight to Grogoff. That shocked him terribly. He confessed as much to me. She had always been so happy and easy about life. Nothing was serious to her. I remember once telling her she ought to take the war more deeply. I was a bit of a prig about it, I suppose. At any rate she thought me one. . . . And then to go off to a fellow like Grogoff!

He thought of it the more seriously when he saw the agony Vera was in. She did not ask him to help her, and so he did nothing; but he watched her efforts, the letters that she wrote, the eagerness with which she ravished the post, her fruitless visits to Grogoff's flat, her dejected misery over her failure. He began himself to form plans, not, I am convinced, from any especial affection for Nina, but simply because he had the soul of a knight, although, thank God, he didn't know it. I expect, too, that he was pretty dissatisfied with his knight-errantries. His impassioned devotion to Vera had led to nothing at all, his enthusiasm for Russia had led to a most unsatisfactory Revolution, and his fatherly protection of Markovitch had inspired apparently nothing more fruitful than distrust. I would like to emphasise that it was in no way from any desire to interfere in other people's affairs that young Bohun undertook these Quests. He had none of my own meddlesome quality. He had, I think, very little curiosity and no psychological self-satisfaction, but he had a kind heart, an adventurous spirit, and a hatred for the wrong and injustice which seemed just now to be creeping about the world; but all this, again thank God, was entirely subconscious. He knew nothing whatever about himself.

The thought of Nina worried him more and more. After he went to bed at night, he would hear her laugh and see her mocking smile and listen to her shrill imitations of his own absurdities. She had been the one happy person amongst them all, and now——! Well, he had seen enough of Boris Grogoff to know what sort of fellow he was. He came at last to the conclusion that, after a week or two she would be 'sick to death of it,' and longing to get away, but then 'her pride would keep her at it. She'd got a devil of a lot of pride.' He waited, then, for a while, and hoped, I suppose, that some of Vera's appeals would succeed. They did not; and then it struck him that Vera was the very last person to whom Nina would yield – just because she wanted to yield to her most, which was pretty subtle of him and very near the truth.

No one else seemed to be making any very active efforts, and at last he decided that he must do something himself. He discovered Grogoff's address, went to the Gagarinskaya and looked up at the flat, hung about a bit in the hope of seeing Nina. Then he did see her at Rozanov's party, and this, although he said nothing to me about it at the time, had a tremendous effect on him. He thought she looked 'awful.' All the joy had gone from her; she was years older, miserable, and defiant. He didn't speak to her, but from that night he made up his mind. Rozanov's party may be said to have been really the turning-point of his life. It was the night that he came out of his shell, grew up, faced the world – and it was the night that he discovered that he cared about Nina.

The vision of her poor little tired face, her 'rather dirty white dress,' her 'grown-up' hair, her timidity and her loneliness, never left him for a moment. All the time that I thought he was occupied only with the problem of Markovitch and Semyonov, he was much more deeply occupied with Nina. So unnaturally secretive can young men be!

At last he decided on a plan. He chose the Monday, the day of the Bourse meeting, because he fancied that Grogoff would be present at that and he might therefore catch Nina alone, and because he and his fellow-propagandists would be expected also at the meeting and he would therefore be free of his office earlier on that afternoon. He had no idea at all how he would get into the flat, but he thought that fortune would be certain to favour him. He always thought that.

Well, fortune did. He left the office and arrived in the Gagarinskaya about half-past five in the evening. He walked about a little, and then saw a bearded tall fellow drive up in an Isvostchik. He recognised this man as Lenin, the soul of the anti-Government party, and a man who was afterwards to figure very prominently in Russia's politics. This fellow argued very hotly with the Isvostchik about his fare, then vanished through the double doors. Bohun followed him. Outside Grogoff's flat Lenin waited and rang the bell. Bohun waited on the floor below; then, when he heard the door open, he noiselessly slipped up the stairs, and, as Lenin entered, followed behind him whilst the old servant's back was turned helping Lenin with his coat. He found, as he had hoped, a crowd of cloaks and a Shuba hanging beside the door in the dark corner of the wall. He crept behind these. He heard Lenin say to the servant that, after all, he would not take off his coat, as he was leaving again immediately. Then directly afterwards Grogoff came into the hall.

That was the moment of crisis. Did Grogoff go to the rack for his coat and all was over; a very unpleasant scene must follow – a ludicrous expulsion, a fling or two at the amiable habits of thieving and deceit on the part of the British nation, and any hope of seeing Nina ruined perhaps for ever. Worst of all, the ignominy of it! No young man likes to be discovered hidden behind a coat-rack, however honest his original intentions!

His heart beat to suffocation as he peeped between the coats. . . . Grogoff was already wearing his own overcoat. It was, thank God, too warm an evening for a Shuba. The men shook hands, and Grogoff saying something rather deferentially about the meeting, Lenin, in short, brusque tones, put him immediately in his place. Then they went out together, the door closed behind them, and the flat was as silent as an aquarium. He waited for a while, and then, hearing nothing, crept into the hall. Perhaps Nina was out. If the old servant saw him she would think him a burglar and would certainly scream. He pushed back the door in front of him, stepped forward, and almost stepped upon Nina!

She gave a little cry, not seeing who it was. She was looking very untidy, her hair loose down her back, and a rough apron over her dress. She looked ill, and there were heavy black lines under her eyes as though she had not slept for weeks.

Then she saw who it was and, in spite of herself, smiled.

'Henry!' she exclaimed.

'Yes,' he said in a whisper, closing the door very softly behind him. 'Look here, don't scream or do anything foolish. I don't want that old woman to catch me.'

He has no very clear memory of the conversation that followed. She stood with her back to the wall, staring at him, and every now and again taking up a corner of her pinafore and biting it. He remembered that action of hers especially as being absurdly childish. But the overwhelming impression that he had of her was of her terror – terror of everything and of everybody, of everybody apparently except himself. (She told him afterwards that he was the only person in the world who could have rescued her just then because she simply couldn't be frightened of some one at whom she'd laughed so often.) She was terrified, of course, of Grogoff – she couldn't mention his name without trembling – but she was terrified also of the old servant, of the flat, of the room, of the clock, of every sound or hint of a sound that there was in the world. She to be so frightened! She of whom he would have said that she was equal to any one or anything! What she must have been through during those weeks to have brought her to this! . . . But she told him very little. He urged her at once that she must come away with him, there and then, just as she was. She simply shook her head at that. 'No . . . No . . . No . . .' she kept repeating. 'You don't understand.'

'I do understand,' he answered, always whispering, and with one ear on the door lest the old woman should hear and come in. 'We've got very little time,' he said. 'Grogoff will never let you go if he's here.

I know why you don't come back – you think we'll all look down on you for having gone. But that's nonsense. We are all simply miserable without you.'

But she simply continued to repeat 'No . . . No. . . .' Then, as he urged her still further, she begged him to go away. She said that he simply didn't know what Grogoff would do if he returned and found him, and although he'd gone to a meeting he might return at any moment. Then, as though to urge upon him Grogoff's ferocity, in little hoarse whispers she let him see some of the things that during these weeks she'd endured. He'd beaten her, thrown things at her, kept her awake hour after hour at night making her sing to him . . . and, of course, worse things, things far, far worse that she would never tell to anybody, not even to Vera! Poor Nina, she had indeed been punished for her innocent impetuosities. She was broken in body and soul; she had faced reality at last and been beaten by it. She suddenly turned away from him, buried her head in her arm, as a tiny child does, and cried. . . .

It was then that he discovered he loved her. He went to her, put his arm round her, kissed her, stroked her hair, whispering little consoling things to her. She suddenly collapsed, burying her head in his breast and watering his waistcoat with her tears. . . .

After that he seemed to be able to do anything with her that he pleased. He whispered to her to go and get her hat, then her coat, then to hurry up and come along. . . . As he gave these last commands he heard the door open, turned and saw Masha, Grogoff's old witch of a servant, facing him.

The scene that followed must have had its ludicrous side. The old woman didn't scream or make any kind of noise, she simply asked him what he was doing there; he answered that he was going out for a walk with the mistress of the house. She said that he should do nothing of the kind. He told her to stand away from the door. She refused to move. He then rushed at her, caught her round the waist, and a most impossible struggle ensued up and down the middle of the room. He called to Nina to run, and had the satisfaction of seeing her dart through the door like a frightened hare. The old woman bit and scratched and kicked, making sounds all the time like a kettle just on the boil. Suddenly, when he thought that Nina had had time to get well away, he gave the old woman a very unceremonious push which sent her back against Grogoff's chief cabinet, and he had the comfort to hear the whole of this crash to the ground as he closed the door behind him. Out in the street he found Nina, and soon afterwards an Isvostchik. She crouched up close against him, staring in front of her, saying nothing, shivering and shivering. . . . As he felt her hot hand shake inside his, he vowed that he would never leave her again. I don't believe that he ever will.

So he took her home, and his Knight-Errantry was justified at last.

XVI

These events had for a moment distracted my mind, but as soon as I was alone I felt the ever-increasing burden of my duty towards Markovitch.

The sensation was absolutely dream-like in its insistence on the one hand that I should take some kind of action, and its preventing me, on the other, from taking any action at all. I felt the strange inertia of the spectator in the nightmare, who sees the house tumbling about his head and cannot move. Besides, what action could I take? I couldn't stand over Markovitch, forbid him to stir from the flat, or imprison Semyonov in his room, or warn the police . . . besides, there were now no police. Moreover, Vera and Bohun and the others were surely capable of watching Markovitch. Nevertheless something in my heart insisted that it was I who was to figure in this. . . . Through the dusk of the streets, in the pale ghostly shadows that prelude the coming of the white nights, I seemed to see three pursuing figures, Semyonov, Markovitch, and myself. I was pursuing, and yet held.

I went back to my flat, but all that night I could not sleep. Already the first music of the May Day processions could be heard, distant trumpets and drums, before I sank into uneasy, bewildered slumber.

I dreamt then dreams so fantastic and irresolute that I cannot now disentangle them. I remember that I was standing beside the banks of the Neva. The river was rising, flinging on its course in the great tempestuous way that it always has during the first days of its release from the ice. The sky grew darker – the water rose. I sought refuge in the top gallery of a church with light green domes, and from here I watched the flood, first as it covered the quays, tumbling in cascades of glittering water over the high parapet, trickling in little lines and pools, then rising into sheeted levels, then billowing in waves against the walls of the house, flooding the doors and the windows, until so far as the eye could reach there were only high towers remaining above its grasp. I do not know what happened to my security, and saw at length the waters stretch from sky to sky, one dark, tossing ocean.

The sun rose, a dead yellow; slowly the waters sank again, islands appeared, stretches of mud and waste. Heaving their huge bodies out of the ocean, vast monsters crawled through the mud, scaled and horned, lying like logs beneath the dead sun. The waters sank – forests rose. The sun sank and there was black night, then a faint dawn, and in the early light of a lovely morning a man appeared standing on the beach, shading his eyes, gazing out to sea. I fancied that in that strong bearded figure I recognised my peasant, who had seemed to haunt my steps so often. Gravely he looked round him, then turned back into the forest. . . .

Was my dream thus? Frankly I do not know – too neat an allegory to be true, perhaps – and yet there was something of this in it. I know that I saw Boris, and the Rat, and Vera, and Semyonov, and Markovitch, appearing, vanishing, reappearing, and that I was strongly conscious that the submerged and ruined world did not *touch* them, and was only a background to their own individual activities. . . . I know that Markovitch seemed to come to me again and cry, 'Be patient . . . be patient. . . . Have faith . . . be faithful!'

I know that I woke struggling to keep him with me, crying out that he was not to leave me, that that way was danger. . . . I woke to find my room flooded with sunshine, and my old woman looking at me with disapproval.

'Wake up, Barin,' she was saying, 'it's three o'clock.'

'Three o'clock?' I muttered, trying to pull myself together.

'Three in the afternoon . . . I have some tea for you.'

When I realised the time I had the sensation of the wildest panic. I jumped from my bed, pushing the old woman out of the room. I had betrayed my trust! I had betrayed my trust! I felt assured that some awful catastrophe had occurred, something that I might have prevented. When I was dressed, disregarding my housekeeper's cries, I rushed out into the street. At my end of the Ekateringofsky Canal I was stopped by great throngs of men and women returning homewards from the procession. They were marching, most of them, in ordered lines across the street, arm in arm, singing the 'Marseillaise.'

Very different from the procession a few weeks before. That had been dumb, cowed, bewildered. This was the movement of a people conscious of their freedom, sure of themselves, disdaining the world.

Everywhere bands were playing, banners were glittering, and from the very heart of the soil, as it seemed, the 'Marseillaise' was rising.

Although the sun only shone at brief intervals, there was a sense of spring warmth in the air. For some time I could not cross the street, then I broke through and almost ran down the deserted stretch of the Canal. I arrived almost breathless at the door in the English Prospect. There I found Sacha watching the people and listening to the distant bands.

'Sacha!' I cried, 'is Alexei Petrovitch at home?'

'No, Barin,' she answered, looking at me in some surprise. 'He went out about a quarter of an hour ago.'

'And Nicholas Markovitch?'

'He went out just now.'

'Did he tell you where he was going?'

'No, Barin, but I heard Alexei Petrovitch tell him, an hour back, that he was going to Katerinhof.'

I did not listen to more. I turned and went. Katerinhof was a park, ten minutes distant from my island; it was so called because there was there the wooden palace of Catherine the Great. She had once made it her place of summer residence, but it was now given over to the people and was, during the spring and summer, used by them as a kind of fair and pleasure-garden. The place had always been to me romantic and melancholy, with the old faded wooden palace, the deserted ponds, and the desolate trees. I had never been there in the summer. I don't know with what idea I hurried there. I can only say that I had no choice but to go, and that I went as though I were still continuing my dream of the morning.

Great numbers of people were hurrying there also. The road was thronged, and many of them sang as they went.

Looking back now it has entirely a dream-like colour. I stepped from the road under the trees, and was at once in a world of incredible fantasy. So far as the eye could see there were peasants; the air was filled with an indescribable din. As I stepped deeper into the shelter of the leafless trees the colour seemed, like fluttering banners, to mingle and spread and sway before my eyes. Near to me were the tub-thumpers now so common to us all in Petrograd – men of the Grogoff kind stamping and shouting on their platforms, surrounded by open-mouthed soldiers and peasants.

Here, too, were the quacks such as you might see at any fair in Europe – quack dentists, quack medicine-men, men with ointments for healing sores, men with pills, and little bottles of bright liquid, and tricks for ruptures and broken legs and arms. A little way beyond them were the pedlars. Here were the wildest men in the world. Tartars and Letts and Indians, Asiatics with long yellow faces, and strange fellows from Northern Russia. They had everything to sell, bright beads and looking-glasses and little lacquered trays, coloured boxes, red and green and yellow, lace and silk and cloths of every colour, purple and crimson and gold. From all these men there rose a deafening gabble.

I pressed farther, although the crowd now around me was immense, and so I reached the heart of the fair. Here were enormous merry-go-rounds, and I had never seen such glittering things. They were from China, Japan, where you will. They were hung in shining, gleaming colours, covered with tinsel and silver, and, as they went tossing round, emitting from their hearts a wild barbaric wail that may have been, in some far Eastern city, the great song of all the lovers of the world for all I know, the colours flashed and wheeled and dazzled, and the light glittered from stem to stem of the brown silent trees. Here was the very soul of the East. Near me a Chinaman, squatting on his haunches, was showing before a gaping crowd the exploits of his trained mice, who walked up and down little crimson ladders, poked their trembling noses through holes of purple silk, and ran shivering down precipices of golden embroidery. Near to him two Japanese were catching swords in their mouths, and beyond them again a great number of Chinese were tumbling and wrestling, and near to them again some Japanese children did little tricks, catching coloured balls in wooden cups and turning somersaults.

Around all these a vast mass of peasants pushed and struggled. Like children they watched and smiled and laughed, and always, like the flood of the dream, their numbers seemed to increase and increase....

The noise was deafening, but always above the merry-go-rounds and the cheap-jacks and the shrill screams of the Japanese and the cries of the pedlars I heard the chant of the 'Marseillaise 'carried on high through the brown leafless park. I was bewildered and dazzled by the noise and the light. I turned desperately, pushing with my hands as one does in a dream.

Then I saw Markovitch and Semyonov.

I had no doubt at all that the moment had at last arrived. It was as though I had seen it all somewhere before. Semyonov was standing a little apart leaning against a tree, watching with his sarcastic smile the movements of the crowd. Markovitch was a little way off. I could see his eyes fixed absolutely on Semyonov. He did not move nor notice the people who jostled him. Semyonov made a movement with his hand as though he had suddenly come to some decision. He walked slowly away in the direction of the palace. Markovitch, keeping a considerable distance from him, followed. For a moment I was held by the crowd around me, and when at last I got free Semyonov had disappeared, and I could just see Markovitch turning the corner of the palace.

I ran across the grass, trying to call out, but I could not hear my own voice. I turned the corner, and instantly I was in a strange place of peace. The old building with its wooden lattices and pillars stood melancholy guard over the dead pond on whose surface some fragments of ice still lay. There was no sun, only a heavy, oppressive air. All the noise was muffled as though a heavy door had swung to.

They were standing quite close to me. Semyonov had turned and faced us both. I saw him smile, and his lips moved. A moment later I saw Markovitch fling his hand forward, and in the air the light on the revolver twinkled. I heard no sound, but I saw Semyonov raise his arm, as though in self-defence. His face, lifted strangely to the bare branches, was triumphant, and I heard quite clearly the words, like a cry of joy and welcome:

'At last! . . . At last!'

He tumbled forward on his face.

I saw Markovitch turn the revolver on himself, and then heard a report, sharp and deafening, as though we had been in a small room. I saw Markovitch put his hand to his side, and his mouth, open as though in astonishment, was suddenly filled with blood. I ran to him, caught him in my arms; he turned on me a face full of puzzled wonder, I caught the word 'Vera,' and he crumpled up against my heart.

Even as I held him, I heard coming closer and closer the rough triumphant notes of the 'Marseillaise'.